# LITTLE BROKEN

**A novel**

**Mollie McGrath**

*For Nelson*

# Chapter 1

Semi-truck brakes squealed outside and the brunette girl at the kitchen table dropped her spoon, sloshing milk on the white laminate. Her attention stolen from her cereal, she rushed to the window, fighting through the outdated curtains, and peered into the street just in time to see an unfamiliar truck turn a corner out of sight.

"Megan, finish your breakfast, please," a tall young man in grease stained, work pants walked out of the bathroom, grabbed a damp washcloth from the sink and cleaned the spilled milk around her cereal bowl, "I can drop you off on my way to the shop or do ya wanna take the bus?"

"I'll take the bus," she shrugged, returning to her chair and refused to look at him.

"You still mad at me?" he dipped his head of short, dark hair, but she just shrugged again and kept her green eyes on the cereal she was pushing around with her spoon, "Well, I'm sorry, I really am, but I gotta work this weekend-"

"Jimmy said he'd take me!" Megan snapped, glaring angrily at her oldest brother's sincere expression.

"Megan, don't start," he said firmly, "I can't trust Jimmy to take you, I'm sorry, hopefully she'll do this again next year and I promise I'll take the day off."

"Yeah, sure, Dan," she scoffed, pushing away from the table hard, "You take a day off! Like that'll ever happen!"

She could tell by the creases in his forehead he was hurt by her words, but also losing patience, and Megan decided not to push further.

Grabbing her old sneakers from next to the front door, she curled her toes uncomfortably while shoving her feet inside, and took a deep breath before turning back to her brother. Neither could continue, however, when the front door squeaked open and the broken screen door slammed as two young men stumbled in, the stench of alcohol and cigarettes a nearly visible cloud around them.

"Jimmy!" Megan jumped at her brother.

"Heya, babygirl," he slurred a little and shook her before letting go, his shaggy, dark hair falling in front of his bloodshot eyes.

"Where ya been all night, Jimmy?" Dan growled, ignoring the scowl their sister trained on him.

"Just havin' a'lil fun bro, s'Jordan's birthday," Jimmy smiled and patted Dan hard on the shoulder, which he immediately brushed off.

"Happy birthday, Jordan," Megan said sweetly to the pudgy, young man grinning at her with glazed eyes.

"It's been good so far," he said and she smelled stale beer on his breath when he leaned down, "I hope some other pretty girls'll wish me a happy birthday."

Megan inclined her head in curiosity of his comment, mostly because of the face he made when he said it, but Dan dragged her towards the table with a finger-pointing order to finish her breakfast.

"You reek," Dan sounded calm, though Megan could hear anger brewing in his tone, "Go take a shower. Jordan go home."

"Dude!" Jimmy retorted incredulously, "We're hangin' out! You can't just send my friends home!"

"Watch me," Dan took an intimidating step at the young men, with only a few inches on each it was surprising how much he towered over them, "Go home, Jordan. Now."

"Siryessir," Jordan attempted to snap himself into a military style salute, but toppled onto Jimmy and they broke into boisterous laughter while trying to steady themselves.

Dan's patience had reached its limit. He grabbed his younger brother's friend by the bicep, lurched open the door and launched a very surprised Jordan through the unlatched screen. Slamming the heavy front door, Dan quickly seized Jimmy by the back of his neck, roughly pushed him into the bathroom, pulled the door shut on the struggling young man in an instant and held it closed.

"Screw you, Dan!" Jimmy was beating on the bathroom door so hard the frame shook, "I'm eighteen! You can't fuckin' tell me what to do anymore!"

2

"Take a shower and cool off, Jimmy," Dan barked over the incessant pounding, "You break this door and see what happens, eighteen or not!"

Very suddenly, the door was still and silent, but Dan waited a few moments to hear the shower start before releasing his grip on the handle. Megan returned to her cereal, eating slowly and tried to ignore her brothers' fight. Lost in the distraction, she forgot to check the time on the microwave and heard the rumble of her bus just as she turned to the window and watched it drive away.

"Shit!" she dropped her spoon, sloshing milk again.

"Watch your mouth," Dan warned routinely, buttoning his work shirt for Jay's Lube 'n' Tires over a 1996 Illinois high school football champions t-shirt.

"I missed my bus," she whined, swinging her backpack on too late.

"I told'ja I'll drop you off," he rolled up his sleeves, grabbed his worn Chicago Bears cap from the counter and opened the door.

Megan led the way to Dan's old, green, GMC pick-up truck in the driveway, wrenched the passenger door open and pulled herself onto the bench seat. For as beaten up as it was on the outside, his truck was pristine on the inside. Like most things in their lives, the truck had been well more than second hand by the time Dan had gotten it and he'd spent the months leading up to his sixteenth birthday fixing it. The day before he'd passed his driver's exam he'd had it running like new. That was over six years ago and it had yet to break down.

Dan hopped behind the wheel, turned the engine over with a loud growl and backed slowly out of the driveway. It wasn't a long drive, but Megan purposefully avoided Dan's repeated attempts to catch her eye.

Her favorite author, A.K. Foreman, would be in Chicago for a book signing the coming weekend and there wasn't anything Megan could remember wanting to go to more. Granted, she hadn't given Dan much warning about the event, but Jimmy had offered to take her to the city, which Dan had immediately refused to allow.

"Megan," Dan began, but she continued staring out the window, "I really wish ya knew how much I'd like to take you to that book signing this weekend," she hunched her shoulders slightly to let him know she

3

was listening, even if she wouldn't give him the benefit of a response, "If I'd known last week I might've been able to get the time off."

"I didn't know last week!" she finally turned, throwing her skinny arms in the air.

"Well neither did I," he responded in a lighthearted, mocking tone, complete with arm flail, and Megan crossed hers, turning again towards the passenger window, "Why don't'cha look into her next few stops with Mrs. King when you're in the library today, okay? Maybe she's goin' to Peoria or Rockford, we could try 'n make another one."

Megan considered this for a moment, knowing Dan was trying to make her happy and it wouldn't be easy for him to take a day off, she found it hard to maintain her anger. Reasonably she knew he couldn't take time off work with three days' notice and, when the librarian had told her about A.K. Foreman's upcoming stop, Megan was sure there was no way she could go. But, when Jimmy had said he'd take her and Dan instantly rejected the idea, she'd dissolved into an angry fit, slammed the door to her bedroom and refused to come out or eat, crying herself to sleep. Suddenly, Megan really wished she'd finished her cereal.

"Yeah, okay," she nodded and gave him a weak smile, just to let him know she wasn't mad anymore.

"Here you go," Dan slowly passed the elementary entrance, pulling the huge truck into the middle-school drop zone and waved to the monitoring teacher, "Oh, here," he dug his wallet from his back pocket and Megan noticed it was empty after he pulled a five-dollar bill out, extending it to her, "Don't get crap for lunch."

"What're you gonna do?" she asked with a quick glance at his wallet as he shoved it back in his work pants.

"I'll figure it out, don't worry," he shook the bill with a grin, "C'mon I'm gonna be late," with one last, tentative glance she took the money and gave him a quick hug, which was promptly returned, "Have a great day, sweetheart, I'll see ya tonight."

"You too, Dan," she smiled and pushed out the heavy truck door, but, before closing it, said, "Love you."

"Love you, too," Dan beamed and the door shut with a thud.

4

He waited until she joined the swarm of students outside the building and slowly crept away from the drop zone. The engine rumbled with building power before the loud growl echoed in the open country air as Dan accelerated out of the parking lot, followed by the middle school boys imitating the sound. Megan had told her brother the reaction his truck always got with them and he indulged her classmates, and himself she was sure, every time he could.

Her morning dragged, unable to stop staring at the beautiful weather outside the classroom windows. The last month of school before summer break always felt like the entire year was being repeated. Lunch finally arrived with the bell and Megan slipped into the library during the chaos of students clamoring into the hot lunch line.

The librarian, Mrs. King, was Megan's favorite adult in the school, she'd always had a soft spot for her. She assumed it was because Mrs. King had babysat her a few times when she was little, but sometimes she'd just visited with Megan's mother. And, a lot of times, when she'd had what everyone called a 'bad day', Mrs. King brought over lasagna. Their mother never ate any, but someone had told Megan that wasn't the point, and leftovers always made things easier on Dan. Mrs. King never made her go back to lunch if she didn't want to and, in fourth grade, when Megan hadn't slept, following one of the worst nights of her young life, the kindhearted librarian had let her nap in the small office behind the check-out desk for the entire afternoon.

"Hi, Mrs. King," Megan smiled at the plump woman, who stopped typing on her computer immediately.

"Megan, how are you today?" Mrs. King's smile was warm.

"M'okay," she shrugged, "I was wonderin' if A.K. Foreman had any other book signings around in a few weeks, Dan can't get the time off 'n he won't let Jimmy take me."

"Well, I can't really blame him for that," she smiled knowingly, "I wish I'd heard about it earlier, I know Dan would've taken you if he could."

Megan nodded in agreement, hiding her bitterness at the librarian's small jab towards Jimmy.

She didn't understand why everyone was so hard on him. Jimmy was always fun and carefree, unless Dan was breathing down his neck about something. He wasn't perfect and had occasionally forgotten to pick

Megan up, or the couple times when she was younger he had left her home alone, but he'd always had good reasons and nothing ever happened. Megan had thought Dan's reactions to these instances were extreme. The last time Jimmy had forgotten to get her from an after-school event, Dan had taken his car keys for a week and promised if he ever forgot about her again he'd lose them for good. Jimmy had been incredibly indignant to the punishment of losing his car, but, after a failed attempt at stealing his keys back, and Dan's threat to keep them another month, he'd accepted it with hidden defiance in the form of rude hand gestures at their brother's back for the duration of his sentence. Since he'd turned eighteen the month before, Megan had caught a few fights between her brothers in which Jimmy reasoned his age allowed him complete freedom, but they ended exactly the same as every fight before his birthday. Dan always had the final word.

"Let me see," Mrs. King turned to her computer and adjusted her tiny glasses on her nose, "Give me a minute, I do love this yoohoo site, although some of the things I've been finding on this web are just- well never mind. A lot of it's really incredible though, and to think just a couple years ago we were all worried about Y2K crashing our computers. Now, Principal Jarsen is telling me the school district is planning to put the whole card catalog on these things. All you'll have to do is type in a word and every book that matches will just pop right up. Amazing, really, but I'm a little nostalgic for the cards, oh, okay, here we are," Mrs. King mumbled to herself as she scanned the computer screen, Megan bounced a little on her slightly scrunched toes, "So, it looks like, yup, Chicago this weekend, but next weekend she'll be in Milwaukee Wisconsin and then starts headin' west, but Milwaukee's not too far, Megan. Here, let me print this for you."

"Thank you," Megan smiled, taking the warm sheet of paper, "I should get to lunch, thanks again."

"Anytime, dear," Mrs. King waved as Megan left the library.

All through her afternoon classes, Megan kept sneaking glances at A.K. Foreman's tour dates, but the only possibility was her Milwaukee stop the following weekend. It would hopefully give Dan enough time to take the Saturday off, but she didn't want to get her hopes up further than they already were. After what felt like the longest hour of her life in math class, her teacher finally called for students taking a bus home to line up in the hall. Megan hurried from the room with more than half her class and, like the rest of them, rushed downstairs to the pick-up area.

6

Megan climbed the steps of her bus, waving to her best friend at the very back. She had some friends in her own class, but Sam was going to high school the following year, while Megan would be in eighth grade, and she wasn't looking forward to being without him. Sam slid his backpack off the bench seat and smiled as Megan sat down.

"Hey," he nudged her with a boney elbow, "How was seventh grade today?"

"Boring," she sighed, "And long. How 'bout you?"

"Same old," Sam shrugged, "You missed the bus this morning. What happened with the A.K. Foreman thing?"

"I know sorry, I lost track'a time. But it's a no go, Dan can't get the time off," Megan said slightly disheartened, "There might be another one we can make in a couple weeks. It's just so frustrating 'cause Jimmy said he'd take me to the city, but Dan won't let him."

"Do you blame him?" Sam asked, unaffected by Megan's nasty scowl, "Hey, I'm just sayin', Chicago's not down the street, and Jimmy doesn't have the best track record of watchin' out for you, or himself."

Megan didn't have a response, but if it had been anyone besides Sam saying that about her brother she'd have punched them. They'd grown up together, just one lonely, decrepit house separated their homes, and Sam had been unfortunately intimate with many of her family's problems.

Before Dan was comfortable leaving Megan by herself after school, she'd spent nearly every afternoon, and the occasional bad night, at Sam's house or the local bar and grill, Pederson's, if his Mom was working later than usual. Megan still frequented their home after school and ate dinner with them several times a week. Sam's Mom, Darlene, as she insisted on being called by her first name, was always nice to Megan and kept her freezer well stocked with pizza rolls. Often, Darlene would shove a whole bag in her hands before she went home, saying her and her brothers were far too thin and needed to come over for dinner more often. And, at least once a month, Dan would join them. Darlene would make a real meal on these evenings, chicken or a roast with potatoes and vegetables. Sometimes, Jimmy would come too, those nights were always the most fun for Megan and Sam.

"Don't be mad," Sam gently tickled her side until she giggled, "Y'know I'm right."

"Yeah, whatever," Megan stuck her tongue out and smiled at him, "Wanna go to the river when we get home?"

"Definitely. Mind if I drop my bag at your place? My mom's workin', I won't have to unlock the door," he grinned when she gave him an expression that he needn't even ask and put his arm around her shoulders, "C'mere, I gotta put my arm up before it falls asleep."

Megan assumed Sam's recent growth spurt had caused the development of his limbs needing certain positions or risk discomfort. She didn't really mind, he was thin, though not so boney it was uncomfortable to lean into his side, and he didn't smell bad. But a few of the boys across the aisle started making kissy sounds at them and Megan caught Sam's rude finger gesture, using the hand on her shoulder, when she turned to glare at them. The exchange had become a fairly common occurrence since Sam had started stretching his arm on the ride home from school.

The bus slowly screeched to a halt at the corner of their street, right in front of Sam's house, and he and Megan followed half a dozen other kids down the stairs. Offering a competitive eyebrow raise, she started sprinting across the yard of the abandoned hovel towards her home next door, but, even with a head start, Sam caught up in a second. They collapsed in her front yard together and Sam pinned Megan's wrists to the ground.

"No fair!" she yelled through a fit of giggles, pathetically attempting to lift her arms, "You're stronger than me!"

"I'm supposed to be," he laughed and started tickling her.

"Sa-s-Sam!" Megan was nearly in tears she was laughing so hard, slapping futilely in his direction and tried to twist her hips from their secure hold between his knees.

"Ge'off my daughter, ya lil pervert!" the broken screen door slammed against the siding and Megan saw Sam's abrupt fear as he scurried to his feet, extending a hand to help her up.

"Dad!" Megan rushed at the potbellied man stumbling down the porch steps and wrapped her arms as far around his middle as she could. He returned the embrace with a quick pat on her back and tousled her hair, looking down with half-closed, bloodshot eyes, and Megan knew his current state required further explanation, "Dad, it's Sam. You know Sam. Darlene's son, they live in the yellow house on the corner."

Her father scrutinized the lanky boy on his lawn, swaying slightly on his feet, "Darlene's boy! Yeah, I know! Heya Sammy, shootin' up like a weed, huh, son?" without breaking for the young man's response, her father chuckled, "Yer momma still good lookin'?"

Megan winced with embarrassment and gave Sam an apologetic glance. He, however, didn't seem phased, as this was a normal question he had to field from her typically absent father.

"I wouldn't know, sir," Sam responded neutrally.

His ample gut quivered while her father snickered, "Might hafta see her 'fore I head out again."

"When're you leaving?" Megan asked with a small pout.

"Firs' thing in the mornin', sweetie pie," he turned to go back up the porch steps, missing the bottom stair on his first attempt, but grabbed the railing just in time, "Goddamn broke shit!"

Megan stayed on the lawn, watching her father stumble into the house and heard his loud warning to Jimmy about staying away from his beer. Grimacing, Megan knew she shouldn't abandon Jimmy, despite her longing to play at the river. Turning to Sam, his face told her he already knew what she was going to say and, as always, was understanding.

"Don't miss the bus tomorrow, okay?" he smirked, grabbing his backpack off the ground.

"I won't," Megan smiled weakly, snatching her bag from beside his and hurried up the porch steps.

Her father was reclined on the couch with his feet on the coffee table, beer can in one hand and the remote in the other. As usual when he was home, the television was unbearably loud and his laugh still managed to cackle over the volume. Megan tossed her backpack under the kitchen table out of habit and slipped into Jimmy's room after a quiet knock on the door.

Her brother was lying on his bed with headphones on, staring angrily at the ceiling, a cigarette burning between his fingers as the smoke poured out the open window above him. Dan didn't like Jimmy smoking in the house, but they no longer shared a room and, as Jimmy put it, 'the place is a dump anyway', so, as long as he kept his window open and door shut, Dan didn't complain. He and Jimmy went toe to toe on so many other things, Megan was glad the smoking argument had ended.

"Hey," she sat hard on Jimmy's bed, startling him, and he yanked his headphones off, but sighed at the familiar intruder.

"Your dad's a piece a shit," he grumbled, but gave her a warm smile, holding eye contact a little longer than usual, "Good thing you're all Mom."

Jimmy said that every time her father was home. He'd been very close to their mother and always reminded his sister how much she looked like her, sharing the same bright-green eyes. Megan smiled at the compliment and ignored the sneer.

His and Dan's father had died when they were barely three and seven, their mother had remarried after she'd gotten pregnant with Megan several years later. Her father had always been gone a lot, even before their mother passed, and though Megan loved him, she understood why her brothers did not, having seen the abuse they'd taken at his hands. She'd been too young when her mother passed to remember much about her parent's marriage, but Jimmy had told her a few times Greg had hit their mother too, Dan had growled at him to shut up when he'd heard these comments. Megan's father had consistently beaten on her brothers, and had even tried to go after her occasionally, an attempt that was always deterred by one, if not both boys, despite the injuries they'd already suffered. A few years ago, however, Dan had laid the older man out during a particularly gruesome brawl and, since then, he'd done little more than throw backhanded comments at his step-sons. Greg had even started showing Dan a surprising amount of respect when he was home, although he was gone at least twice as much after that altercation.

"He doesn't even give a shit I have to work in a few hours," Jimmy snarled quietly and threw a nasty hand gesture at the closed bedroom door.

"M'sorry," Megan mumbled sympathetically, but didn't offer any assistance, she knew better than to ask her father to turn down the television, and Jimmy wouldn't let her anyway.

"It's not your fault," he gave her a playful shove, then tugged her into his side, "And he'll be gone tomorrow."

Megan nodded, understanding why he wanted the trucker back on the road, but still held childish hope they could get along and her father would stick around longer. It was almost summer break and she'd seen him less than half a dozen times since New Year's. When he was home it was only for a day or two, and always in a drunken stupor that often ended in a screaming match with one, if not both, of her brothers.

"You normally home right now?" Jimmy glanced at his alarm clock, "I thought'cha hung out with your boyfriend after school."

"He's not my boyfriend!" Megan implored loudly, immediately covering her mouth with her hand as Jimmy's eyes widened and, for a few moments, they stared at the door, listening for a change in the sounds from the living room.

When the television volume didn't alter, and no pounding stomps were heard, they both sighed with relief before Megan repeated her protest, much quieter this time, "He's not my boyfriend."

"Not yet," Jimmy nudged her with his elbow and jokingly waggled his eyebrows up and down.

"He's my best friend," Megan said matter-of-factly, with a twinge of budding irritation.

"Is that an argument?" he chuckled and her face broke into a frustrated pout, "C'mon, babygirl, I'm just playin' around, and y'know I'd kill him if he was your boyfriend," finishing his statement with a wink, he managed to pull another smile from her.

"You gonna sleep or can I do my homework in here?" Megan was excited to start her report on a series of short stories her English class was reading, but she didn't want to try sitting at the kitchen table with the television blaring and her father yelling, or snoring, over the volume.

"You gonna leave either way?" Jimmy laughed and she shrugged at him, her pout returning, "Yeah, fine, I'm not gettin' any sleep with that shit anyway. Grab me a beer though, would'ja?"

Megan answered with a secret smirk she and Jimmy shared, a long-standing expression of their comradery, and hopped off his bed, slipping quietly from the room.

In the front room, her father's head was lolled back on the couch as he snored loudly. Even though it was unnecessary, since he was an incredibly deep sleeper, and the television was near full volume, Megan tiptoed to the fridge, pulled it open slowly and snatched a can from the half empty case that hadn't been there in the morning. Mission completed, she grabbed her backpack and noiselessly carried everything back to Jimmy's room. With the same wicked grin, Megan proudly handed her brother the cold beer after closing the door without a sound.

"Just the one?" he returned their smirk, but inclined his head with sarcastic disappointment, "C'mon, babygirl where's the ambition?"

"Git'cher own then," she stuck her tongue out, knowing he was joking.

"But you're so much better at it than me," he complimented sweetly and put one hand over the other to mask the sound as he cracked the can and took a long sip, followed by a dramatic sigh, "Thank you, so needed this."

Megan sat cross-legged on the floor, taking out her homework while Jimmy guzzled the cold beer, crumpled the can and hid it at the bottom of the wastebasket next to his bed. He didn't have to tell her not to mention the beer, it was a mutual agreement, knowing Megan would probably be in more trouble for helping him obtain them when her father unwittingly supplied. However, it wasn't her father they were worried about discovering Jimmy's secret drinks.

Dan didn't allow alcohol in the house, he rarely drank and, since Jimmy had been brought home for under-age drinking a few months before, the oldest had put his foot down. It was a constant argument when Megan's father offered an infrequent visit, because he always came with a case of beer and loudly reasoned that the house was in his name so he could do what he liked in it and it wasn't his problem Jimmy was a 'budding drunk'. Thankfully, during the few visits they had to tolerate, Dan and Jimmy were usually a united front against their stepfather and Jimmy would at least hide his insubordination until the veteran truck driver was back on the road.

Snapping his headphones back on his ears, Jimmy lit another cigarette and started thumbing through a street racing magazine while Megan began her paper. Even though she had her own bedroom, and it didn't smell like stale cigarettes, she preferred her brother's company to being alone. Jimmy had always been her friend. Even before Sam, Megan had always had him to laugh at silly cartoons with, avoid being caught fooling around in the church pew when he used to go to Sunday service, and Jimmy's shoulder was where she still cried when Dan was being harsh. Even if they both knew their older brother was right, Jimmy would whisper how unfair and mean he was being whenever she was upset. Recently, Megan's abnormally moody behavior was wearing on Dan, but Jimmy continued making defensive excuses, despite having snapped at her occasionally himself over the last few months.

The late spring sun was still high outside the window when the red numbers on Jimmy's alarm clock showed quarter after five and they heard the broken screen door bang over the television volume. Megan shoved her homework into her backpack and Jimmy slipped his headphones off, tossing the magazine on a pile of clothes crammed in the corner of his bed.

"How ya doin', boy?" Greg was pulling himself from the couch with difficulty as they entered the front room.

"Greg," Dan said indifferently and began washing his hands and forearms in the kitchen sink, "Didn't know you were comin' into town this week."

"What?" Greg scoffed, grabbing another beer from the fridge, "Can't come in m'own house?"

Dan stayed silent, but caught his siblings out of the corner of his eye and approached them with a small shake of his head, pulling Megan into his freshly washed arms, "Jimmy, you workin' tonight?" Jimmy nodded irritably, "Got time to grab a bite with us?"

"With who?" he glanced warily at the man sipping a fresh beer and leaning against the counter.

"Don't worry, junior," Greg snorted and Jimmy averted his eyes quickly, "M'not fishin' fer an invite, meetin' some guys at Pederson's in a bit."

"Can we get pizza?" Megan looked up at Dan's grease smudged face as he released her from his arms.

"Sure thing, sweetheart. What'd ya say, Jimmy?"

"Yeah, okay," Jimmy shrugged, "But I'll follow you, probably gotta head straight to work from there."

Dan nodded, "Lemme grab a shower real quick."

Dan's disappearance into the bathroom prompted Jimmy's immediate retreat into his bedroom, closing the door and left Megan alone with her father.

"S'how's school, girly?" Greg took another guzzle from the can and gave his daughter an unbalanced smile.

"Pretty good," Megan sat on the arm of the couch, letting her legs dangle and stared at her fidgeting hands, "A.K. Foreman is doin' book signings over the next few weeks, Dan might take me to one if he can get off work."

"Who?" her father's question lacked interest as he sipped his beer again.

"The author of the Fire Fox series," she replied, thinking she should have said that the first time, knowing he had no idea what she was talking about.

"You 'n yer books," he chuckled, returning the can to his lips, "Keepin' yer grades up then?"

"All A's," she smiled proudly.

Her father responded with an upbeat scoffing sound and guzzled the last of his beer, crumpling the can as he sucked the last few drops and tossed it in the sink.

"Welp, I best be gettin'," he tousled Megan's hair roughly, barely turning his unfocused, glossy eyes towards her as he said, "Be a good girl fer yer brother now."

Without even waiting for his daughter to nod, Greg left the house, leaving the front door wide open as the screen banged in its frame. Megan sighed, sliding off the armrest, and shut the door after her stumbling father.

Retrieving her backpack from the floor outside Jimmy's bedroom, she set up her normal homework station at the kitchen table and resumed her report. It was already well beyond the page length requirement, but Megan had really enjoyed the story and felt the characters deserved more than a few words of description. Jimmy's bedroom door squeaked open and he peered around the room before walking briskly through the kitchen and opening the fridge. Megan ignored him as he pilfered a few cans from the dwindling box, but giggled to herself, watching Jimmy nearly jump over the threshold into his bedroom as the shower turned off. Cradling the cans in one arm against his side, Jimmy hastily shut his door without a sound.

A few moments later, Dan walked out of the bathroom with a towel wrapped around his waist, running his fingers through his short, damp hair.

"How much homework ya got?" he asked before walking down the short hallway towards his and Megan's rooms.

"Just finishing," she answered without looking up.

Dan returned to the kitchen in fresh jeans and a black t-shirt. Leaning over the table, he inspected the lengthy report with a proud nod just as Megan completed the last swipe with her pen.

"Find anything out about the book signing?" Dan asked, patting her on the shoulder before gathering the littered beer cans and dumping them in the trash.

"She'll be in Milwaukee next weekend," Megan smiled hopefully, grabbing the crushed can from the sink he hadn't seen and pushed it into the overfilling bag Dan was wrestling out of the plastic bin.

"That might work. I'll ask Jay tomorrow if I can get the day," he nodded thoughtfully, tying the bag and setting it next to the front door, "Jimmy! C'mon, let's go, I'm starvin'!"

"I'll meet'cha there!" Jimmy called from the other side of his closed bedroom door.

Megan saw an irritated twinge in Dan's jaw as he bit his lips and crossed his arms, sternly responding, "No, Jim, we're leavin' together. Get'cher ass out here before I start countin' the empties against what's missing and we can really get into it."

Feeling her stomach twist, Megan wished Jimmy would just comply with Dan's request, knowing how angry their older brother would be with her if he found out she'd stolen her father's beer for Jimmy. Megan breathed a silent sigh of relief when Jimmy threw his door open and stalked into the front room, his factory shirt unbuttoned over a Nirvana t-shirt.

"You're a real jerk, y'know that?" Jimmy sneered at Dan.

"Yep," Dan nodded curtly, uncrossing his arms and opened the door, picking up the trash with his other hand.

Locking the front door behind himself, Dan let the screen door bang shut and followed them down the porch steps.

He tossed the bag in the metal can, securing the lid, and called across the yard to Jimmy, "I'll follow you."

Jimmy spun, ready to argue, but, at the look he received from Dan, just rolled his eyes and dropped into his Oldsmobile.

The huge sedan was faded blue and rusting from constant exposure to the elements over its long life and often needed some part or another just to keep it running. Megan hopped into the passenger side of Dan's truck and heard the normal whirring of the Oldsmobile trying to turn over, unfortunately, after a few more attempts pumping the pedal, hitting the dashboard and cussing at it, it did not. Jimmy slammed the driver's door hard.

"Goddamn piece a shit!" Jimmy kicked the fender with his steel-toed boot, "It's the alternator again, I know it!"

"Alright, we got this, Jimmy," Dan said calmly, "I'll drop ya off tonight, grab a new one before the parts store closes and when I get home from work tomorrow-"

"How am I gonna get home from work?!" Jimmy yelled at his car to avoid attacking his brother.

"I'll pick you up in the mornin'," Dan remained calm and put a hand on Jimmy's shoulder, guiding him away from the useless automobile, "You drop me at the shop and take my truck home."

Jimmy nodded at the idea, a smirk creeping onto his face, "Then I gotta go back and pick your ass up?"

"I'll figure it out, don't worry," Dan gave his shoulder an encouraging shake, "Let's eat, huh?"

Jimmy wrenched open the passenger door of Dan's truck, "Scoot over, shrimp," and hopped up next to his sister.

Megan didn't mind sitting between her brothers even though they were much larger and it left her with much less room than before Jimmy had gotten his license. Dan turned the engine over on the first try, as always, and backed out of the driveway. The local pizza place in town, just over a mile from their house, and Dan found a spot on the street right in front.

Megan made a beeline for the arcade games as soon as they walked in, but a tight grip on the back of her shirt stopped her. She scowled at Dan, dramatically rubbing where her collar had choked her throat.

"Can we sit down first, please?" Dan raised an eyebrow and she shrugged stiffly, but didn't try to move again, "Thank you."

"Hey, Dan," a young, blonde woman smiled as she exited the kitchen and approached their group, "Jimmy, Megan, how're you guys?"

"Hi, Lacey," Dan returned her smile while Jimmy and Megan quickly exchanged kissy faces at each other behind his back, "Can't complain. How've you been?"

"Same as always," she giggled, Megan noticed she did that a lot, "Booth?"

"Yes, please," Dan nodded and they followed the pretty blonde until she placed three menus on a table within perfect view of the arcade room.

"D'ja hear O'Malley's havin' a party at his farm Friday night?" Lacey asked.

"He mentioned it when he was in gettin' his oil changed last week," Dan remarked, sliding onto the seat across from his brother and sister.

"Well," Lacey giggled, "You should come! We never see you anymore, the class of ninety-seven misses our star quarterback."

Dan gave her a weak smirk, "I'm sorry, Lace, but I gotta work all weekend, wish I could."

"You're always working," she gave him a playful push on the shoulder, "Gotta get out and have fun sometimes."

"No kiddin'," Megan mumbled, but bit her lips when Dan raised a warning eyebrow.

"Well, if you can make it, a lotta people would be excited to see ya," Lacey smiled sweetly, "What can I get y'all to drink?"

The brothers each ordered a soda and Megan a pink lemonade before Lacey swayed back to the kitchen. Dan briefly stared as she walked away, but shook his head lightly and buried his attention in the menu.

"Y'know you can have a drink here, right?" Jimmy said.

"Little over a year now," Dan retorted without looking up.

Jimmy didn't continue on the subject, to Megan's relief, and Lacey returned shortly with their drinks.

"Can I go play games?" she asked after a long sip.

"Ya got money?" the corners of Dan's mouth curled amusingly.

"I still have two bucks from lunch," she shrugged.

"So, my money?" he chuckled, "Yeah, git."

18

Megan stuck her tongue out jokingly while sliding off the seat and headed towards the game room. A light backhanded swat on her behind instigated one more tongue protruding face at Dan, who made a scissor motion with his fingers.

While working on beating the newest high score in Space Invaders, Megan occasionally glanced at her brothers. Jimmy and Dan were having an animated conversation, but, since they were both nodding and laughing, Megan assumed it was either about Jimmy's car or her father. Something they agreed on instead of one of the many topics that would start an argument. Just as she went to put in the last quarter, Dan whistled from their table and waved her over. Saving the coin from the slot, Megan shoved it back in her pocket and rejoined her brothers at the booth where a hot pizza sat in the middle of the table.

"D'ja win?" Jimmy asked, sliding a slice of pepperoni onto his plate.

"Sure did," she nodded proudly, taking a plate from Dan that already had two pieces of cheese and immediately doused them in parmesan crumbles.

"Got any money left?" Dan asked amusingly and broke into a quick bout of laughter as she produced the final quarter between her fingers, "Good thing I got paid today."

"Is he givin' you any money before he takes off?" Jimmy asked after swallowing a large bite.

"Dunno," Dan shrugged and sipped his soda, his plate still empty.

Dan had developed a habit of waiting to eat until he knew his siblings had had enough and they had long since stopped trying to curb his routine. Jimmy grabbed a pepperoni and cheese on his own plate, leaving a couple pieces of each on the tray and nudged it a little towards Dan.

"All you, bro," Jimmy said and shoved another huge bite in his mouth.

With a small smile at his brother, Dan started in on one of the pepperoni slices and Megan knew it was just in case she would want another piece of cheese, the only kind of pizza she ate. But three dollars bought a lot in the school cafeteria and, after the first bite of her second pizza slice, she already felt full. Dan finished one and started on another before Megan could even managed a third bite and she felt a

19

pang of sadness watching him ravage an early dinner, realizing he probably hadn't eaten lunch since he'd given her his last five dollars and wasn't paid until the end of the day. She took the last few bites, her stomach feeling a little queasy, and uncharacteristically left the crust on her plate, pushing it away from herself.

"Ya done?" Dan asked after a hard swallow.

Megan nodded imploringly at his disbelief, and he shrugged, nearly inhaling the last of the pizza.

"We gotta go, I start in twenty minutes," Jimmy said, checking his watch once Dan had finished Megan's crust.

"It takes less than ten minutes to get there," Dan sipped his soda, smiling as Lacey strolled back to the table.

"How was everything?" she glanced at the younger two before locking her eyes on Dan.

"Great as always, Lace," Dan slid from the seat, standing at least half a foot over the young woman, "We gotta get movin', it was real nice to see ya."

"You too, Dan," Lacey unexpectedly wrapped her arms around him, catching Dan off guard, and he awkwardly patted her back before she pulled away, adding, "It'd be real great to see more'a you."

"I, yeah, uh, that'd be cool," Dan stumbled and Megan saw a rare flush in his normally stoic expression.

Barely before Lacey was out of earshot, Jimmy and Megan turned to each other with puckered faces, smooching into the air dramatically.

"Knock it off," Dan growled quietly, halting their mockery.

Dan tossed a few bills on the table, ushering the younger two out of the restaurant and back to the dark green pick-up outside. Megan pulled herself onto the bench seat and straddled her feet on either side of the 4x4 shifter as her brothers climbed in on both sides. Dan expertly maneuvered a U-turn on the tight street and took off towards the industrial park just outside the city limits.

Jimmy worked third shift at Hollis Inc, a metal fabricating factory, pushing the same button over and over. It wasn't thrilling work and he complained to anyone who would listen, usually just his sister, but it was good money for three to four twelve hour shifts a week, leaving him with a fair amount of free time. Unlike Dan, Jimmy had no interest in picking up extra shifts, even with the time and a half overtime pay, and only worked on a night off if his manager threatened to fire him for not showing up for his last shift. This had happened twice since Jimmy got the job one day after his eighteenth birthday, dropping out of his senior year of high school with less than a couple months left until graduation. Megan would never forget the fight they'd had when Dan found out.

The old truck rumbled to an idle outside the entrance of the factory, Dan threw the shift lever into park and looked over just in time to catch a long yawn from his brother.

"D'ja get any sleep today?" he asked with concern.

"Couple hours before jackass showed up," Jimmy shrugged and reached for the door handle.

"Jimmy, how're ya gonna work like this?" Dan's tone was irritated, though Megan suspected it wasn't directed at Jimmy, who shrugged again, "Can ya flip for tomorrow night?"

"Dude, I got plans tomorrow," Jimmy whined, "I'll be fine."

Dan scowled, but shook his head in defeat, "Okay, but if ya start feelin' like you're gonna pass out tell Mr. Schmidt ya gotta go. I don't need'ja fallin' into one'a those machines and neither does he. Got me?"

"Yeah, 'cause that'd be great for me too," Jimmy rolled his eyes, smirking and pulled Megan's head close in a quick embrace before shutting the truck door with a solid thud and sauntering to the factory entrance.

She slid into the warmth of the passenger seat as they left the parking lot and, for a few minutes, the truck was silent as Dan stared ahead at the road, his brow furrowed. Megan flipped the radio on and played with the knob until she heard Lady Marmalade and turned it up a little, bobbing her head while mumbling the lyrics.

"Y'know," Dan gave his sister a sideways smile, "Somebody at work told me what that French part means."

"What?" Megan asked, she wasn't able to see the movie *Moulin Rouge* yet, but loved the music video and danced along every time she caught it on MTV.

"M'not tellin'," he chuckled.

"Then why say somethin'?" she accosted, throwing her arms up in her typical frustrated fashion.

"I get to have some fun with you, don't I?" Dan poked her side and she moved as far away from him on the bench as she could, "Oh, lighten up."

"What's it mean?" Megan glared challengingly.

A short laugh escaped at her attempt to intimidate him, and relenting, he said, "Okay, basically, they're askin' a guy to walk 'em home."

She scoffed, "That's it? I get that, Sam walks me home like every day."

Dan bit back a laugh and said, "Yeah, Sam's a good kid."

They pulled into the mostly empty auto parts store parking lot and Dan stopped in the first spot by the front door, "You wanna come in with me or stay in the truck?"

"I'll come in," Megan shrugged, knowing how long he could spend in the parts store and would rather wander the aisles than sit in the truck.

"Hey, Dan," the tall, old man behind the counter waved as they walked in, "That can't be Megan, can it?"

"Hi, Mr. Glasby," Megan giggled at his overexaggerated jaw drop.

"You grow a foot every time I see you," he smiled, "Your brother must be feedin' you well, you're gonna be taller than me soon," she giggled again, shaking her head at the white-haired man standing easily three inches over Dan, who was considerably tall himself, "Dan, what can I get'cha?"

"Jimmy's alternator went out again," Dan answered.

"Didn't you just replace it?" Mr. Glasby shook his head.

"Yeah, thinkin' it may've been a defective one, it's still been givin' him issues," Dan shrugged, "We'll probably be in next week for a battery too, but I know the alternator'll keep it goin' for now and I can jump it for him 'til then."

Mr. Glasby's expression faltered for a moment before regaining his smile, "Well, y'know I don't mind if ya pay me next week, boy, save you some time and hassle."

"No, thank you, sir," Dan smiled, refusing any resemblance of charity, as he always did, "We'll be fine."

"Well, at least don't argue with me about Jay's discount today," he pointed a jokingly stern, wrinkled finger at Dan, "That man has you workin' like a plow horse, it's the least he could do even if he doesn't know he's doin' it," and, with a wink, Mr. Glasby turned to the long rows of shelves behind his counter and disappeared.

Megan started running her fingers over displays of window cleaner and discount snow brushes. She accidently pushed one of the brushes a little harder than she meant to and one row toppled out of the rack and onto the floor. Megan froze and slowly turned to Dan, cringing.

"Pick it up," he sighed and watched her replace the snow brushes, balancing them carefully in the rack.

"Okay, Dan," Mr. Glasby returned with a plain brown box, about twice the size of a shoebox, "Bring me the old one and I'll send it back to the company, try 'n get'cha some money back."

"Thanks, Mr. Glasby," Dan said, pulling his wallet from his back pocket, "I appreciate it."

"Okay, son," the older man adjusted his glasses and peered at the screen, "With Jay's discount, comes to one-ninety-seven-fifty-six."

Megan saw Dan's jaw twitch and he closed his eyes for a moment as he opened his leather wallet, pulled out two crisp hundred-dollar bills, gave them to Mr. Glasby, and shoved his wallet in his back jeans pocket. The older man quickly made change, handing Dan a couple dollars and coins.

"Here," Dan slipped the coins in his front pocket, but handed Megan the two dollars, "Lunch tomorrow."

"Thanks," she took the money, folded it twice and shoved it next to the quarter in her jeans.

"Thanks, Mr. Glasby," Dan said, grabbing the box, "I'm sure I'll see ya tomorrow."

"Have a good night, Dan," he smiled, "Megan, stay outta trouble, ya hear."

She giggled and gave the man a thumbs-up while walking backwards out the door her brother held open with his free hand. Megan continued to walk in reverse to the truck, despite Dan's warning to turn around, and knocked the back of her head on the passenger side mirror.

"Told'ja," he chuckled, "You okay?"

"Yeah," she pouted, rubbing her head before slapping the side view mirror and wrenching open the passenger door.

"Hey," Dan scolded across the bench seat as he pulled himself up with the steering wheel, "You wanna get smacked like that?"

"No," Megan pouted.

"Then don't hit my truck," Dan warned, turning the engine over and his truck roared to life.

Megan continued pouting for a minute, rubbing the back of her head even though the pain had subsided almost immediately, and Dan glanced over a few times with an amused grin. Finally, he put his arm around her, pulling her next to him on the bench, and planted a kiss on her head where she'd smacked into the mirror. Megan leaned into his familiar side, her eyelids getting heavier with the darkening sky, and yawned. She was asleep before he finished the ten-minute drive home.

Megan woke with the budding urge to pee, threw her blankets off and climbed out of bed. Grabbing a pair of Jimmy's old sweatpants from the basket of clean clothes on her floor, Megan slipped into the bright hallway, but stopped, hearing her oldest brother and father in the kitchen, and flattened against the wall.

"You gonna be in town for Megan's birthday next month?" Dan asked roughly and she heard the clatter of dishes being put away.

"We'll see," her father said, "I gotta spend a few weeks up north comin' up."

"You've missed her last two. Y'know that, right?" Dan's tone was bitter, but even.

"I was here for her tenth," Greg returned indignantly.

"She'll be thirteen next month," Dan growled and a particularly loud crash told Megan her brother was trying not to lose his temper.

"Shit," her father chuckled, "Better keep an eye on that boy down the street then."

Dan didn't respond, but more dishes clanked before the dishwasher door slammed shut.

"Look," Dan began bluntly, "I need some money," she distinctly heard a mean scoff from her father before the telltale crack of a fresh beer can, "Megan's out growin' everything, and I don't remember the last time you threw me a couple bucks to keep this dump from goin' into foreclosure."

"You live here, not me," Greg spat angrily.

"And I'm raisin' your daughter here," Dan implored, a slight shake in his tone threatened his barely maintained control.

"So yer mother said," Megan's stomach twisted at her father's sneer, though it wasn't the first time she'd heard it.

She twitched as the walls shook from a heavy thud in the front room.

"Don't you ever say that shit about my mom," Dan growled angrily, "I swear to God old man, I'll put you in the morgue instead'a the hospital this time."

"Get off me you little-," Greg struggled through his words.

"Stop bein' a fuckin' deadbeat and gimme some money for your kid!" Dan barked loudly, losing his temper, and the unmistakable sound of a fist breaking drywall made Megan jump.

"FINE!" Greg shouted, "Here! You greedy bitch! Fuck you, fuck your brother, fuck her, fuck this fucking house!"

The front door slammed and the screen door followed, and Megan stood rooted to the dingy hallway carpet, near tears. Dan turned the corner, his livid expression instantly softened and he opened his arms, which she sprinted into, sobbing on his black t-shirt. Rubbing her back, Dan hushed her cries, but, when they got harder instead of subsiding, he bent down, picked her up and carried her to the couch. For a few minutes, he just let Megan cry.

"I'm sorry, sweetheart," he said softly, brushing hair from her face and wiped tears from her cheeks.

"Wh-y does he h-hate me?" Megan sniffled.

"He doesn't," Dan insisted, "Your dad just doesn't, sometimes he just doesn't think before he says things. Alcohol has that effect on a lotta people, but we just gotta do the best we can and pray for him, right?"

Megan nodded weakly, glad he didn't try to push his point. Calmer from the comfort Dan provided, she kissed his cheek, earning his genuine smile, and slid off his lap towards the bathroom.

When she returned to the living room she saw Dan sopping beer from the carpeting with a ragged dish towel. A few feet above him was a gaping hole in the ugly wallpaper about the size of dinner plate.

"Get back to bed, Meg," Dan walked to the sink to wring out the rag, "It's late."

Watching Dan still dressed, cleaning a mess at midnight, knowing he would probably do at least one more chore before turning in and still be up before her, Megan felt the guilt she'd had at dinner return. Even before their mother had died, Dan took care of her, her much older brother had always been there, consistently more of a parent than her own father. Megan didn't remember much from when her mother was alive, except she'd spent a lot of time in bed and going to doctor appointments, but her brothers always told her how active she'd been before getting sick. While not unexpected, their mother's unfortunate

26

passing had landed the responsibility of raising a nearly six and twelve-year-old on the unprepared shoulders of a boy who'd turned sixteen exactly a week before that cold, fatal day. Megan walked up behind her brother as he leaned over the sink, his head hanging with stress, and wrapped her arms around his middle.

"I love you, Dan," she mumbled into the back of his t-shirt and he turned, easily lifting her into his arms again.

"I love you, too, sweetheart," he smiled and walked towards her bedroom, pushing the door open with his foot and dropped her on her bed, "Sleep, you gotta take the bus in the mornin', can't be late."

"G'night," she threw her blanket over herself, snuggling into her pillow.

"Sweet dreams," Dan smiled, flicked the light switch and quietly pulled the door shut.

# Chapter 2

A nearly empty box of cereal and jug of milk were waiting on the table next to a bowl and spoon when Megan entered the bright kitchen the next morning. Pouring the last of the colorful puffs into the empty bowl, she topped it with a splash of milk and left the jug on the table while digging into her breakfast.

"Mornin'," Dan walked out of Jimmy's bedroom, already dressed for work, carrying a hamper overflowing with dirty clothes and set it next to the basement door, "Sleep well?"

"Yep," she nodded, popping the spoon into her mouth again as Dan put the milk away.

"Good, get a move on," he patted her shoulder, "Where's your backpack?"

Peering around the room, Megan didn't immediately see the beaten up Jansport and shrugged at Dan, shoving another spoonful in her mouth. He just shook his head, checked behind the couch and lifted the dark green, hand-me-down bag triumphantly in the air, rolling his eyes at her cheek bulging grin. Dan hung it on the back of her chair, grabbed the hamper and disappeared down the basement stairs. Moments later, Megan heard the washer's normal thump before a gush of water rained into the hollow steel drum.

She finished her cereal, drank the remaining milk and dumped the bowl and spoon in the sink as Dan jogged back up the stairs into the kitchen, grabbed the empty cereal box from the table and tossed it in the garbage. Slinging one backpack strap over her shoulder, Megan followed Dan out the door.

"Have a good day, Sweetheart," Dan called while unlocking his truck and she crossed their front lawn towards the bus stop.

"You too, Dan!" Megan spun around, waving to her brother and hustled to the corner where Sam was waiting.

"Good," Sam smiled, "You're here."

"Told'ja I would be," she pushed his shoulder playfully.

"Everything okay?" Sam's tone was neutral, but worry hid in his eyes, "Got a little loud for a minute last night."

"What were you doin' up?" Megan asked, avoiding his concern.

"I wasn't," Sam raised his eyebrows and she averted her gaze with mild embarrassment, although it wasn't as if the entire neighborhood hadn't heard far worse from her house in the past, "Him 'n Jimmy get into it?"

"Dan," Megan shook her head.

"Shit," Sam's eyes widened and he tried to suppress a grin, "Is your dad okay?"

Megan scoffed, "Yeah, pretty much just yellin', he doesn't mess with Dan anymore."

"He did put the man in a coma," Sam chuckled.

"A day 'n a half is not a coma," Megan insisted with dark humor on the unforgettably awful night three years before.

Her thoughts traveled as the bus approached and Sam followed her to their usual seat in the very back. Greg had been home for nearly a month, due to a lack of available contracts, and had spent every day lazing on the couch in front of the television or drinking at Pederson's, unless he was picking fights with his stepsons. Megan remembered vividly sitting at the kitchen table, doing her homework with Jimmy when her father had stumbled through the front door, fresh from the bar at four thirty in the afternoon, and set his unfocused, raging mad eyes on the sophomore. Jimmy was well versed in the violent dance, but the color had still drained from his face as he'd jumped into a defensive position and pulled Megan by the arm, pushing her towards her bedroom barely before she was out of the chair. Jimmy's agonizing yell still echoed in her memory, watching him dragged to the floor by his dark hair.

Megan had screamed at her father to stop, lunging forward and yanked hard on his forearm, but a sharp strike across her cheek had sent her crashing to the floor next to her brother. Pain creased Jimmy's face as he'd cried in agony from a savage kick to his skinny torso. Incoherent shrieks had filled the room and Megan launched at Greg, who'd easily snatched her by the neck, hindering her heavy, panted breath. She'd kicked wildly into his legs, desperately hoping to hit a spot sensitive enough to force the release of his iron grip. But, just as she'd been sure her own father was going to kill her, Megan had found herself on the floor in a gasping heap, Jimmy's scrawny arms wrapping around her. Megan's eyes had focused slowly and she'd heard an unfamiliar, agonizing grunt as the scene before her had become clear.

Dan had been unrecognizable, angrier than she'd ever seen. It still sent chills down her spine remembering the moment her oldest brother finally snapped after years of enduring and observing abuse. He'd had Greg against the wall and landed punch after solid punch to his face, gut, sides and one exceptionally hard hit to his left temple made the drunk's bloodshot eyes glaze over just before he'd crumpled with a sickening thud on the floor. It had seemed like a long time Dan, Jimmy and Megan had just stood there, staring at Greg's husky form passed out on the living room carpet, Dan's eyes wide with terror as he'd panted over his stepfather. But, Megan could still hear how calm he'd kept his voice while his shaking hands picked up the phone and he'd called for the police and an ambulance. How unbelievably collected he'd seemed ordering his siblings to get their backpacks and an overnight bag together before dialing Darlene to ask if the two could stay the night. Then the cops showed up.

Megan and Jimmy had screamed in protest when the policemen arrested Dan, even as they assured the minors there was more than enough history of Greg's abuse to corroborate Dan's defensive reasoning and he would likely be released shortly. But it wasn't until Dan had raised his voice, scolding them for yelling at the officers, that they'd stopped. He'd been let go after Greg woke up in the hospital, refusing to press charges against the nineteen-year-old. Megan remembered the hours she'd had to sit with their well-acquainted social worker before getting to see her brother, but the hug she'd received when Dan finally walked in was worth the wait. Greg had left the hospital, immediately fleeing town, less than a week later and didn't come back for over six months.

"So, what'd Dan say about the A.K. Foreman signing in Milwaukee?" Sam's question brought Megan back to the bumpy bus ride.

"Maybe, he's gonna try 'n get the time off," she shrugged, changing the subject with an eager smile, "Hey, you maybe wanna go to the movies Saturday night?"

Sam nodded, "I got a couple bucks. Wanna go see Shrek?"

"I wanna see Josie and the Pussy Cats," she scoffed, "But everyone's sayin' Shrek's really funny, I thought it was supposed to be a kid's movie."

"Yeah, but I guess it's not like other cartoons," Sam said, "And Dan's not gonna let you see a PG thirteen movie."

"I'll be thirteen next month," Megan let her head fall back in frustration, but knew no amount of whining would get her brother to bend his rule, even if she was only a few weeks from the liberating milestone, "So, stupid."

"It just came out," Sam nudged her, "How about I take you for your birthday? Just you 'n me."

"So, basically every time we go to the movies," she nudged him back, "Thanks, Sam, I'd like that."

"As long as you'd like it," he smiled and put his arm around her shoulders.

Sam didn't offer the normal explanation about his arm losing feeling, but Megan had heard it enough over the last several months to know his reasoning. She was not looking forward to the following year when he would be a freshman and she would still be at the elementary through middle school building across town. Megan got along with her classmates, but Sam was her best friend and she'd always had him on the bus. In a few weeks, he would graduate eighth grade, leading into a short summer before they'd only have weekends and occasional free evening to hang out.

"Let's go to the river after school," Megan said as she and Sam approached her classroom.

"Definitely," he nodded, "Bet'cha those eggs've hatched."

Megan smiled at his reminder of the robin's nest they'd been observing a little over a week, "I hope so," and a loud ringing filled the halls, "See ya later."

"Later," he smiled and backtracked to his own classroom.

Classes didn't seem to drag as much as the day before and, as usual, her English teacher was very impressed with her report, but as always, math class was brutally sluggish. Megan's good day was dampened when her math teacher handed back their most recent test during the last few minutes before the bus riders were called and a big red B minus hovered next to her name. Even in her most detested subject Megan maintained A's, but their class's recent dive into algebra was proving a struggle. Harder than necessary, she folded the test in half and hardly less than slammed it between the pages of her textbook before shoving the book into her backpack and inching to the edge of her seat in anticipation of the bus call.

"How's your day?" Sam asked, meeting her in the hallway by the main entrance.

"Shitty," Megan mumbled, glaring at a six grader who'd caught the curse on their way out the door.

"What happened?" Sam asked, following her to their bus.

"I hate math," she growled in frustration, joining the line of students pushing up the short set of steps.

"I told'ja I'd help," Sam poked her in the side and she scowled over her shoulder, suppressing a smile, "Don't gimme that look."

"Yeah," Megan admitted, scooting onto the backseat, followed by Sam, "I know, and I have like twenty problems for homework, a worksheet for history and a science quiz tomorrow."

"So, no river today," Sam chuckled, throwing his arm over her shoulders and shaking gently, "We'll go tomorrow, it's Friday. Wanna come over and do some homework? I got a book report due next week, you could help me start it and I'll give you a hand with your math."

"Yeah, okay," Megan appreciated his comforting proposal.

When they arrived at the corner in front of Sam's house Megan followed him off the bus, up the porch stairs and into his house, immediately hit with the comforting smell of scented candles and a hint of menthol smoke. Sam's Mom, Darlene, was sitting on her favorite stool watching a soap opera on her tiny kitchen TV and smoking a cigarette under the exhaust fan.

"Hey, Mom," Sam called, kicking his shoes off inside the front door, "Megan's here."

"Hi, Darlene," Megan waved as the thin woman's head of teased blonde hair swung around, her bright smile framed by high cheekbones.

"Hey, baby. Miss Megan how've you been, darlin'?" Darlene took a drag of her cigarette and blew the smoke towards the vent fan.

"Good," Megan smiled and followed Sam into the kitchen, "The author of the Fire Fox series is doin' book signings, Dan might take me to Milwaukee in a couple weeks."

"How cool!" Darlene exclaimed, knocking her cigarette with a polished finger into a small ashtray between the burners on the stove, "Your big brother is pretty good to you. What're you kids up to?"

"Homework," Sam jerked his head for Megan to follow, "We'll be in my room."

"Okay, there's pizza rolls or I've got some pulled pork from work if y'all want a sandwich, Travis made it," Darlene offered, smirking when they pivoted at the end of her sentence.

She worked at Pederson's as a bartender four to five evenings a week and Travis had been the head cook for years. Due to his mom's job and her father's affliction, Sam and Megan had eaten many dinners made by Travis. Often followed by their attempt to play darts or shuffleboard until Dan stopped by after football practice and took Megan home. Once football was over, and especially the last few years her father had mostly stayed away, those trips became nearly nonexistent.

"I'll take some'a Travis's pulled pork," Megan nodded, "Thanks, Darlene."

"Yeah, me too," Sam said and started to pull Megan away from the kitchen, "C'mon."

Sam's room was a little smaller than Megan's, his blue walls plastered in posters of his favorite rock bands and CD's and video game magazines covered a dusty toybox. Like Megan, remnants of his recent childhood still lingered between new interests. Sam tossed his backpack on his bed, hopping up next to it and slapped his mattress for Megan to join him.

"So, let's see this algebra," Sam leaned closer as she slumped against the wall, pulling the hated text book from her bag.

"I don't know why I'm havin' such a hard time," Megan whined, shoving the less than perfect test at him bitterly.

"Aww c'mon, a B minus is not that bad," he gently nudged her shoulder.

"One more wrong and it'd been a C," she sighed in defeat, "I don't even know why it's hard, it's like one problem I get, but the next just doesn't make any sense even though they're supposed to follow the same rules."

Sam smiled encouragingly, "You'll get it. Y'know, I heard that everybody's either right brained or left brained, so like you're either really good at readin' and creative stuff or math 'n science. You always ace English and the way you remember history stuff is unbelievable."

"So, I'm doomed to be stupid in math?" she whined, but his expression became stubbornly unamused.

"Y'know you're not stupid," Sam said simply, "Don't say shit like that."

"Alright," she scoffed lightly and opened her notebook, "Well, you're good at everything, help me then."

"Hey, kids," Darlene called from the kitchen, "Soups on!"

As expected, the pulled pork sandwiches were delicious.

Assisted by Sam, Megan felt much more confident completing her math homework and even fixed the problems she got wrong on her test to return for extra points, essentially removing the taunting minus symbol from the imperfect score. Once she'd gotten the hang of it, Sam began his book report and Megan occasionally paused her work to discuss some of her favorite parts of *The Phantom Tollbooth*.

Faintly, she heard Dan and peeked out Sam's window in time to see her brother waving to a departing van from their front porch before he disappeared through their front door.

"I should go," Megan began packing her things, "Dan's home."

"Thanks for the help," Sam set his notebook aside, sliding off his bed to walk her out.

34

"You too," she smiled, swinging her backpack onto one shoulder and entered the kitchen where Darlene was washing dishes while immersed in a hospital drama, "Bye, Darlene, thanks for the sandwich."

"You're very welcome, you skinny girl," she smiled, shaking her hands out and pat them dry on the dish towel before picking up a plastic grocery bag, heavy with takeout containers, "Here, I put some of the leftovers from last night in here, pulled pork, coleslaw for Dan and three of Travis's twice baked potatoes."

"Hope you saved me one," Sam mumbled half-heartedly.

His mom rolled her eyes, "Hush, y'know I did."

"Love you, Mom," Sam smirked and held the bag for Megan while she put on her shoes, curling her toes in the too small sneakers.

"Thanks, Darlene," Megan gave her a quick hug and took the bag from Sam, "My brothers would thank you too, y'know, if they were here, but they will next time they see ya I'm sure."

"My pleasure, darlin'," she smiled, but, with a brief falter in her expression, continued, "Y'know I saw your dad yesterday when I was workin'."

"Oh," Megan shifted her gaze to the bag of food in her hands and, for some reason, wondered if he'd eaten the pulled pork too.

"He seemed well," her tone heightened with the lie, "Sounded like he has some big jobs comin' up this summer."

"Yeah, I guess," Megan shrugged, wishing she was walking home already, but, before she could stop herself, sadly admitted, "He's not gonna be here for my birthday next month."

"That's too bad," the corners of Darlene's mouth tugged down, but suddenly widened into an excited smile at Megan and Sam, "I wanted to talk with you two about that. Since Sam's graduating right when you're turning thirteen I was gonna see if you'd like to do a double celebration, a party with all your friends, for both. Of course, I understand if you wanna do your own things, it's up to you two, I was just thinkin' ya might wanna-"

"Awesome," Megan and Sam answered together, following the perfectly timed coincidence with a high five and Darlene chuckled.

Megan said good night and walked passed the decaying ranch between her and Sam's homes to her own front porch. Inside, Dan was searching the barren fridge, but closed the door as she walked in and kicked off her shoes.

"You over at Sam's?" he asked, walking over.

"Yeah, he was helpin' me with my algebra," she said, handing him the bag of take-out.

"What's this?"

"Leftovers from Pederson's, pulled pork 'n twice baked potatoes," Megan slid onto her chair and unzipped her backpack, "I think Darlene said she grabbed you some coleslaw."

But Dan had already found the container, grabbed a fork from the drawer behind him, and dug in with the enthusiasm of a starved wolf.

Jimmy and Megan had never cared for the cabbage side dish, so she wasn't bothered by the few bits dropping from his eager lips back into the take-out bowl to be successfully scooped on another try. After five or six hearty forkfuls, Dan sighed and slowed his last few chews with his eyes closed. Capping the plastic bowl, he set it on a mostly bare shelf in the fridge with the rest of the leftover takeout, tossed his fork in the sink and took a swig of a glass of water he'd left on the counter.

"Thanks, I needed that. Finishing your homework?" Megan nodded and Dan smiled, "Alright, kid, I'll be outside workin' on Jimmy's car if ya need me. Okay?"

"Okay," Megan said absently, her eyes rereading the directions at the top of her worksheet as the screen door banged.

The history worksheet was easy, completing it in minutes, and she started studying her science notes and chapter summary. She wasn't as confident about the quiz tomorrow, but, besides her struggle to correctly spell some of the terms, Megan knew she had a fairly good grasp on light types and sound frequencies. Thankfully, her science teacher was pretty lenient with spelling, as long as it was close enough.

Jimmy's bedroom door creaked as Megan finished the last flashcard of term definitions, Dan always quizzed her on vocabulary words before a test.

"Mornin'," he patted her on the head and leaned against the counter in sweatpants and a baggy shirt.

"Evenin'," she giggled at his chin length hair sticking out in all directions.

"My mornin'," he smiled and ran a hand over his hair, accomplishing nothing to tame it, "How's school?"

"S'okay," she shrugged pitifully, not meeting his eyes.

"What happened?" he asked, crossing his arms and eyeing her with joking hardness, "Who'd I gotta kill?"

That produced a laughing smile as she shook her head at him, "I just didn't do well on a math test."

"What'd'ja get?" Jimmy asked, grabbing a cup from the cabinet and filling it in the sink.

"B minus," she admitted, knowing Jimmy's reaction before it came.

"I'd've loved B minuses," he scoffed and sipped his water, "Ya ain't always gotta be perfect, babygirl."

"I'm not," Megan insisted and Jimmy rolled his eyes, "I just like gettin' A's."

"M'just sayin' don't beat yourself up over one test," he said encouragingly, but a loud growl from his stomach encouraged a sudden grimace, "Man, I'm hungry, wish we had somethin' besides knock off Spaghettio's."

"Darlene gave me some leftovers from Pederson's," Megan pointed at the fridge with her pencil, "Pulled pork 'n potatoes."

"Twice baked?" Jimmy asked excitedly, already grabbing the leftovers from the fridge, popping the lid off the pulled pork and peered inside, "Oooooh my God, thank you Darlene!"

Megan looked up to see her brother picking out cold pulled pork with his fingers and dropping pieces into his mouth, moaning softly.

"Dude, that's gross," she sneered, "We're all gonna eat that."

"I'm your brother," Jimmy smiled, popping another piece in his mouth and set the container on the table, "Same germs."

"Not how that works, Jimmy," Megan giggled, shaking her head.

"I love Travis's twice baked," he groaned happily, unwrapping a wad of foil as Dan walked in drenched with sweat, the broken screen door banging behind him, "Hey, brother."

"Hey, d'ja get some sleep?" Dan asked, turning the kitchen faucet on with his forearm and washed his greasy hands.

"Like a baby," Jimmy smiled, piling pulled pork onto a plate next to the potato he'd claimed.

"Good," Dan dried his hands on the dish towel hanging over the oven handle, "Your beast is runnin', just took her around the block, started right up and there's definitely better power on acceleration. Hopefully it'll keep up for a little while."

"Thanks," Jimmy smiled graciously, tossing his plate in the microwave and it hummed to life, "I get paid tomorrow, I can give ya some money for the alternator."

"I'm gonna take the old one back to Mr. Glasby," Dan shrugged at his brother's offer of repayment, "It was refurbished, but he thinks he can get back some of what that one cost ya."

"Go, Mr. Glasby," Jimmy smiled, taking his car keys from Dan, the bottle opener keychain clinked as he shoved them in the pocket of his sweatpants.

"Yeah, we'll see," Dan sighed, "I'm gonna grab a shower. Megan, how's your homework comin'?"

"Done," she looked up from her text book, "Just studying for a science quiz tomorrow. Will you run through flashcards with me later?"

"Yeah, of course," he nodded and shut himself in the bathroom, the shower turned on moments later.

The microwave beeped and Jimmy joined Megan at the kitchen table with a steaming plate and a glass of water. Unlike Dan, Jimmy took a moment to assess the meal in front of him, deciding the best plan of attack before diving fork first into the twice baked potato. Jimmy was a surprisingly picky eater for someone who hadn't been given a lot of choices in the past and, when he was younger, had often complained about endless nights of macaroni and cheese or hotdogs. Somewhere in the last few years his whines had subsided into the occasional disgruntled comment about their bare pantry, and never within earshot of Dan.

"Oh my God that was good," Jimmy sat back, patting his stomach with a satisfied grin, "I think I'm gonna need to go back to sleep for a bit now."

"Thought'cha had plans tonight," Megan commented, glancing away from her science book.

"Not till later," he shrugged, "Jordan doesn't get off work till nine."

Jimmy dumped his barbeque sauce stained plate and fork in the sink and disappeared behind his bedroom door.

Megan heard the shower turn off with a squeak as she finished the end of the chapter review. Dan walked out with a towel wrapped around his waist and carried his dirty clothes to his bedroom, returning moments later in fresh jeans and a t-shirt.

"So, science quiz," Dan put a heavy hand on her shoulder, peering at her notes, "What's it on?"

"Light 'n sound," Megan craned her neck backwards, catching an unsure furrow between Dan's eyebrows.

"Oh, okay," he hesitated, but asked, "D'ja make your flashcards?" Megan held up the neat stack of white notecards, "Good, I'm gonna switch the loads, I'll be right back," and Dan disappeared down the basement stairs.

"D'ja get to ask Jay about that weekend?" Megan asked hopefully when he jogged back up the steps with a basket full of warm clothes and shut the basement door with his foot, muffling the sounds of the washer and dryer.

"I did," he grinned, setting the basket on the coffee table, "He doesn't think it'll be a problem, but we kinda gotta see how the rest'a this week goes. Armando's visiting family for two weeks and this new part-time kid we got isn't the most reliable about showin' up to work. I wish Jay'd just let me launch him and get somebody worth a damn."

"Me too," Megan nodded in blind solidarity, "Hey, can I go to the movies with Sam this weekend?"

Dan cringed, but quickly hid it with a sympathetic curl in the corners of his mouth, "Sweetheart, I don't really have any extra money right now, especially if ya wanna take a trip to Milwaukee, I'm sorry."

"Sam's payin'," she said, oblivious to his eyebrow raise and quiet scoff, and decided to try her luck, "I really wanna see Josie and the Pussycats."

"Isn't that PG-13?" Dan hid an amused smile at her timid nod, focusing on rolling his sleeves to his elbows, "Well, I'm sure it'll be just as good next month."

Megan shrugged with temperate disappointment, but hadn't had any hope he would bend his movie rule and, since she kind of wanted to see *Shrek* anyway, she wasn't really upset at his refusal.

Dan wasn't unreasonably strict, but, lately, Megan had been arguing more of his rules than usual, and she caught his relieved sigh when she didn't refute his decision. Megan had always been stubborn, but, the last few months, she'd been exceptionally moody and uncharacteristically defiant. After raising Jimmy as best he could, Dan had developed his own tactics for dealing with unruly teenagers, however, he was not prepared for the emotional rollercoaster his little sister was putting him through daily. Just the other night, in the climax of her tantrum about the Chicago book signing, Dan had promised if she slammed her door again he would take it off the hinges, forcing the finale of her fit into silence. Megan didn't even understand why she'd been so edgy, and was sure, from Dan's relaxed smile, he was starting to relish the moments she wasn't fighting him on something.

"Darlene wants to have a birthday and graduation party for Sam n' me. She didn't really say what, probably just over at the park or somethin',"

40

Megan changed the subject, hoping Dan would like the idea as much as she did.

"Do you wanna do that?" Dan asked, rinsing the bowl and plate in the sink before organizing them in the half empty dishwasher.

"Yeah," Megan nodded eagerly.

"Well, as long as you're okay with sharin', it sounds like a great idea, I'll talk to Darlene when we're over for dinner Sunday," he said and picked his truck keys off the counter, "I gotta run that old alternator back to the store. Wanna take a break and come with me?"

"Sure," she smiled, sliding off the kitchen chair, leaving her homework spread out on half of the white table.

Dan held the door for her, pulling it shut behind himself before jogging down the porch steps and hopping into the truck.

An open bag of Skittles sat in the cup holder and, giving her brother a sneaky look, Megan poured a few in her hand, popping them quickly in her mouth. He chuckled, turned the truck's engine over and backed out of their driveway, passing Jimmy's Oldsmobile parked on the street.

The parts store was much busier than their previous evening's trip and Dan pulled into a spot at the end of the small lot. He grabbed a brown box from the back of his truck and gestured for Megan to lead the way inside.

"Behave, please," he sighed, "There's people here today."

She whipped around, sticking her tongue out at him before quickly spinning forward again, remembering how her backwards walk had ended the night before.

"Watch it," Dan warned jokingly, "I'mma cut that tongue off one'a these days."

Megan giggled at his old threat, when she was little she'd actually believed it and refused to speak around Dan for an entire day until he'd finally tickled it out of her why she was giving him the silent treatment. He'd fallen into a fit of laughter when she'd told him she didn't want him to cut off her tongue, but promised he was only joking and would never do anything so terrible to his favorite girl. It had become one of their many inside jokes.

"Hi, Mr. Glasby," she called across the store, waving to the gray-haired man behind the counter, who smiled and waved back, despite the customer checking out in front of him.

Dan, however, raised an eyebrow and lowered his voice, "Don't yell at people when they're talkin'."

"I was just sayin' hi," she reasoned indignantly, crossing her arms.

"It's rude, Meg," his hushed scolding was met by an angry glare, "Stop poutin' at me," but she let out a disgruntled scoff instead, and Dan leaned down, whispering firmly, "If you're lookin' for a reason to pout, I'll give ya one."

And a mild, yet threatening, tap landed on her behind.

Megan flipped around, her face burning with embarrassment while scowling at Dan, but his perfected, no-nonsense, expression made her immediately shift her gaze down and mumble a mostly inaudible apology. Glancing around them, she was relieved the few patrons nearby seemed unfazed and hoped no one had noticed the childish reprimand. When Dan approached the counter with his return, Megan stayed by the display for headlights, pushing the tester button every few seconds to light up the bulbs behind the smiling cartoon car.

Grudgingly, she knew Dan was right about it being rude to interrupt, and it definitely wasn't the first time he'd reproached her about it, but sometimes, a lot of times, she just forgot herself. Dan was always understanding if she apologized for an outburst, but, lately, it seemed even a mild scolding sent her into brooding insolence, occasionally leading to a grand finale fit, complete with stomping feet, shrill cries and throwing things. Dan had resumed an old threat of a warm backside and, even though he'd never landed more than a sharp swat to get her attention, Megan didn't appreciate the timeworn warning, still, it was highly effective.

"Megan, c'mere," Dan called and she unenthusiastically trudged to the counter, avoiding his eyes.

"I got somethin' for ya," Mr. Glasby smiled promisingly and Megan instantly brightened at the expectation of a gift, "My wife found this when she was cleanin' out some old stuff, not me thankfully," he chuckled at his joke and pulled an antique book from under the counter, offering it to Megan, "Dan's always tellin' me how ya love to read and ya like those Disney movies, but these are the original fairy tales, before Hollywood got a hold of 'em."

Megan's smile widened, eagerly taking the dried volume, "Thank you, Mr. Glasby, this is awesome!"

"You're very welcome," he beamed at her enthusiasm for a book that would have ended up in the fifty-cent bin of his garage sale, "They're just short stories, sure you could read one tonight."

"When she's done studyin' for a science test," Dan smiled, nudging Megan on the shoulder, but she kept her eyes on the book, trying to ignore him.

"Boy, your big brother sure cracks a whip, huh?" Mr. Glasby joked and Megan felt warmth creeping to her cheeks, hoping he didn't notice, but his attention had returned to Dan, "I'll let'cha know what I hear back about that busted alternator."

"Thank you, Mr. Glasby, I appreciate it," Dan nodded, guiding his sister from the store with a gentle hand, her eyes fixed on the book.

Megan climbed carefully into the green truck, making sure the collection of tales didn't touch anything. Hans Christian Andersen Stories for Children, in cracked and peeling letters, was still clear across the cover and the smell of crisp, aged paper greeted her as she cracked open the spine. The contents page listed several stories she knew like The Little Mermaid, The Ugly Duckling and Thumbelina, but also a few she'd never heard of and flipped to the page numbered for The Little Matchgirl, tracing the single, sketched illustration with her index finger. A little girl in rags holding a tin cup of matches stood on a brick street, surrounded by bustling people, but completely alone. Megan felt sorry for her and hoped the story had a happy ending.

"Pretty nice of him to think'a you, huh?" Dan said, trying to pull her attention from the pages.

"Yeah," she nodded, closing the hardcover and ran her fingers over the raised letters again, "It's really cool."

"You hungry?" he asked.

"I could eat," she shrugged, stubbornly holding onto a twinge of irritational anger, despite the voice in her head telling her to let it go, wishing she'd just accepted his small criticism about her outburst, because her pouting had caused the real embarrassment.

"Y'know," Dan started and Megan's stomach twisted, hearing the lecture begin, "I'm not tryin' to be a jerk, Megan, I don't tell you not to do things 'cause I enjoy it. Seriously, I wish I could just be your big brother, kid," she looked at him finally, his exhausted eyes, aged well beyond his twenty-two years, glanced at her earnestly before focusing on the road again and Dan continued, "But it is what it is, and we've been doin' alright. Jimmy's a piece'a work, but you, sweetheart, you are so smart, you're gonna go to college, you could do anything you want with your life. I know ya think I'm hard on you, but I just want you to succeed. And lemme ask, when ya see somebody else yellin' and interruptin' people, what'd you think?"

Suddenly being asked to respond, Megan was a little lost for words, but a recent scene came to mind where she'd watched a fifth grader yell at his mother and slam their minivan's sliding door during drop off and she mumbled, "Pretty dumb."

"Okay, dumb," he suppressed a snicker, "And you're not dumb, right?" she shook her head, "And I bet most'a the time you get warned ya probably know you're wrong already. Truth?" she nodded, "So, why not just say, okay Dan, instead'a gettin' all mad at me?"

She shrugged, but the slight raise in his eyebrows said that was not a sufficient response.

"I dunno," Megan shrugged again, "I just get angry."

"Angry or embarrassed?" Dan gave her a sideways glance as he pulled into their driveway.

"Well, it doesn't help when you swat me in public," she mumbled with one last glare of lingering resentment.

Dan, however, laughed aloud and Megan's lips curled unwillingly at his rare amusement, "C'mon, you've seen kids get it in public and that's not at all what I did," she was having a hard time maintaining her pout as he just about pleaded, "Megan, I always try to say stuff to you so nobody can hear, y'know I don't wanna embarrass you, but I also

44

don't want you to embarrass me. And lately, kid, you've been pushin' buttons I didn't even know I had."

Megan felt swirling guilt return to her gut at his frustrated confession. Dan was always discreet if he scolded her around others and, with the culpable consideration that her behavior could embarrass her brother, not only herself, she wrapped her arms around his neck.

"M'sorry, Dan," she sniffled pitifully.

"Just try 'n do better, sweetheart," Dan kissed her hair, "That's all I ask."

Megan nodded and got out of the truck, carefully carrying her new treasure into the house. A light smack crossed her backside as she stepped onto the porch and Megan turned, trying to hide a smile by sticking her tongue out at Dan, but couldn't suppress a short giggle at the scissor gesture he made with his fingers.

"Alright," Dan said, opening the fridge and pulling the leftovers out, "I'm gettin' in on some'a this pork and then we'll run through your science stuff. How much ya want?"

Megan took the fork from him and scooped a decent sized pile of barbequed pork onto her plate, leaving most of it in the takeout bowl, and unwrapped the smaller of the two twice baked potatoes, plopping it next to the pork, before heating it on high in the microwave. A few minutes later, they sat at the table together, as they did most evenings, each with a large glass of milk and a steaming plate. Jimmy used to eat with them, but, since he'd started working third shift, he was usually waking up or leaving around the time they sat down to eat.

Jimmy's door creaked opened and he entered the kitchen in a fresh, black button-down shirt, untucked over dark jeans and his shaggy bangs swooped to the side.

"Where're you headed?" Dan asked, shoving the last piece of twice baked potato in his mouth before standing to clear his plate.

"Goin' to get Jordan," Jimmy nodded, rolling the sleeves of his shirt to his elbows, "I'm not sure what the plan is."

"Just be smart, Jimmy," Dan sighed, leaning against the sink and crossed his arms.

"C'mon, brother, you insult me," Jimmy joked, "I'm always smart."

"Jim," Dan raised a threatening eyebrow.

"Yeah," Jimmy nodded impatiently, "I'll be fine, I promise, no drinkin'."

"Ya better call me if you do," Dan said firmly, "I'll be more pissed if you drive home than if I gotta come get'cha."

"I got it, Dan," Jimmy seemed to be putting effort into not rolling his eyes.

"Bye, Jimmy," Megan said, hiding any concern in her expression with a large bite of pork, and crossed her fingers, wishing he'd keep his promise.

"Bye, babygirl, I'll see ya tomorrow," Jimmy kissed the top of her head on his way to the front door, calling as he left, "G'night, brother."

"You call me, Jimmy!" Dan yelled as the screen door slapped its frame.

Moments later, the Oldsmobile's whine was followed by a high-pitched scratch of the wheels as Jimmy accelerated away from their house.

With a sliver of potato and a few forkfuls left of pork on her plate, Megan pushed it away and hopped off the kitchen chair.

"Ya done?" Dan asked, reaching for her plate.

She nodded, putting a hand over her stomach in emphasis, and he gulped the rest of her dinner in a few bites before dumping the plate in the sink.

Megan grabbed her science flashcards, fanning them with her thumb, but Dan jokingly snatched them and led her to the couch, settling on either side as they always did when he helped her study, preferring to have his feet on the coffee table after a long day at the shop.

"Light 'n sound, huh?" he examined the definitions with a strange grin, "Y'know, pretty soon, I'm not gonna be able to help you with this stuff anymore, you're gettin' smarter than me."

"Never," she stuck her tongue out at him and giggled madly when he pretended to snatch it between his calloused fingers.

# Chapter 3

Blue and red flashed in her dark bedroom as Megan opened her sleepy eyes, hearing deep voices in the front yard and shook the buzz of sleep from her head. She hurried to her window, leaning over her short bookcase and peered through the dusty blinds.

Dan was speaking with two officers at the end of the driveway and she faintly saw the outline of Jimmy's shaggy hair, hanging his head in the back of the patrol car. Her stomach twisted, hoping they were bringing him home, not taking him away, and saw the strained flex in Dan's shoulders as he shook his head at the policemen.

Megan breathed a sigh of relief when one of them wrenched the door open and pulled Jimmy out. Faintly lit by the street light, she could almost see the defiant look he shot the officer, but cowered the moment Dan approached and grabbed him by the back of his neck, practically throwing Jimmy towards the front porch. He shook both of the officers' hands and pivoted threateningly on Jimmy as the police cruiser's lights turned off before driving away.

Jimmy held up defensive hands at his angry older brother, but Dan grabbed his upper arm and no less than dragged him up the porch stairs. Unable to help her curiosity, Megan slipped out of her bedroom, pressing against the hallway wall, out of sight from the main room, just as the banging screen door was overshadowed by the heavy front door's slam.

"-desperate to get outta there 'n now you're breakin' in?! Goddamn it, Jimmy!" Dan yelled and Megan heard the scrapping of a kitchen chair.

The chair creaked under dropping weight as Jimmy grunted, "We were just messin' around, Dan, nobody thought-"

"Obviously!" Dan barked, "How much did ya have to drink?"

"Like, three beers," Jimmy mumbled.

"Don't lie to me, Jimmy!" Megan winced at his livid volume, she hated when Dan yelled.

"I'm not!" Jimmy yelled back, but instantly lowered his voice, "Seriously, dude, like three or four."

"Don't dude me right now," Dan growled, "You're lucky it was my friends who caught'cha or you'd be in jail right now! How many Jim?"

"I had a few," Jimmy admitted quietly, "But I didn't drive."

"Would ya have if the cops hadn't shown up and broken up your little vandal party?" Jimmy didn't respond, "What were you thinkin' Jimmy?" again, Megan didn't hear an answer before Dan continued, "You're done, two weeks, you don't leave this house except for work-"

"I'm eighteen!" Jimmy burst.

"Exactly!" Dan raged, "They ain't bringin' ya home next time, Jim!"

"You can't ground me anymore!" Jimmy's voice shook with frustration.

"How 'bout a month?" Dan challenged.

"I'm not Megan!" Jimmy screamed and she jumped a little when the chair crashed to the floor, "I'm an adult, Dan!"

"Then act like it, Jimmy!" Dan's booming voice overpowered the tantrum, "I'm in charge, and as long as you live in this house, you follow my rules! Now, go to bed, we'll pick this up tomorrow, when you're sober."

"You can't just send me-" Jimmy began furiously, but a fleeting scuffle interrupted and he sniffled, "Screw you, Dan," before his bedroom door slammed.

Megan tried to sneak quietly back into her room, but, just as she shuffled one step to the side, Dan's angry form appeared at the end of the hallway.

"Back to bed, right now," he growled and she quickly shut herself in her bedroom, biting back tears.

Megan had a hard time falling back to sleep, crying quietly until she finally drifted off. Jimmy had been brought home twice before by the police, each time followed by a similar fight.

She hated when her brothers yelled at each other, but worse would be the next few days. Neither would speak to each other, Jimmy would brood in his room and Dan would be unrelentingly strict with Megan, despite her overall innocence. She didn't understand why Jimmy found himself in trouble so much, wishing he wasn't so often in the wrong place at the wrong time. Dan didn't offer the same excuse for his brother, though it was no secret his friendships and previous football team comradery with a few of the local police was the reason they brought Jimmy home instead of jail.

Dan opened her door, knocking loudly, "Hey, up, you're runnin' late."

After one more solid rap on the door, Megan opened her tired eyes in the bright room. She hadn't gotten much sleep after the police left and yawned heavily, dragging herself out of bed. The hallway smelled of bacon and the inviting sound of crackling grease perked her ears, but Megan couldn't shake her exhausted haze.

"Dan," she used her most pathetic tone, hoping he'd relent to her impending request, "I don't feel good."

He looked up from the laundry he was folding on the couch, approaching as concern etched between his eyebrows, and held the back of his hand to her forehead, "You're not warm," then Dan asked, "D'ja have a hard time fallin' back to sleep last night?" Megan nodded pathetically, but a sigh revealed his answer before she even asked, "Make it through the day and you're goin' to bed early tonight."

Dan took a few long strides to the stove, flipping bacon in the frying pan, and Megan let out an exasperated growl, slamming the bathroom door in frustration.

"Hey!" she heard Dan yell from the other side of the door, "I am in no mood today, Megan, straighten up!"

She turned on the shower and gestured rudely at the door.

Megan left her pajamas on the floor of the bathroom and snuck to her bedroom. She took longer than usual to get dressed, trying to avoid returning to the kitchen, despite the enticing scent of bacon and her rumbling stomach.

"Megan," Dan knocked twice on her closed door, "Let's go, you're gonna miss the bus."

Glancing at her alarm clock, she had about twelve minutes to get to the corner or would be sitting through an awkward drive with Dan. Sighing angrily, Megan left her room, actively averting her eyes from the brother who was setting a plate of crispy bacon on the table next to a glass of orange juice.

"C'mon and eat," his tone wasn't demanding, but he clearly wasn't asking.

"I'm not hungry," Megan slipped on her backpack and started walking towards the front door.

"Sit!" Dan barked, pointing firmly towards the table, "I'm not playin' games with you today. Eat'cher breakfast."

"I told you I don't feel good!" Megan implored angrily, throwing herself in the chair.

"Megan, stop it!" Dan growled, "I'm sorry you didn't get much sleep last night, I didn't either! Please, kid, just gimme a break today!"

He emphasized his frustration by tossing the hot frying pan in the sink deafeningly before storming into his bedroom. Megan flinched at the noise and felt tears sting her eyes, the plate of bacon blurred as she bit back sobs of exhaustion, anger and growing guilt. Wiping straggling tears from her cheeks, she started munching the bacon and sipped her orange juice, noticing at least an improvement to her exhaustion as the pork and vitamin C filled her stomach.

She knew Dan hadn't gotten much sleep, if any, after the police had left, yet, he'd had her breakfast waiting where it always was, and juggled the morning chores, before being accosted by a grumpy twelve-year-old who wanted to get out of school for the day. Megan finished her last piece of bacon as Dan returned to the front room, rolling up the sleeves of his unbuttoned work shirt and shoved his feet into his greasy work boots by the front door.

"Dan?" Megan began tentatively.

He sighed, eyeing her sternly as he righted himself, "You're goin' to school, Megan."

51

"I know," she nodded, sliding off her chair and shuffled towards him, looking as apologetic as possible, "I'm sorry for bein' mean."

His expression softened, the corners of his mouth curling while he crouched and wrapped his arms around her, "Thank you, sweetheart, I'm sorry I yelled."

"I love you, Dan," Megan mumbled into his shirt and he squeezed her a little tighter before letting go, reaching for the door knob.

"I love you, too," Dan smiled, opening the front door, "Good luck on your science quiz, I'll see ya when I get home."

"Have a good day at work," she called, hurrying across the lawn towards Sam, reaching the corner seconds before the bus made a full stop.

Friday went by surprisingly fast. Megan was confident she'd known the answer to every question on her science quiz and returned her corrected math test, appreciating that the entire class period was a review of the last chapter, apparently, she hadn't been the only student to struggle on the previous exam. When bus riders were called to leave for the day, Megan rushed through the halls, finding Sam at the front door, and no less than dragged him to the bus. Despite any homework, they had resolute plans to go to the river immediately after dumping their backpacks.

"I'll be over in a minute," Sam called, taking the porch steps to his front door two at a time while Megan hurried across the yards to her own house.

The broken screen door banged as she rushed into the house and tossed her backpack under the kitchen table on the way to her bedroom. Quickly, Megan changed into a secondhand t-shirt and searched for the oldest pair of jeans she could still wriggle into. Dan had gotten really angry when she'd ruined a new pair playing at the river and, since that excruciatingly long lecture, she'd remembered to change into clothes she didn't wear to school or church anymore.

"Hey," Megan looked up at the knock on her open door and saw Jimmy leaning on the frame, his shaggy hair hanging in his face.

"Hey," she grunted, working the too tight jeans over her skinny hips, "You workin' tonight?"

"Not till Sunday," he said, "Where ya off to?"

"Sam 'n I are goin' to the river," she scooted passed him into the kitchen as Sam walked through the front door.

"Hey, Jimmy," Sam waved, wiping his feet even though he didn't venture off the mat.

"Hey, kiddo," Jimmy grinned, "Ya ready for graduation?"

"I found out I gotta make a speech," Sam shrugged, but elaborated at Megan and Jimmy's identical confusion, "I'm valedictorian."

"Sam!" Megan gasped happily, hugging him in her excitement, "You didn't tell me that! When'd'ja find out?"

"Today," he shrugged nonchalantly again when she released him.

"That's awesome," Jimmy smiled, offering a congratulatory high five, "Good job, Sam."

"Thanks," Sam's cheeks were slightly flushed and he turned to Megan, "You wanna get goin'?"

"Yeah, let's go," Megan jerked her head out the door before looking at her brother, "I'll be home before dark, Jimmy. Let Dan know, please?"

"What I live for, talkin' to Dan," he rolled his eyes, dropping heavily onto the couch.

"Please don't fight tonight," Megan pleaded as the screen door whacked the frame behind Sam.

"Not up to me," Jimmy shrugged, turning on the television, obviously trying to avoid the sad eyes trained on him.

"Please, Jimmy," she implored, "I hate when you guys fight."

With a heavy sigh, he turned and said, "I promise I won't start anything, good enough?" she nodded, "Alright, get outta here."

Megan planted a quick kiss on Jimmy's cheek and he squeezed an arm around her in a seated hug before she bolted out the broken screen door.

Sam was waiting on his bike in her driveway, his fishing pole attached to the frame with pieces of a broken shoelace and a five-gallon bucket hung from his handlebars. Megan grabbed her bike, a hand-me-down of Dan's propped against the lattice under the overhang of the front porch, and sped off behind her best friend. The bucket banged hollowly against Sam's bike and the fishing pole bounced wildly as they sped down the low grade of their street three blocks to the river.

Most of the houses they passed were in the same level of mild deterioration as Megan's, although Darlene kept her yard pretty in the warm months with flowers lining the short path to their front porch, and always had the best holiday decorations. Others, however, were foreclosed, abandoned and completely decayed, like the house between theirs, with holes in the roof and boarded up windows.

They pedaled standing up, pumping hard, and raced down the street before slamming their brakes at the dead end, just short of the drop to the river bank.

Megan leaned her bike on the other side of a fire hydrant from Sam, whose fingers were busy untying his fishing pole as she grabbed the bucket from his handlebars. He shoved the frayed laces into his pocket and followed her down the short, steep embankment to the few feet of dirty sand and rocks along the river's edge. Megan set the bucket down and started flipping over rocks, searching for worms. Unfortunately, it hadn't rained much recently and they had to dig with sticks and fingers a few inches down to locate the squirming, pink treasures.

"Hey!" Sam exclaimed, dropping a worm mid extraction and it slithered into its dirty sanctuary, "The nest!"

Megan jumped to her feet, wiping mud on her torn jeans and followed him to a nearby cluster of trees growing from the side of the embankment. Expertly, they climbed the nearest one, using the massive, looped roots to propel themselves onto low hanging branches. Reaching the highest branch with enough strength to hold them both, Sam and Megan scooted as far as they knew they could towards the tree next to the one they were sitting in and tried to breathe softly, despite the raucous they'd made climbing to the lookout post.

Through the leaves, close to the trunk of the neighboring tree, was a small nest with two turquoise eggs situated side by side. They'd found it the week before and had hoped to find newly hatched, baby birds on every opportunity they'd had to sneak to the river since. Today was

54

another small disappointment, but they still sat, whispering and watching, with feeble hope of a change while they waited, eventually returning to the fishing pole and a mostly escaped pile of worms.

Megan didn't have her own fishing pole, not that she wanted one, she only fished because Sam liked it, and he didn't mind sharing. His grandfather had taught him all about fish, but Megan never understood why Sam let some go while others flailed in the bucket, though thoroughly enjoyed how Darlene cooked up the ones Sam deemed good enough for dinner, despite her usual repulsion of restaurant fish. The sun was low in the sky as Megan tossed the line into the water again.

"Hey," Sam looked up from his two successful catches that had finally stopped floundering in the bucket, "We should get goin', reel that in."

"But I haven't caught anything yet," Megan protested, returning her attention to the taught line.

"You never do," Sam chuckled, "C'mon it's gettin' dark, we're already late."

Megan sighed, relenting to his rationality and the rumble in her gut telling her she'd missed dinner, but shielded her eyes from the sudden bright headlights approaching with an unmistakable growl. Her stomach flipped as the green truck made an abrupt maneuver and halted in front of the fire hydrant, followed immediately by a heavy slam.

"Megan Marie!" her eyes went wide seeing her fuming older brother glaring from the top of the river bank, "Now!"

"Dan, I-," she tried, blindly releasing the fishing pole being tugged from her.

"One!" Dan barked and, with a flush of embarrassment warming her face, Megan scurried up the embankment, unable to explain before he ordered, "Get in the truck."

"But my bi-" Megan's protest was short-lived when Dan tugged her by the upper arm to the passenger door and landed an impatient swat on her behind, instantly springing hot tears to her eyes.

Dan silently picked her bike up with one hand and set it in the bed, reaching next for Sam's as the young man climbed the steep incline with a tight grip on his fishing pole, the bucket swinging from his forearm. Megan wrenched open the truck door, far too embarrassed to look at her friend.

"I'm sorry, Dan," Sam said nervously, handing Dan his pole and bucket, "We we're just about to leave, really."

"Get in the truck, Sam," Dan said simply and Megan scooted over at the words, livid she had to sit so close to her mean, bossy, unreasonable brother.

The short ride up the hill to their driveway was silent, though Sam tried to give Megan a few encouraging smiles, all of which were returned with an angry pout. She scooted out the passenger side after Sam and slammed the door as hard as she could, catching an intimidating glare from Dan as he pulled Sam's bike out of the truck bed.

"G'night, Sam," Dan growled after handing the young man his fish bucket and pole, setting his eyes on Megan, standing cross-armed next to his truck.

"G'night," Sam answered timidly and shifted his eyes with another weakly hopeful grin, "G'night, Megan."

"See ya tomorrow, Sam," she ground out, her eyes locked challengingly on her brother's.

"Wouldn't count on it," Dan jerked his head towards the house in a silent order she knew better than to ignore.

And Megan stomped as hard as she could on the porch steps, slamming the front door behind her.

Jimmy looked up from the couch at her livid entrance, but didn't seem at all surprised, "Ya missed dinner, kid."

"I told you I'd be back before it got dark!" she yelled, earning a rare eyebrow raise from Jimmy.

"Looks pretty dark to me," he scoffed, narrowing his eyes, "And you didn't tell me you were supposed to go to bed early tonight."

The screen door banged as Dan shut the front door, his face contorted with anger. Megan rounded on him instantly.

56

"I can't believe you!" she shrieked through the beginning of sobs, tears already streaming down her face.

"You can't believe me?!" Dan returned incredulously, "It's eight o'clock, Megan!"

"It's Friday!" the stupid excuse burst from her lips, but Megan held her angry scowl with conviction.

"And I told'ja this mornin' you were goin' to bed early tonight. Didn't I?" Dan growled and she shifted her eyes to the floor, "Megan, you look at me and you answer, right now, little girl."

"I'm not a little girl!" Megan shouted at the despised nickname that always meant she was in trouble.

"Sure actin' like it," Dan responded habitually, taking a threatening step towards her and Megan instinctually covered her behind, retreating until she bumped into the living room wall, angry embarrassment boiling as he continued, "Were you told to go to bed early tonight? Heck, even if ya hadn't. What time are you supposed to be home?"

"Seven thirty," Megan muttered at the floor.

"So, what is it exactly about what I just did that you can't believe?" Dan tugged her chin up.

"You embarrassed me in front of my best friend!" Megan pushed him away as hard as she could and tried to slide down the wall, but was swiftly stopped by a strong hand on her upper arm as Dan pulled her towards the couch Jimmy had quietly vacated for the solitude of his bedroom. Her heart beat frantically, "Nooo, Daaan!" Megan dug her heels into the carpet, squirming as much as she could, "I'm thir-teen!"

"You're twelve," Dan argued, trying to reestablish his grip while she struggled desperately to be released, "And you're not actin' like that either!"

"I'm sorry!" Megan screeched when Dan's arm wrapped around her middle and lifted her awkwardly into the air, "Please, please, no, Dan! STOP!"

"Are you gonna stop?" he asked firmly.

A tiny sob escaped before Megan sniffled, "Yeah."

He set her on her feet, sitting on the middle couch cushion with his hands holding her shoulders and his eyes focused intently on hers.

"Tell me why you're in trouble," his demand was stern, but lighthearted enough to give Megan hope she could talk her way out of being punished and she blinked a few more tears down her cheeks.

"I was late," she grumbled, her eyes finding her feet, but Dan lifted her chin.

"And?" he asked.

Megan took a deep, shaking breath before admitting, "I threw a fit."

"Does that sound like something a thirteen-year-old does?" his question brought a level of shame into Megan's already fragile emotions and she shook her head with a sob, but Dan continued, "You broke curfew and then had a tantrum 'cause y'knew you were in trouble. Megan I am so disappointed in you tonight."

"I'm r-eally sor-ry, D-an," she managed through a fairly dramatic whimper.

"You're grounded for the weekend," he said simply and, though another sob escaped, Megan nodded, honestly glad it wasn't longer. Dan wiped her tears with his thumbs, gently ordering, "Go wash up and get to bed."

"I am sorry," she swore, throwing her arms around his neck and nearly climbed onto his lap.

"Show me, Megan," he sighed, squeezing her tightly, "Please, be my good girl again, sweetheart."

"I will," she nodded into the damp spot on his t-shirt, "I promise."

"Alright," he patted her back, "Bed."

With a last apologetic glance at Dan's weary eyes, Megan used the bathroom before slipping into her bedroom and changing into pajamas.

Her stomach growled as she pulled on an old pair of Jimmy's gym shorts and she thought about sneaking into the kitchen for a quick snack. Dan wouldn't refuse, even if she'd missed dinner by her own fault. Quietly cracking her door, Megan peered down the hall, seeing the kitchen light still on, but the house was silent, and she slid down the wall, glancing around the corner.

Dan's hands gripped the counter in front of the sink, his head hanging over the basin as his shoulders shook and a repressed sniffle reached her ears. Her throat tightened and she silently backtracked into her bedroom, bursting into muffled sobs after closing her door. Megan's stomach was painfully empty, but finding her unbreakable brother crying alone over the kitchen sink caused a wave of guilt and anguish that pushed away her personal discomfort.

"Hey," Megan found herself being shaken gently awake and blinked in the light as Dan's face came into focus, "I'm headed to work, there's frozen waffles 'n syrup in there for ya."

"Thanks," she mumbled groggily.

"Clean this sty today, huh?" Dan nudged her, glancing around the messy bedroom.

"M'kay," she nodded, her eyelids falling closed while trying to keep her attention on Dan.

"Go back to sleep," he smiled, brushing her hair back and planted a soft kiss on her forehead, "I'll see you later."

"Mhmmm," Megan hummed into her pillow, falling back into the warm darkness of sleep as the latch of her door clicked softly.

Finally, when the birds outside her window were chirping incessantly, Megan rolled off her bed and shuffled into the hallway. Jimmy was sitting on the couch, bent over a plate of waffles drowned in sticky syrup, laughing wildly at the television as she closed herself in the bathroom.

"Mornin', trouble," Jimmy winked when she walked out, "Want me to make you some waffles or ya got it?"

"I'm not three, Jimmy," she sneered, lifting on her toes to open the freezer.

"Just tryin' to be nice," he scoffed, shoving a large bite in his mouth.

Megan popped two cold waffles in the toaster, still plugged in next to the stove, and avoided it carefully while dragging her knees onto the counter to reach the plates in the top cabinet, dismounting expertly.

Jimmy chuckled again at the television and Megan narrowed her eyes at the crude cartoon program.

"Can we watch somethin' else?" she whined, pulling the nearly empty carton of orange juice from the fridge and set it hard on the counter.

"It's a Rocko marathon!" Jimmy implored.

"I'm not supposed to watch it," Megan argued, shutting the fridge door hard.

"I won't tell," Jimmy offered snidely.

"I don't like it!" she nearly yelled.

"Alright, look," Jimmy stood and walked into the kitchen, "We're stuck here together all day, and I'm not dealin' with your moody girl crap," with a single eyebrow raise, he continued, "Guess ya didn't get it good enough last night."

"Shut up, Jimmy," Megan muttered, sure her ears were burning as hot as the steaming waffles that decided to pop at that moment.

"You wanna spend the day in your room?" Jimmy growled and she flipped at him indignantly before forcing a complying head shake, "Cut it out then, I didn't do anything to you."

"Dan's always mean to me when you get in trouble," Megan grumbled bitterly.

"Wait," Jimmy expelled a hard laugh, "So, 'cause you didn't listen, came home late, and had a frickin' tantrum like a two-year-old, that's my fault?"

Megan's eyes found her bare feet, knowing Jimmy was right, but the defiance she felt was stubborn and merely shrugged in response.

"Can we be good now?" he leaned down to make her look at him and she offered a small nod, "Okay, eat'cher breakfast."

Megan covered her waffles in butter and syrup and grabbed a fork from the drawer before joining him on the couch. Jimmy flipped the channel and grinned as delight replaced her lingering scowl when the Recess theme song blared from the television. They sat together for a couple hours, mindlessly absorbed in cartoons, and each had a second helping of frozen waffles before Jimmy wound the cord around the toaster and shoved it in a low cabinet.

"Dan ask ya to do anything today?" he asked, checking the time on the microwave, "It's almost noon."

"Clean my room," she shrugged.

"Wanna hazmat suit?" Jimmy chuckled.

"You're one to talk," she sneered.

"Yeah," Jimmy smirked, "But he didn't tell me to clean my room."

Rolling her eyes, Megan decided to take a shower before starting on the assigned task, spending a bit longer than usual washing her hair. Her pajamas remained on the bathroom floor after she went back to her room and slowly picked through a basket of clean clothes for jeans and a t-shirt.

Clothes, dirty and clean, were strewn around the floor and piled on the worn beanbag chair in the corner. Scraps of magazines and a bottle of Elmer's glue had been shoved to the side of her dresser, the remaining mess of a two-week-old school project she'd moved from the kitchen table to avoid cleaning. Megan sighed at the overwhelming mounds of clutter and glanced at the alarm clock on her nightstand, mostly hidden behind books and empty water glasses. It was noon and Dan would be home a little after three since the shop closed early on Saturdays.

Assessing the chaos, Megan was confident she had time before Dan returned and picked up Fire Fox Embers, the first book in the beloved trilogy she'd started rereading after learning about A.K. Foreman's book signings. Plopping on her bed with a soft creak, Megan opened to the folded corner page and fell back into her favorite story.

"Hey," Jimmy called, knocking on her door and didn't wait for a response before barging into her bedroom.

"Hey, privacy," she snapped, flipping the book closed on her index finger.

"You better get goin'," Jimmy ignored her protest and nudged an inside out pair of jeans with his foot, looking around the disheveled room.

"I'll get it done," she sighed, "Get out."

"It's two," he warned, but softened his tone, asking, "You want some help?"

Brightening at his offer, Megan slid off her bed, "Yeah, thanks, Jimmy."

"What's dirty?" he kicked a wadded-up t-shirt onto the already covered beanbag chair and she shrugged. Jimmy chuckled, pointing to the basket of semi-folded clothes, "Okay, those are clean, put 'em away."

He disappeared briefly and returned with the hamper, proceeding to shovel her dirty clothes in by the handful while Megan shoved what was clean into her dresser. She pulled open the middle drawer and crammed in an armful of clean shirts without refolding them and snapped it shut. Then tossed a pair of jeans in the bottom drawer and kicked it closed with a loud crack. Jimmy shook his head.

"Ya got too many clothes, girl," he scoffed, putting his foot on top of the swollen hamper and Megan laughed as he overexaggerated his effort to stomp them down, "I'm gonna start this, keep goin'."

With her clothes put away, or on their way to the wash, Megan felt far less overcome by the mess that was left and picked up the pieces of scrap paper from her collage, squishing them into the wastebasket under her nightstand that begged to be emptied. Jimmy reappeared in the doorway, slightly out of breath from jogging up the basement stairs, and nodded at the improvement. But his eyes caught the congested wastebasket as Megan was straightening her blanket and Jimmy took the trash to the kitchen garbage can.

"Thanks," Megan smiled when he set it back under her nightstand.

"So, this is where all the cups went," he joked and picked up the half empty water glasses, squeezing a couple against his side to avoid a second trip.

Leaving Embers on her bed, Megan picked up the other books from her nightstand and around the floor, including the short stories Mr. Glasby had given her, and organized them in the bookcase under her window. Turning to evaluate the progress they'd made, she smiled sweetly at Jimmy when he returned, putting his hands on his hips and nodded with satisfaction.

"Nice work," he said, "Want me to get'cha the vacuum?"

Her shoulders slumped and she rolled her eyes, "It's fine."

"Babygirl," Jimmy sighed, "C'mon cross the finish line, you're almost done, I'll grab it."

Megan flopped onto her bed and cracked open her book again, ignoring Jimmy as he wheeled in the black Dirt Devil. However, she was unable to ignore the book being torn from her hands and quickly whapped on the side of her hip.

"Hey!" she said crossly.

"I'm not kiddin', Megan," Jimmy tossed the book on the foot of her bed, "It'll take two minutes, let's go."

With a heavy sigh and dramatic eyeroll, Megan slid off her bed, snatching the meticulously wound cord from the neck of the vacuum and roughly shoved the plug into a wall socket. Jimmy shook his head, but said nothing as he left her room and a few moments later, she heard the screen door bang over the whir of the old upright. Her room wasn't very big, and Megan wasn't trying to do a very good job, ignoring the corners that seemed clean enough, before looping the cord messily around the handle and dragging the vacuum out of her room.

Outside the window behind the television, Jimmy was smoking a cigarette on the porch, leaning over the railing on his forearms. Leaving the vacuum in the middle of the front room, Megan walked outside, letting the screen door bounce in its frame, and plopped on the steps.

"Why'd you do that?" she sneered slightly as he took a deep drag off the tan filter.

"I like it," he shrugged, blowing the smoke away from her.

"It's gross," Megan stated matter-of-factly.

"Glad ya think so," he retorted, "Don't hafta worry about you doin' it then."

"Eww never," she grimaced.

"Why don't'cha go read your book or somethin'?" Jimmy said impatiently.

Megan shrugged, "I'm bored."

"Yeah," he rolled his eyes, "Bein' stuck here with a bratty little girl is thrilling for me," she scowled at him and he scoffed, "Yeah, y'know it's true."

With a frustrated huff, Megan slammed her feet on the step as she stood and stomped into the house. Dropping dramatically on the couch, she turned the television back on, mindlessly flipping through channels when Jimmy walked in and the bouncing screen door fanned the trailing smell of smoke further into the front room.

"Hey, put the vacuum away," he ordered.

"I'll get to it," she mumbled, not looking away from the infomercial she had no interest in.

"Megan," Jimmy begged in frustration, "I helped ya out. Can you, please, just get it done all the way? Dan'll be home in a few minutes and it'd be great if you didn't immediately put him in a shitty mood."

Letting out another exasperated growl, Megan slammed the remote on the couch as she pushed herself off, grabbed the vacuum roughly, avoiding Jimmy's scowl, and dragged it to the closet by the basement door. When she turned around, Jimmy was reclined on the couch, his feet on the coffee table, and the channel returned to his vulgar cartoon marathon.

"Hey!" Megan yelled at him, "I was watchin' that!"

"No you weren't," Jimmy didn't even turn his head, but the remote was firmly clasped in his hand as she jumped over the couch and tried to pry it from his fingers, "Megan, stop it! I let'cha watch your shows all morning and helped with your room, now you're just bein' a jerk!"

The screen door banged at the same time she was lifted off the back of the couch, helplessly wrapped under one of Dan's strong arms and carried to her bedroom. He unceremoniously dropped her on the freshly made bed and turned to leave without a word.

"Dan!" Megan whined, but swiftly withdrew on her bed when he rounded in the doorway.

"I heard that, Megan," he said firmly, "I don't know what's gotten into you lately, but I'm done! Stay in here 'til you can be a nice kid."

With unwavering rigidity, he shut her door and Megan fell on her pillow, stifling an abrupt, nonsensical yell, and hit her mattress with an increasingly unenthused fist.

She had no idea why she'd been so moody, there had been a lot of emotions she didn't understand, and couldn't control, growing over several months. Her brothers didn't deserve the attitude she kept giving them, Megan knew that, but, despite the guilty feelings after an unnecessary outburst, she couldn't stop herself during the emotional eruption. Peering around her newly cleaned room, she felt a pang of remorse at how she'd treated Jimmy after he'd helped with the mess. Hearing her brothers' voices muffled on the other side of the wall, Megan knew they were talking about her.

She pulled her door open without a sound and walked slowly into the front room, looking as regretful as possible. They stopped talking and turned to her with identical severity.

"Jimmy?" Megan sounded as contrite as she could and he raised his eyebrows to show he was listening, "M'sorry."

"For what?" he asked.

"Bein' a jerk," she squirmed her right toes into the carpet, glancing from her feet to his eyes and back again.

"Good," Jimmy nodded curtly, "I don't deserve it," she shook her head in agreement, "Okay, brat, be nice to me then," he smirked, poking her side.

Without waiting for an invitation, Megan threw her arms around Jimmy's skinny neck, feeling better when the embrace was sincerely returned.

"Megan, c'mere," Dan sat in the worn arm chair and crooked his index finger, but Megan leaned into Jimmy, looking nervously at Dan, who sighed, "I'm not gonna swat'cha, just c'mere," his tone was soft and she trustingly closed the gap as he leaned his forearms on his knees, continuing, "After our talk last night I'm really surprised to hear about how you're behavin', especially when Jimmy helped ya with the one thing I asked you to do. And so y'know, he's been told not to help you with your chores anymore. You're a big girl, as you like to remind us, even if you're not actin' like it lately," he lifted her disheartened face gently, "I'm serious, Megan, you're on thin ice and I'm done with this attitude."

"We both are," Jimmy chimed in, earning a brief sideways glance from Dan.

Megan's throat tightened and tears stung her eyes as she nodded.

"What's up, sweetheart?" Dan brushed her hair behind her ear and spoke quietly, "What's goin' on in that brilliant brain'a yours?"

She smiled weakly at the habitual compliment, but a few stray tears fell down her cheeks, promptly wiped away by Dan's calloused thumbs. Unable to find words, or trust herself to speak them without her voice cracking, Megan shrugged and unsuccessfully bit back a sob. With his adored little sister in such a miserable state, Dan pulled her onto his lap and let Megan bury her face in his greasy shirt, shaking his head at his brother in complete confusion. Jimmy scoffed quietly, equally perplexed.

66

# Chapter 4

Sunday morning arrived offering another warm, cloudless day, but Megan knew she didn't have a chance of enjoying it since she was still grounded and got dressed for church without being told. After she'd calmed down the previous afternoon, they'd had a pleasant night and Jimmy hadn't even complained about watching a PG movie for once, probably realizing his other option would be to sit in his room, instead of his usual, rusty escape, neglectfully parked by the curb.

Dan knocked on her door to tell her to get dressed and was visibly surprised to find Megan brushing her hair into a long, dark ponytail, already in clean jeans and a purple sweater.

"Mornin'," he leaned against the doorframe in his best jeans with a white button up tucked in and the sleeves rolled to his elbows, dropping a basket of folded clothes on her bed, "Get these put away when we get home, okay?"

"Okay," she nodded, and raised her voice pleadingly, "Hey, Dan?"

"Yeah?" he smirked.

"I know I'm still in trouble," Megan shifted her eyes from her feet to his patient gaze and back, mumbling, "But we were supposed to go to Sam 'n Darlene's for dinner tonight," she let her last couple words trail off, knowing he understood her concern.

"I'm not missin' Darlene's cookin' 'cause you were a brat," Dan chuckled, but raised a single eyebrow when she smiled at him, "Although," Megan's stomach turned at the beginning of his conditional statement, "I expect you to apologize to Sam for your little outburst the other night," she couldn't hide a flash of stubborn mortification from her eyes and Dan didn't miss it, "Hey, I'm not tellin' you to make a speech or somethin', but that's your best friend and you should at least pull him aside and tell him you're sorry he got in the middle'a that," she nodded, knowing Dan was right and at least appreciated he wasn't going to oversee the impending conversation, "Alright, get'cher shoes on, let's go."

"They hurt," she said, remembering the dull pain that had been growing constant in her toes from being slightly curled for weeks.

"Your shoes?" Dan inclined his head and she nodded at him, with a sigh he asked, "How long have your shoes not fit?"

"Little while," Megan shrugged and her brother hung his head in frustrated amusement, chuckling to himself.

"Can you make it through church with those and we'll get to the store after?" she grinned and followed his gesture into the front room, "And can ya let me know next time you outgrow your shoes before they hurt?"

"Sorry," she said pitiably, pulling the too tight sneakers on her feet by the front door with a dramatic grimace.

"I'm not the one whose shoes don't fit," Dan scoffed lightheartedly, holding the door open.

Jimmy had stopped going to church with them a few years before, it was thankfully never an argument between him and Dan, but Megan still missed her goofy brother's presence. Sunday service wasn't as entertaining without him to play thumb wars or tick-tack-toe on the back of the bulletin, although, she did get in a lot less trouble without Jimmy's influence in the pew. But half the fun had been avoiding Dan catching them fooling around.

The green truck growled into the church parking lot as couples and families walked up the cement steps into the large brick building and Dan maneuvered expertly into a back spot. Megan hopped out of the passenger side as he walked around the truck bed and swung his arm around her shoulders as they joined the crowd shuffling into 9 a.m. service.

As usual, they were stopped several times on the way. Dan shook hands and briefly talked shop with a few older men as Megan patiently shifted her weight from one foot to the other behind him. A tap on her shoulder was a welcome distraction and she turned to Sam, Darlene behind him in an active conversation with Mrs. King.

"Missed'cha yesterday," he poked her gently in the side, "You guys still comin' for dinner?"

"Yeah, we'll be there," Megan smiled and felt Dan's hand squeeze her shoulder.

"Hey, Sam," Dan shook the young man's hand, among other things, Dan had taught him to shake hands the way he said a man needed to since Sam's dad left when he was a baby, "I heard a rumor about you," Dan raised his eyebrows and Sam looked almost nervous for a moment before he continued, "Mister valedictorian."

Sam smiled sheepishly, "Yeah, well, it's not a big class."

"Hey," Dan's encouragement bordered on mild warning, "Don't sell yourself short, kid, you should be proud."

"That's what I keep sayin'," Darlene joined their conversation as Mrs. King waved to Megan and Dan, but allowed her husband to guide her through the church doors, Sam's mom released a quiet, yet relieved, sigh, "Hi, Dan, sweetie, how are you?"

"I'm good, Darlene. How've ya been?" Dan returned her hug, but Darlene's hand dawdled on his lower back.

"Can't complain," she shrugged, slowly withdrawing her hand and smiled at Megan, "You guys still comin' over tonight?"

"Yes, ma'am," Dan nodded and was immediately rewarded with a light slap across the arm for his manners.

"I hate when you call me that," Darlene gave him a half smile, rubbing where she'd made gentle contact and Megan saw her brother's ears pinken.

They followed Sam and Darlene through the double doors, but Megan stopped when Dan held her shoulder, letting other people pass, and gently guided her into their usual back pew. She listened to the minister on and off, muttering the routine responses and read the bulletin cover to cover slowly until the organ began playing again and the congregation flooded the aisles to leave.

"Dan!" Megan's head turned with her brother's as they passed over the threshold of the wide doors and saw a tall, heavy set young man waving from the bottom of the steps.

"Hey, Mike," Dan said brightly and Megan followed him down the stairs, happy to see the familiar face of Dan's high school friend, the young men clasped hands, pulling into a quick embrace with a hard pat on each other's backs, before Dan asked, "How ya been?"

"Good," Mike nodded, "Ya missed a helluva party Friday."

"So, I heard," he remarked.

"Holy crap," Mike's shifting eyes widened, "Is that Megan?"

"Hi Mike," she giggled, returning his hug the best she could, but her arms couldn't reach very far around his large middle.

"Well, ain't you 'bout to have trouble on your hands," Mike chuckled, nudging Dan with his elbow.

"Already do," Dan shook Megan's shoulder, gesturing a scissor motion at the impish tongue she stuck out, and, returning his attention to his burly friend, said, "Didn't think you came to service anymore. What'cha doin' here?"

"Datin' a church girl," Mike shrugged, "Gotta give a little y'know."

"Who?" Dan inclined his head.

"You remember Lacey from our class?" Megan saw Dan's jaw twitch as he nodded and Mike continued, "Her little sister, Kayla, she was a couple years under us."

A smile broke out on Dan's face, "That's great, Mike, good for you."

"And here she is," Mike grinned, putting his arm around an undeniably attractive, plump, dark-blonde, "Kayla, I dunno if y'know Dan."

"Everybody knows Dan," she smiled, extending her hand and shaking Dan's, "But no, we've never actually met, I'm Lacey's sister."

"Nice to meet'cha," Dan smiled awkwardly, "How, uh, how's your sister?"

"Great! Actually-" Kayla exclaimed, waving over Dan's shoulder, "Lace, c'mere!"

Dan whipped around as the pretty waitress skirted through the remaining parishioners huddled in small groups around the church steps, her wavy blonde hair bouncing a little with each step. Megan sighed from boredom and sat on the short brick wall, picking at a cluster of clovers in the flower bed.

70

"Hi," Lacey smiled sweetly, stopping right in front of Dan, a bit closer than comfortable conversation usually allowed.

"Hey," Dan grinned and pulled on the back of his neck, "D'ja have fun at O'Malley's party?"

"Would've been more fun if you'd been there," she giggled, and Megan rolled her eyes.

"Yeah, well," Dan hesitated, "Maybe next time."

"Hey," Mike interjected, "Why don't'cha come out with us this Saturday?"

Megan's head snapped up as her stomach dropped, praying he hadn't forgotten about the book signing.

"I'm goin' outta town this weekend," Dan said and Megan smiled, digging her index finger further into the soft soil, having given up the fruitless search for a four-leaf-clover.

"Next weekend then," Lacey's hand found his arm and Dan's ears turned pink.

"Um, yeah," he stammered, "That, uh, should, that'll work."

"It's a date then," Lacey lifted on her toes and planted a quick kiss on his cheek.

"Okay, yeah, cool," Dan smiled, squeezing an arm around Lacey, his ears bright red, and turned to his very bored sister, "C'mon, Meg, we got stuff to do. Bye, Lacey, uh, Kayla it was nice to meet'cha, Mike I'll see ya."

"Next weekend, pal," Mike smirked, "I'm gonna hold'ja to it. And Megan, stop growin', you're makin' me feel old."

Megan held back an eye roll and returned Mike's high five with the hand she hadn't been using to dig through dirt, offering a tiny wave to the sisters as she followed Dan to his truck.

He was staring off into the distance with a funny smile and strolled a few feet passed the truck bed until Megan laughed and opened the passenger door. Shaking his head, finally relieving his face of the goofy, absent grin, Dan got in the driver's seat.

"Thanks for bein' patient," he said, "I didn't mean to be so long."

"S'okay," Megan shrugged, asking her next question with hopeful hesitation, "So, um, are we goin' to Milwaukee?"

He smiled, but raised a single eyebrow, "Long as you behave yourself, yeah, I got the day off, for sure."

Megan squealed, jumping onto her knees on the seat and wrapped her arms around Dan's neck, "Thank you, thank you, thank you!"

"Just be good, okay?" she nodded eagerly at his request, retreating happily to her side of the bench seat as Dan pulled the shifter down and said, "Alright, let's get'cha some shoes, kid."

Their stop at Walmart was longer than expected. It took Megan several minutes to choose sneakers she liked, but finally settled on white ones with bright green stripes up the sides. Since they were already there, Dan grabbed a few household essentials and Megan patiently followed him around the store, carrying her shoebox and excitedly peeked inside every few minutes instead of putting them in the cart. After what she considered an obnoxious amount of time spent choosing toilet paper, Dan led them to the register.

Her old shoes felt even tighter walking back to the truck and Megan immediately changed into her new sneakers, shoving the old ones in the box on the floor of the passenger side while Dan loaded the bags in the bed. Wiggling her toes freely, Megan smiled when he pulled himself behind the steering wheel.

"You happy?" he asked, beaming at her enthusiastic nod, "All that matters."

As soon as they arrived home, Dan reminded Megan to put her clothes away and start her homework for the next day. With brand new shoes on her feet and the promise of meeting her favorite author the following weekend, she contently did as she was told, quickly shoving already folded clothes from the basket into her dresser drawers before jumping through the doorway in her new sneakers. Dan chuckled, disappearing into the bathroom with the well thought-through toilet paper, where it was always stacked under the sink. Megan bounced to the kitchen table on her unsquished toes and grabbed her backpack from its discarded spot underneath, tossing it on the white laminate as she plopped in her usual chair.

Since the school year was winding down, her teachers weren't giving as much homework, but Megan had a couple worksheets due and a few tests to get ready for. History and English wouldn't be so bad, but she wasn't looking forward to the next five days of math, reviewing everything they'd learned before the last test. At least it was the last full week of classes before field day and an end of the year pep rally would conclude days of exams the following week. Then, finally, summer vacation would start.

Dan left the bathroom with her pajamas balled in his hand, tossed them into the empty hamper right outside Jimmy's closed bedroom door and didn't lose a step as he moved to the sink and turned on the faucet. He rinsed the plates and bowls before organizing them in the dishwasher and started it after pushing the door shut with his foot. Scanning the tidied main room and stopping a moment on Megan, head bent over a worksheet, Dan ran a tired hand through his short hair and sighed.

"Hey, Meg," she looked up at his drained tone, "I'm gonna rest my eyes for a bit, wake me up in a few hours for dinner. Okay?"

"Okay," she nodded, returning to her assignment, and Dan patted her shoulder as he passed.

Megan finished her few pieces of homework, jealously listening to neighbor kids whooping down the street on their bikes, but reminded herself she would be meeting A.K. Foreman next weekend. And, while being restricted to the house on such a beautiful afternoon was frustrating, Megan was at least happy dinner at her best friend's house hadn't been excluded, eager for the dinner Darlene would make. Whenever Dan joined them for dinner, Sam's mom never simply heated leftovers or frozen pizza, always putting together a delicious homecooked meal, despite Dan's insistence she needn't go overboard on his account. Megan hoped there would be mashed potatoes, real ones with bits of skin mixed in, not from dehydrated flakes out of a box, sometimes Darlene would even add bacon bits and shredded cheese. She smiled in anticipation of the dinner she'd be having in a few hours.

Megan repacked her homework, tossed her backpack next to the front door and quietly entered her room, pulling a familiar story from her bookshelf and flopped on her bed, trying to ignore the laughter outside. Hardly paying attention to the book she knew so well, Megan repeatedly checked the time. She and Dan, and occasionally Jimmy, always arrived at Sam's house around 5:30 for dinner on Sundays, so, when the alarm clock on her freshly decluttered nightstand read 4:57, even though it took less than a minute to walk across the yards, Megan couldn't wait any longer and tiptoed across the hallway into Dan's room.

The blinds were closed in his bedroom on the house's east side, making it much darker despite the bright sun still shining outside. For years, Dan and Jimmy had shared Jimmy's bedroom, but, when Dan had gotten home after sending Greg to the hospital, he'd cleared the rarely used master bedroom of his stepfather's possessions and staked claim on the room. Megan remembered how nervous she'd been, expecting her father to be furious at the eviction, his things becoming basement storage. But, when Greg had finally returned over half a year later, he hadn't said a word, and would pass out on the couch the few nights he'd stayed there since.

Dan's large frame faced the long wall his queen-sized mattress was pushed against under the window, the blanket rising and falling with his soft snores. She remembered to kick off her new shoes before climbing onto his bed and curling up behind him, lightly dragging her index finger along the dark freckles on his upper back and shoulders in a long-standing game of connect-the-dots.

"That tickles," he mumbled, shrugging his shoulders.

"You're not ticklish," Megan scoffed, poking him in his armpit crease to prove her point.

"You're right," Dan quickly flipped around on his knees, gently grabbing Megan's sides, sending her into shrieks of laughter, "But you are."

"St-op! Da-an!" she twisted wildly, unable to get away from the affectionate attack.

He chuckled and pushed off his bed, yawning as he stretched his long arms over his head. He picked the jeans he'd worn to church off his dresser and slipped them on over his black boxer briefs, the metal buckle of his belt clinked as he cinched it around his hips.

"Dan?" Megan leaned against his pillow, picking at a few stray threads poking out of his comforter.

"Yeah, sweetheart?" he slipped a fresh t-shirt over his head.

"You gonna date Lacey?" she asked hesitantly.

A lot of the seventh and eighth graders had started dating each other and, while Megan didn't really get why, she wasn't oblivious to Lacey's flirting or her brother's welcoming grins when she did.

Dan scoffed, clearly not expecting her question, but said, "I'm gonna take her on at least a date. Why'd ya ask?"

"Just wonderin'," she shrugged, pulling a thread from his blanket.

"Is that okay with you?" he smirked, leaning against his dresser and pulled on black socks.

"She's alright," Megan shrugged again, "She giggles a lot."

"So do you," Dan poked her in the side producing an irrepressible laugh, "C'mon, let's get goin', I'm starvin'."

She hopped off his bed, grabbing her new sneakers from the floor, and followed his gesture into the hallway. Jimmy left his room as they walked into the kitchen, his dark, shaggy hair sticking in all directions and stretched his thin arms across his chest before shoving both hands in the pockets of his baggy sweatpants.

"Workin' at seven?" Dan asked.

"Yup," Jimmy nodded at the end of a yawn.

"We're goin' over to Darlene's for dinner," Dan inclined his head with a mild warning, "I'll see ya before I leave for work in the mornin'."

"Yeah, I know," Jimmy turned to the fridge, rolling his eyes as he wrenched the door open, but, seeing a six-pack of his favorite soda on the shelf, he gave his brother a contrite glance and muttered, "Thanks."

"You're welcome," Dan said, Megan's backpack catching his eyes as he grabbed his clean boots from near the front door, "Is your homework done?"

"Yep," Megan confirmed, slipping on her new sneakers and bounced to her feet.

"Think you can bring me some leftovers?" Jimmy gave Megan their secret smirk and she returned it with a tiny nod.

"If Darlene offers any," Dan glanced between them before bending down to tie his boots, allowing Megan the chance to mouth 'I got it' and Jimmy threw her a quick thumbs-up before Dan stood and said, "Have a good night at work, Jimmy."

"Thanks," Jimmy cracked open his soda can, sighing dramatically, "Wish I could come to dinner with you guys, love Darlene's cookin'."

"We'll see what we can do," Dan scoffed lightheartedly, opening the front door for Megan to push out the broken screen.

Closing her eyes to the warm sun, she spread her arms, spinning in the yard after jumping down the porch steps. Dan chuckled, descending the stairs with less enthusiasm.

"You'd think you'd been locked up a year," he joked, putting an arm around her shoulders.

"Almost two days," she pouted.

"And ya deserved every bit of it," he shook her shoulders playfully and she couldn't help a guilty blush, "Remember what I said about talkin' to Sam," Dan reminded, removing his arm when they reached the flower-lined walkway.

"I know," Megan rolled her eyes a moment before turning and grimaced apologetically when she caught Dan's characteristic eyebrow raise.

Instead of opening the door, like she usually did, Megan knocked, having been told enough by Dan it was rude to just walk into someone else's house, even though Sam and Darlene didn't mind. Sam opened the door right away and Megan yanked open the screen, almost jumping into the front room.

"Heya, Sam," Dan followed and looked up as Darlene walked out of the kitchen, "Thanks again for havin' us."

"Oh, you," Darlene scoffed happily, embracing Megan first and then wrapped her arms around Dan with a quick peck to his suddenly pinkening cheek, "I'm glad you could come. No Jimmy tonight?"

"He's gotta work," Dan shrugged as they shuffled into the kitchen and the scent of well-orchestrated spices grew stronger, "Somethin' smells good."

"Fried pork chops with that cheese sauce y'all like, mashed potatoes and peas 'n carrots," Darlene listed, lifting a pot lid and steam dissipated over the stove, currently ashtray free. She twirled a wooden spoon in the simmering vegetables and casually ordered, "Sam, finish setting the table, please."

Megan caught Dan's satisfied nod when she moved to help Sam grab silverware, placing forks, knives and spoons around the four red plates on the woven placemats. Dan leaned against the counter, thanking Darlene for the soda she handed him before flipping a pork chop in the skillet.

"Can we watch America's Funniest in a bit?" Megan asked Sam when they'd finished.

"Not tonight," Darlene said over a sizzling hiss just as Sam shook his head, his cheeks blotching pink.

"You're not the only one who got in trouble for comin' home late," Sam mumbled and Megan offered a hidden eyeroll in solidarity.

"Wanna play checkers?" she asked, glad when Sam nodded and rushed to his room, returning shortly with the cardboard, game box held together by masking tape.

"I'm sorry, Darlene," Megan heard Dan's deep voice in the kitchen as they arranged their pieces on the checkerboard flattened across the coffee table and strained to listen, "I meant to thank you for the leftovers the other day."

"Don't even mention it, darlin'," Darlene brushed him off sweetly, "Did Megan tell you about my little party idea for them?"

"Yeah," Dan said, "It's a great idea, Megan's all about it, and, well, it would make it easier for me. I'm not really sure what to do for a thirteen-year-old girl's birthday," he scoffed, "Or in general."

"Dan," Darlene encouraged, "You're doin' great, that girl is happy, healthy and sharp as a tack. Talk about sellin' yourself short, young man. Where would your brother 'n sister be without you?" Darlene continued after a pause, "Exactly. Oh, Megan mentioned some book signing you might take her to, seemed pretty excited about it."

"Yeah," Dan sounded like he was smiling, "I'm takin' off this Saturday and we're goin' to Milwaukee."

"Oh, I bet she's thrilled!" Darlene exclaimed, adding, "I'm pretty sure you just won big brother'a the year."

"Maybe," Dan scoffed, "Jimmy doesn't have to be the hardass though, so I'm pretty sure he's always her favorite."

Sadness sunk in Megan's gut, overwhelmed with the urge to assure Dan she didn't prefer Jimmy to him, but understood why he'd think so, and absently moved a red checker into the perfect square for Sam to jump it, which he did.

"It may seem like that sometimes," Darlene sympathized, "But she needs you, trust me, Megan is gonna appreciate every sacrifice you've made someday. Speakin' of," her tone brightened, "Saw ya talkin' to Lacey Peters on our way outta church this mornin'. She's a beautiful girl, Dan."

Dan cleared his throat awkwardly, "Yeah, nothin's changed there. I'm, uh, well, I guess I'm takin' her out next Saturday."

"Good!" Darlene said excitedly, "You need to get out and have some fun, I'm happy for you. If Megan needs to stay over y'know that's fine."

Dan chuckled, "Thanks, I don't think it'll be the whole night, but if you wouldn't mind me pickin' her up around eleven?"

"Whatever you need, darlin', y'know that," Darlene stuck her head around the corner, "Dinner kids."

They hurried into the kitchen, leaving the nearly finished game she was losing terribly, but Megan's typical competiveness was indifferent.

Darlene set a steaming pot of mashed potatoes next to a bowl of peas and carrots while Dan still leaned against the counter. He knew better than to offer assistance, having been politely chastised several times in the past for trying to help, but they'd end the meal with a playful argument anyway when Dan wouldn't let Darlene stop him from washing the dishes. Megan sat across from Sam, beaming at Dan when he settled on an end chair, and he squinted at her seemingly unprompted grin with suspicious amusement. Darlene carried the skillet to the table with a pot holder wrapped around the handle and plopped a hot pork chop on each plate, the largest on Dan's.

"Thank you, Darlene," he said.

"Anytime," she reiterated, putting a gravy boat next to the potatoes before taking her seat.

All four bowed their heads over clasped hands as Darlene said a prayer, then, a bit forcibly, encouraged them to fill their plates. Megan plopped a large helping of mashed potatoes next to her pork chop and suddenly found the vegetable bowl hovering inches from her plate. She scooped a small serving but, when the bowl wavered in a silent command, looked sideways at Dan and his pushy smirk made her take a larger helping of peas and carrots. He ladled cheese sauce on Megan's pork chop before his own and passed the serving boat to Sam. Darlene never let Dan wait to eat, insisting there was always more if it was needed.

"D'ja start your speech for graduation yet?" Megan asked Sam, remembering to swallow a mouthful of mashed potatoes first.

He shook his head, "I'm tryin' to get out of it."

"Not a chance, young man," Darlene said flatly, hardly glancing at her son while spooning a large serving of vegetables on her on plate.

"I wouldn't wanna talk in front of everybody either," Dan admitted empathetically, "But y'know, it's really awesome that you're the top of your class, it's always nice to be number one. Just make it short 'n sweet. You don't wanna use up all your material, you're gonna need somethin' for when you're high school valedictorian."

Sam laughed, seeming a bit more confident, and dove into his potatoes. Megan saw Darlene wink across the table, mouthing 'thank you', but Dan just shrugged modestly.

The conversation shortly switched to plans for the joint party in a few weeks. Megan and Sam were set on the park by the river so they could set up a football game in the big field next to the playground. Darlene was content with the idea and Dan only had an opinion on the day.

"Of course it'll be a Sunday," Darlene chuckled, "I'm gonna need your help keepin' tabs on all of 'em, and the boys are gonna wanna play football."

"Y'know I'm okay at that," Dan remarked, standing to clear his empty plate and raised an eyebrow Megan knew all too well, effectively stopping Darlene's protest before it began, "I'm helpin' with the dishes."

"You're a brat, Dan," she giggled and he stacked Megan's and Sam's empty plates under his, chuckling at Darlene's light slap as he reached for hers.

"Darlene?" Megan asked sweetly, "Could I bring Jimmy some'a your mashed potatoes, please?"

She kept her eyes on Sam's mom while Dan's stare warmed the side of her face.

"Jimmy's all set," Darlene's kind assurance accompanied her finger pointing to the covered pans still on the stove, "Extra pork chop, potatoes and vegies, I'm gonna put it in a Tupperware or two."

"You don't have to do that," Dan said, "But thank you, that'll make his day tomorrow."

"My pleasure," Darlene insisted and, with a concerned tone, asked, "How is Jimmy?"

Megan and Sam shared a look, understanding that the conversation was no longer for them, and returned to their game of checkers in the living room, but she kept an open ear to the kitchen, listening intently.

"He's, uh," Dan released a heavy sigh, "He's a pain in my ass. And now that he's eighteen, I dunno, just tryin' to keep him outta trouble."

"Yeah, I saw the cops at your place the other night. Everything okay?"

Megan's stomach turned and she wished Darlene would mind her own business.

"This time," Dan said bitterly, "But Andy made it clear, if they catch him again, it's not gonna matter how many football games we won together."

"Drinkin' again?" Darlene asked.

"Always," Dan groaned, "But this time, him 'n his buddies decided to break into the high school and get liquored up in the gym."

"Why?" Darlene almost laughed in surprise and Megan sighed quietly at the new information, somehow, it wasn't entirely shocking.

"Your guess is as good as mine," Dan expelled a frustrated chuckle, "He didn't have an answer either. I don't know what to do with him anymore. Groundin' him just pisses him off. It's like I'm tryin' to hold onto a lit rocket."

"It's a good thing ya got such big shoulders. Not that these should be your burdens," Megan's throat tightened a little, but she listened closely to Darlene's soft-spoken support, "But I know a lotta full grown men who wouldn't be able to do half of what you do every day."

Megan heard a deep mumbled and tried to return her attention to the checkerboard as Sam finished setting up a new game, after destroying her in the first. But the word 'burden' echoed in her head and sadness and guilt swirled in her gut, carelessly pushing a red piece into the middle of the board. Hearing it used to describe her brought the return of a painful realization Megan had recently started forming, having never given it much thought in the past, but the door had been opened and she understood she couldn't be anything except a burden to her oldest brother. Intrusive thoughts of the problems she and Jimmy caused Dan distracted her into losing horribly at checkers again.

"Hey, Megan," Dan stuck his head around the corner and her guilt worsened with the lighthearted command, "Say good bye, we're gonna head home in a minute."

"I'll see ya on the bus tomorrow," Sam said, following her to the door.

"Yeah, see ya," Megan smiled weakly, trying to look as unaffected as possible by the words she wasn't supposed to have heard, and returned Darlene's hug, "Thank you for dinner, it was really great."

"I'm glad you could come," Darlene said, then squeezed Dan's bicep, "You take care'a yourself, Dan, I'm always here if ya need me."

"I know, Darlene," he smiled and lifted a plastic grocery bag of leftovers in his hand, "Thank you, really don't know what I'd do without'cha."

"Well you certainly wouldn't eat enough, ya hardly do now," she declared, opening the front door, "G'night, you two."

"G'night," Megan and Dan said together and descended the porch steps.

"D'ja have fun?" Dan asked, putting his free hand on her shoulder.

"Mhm," Megan nodded, keeping her gaze on the next few feet of grass ahead.

"Dinner was great," Dan pried, giving her a tiny shake, but gained no more than a quick, sad glance, "What's up, sweetheart?"

She shrugged, walking ahead of him up to their front door, but Dan gently took her hand, stopping her on the third step and tilted his head, forcing eye contact.

"Megan," he said softly, "I can't read your mind, talk to me please."

"I don't wanna be a burden to you," she mumbled, watching Dan's eyes widen in shock as he scoffed.

"Megan, why would-" but sudden understanding narrowed his eyes and curled the corners of his mouth, "Weren't snoopin' were ya?"

The sob Megan couldn't hold back was response enough.

She expected him to be angry, so was very surprised to find his arms suddenly wrapped around her.

"No, Megan," he leaned back, holding her at arm's length, and pain lined his brow while he emphasized, "You are not, never have been, and never will be, a burden to me. You're my favorite girl, so don't ever think you're anything besides one'a the two most important people in the world to me. We got dealt a shitty hand. But I wouldn't trade you or Jimmy for anything."

"Really?" she asked as he picked up the plastic bag and walked up the steps, towering over her as usual.

"No, I found a new little brother 'n sister who actually put their dishes in the dishwasher and pajamas in the hamper," Dan joked, pushing the front door open and smirked at the tongue she stuck out, "C'mere, the kitchen scissors are clean 'cause I just took 'em outta the dishwasher."

Megan giggled madly as he pretended to grab the shears from the knife block on the counter and ran to the couch, falling onto the safety of the cushions.

"Hey, there's fifteen minutes left of America's Funniest," Dan nodded at the television and Megan looked at him hesitantly, she was technically still grounded until the end of the night, even if she'd gone to her best friend's for dinner and gotten new shoes, but Dan dropped beside her, picking up the remote and said, "I'm a crappy excuse for a dad, but I like to think sometimes I'm a good big brother."

"I don't think you're crappy at anything," Megan pecked his cheek and settled against his side, "And you're the best big brother."

"Can I tell Jimmy you said that?" Dan joked, chuckling at her scrunched nose head shake and planted a kiss on her hair.

# Chapter 5

Dan made eggs with buttered toast Monday morning and it was one of the rare occasions they ate breakfast together. Megan had gotten up earlier than usual, and the microwave clock promised half an hour until her bus, instead of the usual ten to fifteen minutes. After a mostly one-sided chat about her anticipation for the upcoming weekend, Dan finished his toast and left the table to take the hamper downstairs.

The front door swung open and Jimmy walked into the house, sweaty and tired as the screen door banged behind him.

"Mornin'," Megan smiled and he grunted indifferently, "How was work?"

"Shitty," Jimmy scoffed, shaking off his second boot and clomped to the refrigerator.

"There's leftovers from Darlene's in there for ya," Dan said, jogging up from the basement and cleared Megan's plate as she munched the last bite of crust.

"Thanks," Jimmy muttered, closing the fridge and cracked a can of soda.

"You workin' tonight?" Dan asked, picking Megan's backpack off the ground in the living room and hung it on the back of her chair.

"Tomorrow," Jimmy sipped his soda and opened the refrigerator again, staring at the shelves.

"Y'know what's in there," Dan said exasperatedly, "Stop wastin' power holdin' the door open."

"Fine," Jimmy snapped and slammed it shut, "Should've stopped at McDonald's on my way home anyway," but his attempt at the front door was quickly blocked, "Dude, I'm hungry!"

"There's food here Jim," Dan growled, "Y'know you're not leavin'."

"You're such a dick y'know that?!" Jimmy yelled, but stepped back into the kitchen, and Dan didn't move from his cross-armed position in front of the door as the rant continued, "Jordan's parents had to bail him out and he didn't get shit for it! His actual dad didn't ground him or threaten to beat his ass! And the old man had to pay like five hundred bucks! I didn't even cost you anything 'cause you're buddies with all the cops!"

Megan stared wide eyed at Jimmy, breathing heavily in his rage on the opposite side of the kitchen from Dan, whose calm demeanor was cracking.

"You don't think ya cost me anything?" Dan began, his irritation steady, but gained volume, "Really, Jimmy? Yeah, maybe I get a favor or two on account'a my asshole brother can't keep his goddamn self outta trouble! But trust me, kid, they're done, you better not have a next time 'cause I ain't got five hundred bucks like Jordan's parents to bail your ass out, and you'd be thankful, 'cause your ass would be safer there anyway!"

"You're not Dad!" Jimmy yelled again, but with much less conviction, "Jordan's parents-"

"I don't give a shit Jimmy!" Dan barked, "Jordan's not my problem, that kid can rot in a gutter for all I care! You don't get that chance. I will ride your ass everyday till your head's on straight 'cause I'm not watchin' you keep goin' down this path, I'm not losin' anybody else I care about!" Dan stopped hollering, but continued firmly, "And you're right, I'm not Dad, but I'm what'cha got, little brother."

Jimmy's eyes were locked on the kitchen floor, but he looked up when Dan walked around the table and retreated a nervous step. His expression was stone, stopping right in front of Jimmy and flattened a hand expectantly.

"Gimme your keys," Dan demanded.

"C'mon, I'm sorry," Jimmy flat out whined.

"It's not about this," Dan shook his head, "We talked about this Friday. Keys Jim, now."

"Dude," Jimmy implored, "What if there's an emergency or somethin'?"

"Phone's over there, number's nine one one" Dan pointed to the kitchen wall before holding out his upturned palm again.

With a frustrated, relenting growl, Jimmy shoved his keys into Dan's hand, grabbed his soda and stalked to the bathroom, shutting the door hard. Dan slipped the Oldsmobile keys into the pocket of his work pants and sighed, glancing at Megan on his way to the front door.

"Hey," he jerked his head at the fridge while pulling on his boots, "I got'cha a few of those Lunchable things, left drawer'a the fridge."

"The pizza ones?!" she slid excitedly off her seat.

"Yeah," he chuckled, "And a couple others, you're not gonna want that ketchup cracker crap every day."

"They're good," she shrugged defiantly, grabbing a pizza Lunchable, and shut the drawer.

"They're crap," he stated, but still tugged the yellow box from her eager grip, dropping it in with her books and zipped the bag while flipping it around for Megan to slip her arms through the straps before casually conceding, "But if you like 'em, that's all that matters. Alright, get goin', I can hear your bus."

Megan didn't know how he did that, she couldn't hear the bus until it was on the street. But, sure enough, halfway across the yard of the abandoned house, her bus turned the corner into view. Dan said it was the 'mechanic ears' he'd gotten from his father. Megan never heard much about him, Dan and Jimmy rarely brought him up except for the occasional comment that only they understood. She knew he'd been a mechanic after a few years of military service and had died suddenly in a car accident, but, beyond that, she could only make guesses about her brothers' dad.

"Megan!" she turned to the sound of her name, pausing just before she walked out the front doors to her bus and saw the school nurse hurrying towards her through a crowd of students, "D'ja get that permission slip signed for next year's volleyball team?

"I, uh, left it at home, Mrs. Olsen," Megan looked down at the lie, remembering the form crumpled at the bottom of her backpack for over a month, "I'll bring it tomorrow."

"Good, we need you on the team," Megan smiled weakly at Mrs. Olsen's compliment, "But I wanted to remind ya to get your physical done, the school district's cut off is May twenty-third for athletes so make sure ya get to the doctor in the next week or two," with an eyeroll she mumbled, "This new administrator's not much of a rule bender. Get it done soon, okay?"

"Yes, ma'am," Megan internally cringed, she'd been reminded several times over the last few months about the required physical, but it had repeatedly slipped her mind to tell Dan.

"Thank you," Mrs. Olsen smiled and nodded at the front doors, "I won't make you miss your bus. Bring me that form tomorrow."

"I will," Megan promised while rushing out the front door and hurried to her waiting bus, ignoring her bus driver's grumble about tardiness on her way to the backseat next to Sam.

"Almost missed it," Sam warned, sliding towards the window.

"He'll wait," she shrugged, setting her backpack on the dirty floor and opened it to find the crushed athletic form under her books, "Mrs. Olsen wanted to reminded me about the volleyball permission slip and the physical."

"You haven't done that yet?" Sam asked, more amused than surprised.

"I keep forgettin' to tell Dan," she pulled several crumpled and torn pieces of paper from the bottom of the dark green bag, unfolding each and shoved them back until she found the one she was looking for, "Yes!"

"They gave that to us in March," Sam chuckled, shaking his head as she tried to iron the crinkled paper with her hands.

"I just forget stuff sometimes," Megan shrugged, her eyes widening, "Speakin' of!" but lowered her voice so she was sure only he could hear, "I'm supposed, well, I'm really, really sorry 'bout the other night. You shouldn't've gotten in the middle'a that with me 'n Dan."

"Yeah, he was pretty pissed," Sam tried to laugh at the recent memory, "But it didn't help when ya slammed his truck door."

Megan grinned with guilty agreeance, "Yeah, I kinda acted-"

"Like a spoiled brat," Sam offered when her thought trailed off without completion.

"I'm not spoiled," she scoffed, deciding not to indulge her curiosity at his smirk, and actively changed the subject, "Ya wanna go to the river?"

"Can't," Sam shrugged, "I'm not allowed 'til this weekend, plus I got homework."

"All week?" Megan whined, pouting at Sam's nod, "But the nest."

"You'll hafta check on it without me," he said with disheartened acceptance, "You think Dan was pissed? My mom's just not as loud."

The bus rolled to a slow, screeching halt in front of Sam's house and they jumped from the last stair onto the grass beyond the gutter. With a quick wave good-bye, Sam jogged up the steps to his front door, unlocking it with a key from his pocket, and Megan ambled across the yards to her front porch.

Jimmy smiled from the couch when she walked in.

"Hey, babygirl," he turned down the television volume, "How's school?"

"Okay," she offered an upbeat shrug, kicking her shoes off at the front door, "So many tests next week though."

"Can't say I'm jealous," he smiled, "But you're like a genius, so no sweat right?"

"Yeah," she laughed sarcastically, plopping next to him on the couch, "Sure, no sweat."

"I'm watchin' TRL. Don't change it," Jimmy ordered, snatching his empty soda can from the coffee table and walked towards the kitchen.

"I won't," she mumbled, but, with a sneaky grin, Megan grabbed the remote, causing him to stop and raise an eyebrow, scoffing lightly when she turned up the volume.

Jimmy slouched back on the couch, setting a soda and lemonade on the coffee table, and mockingly ripped the remote from her hands, but situated it on the other side of himself anyway.

"You got homework?" Jimmy asked.

"Some," Megan shrugged, settling further into the couch and Jimmy shrugged too, returning his attention to the television.

A little after five, Megan heard the truck's familiar growl and Jimmy chuckled as she hurried to the kitchen table. Dan walked in the moment she'd finished writing her name on a worksheet.

"Hey, kids," he said, kicking off his boots and tossed his hat and keys on the kitchen counter.

"Hey, brother," Jimmy waved without glancing away from the television.

"How's your homework comin'?" Dan asked on his way to the fridge.

"Good," Megan muttered guiltily at his sideways smirk.

"Mhm," he peered at the empty worksheet, setting a freshly opened soda on the table, "I'm gonna grab a shower."

Before they ate leftover mashed potatoes and a Hamburger Helper meal, Megan shoved her assignments carelessly into her backpack and tossed it on the floor by the couch. Jimmy gave her an 'I told you so' look during Dan's mild reprimand about homework being done before dinner, to which Megan responded by sticking out her tongue, when Dan wasn't watching.

"Megan," Dan began, clearing his plate and evaluated what she had left on hers, "Finish up, I don't want'cha stayin' up late. How much ya got left?"

"Just that one worksheet," she said, but remembered, "Oh, but you gotta sign my permission slip for volleyball next year."

"Yeah, of course," he nodded, taking Jimmy's plate and dumped it in the sink with his own.

"And I gotta get a physical before May twenty-third," she added, shoving the last forkful of ground beef casserole in her mouth.

"No chance they told'ja about this earlier?" Dan put his hands on his hips, shaking his head at her noncommittal shrug, and sighed, "I'll call Doctor Summers tomorrow."

Megan smiled, sliding off her chair to grab her backpack without clearing her plate, which was gone in the few seconds before she returned to the table. Plucked the almost finished worksheet from her text book, Megan unfolded it on the table, but a hard throat clear stole her attention.

"Permission slip," Dan crooked his finger.

"Oh, yeah!" she giggled and slid the half sheet of paper from between her two heaviest text books.

Dan expelled a laugh, taking the freshly flattened form from her, "Haven't had this long, have ya?" she smirked contritely and he chuckled again, ruffling her hair, "Good thing this is attached."

Dan grabbed a pen out of the junk drawer, trying to flatten the creases further with the edge of the counter, before signing the bottom and pushing it across the table. Megan continued her homework while Dan started the dishwasher and disappeared into the basement. Jimmy had returned to watching television, occasionally emitting a loud bout of laughter from the couch.

"What tests do you have this week?" Dan asked, carrying a basket of clean clothes and kicked the basement door shut.

"English 'n music on Friday, everything else is next week," Megan said.

"How'd ya take a test in music?" Jimmy joked, sliding to the far side of the couch when Dan set the basket on the coffee table.

But, before Megan could answer, pounding boomed from the front door, followed by an off-key voice singing, "Jimmmmmmmaaaaay come out 'n plaaaaaay!"

Dan's jaw twitched as he scowled at his brother, who immediately threw his hands up defensively, Jimmy's shock obvious as he implored, "Dude, I didn't know he was comin' over."

Dan scowled at the door as it shook again, dropping the shirt he'd been about to fold, and wrenched it open. Jimmy's friend Jordan grinned goofily, the screen door propped open with his foot, and looked passed Dan to Jimmy.

"C'mon Jimmy," Jordan was slurring a bit, "Some'a the guys're meetin' at the park-"

"You're hammered," Dan scoffed, "'Cause ya ain't normally this stupid, kid."

"I'm twenty now, kid," Jordan sneered.

"And still hangin' out with high schoolers," Dan retorted meanly, "You must be proud."

"Fuck you, man," Jordan shot back, but his angry eyes widened when Dan seized his shirt and forced him backwards.

Megan and Jimmy shared a worried glance before hurtling through the screen door, bashing its frame as they skidded to a halt on the porch.

In the front yard, Jordan took a badly aimed swing at Dan, but he leaned back, almost lazily, to avoid it, and roughly shoved the younger man away. Jordan stumbled, but managed to stay on his feet, staggering a moment before squaring again on Dan.

"You always been an uptight asshole," Jordan's voice shook, "Ya don't gotta make yer brother one too."

"Go home, Jordan," Dan's instruction was nearly calm, but he maintained a defensive stance on the walkway.

"Yer not the boss'a everybody," Jordan balked, "M'just here fer my buddy 'n we'll go."

"Y'know he's not leavin'," Dan growled, "Don't be startin' shit, Jordan. I really don't care where you go, just get the hell away from my house!"

"Pretty sure it's Greg's house," Jordan's scornful statement made Dan's shoulders tense, but, before he could react, Jimmy jumped from the porch.

"I'm not comin' Jordan, just go!" anger bubbled in Jimmy's words at the name his friend had had the audacity to use.

"Dude!" Jordan scoffed, "Ya don't hafta follow his bullshit rules!"

"Jordan!" Jimmy roared and Megan jumped at the unexpected volume towards his friend, "Just go, man, please!"

Jordan shook his head in disbelief before glaring at Dan again, "Didn't get enough people in high school worshippin' you, huh?"

"You'd've gotten to see more of it if ya hadn't gotten yourself held back in middle school," Dan remarked, "But seems like you enjoy tryin' to influence the younger crowd, or maybe you just can't make any friends your own age."

"Screw you, Dan!" Jordan lunged, but Dan's quick sidestep sent him falling onto the small patch of yard before the driveway.

Dan roughly picked the younger man off the ground by the back of his shirt and pushed him towards the sidewalk with a harsh admonishment, "Don't come around here drunk tryin' to start shit, Jordan! It's Monday night for Christ's sake! Megan's got school in the mornin'!"

Jordan looked passed Dan, exaggerating a smile at Megan, and waved, "Hiiiii, Megan," she wished Jimmy hadn't left her alone and heard his drunk friend slur, "Gonna hafta watch out pretty soon wi'that one."

Jimmy rushed between the opposing pair as Dan's fists clenched and pulled his older brother back before rounding on his friend.

"Dude, you're messed up and you're askin' for it! Go!" Jimmy shoved him onto the sidewalk.

"Whatever," Jordan tried to brush off his surprise with a bitter scoff, "I'm out, this shit's bogus."

Jimmy and Dan stood shoulder to shoulder as Jordan stalked down the sidewalk, kicking an empty soda can until it rolled into the street and he rounded the corner towards the park. Without a word, Dan spun and strode to the porch, taking the steps two at a time, and gestured Megan inside.

"Homework, c'mon," he held the screen door for her and turned, waiting while Jimmy abashedly trudged up the steps.

"Dan, I didn't know he was gonna come by," he repeated.

"I know, Jim," Dan nodded, "I'm not mad at'cha, thanks for steppin' up," he patted him on the back as Jimmy walked passed, then closed and locked the front door, unceremoniously adding, "Really wish you'd stop hangin' out with that low life though."

"He's not that bad," Jimmy urged a bit begrudgingly, "He's just drunk."

"He's drunk a lot," Megan observed, but returned to her homework after a glower from Jimmy and Dan's 'I don't need your help' expression.

"Jordan's a punk," Dan drew Jimmy to the couch and lowered his voice, "He's always been a punk, and he's done nothin' except get'cher ass in trouble since you started hangin' out with him."

"Dude, he's my friend," Jimmy started helping Dan fold clothes, something he often did when he was trying to get back in his brother's good graces.

"He's a bad friend, Jimmy," Dan's tone was soft and full of concern, "Why don't'cha ever hangout with Brad or Travis anymore?"

Jimmy shrugged, "I still see 'em sometimes, but they got school and our schedules are different."

"Y'know you only missed a month," Megan's stomach twisted as Dan spoke, "I bet you could make it up 'n still-"

"Dan, stop," Jimmy growled and Megan shut her eyes, praying they wouldn't start fighting about school again.

"I'm just sayin'," Dan continued anyway, "Havin' your diploma's gonna make life a lot easier, kid."

"I'm not goin' back to school," Jimmy raised his voice, but wasn't yelling, "I'm workin' full-time, and I know that's made things easier around here-"

"Don't," Dan warned, "Don't pull that crap, y'know you didn't need to work full-time, I make enough to keep this place together. And you were so close, Jim-"

"I was gettin' D's in half my classes!" he challenged.

"So, you give up?" Dan scoffed, "That's not like you, Jim."

"No, Dan," Jimmy stood and walked around the couch, "That's not like you. I'm the screw up. The piece'a shit little brother of the town football hero. Everybody knows it! I've accepted it! Why don't you?"

"You're not a screw up, Jimmy," Dan maintained, "But you could do a lot better than the path you're choosin'."

"I'm not the one goin' to college in this room!" Jimmy yelled, Megan winced.

"But why not a trade school?" Dan suggested calmly, "Be an electrician or build houses, but, Jimmy, ya don't wanna work night shifts half your life."

"Dan," Jimmy's anger was weaker, betraying his lack of response, "Just, leave it alone, okay? I'm goin' to bed," and he shut himself in his room.

Dan shook his head and returned to the laundry, but stopped midway through folding one of Megan's shirts and tossed it back in the basket. He walked out to the front porch and Megan watched through the bouncing screen door while Dan hung his head. Stress was evident between his broad shoulders, before he withdrew from sight and she heard the scrapping of a wooden chair. Megan abandoned the last question on her worksheet.

"Dan?" she hesitated, shutting the screen door slowly.

"Homework, Meg," he responded automatically, his eyes on the concluding sunset.

"I'm almost done," she said, approaching him with a sweet grin.

94

Dan held out an arm and she wrapped hers around his neck, noticing the tight strain in his muscles.

"Thanks, sweetheart, I needed one'a those," he gave her a small shake and an even smaller smile, "Do me a favor, huh, don't ever hangout with people like Jordan," she shook her head, grimacing, and he squeezed her, planting a quick kiss on her hair, "Good. Alright, get'cher homework done."

Megan turned before slipping inside, Dan's brief grin had disappeared as he dropped his head, pulling a hand across the back of his neck. She didn't understand why guilt rolled through her stomach, it wasn't her friend that had come over starting a fight. But the distracting emotion made Megan take a little longer than anticipated to finish her worksheet and she was packing her bag when Dan walked back in.

"Get ready for bed, Megan," he said, returning to the basket in the living room.

"D'you want some help with the laundry?" she asked.

"Thanks, sweetheart," his kind refusal was expected, "But I'm almost done, go brush your teeth."

Megan put on pajamas and made her way to the bathroom while Dan sat on the couch, folding laundry and watching The Simpsons. Lifting on her toes, she leaned over the back of the sofa and wrapped her arms around him.

"G'night," she kissed his cheek, "I love you."

"I love you, too," he squeezed his arms around her as best he could from the awkward position, "Sweet dreams."

Megan closed her door and climbed into bed, opening her book on the nightstand and settled into her pillow.

"No readin', Meg, go to sleep," Dan's direction was barely muffled by the wall between them.

She didn't know how he always knew, but sighed, setting her book down again and flicked off her light behind the alarm clock. Megan listened to the low sounds of the television, sporadically highlighted by Dan's deep chuckle, until she drifted into sleep.

The next few days were pleasantly uneventful and, as the end of the week got closer, Megan was exceptionally careful to behave, bursting with excitement for the book signing on Saturday.

Before math class ended on Friday, however, her name echoed over the loud speaker, beckoning Megan to the principal's office and her ears burned as the entire class turned, snickering jeers while she left the room. She wracked her brain for anything she might've done to get in trouble, but couldn't think of a thing.

Mrs. Todd, the front desk receptionist, smiled when she walked into the main office and held up a finger, poking her head through the doorway behind her chair.

"Megan," she waved, opening the door fully, "Mr. Jarsen's ready for you."

Megan forced a smile, walking into the small, interior office where her principal, Mr. Jarsen, sat behind his desk and a severely dressed, unknown woman stood beside it.

"Hello, Megan," Mr. Jarsen greeted her warmly, "Please have a seat. Are you ready for all your tests next week?"

"Yes, sir," she nodded, trying not to sound as nervous as she was, and chanced a swift glimpse at the woman's harsh features.

"Your grades were fantastic this year," he commented and Megan nodded again, "But that's hardly anything new, huh?" her grin was weak and Mr. Jarsen's finally faltered, leaning forward on his desk, he said, "Megan, a small problem has come to the school's attention for, uh, next year's volleyball team," her stomach twisted as he fumbled to the point, "It's required that a parent or a legal guardian signs your permission slip-"

Megan couldn't confine her dire protest, "But, Dan always signs my permission slips."

"Yes," Mr. Jarsen agreed, avoided the glaring eyes of the unknown woman, "Unfortunately, new administration has found an issue with the, technicalities of your-"

96

"It's not a technicality," the woman snapped abruptly, "It's a legality. And it's well beyond a permission slip for the volleyball team."

Megan felt tears sting her eyes and her throat tightened. Swallowing hard, she did everything she could to not cry in front of Mr. Jarsen and the mysterious, cold woman.

"Ms. Craft," he retorted testily, "Do not suggest you will keep her from enrolling in next year."

Megan quickly wiped a few tears that slipped down her cheek.

"She must have parent or legal guardian sign her forms," Ms. Craft said matter-of-factly, "I can't believe how long your school has allowed this to slip by," and pointed directly at Megan, who burst with an unrestrainable sob, but she stifled it quickly with a hand over her mouth.

"Ms. Craft," Mr. Jarsen stood, resentment in his tone, "Her brother is on his way here, we can wait to have this conversation with him."

"Dan, can't-" Megan attempted to object, knowing how hard it was for him to leave work, but neither adult was paying her any attention.

"I really don't feel comfortable having this conversation with anyone besides her father," Ms. Craft maintained.

"That's not going to happen," the principal said simply, and a knock interrupted their heated debate.

Mrs. Todd opened the door and Megan sighed with relief as Dan entered in his work uniform.

"Dan, I'm sorry to pull you away from work early," Mr. Jarsen said, shaking the young man's hand, "This is the new school administrator, Ms. Craft," Dan offered the same curt nod she gave him and returned his attention to the principal's statement, "It seems there's a bit of an issue with the, uh, legality of Megan's school forms."

"You've got her birth certificate 'n social," confusion creased Dan's forehead, "Did I forget to sign somethin'?"

"No, Dan-" Mr. Jarsen began, but was halted a sharp throat clear.

"You should not be signing anything," Ms. Craft interjected, "Are you her legal guardian?"

"Well, no, but-" Dan defended, but was swiftly interrupted.

"Then we have a problem," she said decisively.

"Wait," frustration grew in Dan's voice, "I've been signin' for her since second grade. Why's it an issue now?"

"Because somebody is paying attention now," Ms. Craft sneered at Mr. Jarsen.

"Dan," the principal said after a quick glare at the administrator, "Is there any chance you can get Greg to-"

The older man trailed off because Dan was already shaking his head, "He won't be back for a couple months, Mr. Jarsen, maybe longer. His phones don't stay in service long, heck, I haven't had a working number since last year. But, I thought he signed somethin' a long time ago puttin' me in charge of her school stuff?"

"That was something this school made up for your, specific situation," Ms. Craft's tone was still hard, but not as severe, "I can appreciate the difficulty tracking her father down may cause-"

"I really don't think you do," Dan's uncharacteristic disruption was bitter.

"Still," she continued robotically, "Unless you are her legal guardian, we need his signature."

The conversation hit a standstill after her proclamation, and Megan followed Dan to his truck in the parking lot just as the bell rang for the end of the day. He paused, staring out the windshield, before turning over the engine and accelerated towards their home.

"Dan?" Megan mumbled after a minute of silence and he nodded to show he was listening, "Am I gonna go to school next year?"

"Yeah," he sighed, "Yeah, sweetheart, you're goin' to school, don't worry. I'm gonna figure it out."

Megan gave him a confident smile, Dan figured everything out, but concern still tumbled in her gut. Ms. Craft had seemed very firm about the necessity of her father's signature on all of her school forms and she had no idea how he was going to accomplish that before the deadline.

Jimmy was reclined on the sofa, his feet on the coffee table, and inclined his head quizzically as his brother walked through the front door.

"What's up?" he asked, sliding his feet to the floor, and turned down the television volume.

"Nothin'," Dan said, kicking off his work boots, "Just handling some stuff at the school."

"What'd you do," Jimmy jeered jokingly at Megan, a perfect echo of her classmates, but clearly didn't expect the sob that broke passed her lips and opened his arms, "Oh, babygirl. What happened?" he consoled, brushing her hair back and insisted, "Who is it, huh? Lemme at 'em."

"I might pay to see that," Dan grumbled, turning the kitchen faucet on and washed his hands.

"They're not gonna let me go to school," Megan whimpered pathetically.

"Megan, stop it," Dan sighed, drying his hands with the towel hanging on the oven door, "You're goin' to school."

"What's goin' on?" Jimmy asked, shifting Megan onto the couch next to him with an arm around her shoulders.

"New administrator," Dan shook his head, "Just bein' a pain in the ass about me signin' her forms."

"Why?" Jimmy narrowed his eyes.

"'Cause I'm not her legal guardian," he scoffed, but poked Megan gently on the head, "Don't you worry about this. I got it. Okay?"

"Okay," she agreed to placate him and Dan retreated to the bathroom.

"What'd they say?" Jimmy asked when the door latched.

"They asked if we could find my dad," Jimmy scowled as Megan mentioned the stepfather he loathed, but she continued recapping the recent meeting, "This lady, Ms. Craft, said I have to have a parent or legal guardian sign me up for school 'n volleyball. I dunno what Dan's gonna do-"

"Hey," Jimmy stopped her renewed sniffles with a gentle shake, "He'll figure it out, y'know he will. Wanna watch some TV?"

Jimmy had worked the night before and didn't have another shift until Saturday evening, so the three of them had a quiet night of microwavable dinners, settling into a movie afterwards. Since they were leaving at dawn the next morning, Dan told Megan she needed to go to bed early, completely unnecessarily because she fell asleep before the end of the movie with her head resting on Jimmy's leg. For a few minutes before drifting off, Megan laid on the couch with her eyes closed, listening to the television and a short exchange between her brothers.

"We'll be back tomorrow night," Dan reminded.

"I know," Jimmy said a little bitterly, "I'll be at work."

"Just so long as that's all," Dan cautioned.

"I know, Dan," Jimmy sighed, gently brushing Megan's hair.

"Okay," Dan pressed, "Y'know I'm not tryin' to be an asshole here, Jim."

"Do a pretty good impression," Jimmy muttered, but yielded a moment later, "I know, Dan, I'll be here."

"Talk to Jordan lately?" Dan barely hid his disdain.

"Naw," Jimmy scoffed, "I'm sure he's still salty. Not like it matters since I'm a prisoner here another week."

"Yup," Dan patted his little brother's uninhabited knee, "Simpsons?"

"Yeah, fine," Megan felt Jimmy stifle a chuckle as she finally fell into a dream.

She was shaken awake while her room was still mostly dark. Dan sat on her bed in the pale, dusky light.

"Hey," he said softly when her eyelids stopped fluttering, "Ready to meet A.K. Foreman?"

An enthusiastic smile erupted on her face and Megan leapt off her bed. Dan chuckled, leaving her to change, already fully dressed himself, and told her to meet him in the kitchen when she was ready.

The sun was still rising, leaving the front room in near darkness as they munched cereal and Dan reviewed a road map at the table. He was wearing his nice jeans, a black t-shirt and a blue, zip-up hoodie. Megan liked when Dan wore comfortable clothes, he looked more like her brother before he'd had to work all the time.

While slipping her shoes on by the front door, she gasped, "My books!" and started towards her room, but a firm hold on the back of her jeans kept Megan from advancing further.

"Backpack," he pointed to her backpack slumped against the couch, "Your school stuff's in your room, I packed those last night."

"All of 'em?" she asked, grabbing the unusually lightweight bag.

"Check," he said, "I'd hate to be wrong."

Megan confirmed the three, well-read novels were stacked on top of each other before zipping it up and following Dan out the front door. The street was bright, but their house's shadow darkened the yard, stretching just passed the sidewalk in the cool early morning breeze. Goosebumps shivered along her arms and, remembering her jacket inside, Megan turned back to the porch, but saw Dan had it slung over his arm while he locked the front door.

"You're gonna want this," he predicted, tossing her the denim jacket as he jogged down the steps.

Dan dropped the map on the seat between them and they were backing out of their driveway shortly after the truck rumbled to life. The sun was fully risen by the time they hit the highway and Megan yawned, turning up the volume on the classic rock station. She grabbed the map, opening it randomly, as if she knew how to assess the distance between their unknown location and the even less known destination.

"Right around three hours," Dan answered the unasked question, "You excited?"

"Yesssssssssss," she smiled goofily at him, earning a chuckle from the lengthy hiss in her reply.

They listened to music and discussed her upcoming party with Sam as well as other plans they had for the summer. In July, their town would have a week-long carnival only a few blocks from their house and, since she'd be thirteen, Megan reminded Dan he'd said she could go with just Sam this year.

"Y'know," he smirked, "Bein' thirteen's gonna give you more freedoms, but only if ya earn 'em. Jimmy'll tell you, age don't mean much in our house."

"I know," she shrugged, "I'm just sayin'."

"I'm glad you're excited," he said, "Got any ideas what'cha want?"

"Not really," Megan lied, there were a few things she'd recently found interesting, but, knowing their financial situation was perpetually minimal, she was trying to keep frivolous wants to herself.

"Nothin'?" Dan asked in disbelief.

"I mean," she smiled, "This is pretty awesome."

His eyebrows raised in surprise before returning her smile, "I'm really glad I could take you, sweetheart."

More cars surrounded them when the highway widened through the western suburbs of Chicago and Megan gawked at the distant city skyline. It seemed so close, but Dan told her it was at least a half an hour from where they were, the buildings were just that tall.

He asked if she remembered when they'd gone to Chicago with their mother.

"I remember the hospital," she nodded.

"Ya don't remember Jimmy 'n I takin' you to the top of the Sears Tower?" Dan poked her gently in the side, instigating a giggle.

"Oh, yeah," Megan smiled, "And then we got that huge pizza!"

"Yup," Dan chuckled, "That you had three bites of before passin' out at the table."

She remembered the pizza and the red checkered tablecloth, but not much else from that trip except the overly clean smelling hospital. Their mother had been in a section they could only enter after extensive hand washing and had had to wear itchy blue masks. She'd cried because a man in scrubs had yelled at her for taking it off, but Dan had quickly stepped in, explaining the mask was keeping their mother, and everyone else on the floor, from getting sicker, so she'd left it alone, wiggling her nose under the scratchy fabric occasionally for relief. That had been one of the last hospital visits Megan could recall.

Their mother had been frail and gray while lying on a small bed, hooked to machines. Her long, dark hair had fallen out well before that trip and, behind the private doors of the hospital, she'd relieve her head of the wrap, lolling bare and exhausted on her shoulder. Jimmy had hardly left the chair next to her bed, but Dan had taken Megan on a few trips to the hospital's play area, and once to the chapel.

"Megan, check this out," Dan pointed out his window to a large car dealership below the highway, "That's where my dad worked."

"That place is huge!" she gaped at the massive lot of gleaming automobiles.

"Yeah," he stared longingly as they passed, absently reminiscing, "He used to take me with him on Saturdays sometimes to wash cars, but that was the eighties, you couldn't do that nowadays."

"What was he like?" Megan asked, expecting him to casually dismiss the question, and was relieved when Dan smiled proudly.

"He was tough," Dan said, "But a lotta fun. He always had a project car in the garage we'd be workin' on, not that I did more than hand him the tools. But when he'd finish, he'd take me to this empty road behind some warehouses and we'd tear it up."

"What happened to the cars?" she asked, enjoying the light in Dan's eyes as he reminisced private moments with his father.

"He'd sell 'em and start a new one," Dan said, "My dad could build a racecar from the ground up," Megan was impressed and Dan clearly appreciated her awe, "Yeah, he was pretty cool."

She looked around the wide highway and down to the streets below, realizing that somewhere nearby was where her brothers had lived until their dad had died, before her father had come into the picture, shortly followed by her. Megan knew her father hadn't married their mother until after she was born and, with the little she knew about her first husband, she didn't quite understand why their mother had chosen the second. A swirl of guilt rolled in her gut, glancing at her brother and considered the life he was supposed to have had.

While they never talked about it, Megan remembered the men in suits who'd stopped Dan after football games, a few had even come to the house, imploring him to let them help with his future. But Dan had refused every one of them. Jimmy had told her they were college recruiters, though Megan hadn't understood what that meant at the time, but, since then, she'd heard enough around town to realize she had unknowingly halted Dan's promising football career.

A little over half an hour after passing the dealership, she bounced on the bench seat seeing the 'Welcome to Wisconsin' sign, shortly followed by billboards for fireworks and cheese stores off the next few exits.

"How close are we?" Megan asked eagerly.

"Maybe an hour," Dan checked the clock on the radio and then the dashboard, "We gotta stop and get gas soon, though."

The green truck rumbled off the highway at the next exit and Dan pulled into a truck stop gas station, eyeing a white tent in the neighboring field with a hand painted sign for fireworks propped against one of the posts.

"Mind if we check that out real quick?" his eyebrows raised pleadingly and, even though Megan wanted nothing more than to get back on the road, she smiled, surrendering a bit of time for Dan's amusement.

After filling the tank, he parked the truck near the tent and Megan followed Dan inside the tethered shelter. There were dozens of folding tables set up with hundreds, maybe thousands, of fireworks, all different sizes and all expressing their ability to be loud, bright or both. For a few minutes, Megan patiently trailed Dan, reading the DO NOT TOUCH signs every few feet, and, regardless of the urge, she did not, eventually shoving her fidgeting hands into her jacket pockets.

"Jimmy loves these things," Dan nudged her shoulder and nodded at the Roman Candles.

He didn't take much longer, probably noticing the amount of effort Megan was putting into trying not to look bored, and, after a fast transaction, Dan led her to the truck, setting a box in the bed.

"Why'd we have to buy those here?" Megan asked, climbing onto the bench seat.

"'Cause they're illegal in Illinois," Dan said nonchalantly, but smirked at her sudden anxiety, "Hey, I get to have fun sometimes too."

"But-" Megan began to protest.

"Relax," he chuckled, shaking her by the shoulder, "I know what I'm doin'. How many times have you seen Jimmy 'n me shoot off fireworks?"

"A lot," she shrugged, thinking of the few shows her brothers had put on in the field by the river with practically the entire neighborhood as an audience.

"And how many times have I been arrested?" he asked and Megan glanced at him sideways, causing Dan's ears to flush before he clarified, "For fireworks."

"Never," she agreed.

"Well, okay then," he scoffed, turning the engine over, and left the makeshift parking lot.

Milwaukee finally appeared, seeming to come out of nowhere all at once, and Megan twisted her head around to see an arched bridge in the distance. Steeples popped between newer construction and a very large clock was situated in one of the more ornate peaks. But the city wasn't quite as impressive as Chicago, and Dan agreed with her assessment while flicking his attention between the map and the road. After one wrong turn, he found a parking garage near the venue, but they had to go nearly to the top to find a vacant spot not labeled 'compact' and took the elevator down.

Megan bounced on her toes as the floor numbers flashed, sighing when the elevator stopped at three to let a few people on, but, noticing Dan's cautionary eyebrow, she hid her exasperation. His firm grip on her backpack when the doors finally opened was annoying, but Megan silently acknowledged she might have barreled through a group of strangers had he not, and took a deep breath, trying to calm her excitement. Until the moment they turned the corner to the convention center, when there was no amount of self-control that could keep Megan from squealing and jumping up and down. Dan however, looked completely dumbfounded by the line they encountered.

"So, uh," he stammered, "This Foreman lady's pretty popular, huh?"

Megan nodded enthusiastically, dragging him to the back of the line mostly comprised of girls around her age and their mothers. Dan grinned a little warily and exhaled, resigned to standing in a train of estrogen for an undetermined amount of time. More groups of mothers and daughters filed in behind them as the line slowly crawled towards the double doors into the building.

She saw a few girls ahead turning to look at them before whispering to each other and repeating the process. Shrewdly, Megan rolled her eyes up at Dan and he laughed, having just then caught the group of young teenagers, who instantly blushed and flipped straight ahead.

"You excited about your date with Lacey?" the giggling girls reminded Megan of the flirty waitress.

"Yeah, actually," he nodded, "I am."

"She's pretty," Megan shrugged.

"She is," Dan agreed, continuing with a wink, "Think she likes fireworks?"

"Yeah," Megan said pragmatically, "Who doesn't?"

106

They were still at least twenty feet from the door after almost an hour and, while he looked thoroughly exhausted by the situation, Dan seemed relieved to occasionally see men leaving with equally excited girls clutching freshly signed books. As they took another few steps closer, Megan felt Dan turn as a woman spoke behind them.

"I'm sorry to bother you," the middle-aged woman smiled, but her eyes narrowed with scrutiny, "But you can't possibly be her father?"

"I'm her brother," Dan said simply.

"Oh, of course!" she clapped her boney hands together, shaking her head of short, platinum blonde hair, "I'm sorry, you just look so young, I had to ask."

"Not a problem," Dan said curtly, pivoting again, but was stopped halfway through his retreat.

"It's so sweet of you to take her," she crooned, "I wish my son would let me have a day off. Your mother must just adore you."

Dan squeezed Megan's shoulder, silently instructing her not to insert a comment, as he said, "I do what I can."

"Well you tell her some lunatic lady said she's lucky," the woman laughed and Dan gave her a forced, tight lipped grin, spinning Megan around as he faced forward again.

Assumptions from strangers were something Megan had gotten used to, though sometimes she still needed a reminder that not everyone deserved an explanation of their lives. Their mother having passed and her father hardly home was information best kept at home, as past experiences had taught.

The year before Dan put Greg in the hospital was when Megan had met their social worker, Dotty Clark, after she'd told a new teacher her father hadn't been home in a while. The first evening Dotty had stopped by their house, Dan had been a nervous wreck, despite her smiling that everything was fine and promised she was just there to look around. She'd asked when the last time Greg had been there and Dan had under exaggerated by about a month. His ability to polish the truth had been impressive throughout Dotty's questioning, but then she'd asked how many hours the eighteen-year-old worked a week. Megan didn't remember the number, but Dotty had seemed concerned that he was still in his last semester of high school and might be taking on too much. Dan had assured her, since football season was over, he was more than capable of handling all of it. Jimmy had then piped up that he worked part time at the gas station, cleaning after hours a few nights a week for cash, and Dan had looked like he would've hit him if given the chance. Dotty, however, had smiled and shook her head at the admission, saying something about how every little bit helps. Finally, she had interviewed Megan in the living room after kindly asking her brothers to let them have a few minutes alone. Megan remembered admiring Dotty's pinstripe jacket while she'd answered questions about what her normal day was like.

Who got her ready for school? Dan. Who made sure she had lunch? Dan. Who washed her clothes? Dan. Who made dinner? Dan. And who told her to go to bed? Again, Dan. Then Dotty had asked what else she and Dan did together and seemed happily surprised to learn he took his younger siblings to church every Sunday, questioning if her father ever went with when he was home. Megan had been unable to retrain a laugh in response.

Dotty had stopped by a few times after that, however her visits became regular for the few months following Dan's arrest, though she'd seemed secretively supportive of what had happened to Greg.

Finally, Megan and Dan were just outside the doors, looking into the enormous space swarmed with people lumbering slowly through velvet rope partitions. The commotion was intoxicating, at least to Megan. Dan, however, seemed less than thrilled at the more cramped line they were being ushered into.

"Christ, we should've left earlier," he sighed and Megan giggled, taking another few steps forward and tried to peer through the mass of bodies to where A.K. Foreman had to be sitting.

She could see girls, and a few women, practically skipping away from the very end of the crowd and held her breath in anticipation of how close they were, certain the line was moving faster.

Halfway through the velvet roped maze, Megan heard an impressively loud growl and glanced from Dan's middle to his eyes.

"We're eatin' like right after this," he mumbled and she nodded, noting her own hunger.

108

"Mom, I need that Embers t-shirt," a girl in the row next to them pointed to the merchandise counter.

"Honey, you have that shirt," her mother said gently.

"But Heather likes it and I told her I'd get her one," the blonde girl whined.

"Well, honey," her mother sighed, "Why would you tell her that?"

"Mom!" the little blonde snapped, "It's like twenty bucks, and I told her I would!"

Several people were trying to avert their attention, but a few just stared at the indignant preteen on the verge of a tantrum, waiting for her docile mother's reaction. Dan squeezed Megan's shoulder, a gesture she understood as a compliment to her own behavior while a girl her age had a public fit.

"Fine, but then she's getting the one you would've," the girl's mother informed her passively.

"That's not fair!" Megan leaned into Dan as the bratty girl screeched and a few other people actually jumped.

"Okay, honey," her mother bowed, begging softly, "Listen, please, stop, you're making a scene."

She shrugged and spat through gritted teeth, "I want my shirt too."

"Okay, fine, that's fine," her mother nodded defeatedly and Megan felt Dan stifle a chuckle.

A satisfied smile emerged on the girl's face and she uncrossed her arms, contented immediately with the promise of undeserved gifts. Megan looked at Dan, who was already regarding her proudly, and they shared an amused eye roll over the appalling public conduct they'd witnessed. Some bystanders shook their heads, but most simply returned to their own conversations, the brief entertainment having ceased. The girl's mother buried her blushing face in her Blackberry as everyone shuffled forward a few more feet.

Megan bounced on her toes again as they took the last turn and, finally, A.K. Foreman was unobstructed, sitting at a long table with stacks of books. Nodding as she listened with a beaming smile, the author simultaneously signed the inside covers of her fan's books and waved a wrinkled hand, still contorted around her pen, as a handler ushered each away for the next.

When it was finally their turn, Megan withdrew a half step into Dan, but he was well versed in her anxious dance and, with a gentle, encouraging hand, pushed her ahead of himself to the table.

Her stomach fluttered when A.K. Foreman peered over her small framed glasses and smiled.

"Hi, darlin'," her voice was sweet and she held her thin hands out for the books Megan anxiously slid across the table, "What's your name?"

"Megan," she mumbled, glad Dan's hand stayed on her shoulder.

"Thank you for comin' today, Miss Megan," she smiled, opening the first book and signed the inside cover, "Who's this with you?"

"My brother, Dan," Megan looked up and felt less nervous.

"Well, hi brother Dan," A.K. Foreman peeked at him as she opened the second book cover, "How nice of him to bring you here today. Most of these girls' moms are about to keel over in this line."

"My mom passed away," Megan muttered.

"Megan," she heard the growl Dan tried to hide as he squeezed her shoulder.

But the damage was done and the author looked up slowly from the third, unopened book.

"I'm very sorry to hear that, darlin'," her blue eyes glisten with honesty in the statement, "That's just, well, that's just awful. Is it just you and your brother now?"

"And Jimmy," Megan nodded, "Our other brother."

For a moment, before she swiped her pen several times inside the final cover, A.K. Foreman smiled sadly between Megan and Dan.

"Well, Megan," she closed the third book and held up a finger at the approaching handler, "You seem to have a wonderful brother, two I'm sure," A.K. Foreman reached across the table and squeezed her hand, kindly adding, "You take care of yourselves, ya hear."

"Thank you, ma'am," Dan nodded, gently tugging her away from the table.

"M'sorry," Megan mumbled when they were out of earshot from the still massive line.

Dan just sighed and threw an arm around her shoulders, "Let's get some food, kid."

As they walked a few blocks to a burger joint Dan had spotted on the way in, Megan found herself surprised he wasn't upset at her for what she'd blurted out to A.K. Foreman. Maybe he knew she was really nervous, or maybe the author's kind reaction had affected his normal compulsion to chastise her outburst. Either way, Megan appreciated that Dan seemed to be letting it go.

"Thank you, today was awesome," she smiled after washing a waffle fry down with her chocolate shake.

"No problem, sweetheart," he snatched a few of her fries and grinned after popping them in his mouth.

The ride home late that afternoon was pleasantly quiet. They were both exhausted and Megan eventually fell asleep across the bench seat, while Dan's hand brushed over her dark hair. Even though he'd spent hours in a line with nosey women and overindulged girls, he smiled from the remanence of a great day, having seen an uncompromised smile from his little sister the entire time.

# Chapter 6

When Sunday service let out the next morning, Dan and Megan bumped into Darlene and Sam on their way to the truck. While Darlene pulled Dan aside with the allurement of a few party ideas, Sam took the opportunity to confront Megan.

"What happened on Friday?" he whispered eagerly, "I heard you get called to Mr. Jarsen's office."

Megan blushed, "I'll tell ya later," and changed the subject brightly, "Wanna go to the river when we get home?"

"Yeah," he nodded excitedly.

"D'ja forget about the lawn?" Darlene called over her shoulder.

"It'll take ten minutes," Sam sighed, rolling his eyes with his back to her.

"Good," his mom smiled, "You can go as soon as you're done."

"Megan, don't'cha have a few tests tomorrow?" Dan asked, even though he knew the answer, but, when Megan turned down the corners of her mouth pleadingly, he sighed, "Ya got two hours and then you're studyin'."

"Softie," Darlene joked, poking Dan's side, "We'll see you two later, c'mon Sam."

"Alright, let's go," Dan gestured towards the other side of the parking lot with a large hand, but, just as she took a step, Megan turned, hearing their names called.

"Megan! Dan!" Mrs. King was hurrying through the crowd of parishioners in a strange sort of waddle, panting a bit when she stopped in front of them, "I'm glad I caught you, I heard from Mr. Jarsen about the," she cleared her throat forcefully, "administration problem-"

"Oh, yeah," Dan nodded, his ears turning a light shade of pink, "I'll figure-"

"All the teachers are in complete outrage," she continued, shaking her head incredulously, "We're all going to the next board meeting and I wanted to encourage you to as well. It's next Monday night at seven, it's the last one before next school year," Dan raised his eyebrows, nodding thoughtfully, and Mrs. King added, "I also don't think it would hurt to reach out to Dotty Clark, she might be able to help."

"Ya think?" Dan considered the idea with a curious expression.

"Wouldn't hurt to try," Mrs. King said encouragingly, "I should get going. Megan, I'll see you tomorrow, Dan, dear, just remember, you got a lotta people in your corner."

"Thanks, Mrs. King," he said, offering a compulsory smile, and practically pushed Megan towards the truck.

"Are you gonna call Dotty?" Megan asked when the solid doors shut.

"I'm thinkin' about it," Dan nodded, sincerely inquiring, "You like her, right?"

"Yeah, she's okay," Megan shrugged, "Just asks a lotta questions."

Dan chuckled, "Well, that's kinda her job, kid."

"I know," she sighed, rolling her eyes, "But she never makes you sit with her for five hours."

"Precisely five hours," Dan joked, snipping his fingers at the tongue she stuck out before explaining, "And that's 'cause I'm over eighteen. Remember when Jimmy used to do the same thing?" Megan nodded, thinking of her walks with Dan when it was Jimmy's turn for an interview, understanding when Dan said, "And she might have some advice for this administrator."

Megan wanted to be hopeful, but knew her brother's smile was forced, the concern in his eyes was too great to hide.

Jimmy had only been asleep a few hours when they walked in and Dan caught the screen door with his foot, reminding Megan to be quiet. She changed into her too-tight jeans and a t-shirt she never wore to school anymore before hurrying to the front door, but Dan halted her escape.

"Breakfast," he reminded, "And Sam's gotta mow his lawn first. Why don't'cha get some studyin' done while ya got the time?"

"I'll just go over it later," she shrugged, sitting on the couch and reached for the remote.

"Got flashcards made?" his question was answered with a guilty slouch, "C'mon, y'know it'll be easier later, just get some done before you go out."

Megan slumped off the worn sofa, rolling her eyes on the way to her school books still stacked on top of the short bookcase under her window. After setting up at the kitchen table, it really didn't take long to breeze through several points on her history study guide and, once she got started, Megan really did find satisfaction in the completed flashcards.

Dan made french toast, allowing enough time to write a few definition cards before she cleared her books and he put a steaming plate in the middle of the table. Megan grabbed the syrup while Dan set two plates on the table with forks, caught the closing fridge door and grabbed the orange juice carton as she added empty glasses. Jimmy's door creaked and he yawned into the kitchen just as they were sitting down.

"Hey brother," Dan said, "Didn't wake ya up did we?"

"I smelled french toast," Jimmy mumbled, trying to push his shaggy bangs out of his eyes, and grabbed a plate from the high cabinet.

"Dig in," Dan encouraged, waiting for them to stab a few slices, and slid the last three on his own plate.

Megan heard a lawn mower roaring out the window while pouring more syrup on her second piece of french toast and hoped it was Sam's, though was sure he'd underestimated how long the chore would take. Jimmy's eyes were barely open as he devoured his breakfast, finishing even before Dan, and dumped his syrup covered plate in the sink after downing the last half of his orange juice.

"Thanks," he patted Dan on the shoulder, "I'm goin' back to bed."

"Night," Dan chuckled, pushing his chair back.

Jimmy's door shut and Dan turned on the faucet, rinsing the plates before organizing them in the dishwasher. Megan finished her orange juice and slipped off the chair, but stopped as she turned away from the table and brought her dirty dishes to Dan at the sink.

"Thanks," he said, but raised an eyebrow asking, "Do y'know where your watch is?"

"Somewhere," Megan shrugged, "Sam has one, though."

"Well, make sure you're home in two hours," he reminded as she pulled on her shoes, "You 'n Sam are gonna have all summer to hang out after this week."

"I know," Megan called on her way out the front door, "I will."

Sam was just finishing his front yard with a push mower, and Megan jumped down the steps, grabbing her bike from under the porch overhang. She stopped on the sidewalk in front of Sam's house, waiting as he put the lawn mower back in the garage and grabbed his bike, neglecting the fishing rod and bucket because he said it wasn't a good time of day to catch anything. They didn't race to the river, lazily coasting down the low grade of their street.

"So, what happened?" Sam insisted his earlier question almost immediately.

Megan sighed, "The new administrator said Dan can't sign my school stuff, she basically said unless they get my dad's signature I can't go to school next year."

"They can't do that," Sam scoffed irritably, "I mean, what's the problem? Dan's an adult and he's been takin' care'a you for forever."

"I know," Megan agreed with equal disbelief, "But now it's a problem I guess."

"Bullshit," Sam said bitterly, leaning his bike on the other side of the fire hydrant as Megan and she offered a smirk of appreciation for his solidarity.

Sliding down the steep embankment to the river's edge, Megan led him immediately to the gnarly rooted tree, climbing onto their branch and scooted as far out as she knew she could while Sam inched close behind her. They could hear the tiny chirps before two, gray puffs, weakly wobbling their yellow beaks in the nest near the trunk of the neighboring tree, were visible through the thickening leaves. For a little while, they watched in silence as the baby birds wiggled and squeaked, until an adult robin returned to the tree, jumping frantically from one branch to another around the nest. Sam tapped Megan's shoulder and she followed him backwards down to the river bank, away from the flustered mother bird.

"That was cool," Megan said when her feet touched the ground.

"Yeah," he agreed, "Hey, I forgot to ask. How was the book signing?"

"Awesome," she exclaimed, "It was a really long line, but A.K. Foreman was nice, and Dan bought fireworks while we were up there."

"Awesome," Sam grinned and Megan knew it was more related to the fireworks than her recount of meeting her favorite author, confirming the assumption when he asked, "Think he'd light some off after the party?"

"Yeah, I'll ask," she shrugged, "I'm sure he wouldn't mind doin' a couple. Hey, y'know I'm comin' over Saturday?"

"Yeah," Sam smiled, "Wanna go to the movies?"

"Totally," she agreed.

About an hour and a half later, Megan and Sam pumped their bikes hard up the slight incline towards their homes. Dan was almost done mowing their front yard, his sleeveless t-shirt sticky with sweat. Wearing his athletic shorts and old sneakers, Megan thought he looked like he used to after practice, but it had been many years since Dan had played football. He let go of the push mower as she stopped in the driveway, dropping her bike under the overhang of the front porch.

"Those bird eggs hatched," she informed Dan immediately.

"Cool," he smiled, "Didn't get too close did'ja?"

"No," Megan shook her head, sitting on the third porch step, "The mom came back and we left."

116

He nodded approvingly, having told her the nest was an incredible find, but reiterated that she and Sam needed to keep their distance.

"What'd they look like?" Dan sat next to her, wiping his sweaty hands on his mesh shorts.

"Not like birds," she laughed, shaking her head, "I knew they'd be tiny, but they're like, puffy, and kinda ugly."

Dan chuckled, "That's what we said when you were born," and made a scissor motion at the tongue protruding from her scrunched face, "So, what'd ya say I pick up pizza for dinner later?"

Megan smirked, crooning, "So you can talk to Lacey?"

"Maybe," he mocked her tone, but Megan saw his ears blush a little.

"Pizza sounds good," she said.

"Pizza it is," he stood, stretching his long arms over his head, "Go get goin', I want all your flashcards done before we eat."

She trudged up the porch steps, slowly, and shut the front door behind her as the mower roared back to life. Jimmy was still sleeping and Megan was careful to be quiet while changing out of her dirty clothes before sitting at the kitchen table with a stack of blank flashcards and her study guide. She'd made good progress when the mower sputtered to a stop again and Dan walked in a few minutes later.

"How's it comin'?" he asked, pulling his sweaty t-shirt over his head while kicking his grass stained sneakers off by the front door.

"History's done," she pointed proudly to a stack of completed index cards, "Just starting science."

"What else ya got tomorrow?" he paused on his way to the bathroom.

"That's it," she assured him, "Math's on Tuesday."

"You ready for that?" Dan knew she'd recently been having a hard time in the subject.

"I hate math," she sighed, dramatically slumping on the table.

Dan chuckled at the overreaction, "I know, but maybe Sam'll have some time to help ya study for it," he shook his head at her questionable look, "Hey, y'know I'm happy to, but if your best friend happens to be a bit of a math whiz, I mean," he put his hands up in an exaggerated shrug and Megan giggled.

"I'll ask him, I'm sure he will," she nodded and returned to her index cards.

"Yeah, I'm sure he will," Dan seemed to be talking to himself as he shut the bathroom door.

Jimmy dragged himself out of bed just as Dan was leaving to pick up pizza, freshly showered and his short hair gelled. Megan had finished writing flashcards and was reviewing them when Jimmy landed on the couch and turned the television on.

"Hey, turn that down," Dan requested firmly, "She's tryin' to study."

"Take a break, Meg," Jimmy jerked his head towards the screen.

"Jimmy," Dan growled, but Megan's pleading expression made him sigh, "You ready to go over everything after dinner?" she nodded earnestly, "Alright, I'll be back in a bit."

Megan slid off her chair and joined Jimmy on the couch as Dan left, the screen door banging while his heavy steps descended the porch stairs. Jimmy nudged her with his boney elbow and gave Megan their secret smirk.

"Ya know he wants to talk to Lacey alone."

"They have a date this weekend," Megan said pointedly.

"I know," Jimmy inhaled dramatically, tossing his head back, "Man she's hot!"

Megan giggled, shaking her head, and snatched the remote while he was still staring upward dreamily, but, since he was content with Malcolm in the Middle as her choice, Jimmy let her keep it. But when the episode ended, and the Family Guy theme song started, he made her give it up and grudgingly changed the channel from the show he enjoyed, knowing Dan didn't allowed Megan to watch the crude cartoon. Jimmy flipped through channels, but, before he could find

118

anything mutually entertaining, Dan's truck growled into the driveway and he shut off the television.

"Move your stuff," he pointed at the table and the truck door shut outside.

Megan tossed everything on top of her backpack in a heap next to the couch, and, as the front door opened, the delicious smell of fresh pizza filled the front room. Dan set the flat, white box in the middle of the recently cleared table, taking a six pack of soda to the fridge, and Jimmy grabbed three plates from the top cabinet. Megan lifted the top of the box and closed her eyes to the escaping steam, inhaling the aroma. The top slid out of her hands and Dan flipped it under the hot bottom.

"So, how's Lacey?" Jimmy's question came with a sneaky grin.

"She's good," Dan said, setting a glass of milk in front of Megan and cracked a soda for himself as he joined them at the table.

"She's hot," Jimmy repeated his earlier statement and Dan chuckled, offering an agreeable sideways nod to his brother, who continued with a mouthful of peperoni pizza, "Wha'd'r'y'doin' wif'er fadurday?"

"I don't know yet," Dan shrugged, his plate still empty as he sipped his soda and watched them devour their first slices, "I think Mike has a plan, haven't talk to him yet. Are you workin' Saturday night?"

"Not this week," Jimmy shook his head after a long gulp of soda.

"I'm plannin' on her bein' over at Sam 'n Darlene's," Dan jerked his head at Megan, "You gonna be home?

Jimmy grimaced, "I wasn't plannin' on it. Kinda my weekend'a freedom."

"Well, make sure it's not short lived," Dan said, raising a characteristic eyebrow, "Don't do anything stupid."

"I won't," Jimmy sighed, but refrained from rolling his eyes, "We're just gonna cruise around, probably get midnight breakfast at the truck stop in Sheridan."

"Who's we?" Dan's question was almost accusatory.

"Brad 'n Travis," Jimmy shrugged, shoving another bite of pizza in his mouth, "Vey're done wiff claff on Wenvday," he swallowed hard, "We're celebrating. No beer," he did roll his eyes with the clarifying statement.

"Alright," Dan nodded, finally taking a few slices of pizza on his empty plate, "Have fun."

"Thanks," Jimmy said, "You too."

"Sam 'n I are goin' to the movies," Megan announced in the few moments of silence while her brothers shoveled pizza into their mouths.

"So, I'm the only one without a date this weekend?" Jimmy joked.

"Shut up, Jimmy," Megan sneered, but Dan's loud finger snap caught her attention.

"Don't tell people to shut up," he reminded firmly and flipped his attention to Jimmy, "You, just, don't."

"Just a joke," Jimmy rolled his eyes and chomped his crust.

"Goin' to see Shrek?" Dan asked Megan after breaking his lingering stare on Jimmy.

"I still wanna see Josie and the Pussycats," she said pitiably.

"Sure," Dan agreed and Megan's eyes went wide with shock.

"Really?" she asked excitedly.

"In two weeks," he chuckled at her defeated pout.

"Holy crap that's right," Jimmy poked Megan playfully in the shoulder, "Gonna be a teen soon."

"Two'a you," Dan scoffed humorously, "Lucky me."

When they'd finished and the table was cleared, Jimmy settled on the couch, but Dan called from the kitchen just as he grabbed the remote off the coffee table.

"Megan 'n I are gonna study in there," he barely looked up while rinsing the plates and organizing them in the dishwasher.

Jimmy didn't argue, sliding his feet from the coffee table onto the floor, and asked, "Can I have my keys then?" completing his request quickly when Dan shot him a glare, "So I can wash my car?"

Dan relaxed and jerked his head at the hallway, "They're on my dresser."

Jimmy disappeared down the hall and Dan gestured Megan to the sofa with the promise that he'd be right back. She sunk into the soft, worn cushions and shuffled her index cards, reviewing the first few.

Changed into a pair of athletic shorts, Jimmy tossed his keys in one hand and followed Dan, the screen door banging while they clomped down the porch steps. Outside the window behind the television, Megan saw Jimmy hop into his Oldsmobile as the truck started with a loud growl and Dan backed out of the driveway, parking on the street for Jimmy to pull his large sedan into the driveway. Dan jogged back through the front door, tossed his keys on the kitchen counter and snatched the index cards out of Megan's hands as he landed on the other side of the couch.

"Hey!" she protested.

"Thought'cha were ready?" Dan teased and she crossed her arms, slumping against the armrest.

"Still don't have to grab shi-stuff," Megan caught herself before completing the cuss word and grinned innocently, but Dan shook his head with a light chuckle and she giggled.

When they finished and the sun had almost set, Jimmy walked through the front door, his t-shirt and shorts slightly damp and shaggy hair hung limply in front of his eyes.

"I'm gonna switch the cars," he picked Dan's truck keys off the counter, jingling them to get his brother's attention.

"Leave 'em," Dan shrugged, handing Megan her index cards with his usual end of the night instructions, "Pack up and get ready for bed."

"It's not even eight," Megan whined, but slid off the couch and started putting her school work into her backpack.

"It's almost eight," Dan corrected, "C'mon don't argue with me."

"Fine," she rolled her eyes, dumping her bag next to the front door and shut herself in the bathroom.

After showering and brushing her teeth, Megan left her clothes on the tile floor and walked down the hall in a towel. When she returned to the living room, raking a comb through her hair, Jimmy cleared his throat hard and rolled his eyes while tossing her dirty clothes into the hamper just outside the bathroom door and shut himself behind it, the shower turned on a moment later. Dan's heavy footsteps echoed up the basement stairs before he entered the kitchen with a basket of clean clothes.

"Hey, Megan," Dan caught her attention before she sat on the couch, "I haven't really seen those books A.K. Foreman signed yet."

"Oh, yeah," Megan brightened and hurried back into her bedroom, grabbing the three books off the top of her dresser.

After leaving the convention center, Dan had told her to keep them in her backpack while they ate and, since Megan had slept for most of their ride home, she'd only snuck a peak at the inside cover of one in the busy day since they'd returned from Milwaukee. Dan was on the far side of the couch with the basket of clothes on the floor between his feet when Megan skipped back in and landed on the cushion next to him. She handed him the first book and opened the cover of the second, both were nearly identical on the inside with a messy, swooped signature and quickly scrawled thank you. She opened the third book cover, expecting the same, but was surprised to see a whole sentence hurried under the illegible signature. 'Megan, I wish you, Dan and Jimmy the best, stay strong always!'

"Hey, look," she scooted closer to Dan, holding the book open for him to see the inscription.

"Wow," his eyebrows jumped as he read the words, "Megan, that's really cool!"

She traced A.K. Foreman's thin handwriting with her finger and smiled at the permanent evidence of her favorite author's special attention.

Briefly shifting her happy gaze up to her brother, Megan leaned into his side and returned to examining the inside of the third book cover.

"I had a great weekend," she announced and felt him kiss her damp hair.

"I'm glad, sweetheart," Dan said, "I did too."

He clicked on the television and began flipping through channels, landing briefly, to Megan's mild irritation, on the news. Jimmy left the bathroom with steam billowing behind him and dumped his clothes in the hamper before closing himself behind his bedroom door.

"Jimmy look," still clutching the book in her hand, Megan turned on the couch excitedly when she heard his door open again and he walked out in sweatpants and a clean t-shirt.

"Hey that's me," he smiled, pointing to the inscription inside the cover, "Very cool, babygirl. How was the trip?"

"Easy drive," Dan shrugged before expelling a laugh, "Couldn't believe that line though, Christ."

"It wasn't that bad," Megan insisted, "Oh! Dan showed me where your dad used to work by the city!"

"I just pointed it out," Dan clarified, "Oh, and I, uh, picked up some toys while we were in Wisconsin."

"Roman candles?" Jimmy asked eagerly.

"And some others," Dan smiled, "The box is in the garage."

"Sweet," Jimmy tightened his fists happily and fell into the arm chair.

"Will you light off a few at Sam 'n my party?" Megan asked hopefully, remembering Sam's request.

"Yeah, a few," Dan agreed, "That's comin' up next weekend, huh?"

"I'm gonna be thirteen," she sang goofily at him, getting both her brothers to laugh, but a long yawn caught her off guard.

"Alright, Miss almost thirteen," Dan said, "Get to bed."

Even though it was fifteen minutes before her actual bedtime, Megan didn't argue and returned Dan's hug. Slipping off the couch, she leaned into Jimmy, who squeezed her so tight she giggled, before grabbing her books and leaving the front room. She couldn't take her eyes off the encouraging words from A.K. Foreman and laid on her side under her blanket rereading them over and over in the soft light of her bedside lamp. But, in the morning, her lamp was off and the precious book was resting on her nightstand.

Megan made it through the last test days and, after studying with Sam on Monday night, she was even confident about her final math exam, but couldn't wait for Thursday. The last day of school was a morning of field day activities, with a break for lunch, before the end of the year assembly and awards. Megan knew she'd made high honor roll, but there were others to be recognized for and her competitive nature was instinctually eager whenever acknowledgement was involved.

Field day games went by too quickly and, when Megan ran with her classmates inside for lunch, she caught Dan's green GMC in the parking lot. She hadn't done anything to get in trouble, if she had her teachers wouldn't have let her participate in the end of the year festivities. But her gut still twisted nervously on her way into the school.

Chancing a peek towards the main office, Megan saw Dan speaking with Mrs. Todd, his back turned to the main hall, but, before her class shuffled passed the office windows, he turned and caught Megan's eye. With a tight lipped, embarrassed smile, she waved at her brother and, when he jerked his head, turned back towards the office door to meet him, rolling her eyes at a few of the giggling girls in her class as they snuck glances at Dan.

"Hey, how was field day?" he smiled, grease smudged on his face.

"S'okay," she shrugged, "Why're you here?"

"Don't worry I'm leavin'," Dan chuckled, "Just stopped on my lunch to talk to Mr. Jarsen."

"About the paperwork problem?" she asked.

"I'm figurin' it out," he grinned confidently, but Megan saw the worry in his eyes, "Get to lunch, I'll see ya later."

"Bye, Dan!" she called, waiting until she'd passed the office window before bolting down the unsupervised hallway.

After lunch, Megan and Sam walked into the assembly together. The gym floor had folding chairs lined up for teachers and administrators to sit beside the podium that had been dragged into the middle. Megan saw Ms. Craft sitting by herself, looking disinterested, while the teachers talked amongst themselves and ushered students to their seats on the accordion bleachers.

"That's her," Megan whispered, poking Sam lightly and using the same finger to point inconspicuously at the rigid woman, "Ms. Craft."

"Looks more like bitchcraft," Sam mumbled and Megan clapped a hand over her mouth to stifle a loud laugh.

The assembly started once everyone took their seats and Mr. Jarsen stood at the podium, droning on with a slightly updated rendition of his end of the year speech. But Megan kept stealing glances at Ms. Craft, who seemed completely indifferent to the ritual happening around her and checked her watch at least every five minutes. Finally, Mr. Jarsen began announcing awards.

Megan was called up for high honor roll, but also received an exclusive award for 'most hours spent in the library', Mrs. King's terribly obvious, feigned surprise was hard to miss. Sam earned high honor roll and was recognized as the eighth-grade valedictorian, but his class had also voted him 'best taste in music' and 'most likely to succeed'. Megan watched Sam's smile become more strained every time his name was called.

Mr. Jarsen concluded with a short reminder about being safe over summer break and to open a few books before they'd return in August, finally dismissing the eager crowd of students. Megan and Sam were the first on their bus after hurrying out of the school as soon as they were allowed to leave. Neither could wait to get home and drop their backpacks for the last time, until summer was over.

She hopped off the bus with Sam right behind her, calling for him to come over when he was ready while running across the small yards and up the steps of her front porch. In her excitement, Megan shut the front door hard just as she noticed Jimmy's bedroom door was closed and cringed, remembering he had to work in a few hours. But when no sound came from his room, she sighed, dropped her backpack under the kitchen table out of habit and hurried to her bedroom. Her old jeans were still crumpled on her beanbag chair from the day before and she wriggled them on with effort.

Megan had already cut the bottoms into capris when they'd gotten too short, but the last few weeks she'd found them very tight around her hips. After securing the button, she relaxed her middle and poked at the protruding skin sticking over the top of her waistband before pulling on one of Jimmy's old t-shirts. Megan quietly rushed into the kitchen, plopping on the floor to slip her sneakers on, just as Sam opened the front door.

"You ready?" he asked, standing in the doorway, the broken screen propped open with his foot.

"Yeah, let's go," Megan jumped to her feet and hurried after Sam, careful to shut the door quietly and set the screen in its frame.

Several other neighborhood kids were already in the large field next to the playground, putting together a soccer game, and called to Sam and Megan. They dumped their bikes in the established pile and hurried to join the forming teams. Megan wished someone had brought a football instead, but that didn't stop her from chasing the ball with the others, reveling in their recent freedom.

The goal Megan's team was aiming for was between two evergreens against a chain link fence blocking a private yard. After managing to steal the ball from one of the boys, she heard her team cheering as she kicked and sprinted towards the evergreens, but a familiar presence started looming closer. Megan scoffed breathlessly, seeing Sam gaining next to her, but, before she could push her legs any harder, his scrawny arms wrapped around her and she landed on top of him, both laughing madly.

"FOUL!" Mark, the boy who'd brought the ball, and appointed himself Megan's team captain, pointed at the pair angrily.

"I was totally gonna score!" Megan giggled and pushed Sam's shoulder as they both sat up on their elbows.

"That's why I did it," he chuckled, offering his hand and they pulled each other to their feet.

"Well, we get a free shot," Mark admonished.

"Good for you," Sam shrugged indifferently.

Mark had to recline his head to scowl at Sam, he was a few months younger than Megan and hadn't hit a growth spurt yet, unlike Sam who stared down with unamused disregard. A low growl, however, interrupted the impending altercation and Megan tapped Sam's shoulder, rolling her eyes at the green truck stopping by the pile of bikes. Sam gave her a questioning look and Megan shook her head, silently assuring him she hadn't done anything to be in trouble, and, in the back of her mind, prayed that was true.

Dan got out of his truck and waved her over. He didn't seem angry, but was home hours before he should've been.

"I'll be right back," she told Sam, glaring at the boys who'd started mockingly asking what she'd done, and ran across the field, panting when she slowed in front of Dan, "What's up?"

"Dotty called me back at work today," he said, "She managed to swing out here on short notice, c'mon grab your bike."

"But we just started," she protested.

"I'm sorry, sweetheart," he sighed, "I had to leave work early, but we gotta get this handled. Okay?"

"What does she need me for?" Megan whined.

"Megan," Dan growled, "Please, you are gonna have all summer to play out here," she rolled her eyes and crossed her arms, "Keep it up and I'm puttin' your bike in the truck," immediately, Megan uncrossed her arms and did her best to wipe the scowl from her face, "Okay, let's go," he jerked his head at the old mountain bike laying on the ground.

"Can I at least tell Sam I'm leaving?" she asked bitterly.

"Yeah, but hurry up, Dotty's probably at the house already," he pulled himself into his idling truck and chuckled, noticing the imitating growls from the boys in the field, and revved the accelerator, earning enthusiastic cheers.

"I gotta go," Megan said when Sam approached.

"What's goin' on?" he asked, following her to the pile of bikes.

"That social worker lady's comin'," Megan muttered, "It's about school."

"Shitty," Sam shrugged, picking up his bike too.

"You're not stayin'?" she asked.

"No," he scoffed, "You're the only twelve-year-old I can stand."

"Almost thirteen," she reminded pointedly.

"Almost!" he teased, jumping on his pedals and hurried up the street with Megan chasing him.

A red Honda sedan was parked behind Jimmy's Oldsmobile when Megan dumped her bike under the porch overhang and she knew Dotty was already inside. Megan didn't dislike the social worker, but between playing at the park and sitting on the sofa answering an endless list of questions, she much preferred the soccer game she'd had to leave. The front door was open and she saw Dotty at the kitchen table before walking in, letting the screen door whack the frame behind her.

"Miss Megan," Dotty smiled brightly at Megan, kicking her sneakers off, "How've you been, darlin'?"

"M'good," she nodded and a small eyebrow raise from Dan reminded her to ask, "How are you?"

"Peachy as always," Dotty replied, winking as she said, "I heard you got all A's this year," Megan averted her eyes, but smiled proudly when she saw Dan beaming from the other side of the table, "Good job, Miss smarty-pants."

"Thanks," Megan blushed a little at the nickname.

"Why don't ya wash up 'n change real quick," Dan suggested and Megan giggled, holding up her grass stained palms.

After washing her hands in the bathroom, Megan went to change, but left her door open, listening intently to the conversation in the kitchen.

"Dan, you're doin' great," she heard Dotty say reassuringly, "She's growin' up so well, look at that girl. Young man, that's all your doing!"

"Thanks, Dotty," Dan's appreciation lacked confidence, "I don't know what to do here with this school stuff though."

"I'm surprised this new administrator is causing waves over it," the social worker said, "Are you goin' to that board meeting Monday night?"

"Yes, ma'am," he assured her, "Seven o'clock."

"Good," Dotty began, "But I'm afraid even if we finagle through the next year in middle school there's still gonna be the same issues in high school."

"I know," Dan sighed, Megan heard the defeat in his voice and felt her stomach sink.

"I think we need to seriously discuss the permanent option," Dotty resolved.

"We still need him," Dan pointed out.

"Just to sign," Dotty promised, "Then, none of you ever has to deal with him again. But I won't suggest it if you're not up for it," Megan heard her brother's loud scoff, "No, Dan, I know you've been doin' it for years anyway, but if you do this, she's yours, forever."

"She's already mine forever," Dan said simply and, even though Megan didn't understand entirely what they were discussing, she knew he was talking about her and a smile warmed her face.

"Then we need to get this process moving," Dotty said and Megan heard papers shuffling, "Do you know when Greg will be in town next?"

Dan expelled a bitter laugh, "He was a here a few weeks ago, so, I don't know, Christmas maybe."

"My office can call him and try to intervene some," Dotty offered.

"Naw," Dan rejected the idea instantly, "That'll just piss him off. If I call his company they're usually able to give me his current number, or at least track him down to call me back."

"You can't even reach him?" Dotty asked incredulously, "What a piece of, ugh, Dan what you have to deal with. When did you last have a working number for him?"

"It's been almost a year," Dan told her, "He keeps runnin' through burners."

"Is he still gambling?" Megan had to strain to hear Dotty's hushed tone.

"I don't doubt it," Dan said, "Hasn't stopped drinkin' that's for sure."

"Probably tryin' to avoid certain people," Dotty speculated.

"Wouldn't surprise me," Dan said and she heard Jimmy's door creak, "Hey, Jimmy, you remember Dotty Clark."

Megan left her room with the additional company in the kitchen, just as Jimmy offered Dotty a tired smile and mumbled greeting.

"How are you, James?" Dotty smiled, she'd always called him James, saying he reminded her of James Dean.

"I'm good, ma'am," he said, shifting his weight from one foot to the other.

"Stayin' outta trouble?" she asked and Megan saw Jimmy's gaze flicker to Dan quickly before addressing the question.

"Tryin' to," he shrugged.

"Don't try, boy, just do," Dotty chastised lightly, her pearly white smile never faltering.

"Yes, ma'am," Jimmy nodded.

"You workin' tonight?" Dan asked.

"Tomorrow," Jimmy said, leaning against the arm of the couch.

"How's the night shift treating you?" Dotty's question wasn't without a small eyebrow raise, as if expecting Jimmy's sulky response.

"Sucks," he scoffed, his cheeks flushing a bit at Dan's glare, "Sorry, I mean, it's okay."

130

Dotty smirked, "Well, I won't lecture you about how stayin' in school could've got'cha a better job," she nodded towards Dan, "Pretty sure you've heard it enough."

"You have no idea," Jimmy muttered, refusing to look at his brother as he and Dotty shared a small laugh.

"Oh, James," she shook her head, "What are we gonna do with you?"

Jimmy smiled shyly and shrugged again, Megan saw his shoulders relax when Dotty returned her attention to Dan.

"Can I get a few minutes with Megan?" she asked the same sweet way she always did, but it wasn't a request.

"Yeah, of course," Dan stood and jerked his head at Jimmy, "Throw some clothes on, we're gonna go grab dinner."

"Man, I don't wanna see your girlfriend," Jimmy joked, ducking quickly passed Dan and shut his bedroom door.

"What's this?" Dotty crooned.

"I don't have a girlfriend," Dan assured her adamantly.

"He's goin' out with Lacey Peters on Saturday night," Megan interjected casually while sliding onto the chair Dan had just vacated.

"Megan," he groaned, running a hand over his short hair.

"Dan that's great," Dotty seemed genuinely excited.

"Megan's gonna be at Darlene's," he began insistently, "I'm not gonna be later than eleven."

"Dan," Dotty chuckled, "I'm sure you covered all your bases, I'm very happy for you," Dan's ears colored and Dotty turned to Megan with a playful smile, "Is she pretty?"

"Mhm," she nodded, "Jimmy said she's hot."

"Megan!" Dan exclaimed, trying not to laugh while Dotty threw her head back in brief amusement.

"Well, your brother's a pretty good lookin' guy himself," Dotty gave Dan a good-natured wink and Megan rolled her eyes, "Oh, you don't think so?"

"No, it's just," Megan shook her head, "All my friends have crushes on him."

"Sam has a crush on me?" Dan asked, almost keeping a straight face.

"No!" she laughed, "The girls in my class."

"Ah, yes," he nodded, "The giggle squad."

"Got a fan club?" Dotty inclined her head at Dan.

"Apparently," he scoffed and Jimmy opened his bedroom door, wearing jeans and a t-shirt, "We'll be back in a bit. Megan ya hungry for anything?"

"Pizza?" she offered snidely, sharing a smirk with Jimmy.

"I don't want pizza," Dan said flatly.

"Gonna have plenty tomorrow," Jimmy mumbled on his way to the front door and Dan nonchalantly cuffed him on the back of the head, "Hey, what the-" but Jimmy caught himself before cussing in front of Dotty.

"You two got jokes tonight, huh?" Dan shifted his gaze from his brother to his sister, "I'm choosin' then. Coleslaw 'n catfish for everybody."

Jimmy and Megan shared the same disgusted expression before the three of them laughed together and her brothers left, the screen door banging as they tramped down the steps.

Megan smiled timidly at Dotty, she always felt more comfortable when Dan was around because the social worker spoke more with him than her, but their separate conversations were inevitable. Fidgeting with a stray string poking out of her sleeve, Megan looked up when she was addressed from across the table.

"So, Megan," Dotty began, "I heard your father was in town a couple weeks ago."

132

Megan nodded, silently agreeing that he had been, and that she'd heard Dan tell the social worker, of course her nod didn't confess the second part.

"Did you get to see him much?" Dotty pried and Megan shook her head, but, receiving a characteristic expression, knew she had to elaborate.

"He was here when I got home from school," she said quietly, "But he went to Pederson's and then, well, he left before I got up."

Dotty nodded slowly and asked, "Was it a good visit?" Megan shrugged, but followed Dotty's gaze to the sloppily patched hole in the wall.

"Dan didn't hit him," she squeaked, sighing a little with relief when Dotty's eyebrows said he would have deserved it.

"Your brother has a lot of restraint," Dotty grinned bitterly, "Do you know what happened?"

Megan's stomach twisted. She wasn't supposed to lie, but wasn't sure if Dan would want her to tell Dotty about the last night her father was home. Finally deciding a version of the truth would suffice.

"Dan asked him for some money, for the house 'n stuff," Megan couldn't help focusing on her twisting fingers, she knew Dan didn't want people to know about their finances, "And my dad said no, but, uh, then he said somethin' about our mom," Dotty's eyebrows raised and Megan rapidly insisted, "Dan hit the wall, but he didn't hit him."

"Megan," Dotty initiated after a few moments of silence between them, "Do you miss your dad?"

"Sometimes," she shrugged.

"What'd you miss when he's not here?" she asked kindly, but Megan couldn't think of anything and shrugged again, "What does he do with you when he is here?" she offered a disheartened head shake, silently admitting he did nothing with her, "Do you enjoy talking to him when he's home?"

Megan shook her head more adamantly and Dotty couldn't stifle a tiny scoff, giving up on the line of questioning for one she knew would garner actual responses.

"What've you 'n Dan done lately?"

Megan brightened immediately and slipped off her chair, holding up a finger as she rushed off to her bedroom and came running back a moment later, clutching the Fire Fox trilogy. With a wide smile, she set them in front of Dotty, dragging the chair closer as she slid onto it.

"Dan took me to Milwaukee last weekend to see A.K. Foreman, look!" she couldn't hide her excitement, flipping open the cover of the third book and watched Dotty's face as she read the author's inscription.

"Well isn't that somthin'," she tapped a well-manicured nail on the page and smiled, "So, just you 'n Dan?"

"Jimmy had to work," she said, "It was a long drive, but we drove passed Chicago and Dan showed me where their dad used to work and then he got fireworks 'cause he said they're-" Megan's eyes went wide, slapping both hands over her mouth too late to cover the confession.

Dotty chuckled, shaking her head, "I won't say a word, I promise," Megan grinned apprehensively, but nodded, trusting she wouldn't, and Dotty continued, "Was it a long line at the book signing?"

"Yeah," Megan giggled, "And it was like all girls and their moms, and this weird lady asked Dan if he was my dad."

"You're kiddin'," Dotty shook her head, "Some people. But it sounds like a great trip, Megan. Y'know, your brother really loves you."

"I know," Megan smiled, that was never a doubt in her mind, from either brother.

"Megan," Dotty regarded her more seriously, "Do you like living with your brothers?" she nodded like she always did at the question and Dotty asked, "Is Dan good at bein' in charge?"

This was a new question, and Megan wasn't prepared for it, but it only took her a second to nod again, admitting, "Yeah, I mean, he does everything."

"Y'know," Dotty smirked, "I've been washin' my own clothes since I was able to reach the dials, young lady," Megan flushed a little, used to the social worker's occasional insinuations that Dan spoiled her, and certainly wasn't going to admit she still forgot to even throw her dirty clothes in the hamper, "How about when you get in trouble now? What does Dan do?"

Megan shrugged, refusing to confess to anything about the weekend before when Dan picked her and Sam up at the river well passed curfew, "He's okay, I mean, I don't really get in trouble."

"Is that so?" Dotty asked skeptically, but she didn't push any further, the answers had been the same for years and the experienced social worker had no reason to worry about Dan hurting his siblings, "So, you like havin' your brother around to take care of your school stuff and make sure ya got what'cha need?" Megan nodded and Dotty asked, "If you had to choose between your dad takin' care of-"

"Dan," Megan said quickly, offering an apologetic grimace for interrupting.

"I figured," Dotty chuckled with an understanding wink.

Their conversation continued a while longer. Though, when Megan complimented the purple, high heeled booties Dotty was wearing, the mundane repeat of previous interviews turned into a rather enjoyable girl chat. The always stylish woman assured Megan, when she was a bit older, heels were as simple to walk in as her sneakers, though Megan doubted that was true. They were giggling over their shared opinion on how awful crop tops were when the front door opened and Sam walked in ahead of Jimmy and Dan, each brother carrying a take-out bag.

"Hey, what're you doin' here?" Megan asked happily.

"Found him on the side'a the road," Jimmy shrugged, "Looked useful though."

"Is that Sam?" Dotty's eyes widened, "My goodness, boy, did you get some legs on you. How tall are ya now?"

"Five seven," Sam mumbled, looking at his large feet, Megan knew he didn't like attention and, lately, everyone had had the same comment.

"Got me beat," Dotty chuckled, standing from the chair, taller than Megan, but both brothers towered over her as she said good-bye, "Megan, Jimmy, Dan dear, I had a lovely visit. I'm leavin' these with you," her fingertips tapped the tan envelop on the table and Dan nodded, "Please call me whether you have questions or not, I'd like to know what's happening."

"Yes, ma'am," Dan said, holding the screen for her while they shook hands and Dotty left for her car as he pulled the broken door into its frame.

"Is that Pederson's food?" Megan knew the delicious smell and generic takeout bags promised a familiar favorite.

"My mom got stuck workin' late, so she dragged me back with her on break, but then Dan 'n Jimmy showed up and now I'm here," Sam smiled, obviously satisfied with the turn of events.

"Awesome," she shared his enthusiasm, especially since their first afternoon of freedom had been hijacked by Dotty.

"So, Sammy," Jimmy teased, "Graduation's Saturday. Got'cher speech done?"

Sam paled as he shook his head.

Apparently realizing there was no joke, and the fourteen-year-old was genuinely terrified of the impending event, Jimmy tried to be encouraging, "C'mon kid, don't look so excited, you'll be fine."

Sam made a noncommittal sound with a doubtful nod.

"How 'bout we run through it a couple times tonight?" Dan offered, grabbing a two liter of soda from the fridge.

"Yeah," Jimmy agreed, setting four glasses on the table, "I'm a great audience, I'll even hang out in my boxers if that'll help."

"That's not gonna help anyone," Dan scoffed and the others laughed.

Megan liked having Sam over for dinner and knew he liked joining them. Unlike Sam's house, dinners at Megan's were much louder.

Dan opened the lid of the first white container and handed Megan a box of chicken strips, honey mustard and fries, then gave Jimmy his cheeseburger and set a broiled catfish meal in front of Sam.

"Thanks," Sam said while Megan and Jimmy were already devouring their dinners.

"No, thank you," Dan chuckled, popping open the lid on his catfish and coleslaw combo, "I think your mom loaded us up with food for the week, definitely way more than I paid for."

"Yeah, she's good at that," Sam slid out of his chair before Dan and grabbed two sets of forks and knives.

"Thanks," Dan took the utensils with a little surprise in his smile.

"I don't know how you two eat that," Jimmy sneered over his burger at the charbroiled catfish in front of Dan and Sam, "Reeks."

"Well we can't all have palates refined to strictly burgers and pizza like you," Dan said flatly, shoved a large bite of flaky fish in his mouth and gave Jimmy a tight lipped grin, swallowing a moment later and pointed his empty fork as he spoke, "Hey, don't forget Doctor Summers at quarter to one tomorrow, I'll leave the co-pay and insurance card on the counter before I go to work."

Jimmy nodded while chewing a large bite and Megan took the opportunity to interject her concern, "Do I have to get shots?"

Dan smiled weakly at his sister, "Only a couple I think. I know you hate 'em, but Doctor Summers is always really fast, it'll be over before y'know it."

"I hate shots," Megan mumbled, drowning her last chicken strip in honey mustard longer than necessary.

"I'll trade ya," Sam piped up humorously, "You can do my speech."

"Deal," she giggled.

Jimmy and Dan had given up trying to end Megan's fear of needles, simply dealing with it as patiently as they could during the few times it was an issue. But they were determined to convince Sam his speech was nothing to worry about. Dan continued to remind him to make it short and sweet, while Jimmy promised to run through the gymnasium naked if Sam started stumbling, even Dan laughed at that.

By the time Darlene's headlights lit up the driveway two doors down, Sam was reciting his speech almost confidently, hardly referencing the note cards twisted in his hands.

# Chapter 7

Megan woke on Friday in the late morning sun and stretched lazily on her bed, relishing the first morning of Summer vacation before her stomach reminded her Dan had bought good cereal. Jimmy's door was still shut as she entered the kitchen, glancing at the clock on the microwave and realized it was quarter to noon. Megan poured herself a large bowl of cereal and carefully carried it to the coffee table, flipping the television on and changed channels until she found Judge Judy. It wasn't a program she particularly liked, but, with nothing else to choose from, the tiny, angry woman was entertaining enough. When the losing defendants were complaining in an exit interview, Jimmy's door creaked open and he walked into the front room, running a tired hand through his dark, shaggy hair.

"Mornin'," he yawned, moving towards the fridge.

"It's noon," she told him and he was suddenly, very awake.

"Why didn't'cha wake me up?" he implored angrily as the phone started to ring and Jimmy snatched at it, shaking his head at Megan, "Yeah?- Oh, hey- Sometimes- The hell does it matter Dan? I answered the phone, you're the only one whoever calls here anyway- Okay, jeezus, yeah, fine, I'll say hello next time. What'd'ja call for?- Quarter to one," Jimmy nodded slowly, offering Megan an apologetic grimace, "Yup, I got it- Money 'n card on the counter, see it, got it, we're good brother-Yeah, seven- See ya later," Jimmy hung the phone in the cradle on the wall and turned to Megan, "I, uh, thought it was quarter to noon," he chuckled apologetically at her scowl and she couldn't be mad at him for yelling.

She could never stay mad at Jimmy. Dan, however, Megan could sulk at for days.

"I'm gonna grab a shower. Get goin', babygirl," Jimmy said, "Put your bowl in the sink when your done and get dressed."

The next episode of Judge Judy was starting and Megan munched the last few bites of cereal slowly listening to a man explain how he was not responsible for a vehicle he'd totaled because it was in the plaintiff's name. It hardly made sense, but it was funny when Judge Judy yelled at people for saying thoughtless things, or talked when she was talking. She seemed to really hate that, and Megan was glad she wasn't on the show because she had a habit of interrupting people.

"Hey," Jimmy stepped out of the bathroom with a towel wrapped around his waist and scowled, "What'd I say?"

"I'm going," Megan sighed, but made no moves to clear her bowl or turn off the television.

Jimmy made one decision for her, snatching the remote and clicked the program off just as it was returning from a commercial.

"Jimmeeeee," she whined, something that usually made him give her whatever it was that she wanted, but, recently, hadn't had the same effect.

"We have to be at the docs in less than thirty minutes," he said, tossing the remote on the arm chair, "Get dressed, I'm not gettin' my ass chewed out 'cause you're slower than a turtle in peanut butter."

Megan wanted to argue, but knew if she opened her mouth she'd laugh at the image in her head of a turtle slowly making its way through a field of peanut butter. After dumping her bowl and spoon in the sink noisily, she turned to Jimmy with the smuggest look she could muster and stalked to her bedroom, shutting the door hard.

"I'm really lookin' forward to spendin' time with this today!" Jimmy called and Megan gestured rudely at her closed door, "I saw that."

Her stifled giggle was inevitable. Jimmy often said that when she walked off in a huff, but sometimes he was right, and it was funny.

She changed into a stiff, new pair of jeans that were too long at the bottom and a green t-shirt, remembering to grab socks and spun back into her room the first time she stepped into the hall. Jimmy chuckled when she plopped theatrically next to the front door to pull on her shoes and offered Megan her jean jacket after helping her to her feet. He shoved the insurance card and cash on the counter in his pocket just before they walked outside, the screen door banging after Jimmy locked the deadbolt.

The sun was hidden behind a curtain of billowing clouds, dark in the distance, but it was warm as they made their way to Jimmy's car on the street. His Oldsmobile was nothing like Dan's truck, the inside matched the outside in general crappiness, but Jimmy wasn't proud of his car, proving that with takeout bags, straw wrappers and empty cigarette packs littering the floor of the backseat and passenger side. Megan had gotten used to stepping carefully around, or on, the garbage whenever she had to ride with him. The high-pitched whine faded as he pumped the gas pedal a bit before pulling the shifter down and accelerated up the road.

"Watch it, it's supposed to rain later," Jimmy grumbled when she put her finger on the window button and Megan hid an annoyed eyeroll.

She was mindful to only roll the window down halfway, if it went any further Jimmy would have to push it closed. Once, Megan had forgotten and, before he could stop her, had fully sunken the window into the door. He'd gotten upset and yelled for a minute, but Jimmy's anger never lasted long, especially when Megan mumbled 'sorry' with an added pathetic sniffle and focused her apologetic, damp eyes on him. He and Dan had had to take the door apart to get the window back in place, something Dan had clearly been less than thrilled about doing immediately upon getting home from the shop. Since then, Megan had been careful to remind herself about it, even though Jimmy did every time she got in his car anyway.

The driver's side window had no trouble rolling up, which was good because Jimmy smoked in his car, even though Dan told him not to with Megan. But he was at least good about blowing his smoke out the window and held the cigarette outside at stop lights.

"Are we gonna get ice cream after?" she asked, her brothers always took her to get ice cream after she had to get shots.

"Ya got money?" he smirked and chuckled at her intentionally dramatic pout, "Yeah, maybe."

Megan smiled, Jimmy's maybes always meant yes.

Dr. Summers's office was in the short, main street of town, just a few doors from the pizza place where Lacey worked, and had a green awning jutting out above the sidewalk. Megan's stomach turned as Jimmy parked in front of the office, she was really not looking forward to getting shots.

"C'mon, babygirl," Jimmy shook her shoulder reassuringly before kicking his door open, "It'll be over before y'know it."

Thinking, that was easy for him to say, Megan pushed the passenger door open and followed Jimmy into the clean waiting room of Dr. Summers's office. The lady behind the desk smiled, she'd worked there as long as Megan could remember and never seemed to look any different. Jimmy returned her friendly greeting as he dug the insurance card and co-pay from his pocket, sliding both to the older woman and signed Megan's name on the waiting list, even though they were the only people there.

"How've you kids been?" the rosy faced receptionist asked, glancing between them and her computer.

"Can't complain," Jimmy grinned, "Wouldn't do any good anyway."

"Ain't that the truth," she chuckled, handing Jimmy back the insurance card and taking the twenty-dollar bill from the counter, "You're all set, have a seat, Doctor Summers will be with you shortly."

Jimmy sat in a chair across from the television and Megan sat next to him after snagging a Highlights magazine off the squat table. But the puzzles and picture games were all already completed, in pen, and extremely sloppily. Megan emitted a frustrated sighed, tossing the magazine back on the pile, where it stopped just short of sliding off the table and Jimmy gave her a sideways glare, shaking his head, but returned to watching the news with large black captions scrolling along the bottom.

They didn't wait long before a nurse in blue scrubs opened the heavy door to the back offices and called Megan's name.

"Jimmy?" she turned, halfway to the nurse, realizing he hadn't moved.

"Want me to come?" he asked, glancing at the nurse before looking back at his nervous little sister.

She nodded pitiably at him and the nurse smiled, "Big brothers are always welcome."

Jimmy pushed off the chair, taking two long strides next to Megan and put a hand on her shoulder, she leaned into him and he gently steered her to follow the nurse. The young woman smiled warmly, gesturing to a tall, white scale in the hallway and Megan stepped onto the black base. First the nurse slid the large weight over and back once before nudging the smaller one until the bar balanced in the cradle.

142

"Seventy-eight pounds," she nodded, jotting the number on her chart before sliding the height stick out and adjusting it until the flat metal was resting on top of Megan's head, "Look at that, exactly five feet," she smiled, gesturing Megan towards the open door of a small exam room.

"Gettin' too big, kid," Jimmy said, tugging her jacket collar until she shrugged out of it and tossed it over his arm.

She hopped onto the exam table, the white cover crinkling loudly, and Jimmy sat on the chair near the door as the nurse left her chart on the desk and picked up a digital thermometer, sliding the metal rod into a box for a plastic cover. Megan was familiar with the routine and let the nurse slip the thermometer under her tongue, she removed it after the beep and jotted on her chart again. The blood pressure cuff made her giggle, not because the tightness tickled a little, but it reminded her of Jimmy getting his arm caught in the test machine inside Walmart. She'd been sure Dan was going to rage at him when he'd turned the aisle and saw Jimmy trying to wrench his arm from the machine while Megan wedged her tiny fingers into the cuff to help pry him loose, but their brother had stared at them for a moment before doubling over in near hysterics. He'd laughed so hard he was crying when he unplugged the machine to release the pressure on his little brother's arm. Despite Jimmy flushing with embarrassment, Megan knew they'd both appreciated seeing Dan laugh like that.

"Well, Megan," the nurse smiled, gathering her chart and said, "You look like a happy, healthy girl to me. Doctor Summers will be with you shortly."

Megan and Jimmy nodded as she shut the door, leaving them in the exam room. Jimmy stood up and started pulling open drawers, pushing their contents around gently before moving onto the next.

"What're you lookin' for?" she scoffed.

"I don't know," Jimmy grumbled, pulling on a locked cabinet.

Dan normally took Megan to Dr. Summers's, but, considering she'd forgotten to tell him the deadline of her required physical, he'd been unable to set an appointment in time that would coincide with his schedule. Megan liked spending time with Jimmy, they always had fun together, but, watching him poke through the exam room, she wished Dan was there instead. A soft knock on the door made Jimmy straighten and take a quick side step, sliding back onto the chair just before the door opened.

"Hello, Miss Megan," Dr. Summers smiled widely, pulling her red-rimmed glasses off her short, gray curls before perching them on her nose, "Jimmy, how are you both?"

They mumbled that they were fine.

"Well," she glanced at her chart, approaching Megan on the table, "Everything looks great, you've always been a skinny-mini," she gently pinched Megan's arm, producing a small giggle, "But perfectly healthy size. My goodness are you getting tall too!"

"Tell me about it," Jimmy scoffed lightly, sharing a smile with the doctor.

"Oh, I don't think you'll ever have to worry about her reachin' you, Jimmy," Dr. Summer's smiled, "You're as tall as Dan now I bet."

"Almost," Jimmy shrugged, but sat up a bit in the chair.

"Better quit smokin'," the older woman said wisely and Jimmy furrowed his brow, about to respond indignantly, but she continued her amused chiding, "I can smell it on ya boy, don't tell me stories."

He blushed a little, his head dipping in admittance, but the doctor's attention was already moving to her desk with her back to them and Megan quickly stuck her tongue out at Jimmy in solidarity of Dr. Summer's statement. He responded with a funny nostril flare.

"You're gonna be thirteen soon, big age," after a brief look at the chart, and Megan's happy nod, the doctor asked, "Have you been sick at all in the last few months?"

"I had the flu after New Year's," she said, "But Mrs. Olsen said it was goin' around."

"It certainly was," Dr. Summers scoffed, "How long did you have it?"

"It was a weekend thing," Jimmy answered, "Left school sick Friday, but she was better by Monday."

"No other illnesses?" she directed her question as much to Jimmy as she did Megan, both shook their heads, "And, Megan," lowering her voice as she continued, "Some girls your age start getting their periods around now. Do you know what that is?"

Megan felt the heat all over her face, refusing to look anywhere except her hands, sure her brother was also blushing and tying to pretend he wasn't in the tiny room. She nodded. The girls and boys in her class had been separated a few times over the year and taught about changes they should expect, she was also aware many of the girls in her class had already started their cycles.

"And has yours started?" she asked in the same low tone, but there was no way Jimmy hadn't overheard, and Megan shook her head at her hands, wishing the table would swallow her whole, "Not a worry, it'll come, believe me," Dr. Summers chuckled quietly, "Alright, Miss Megan," she set down the chart and took the stethoscope off her neck, "Let's get started. Can I pull up your shirt a little?"

Megan nodded, wondering why the doctor even asked when she was going to do it anyway, and shuddered when the cold metal circle touched her back. She didn't mind having her ears and nose checked, even sticking her tongue out so Dr. Summers could shine the tiny light down her throat wasn't so bad, but Megan knew, when faced with a familiar, encouraging smile, the dreaded moment had arrived.

"We've only got two shots we gotta do," she told Megan, who refrained from asking who the 'we' the doctor was referring to was, fairly certain she was the only one getting stuck with two needles.

She glanced at Jimmy apprehensively and he shook his head with amusement, pushing off the chair. He put an arm around her shoulders and pulled Megan into his side.

"You're gonna be fine," he squeezed her before moving his hand to the back of her neck, allowing the doctor room to roll her short sleeve.

Megan turned her head into Jimmy's chest and closed her eyes, biting her lips when the cool alcohol swab touched her skin. Jimmy's hand tightened gently on her neck, her heart beat faster and she couldn't help a little gasping whimper at the expected pinch. As always, Dr. Summers was fast, finishing the second injection moments after the first, and was applying a small bandage to the affected spot by the time Megan opened her eyes.

"All done," Dr. Summers smiled, "You did great."

"Not one tear, huh?" Jimmy remarked proudly, "Really are gettin' big."

"Thanks," Megan sniffled hard, fighting the tingle of brewing tears.

They left the doctor's office a few minutes later, greeted by suddenly increased humidity. Jimmy repeated the process of pumping the gas after turning the engine over before the whining quieted and they accelerated down the street.

"Ice cream," Megan reminded, stripping her jacket from the muggy heat.

"I said maybe," he clarified.

"Please, Jimmy," her fixed gaze was as pleading as her tone.

"Yeah, fine," he chuckled, "Only 'cause ya didn't cry."

Triumphant and satisfied, Megan sat back with a smile, grateful that sometimes her old tactics still worked on him. After a few blocks, they pulled into Robert's Drive Thru, barely more than a shack in a parking lot, but it was a very full parking lot, and Jimmy waved at a group of high schoolers before maneuvering into a spot.

"Be cool, okay?" he urged and pushed out his door.

"Yeah, okay," she rolled her eyes and followed him.

The small building had a walk-up window and a drive-thru, if it qualified to be called that since the speaker hadn't worked for as long as Megan could remember, but people would pull up to the window when it was cold to order anyway. With school out and the weather warm, the picnic tables were covered with teenagers and families. She followed Jimmy to his friends, most she recognized, but only remembered a few of their names. It didn't matter, she was supposed to be quiet.

"Hey, Brad, Travis, what's up?" Jimmy and his friends swiped their palms before bumping fists.

"Jimmy, man, what's up?" Brad said, but did a small double-take and scoffed, "Megan? Man, you're gettin' big, girl."

146

"Five feet exactly," Jimmy commented, patting her on the head, "Just came from the doc, she twisted my arm into ice cream."

"Good job, kid," Travis interjected, grinning at Megan, "Get'cher money's worth. Ya have to get a shot?"

"Two," she mumbled.

"Fuck that," he scoffed, before grimacing apologetically at Megan and Jimmy, who shrugged, and the young man chuckled before continuing, "I hate shots. Used to take two nurses and my dad to hold me down."

"Yeah, that's this one," Jimmy gave Megan's shoulder a tiny shake, but continued after catching her hurt scowl, "But she did great today, real trooper."

Megan smiled a little at his compliment, but mostly in appreciation of Travis's comradery against shots. Patiently, she waited a few minutes for Jimmy to talk to his friends, but, when he hopped up next to Travis on the picnic table, she crossed her arms and sighed.

"What?" he scoffed.

"Ice cream," she said simply.

"Here," he dug into his jeans pocket and handed her a five-dollar bill, "Get me vanilla," she didn't offer a response, but tried to take the money, except Jimmy didn't let it go, explaining, "Them's the rules, kid, I buy, you fly," and, with a joking, hard stare, he let go of the bill.

There was a mother and her two young boys at the counter and Megan waited as the woman tried to get her toddlers to decide on a sundae flavor. Finally, it was her turn and she ordered a vanilla cone for Jimmy and a chocolate one for herself, shoving the two dollars in change into her pocket. The girl behind the counter handed her the two cones and Megan returned to the table Jimmy and his friends were occupying.

"Change?" he asked, taking the cone she handed him.

"Flyers fee," Megan shrugged, hiding her smile behind her ice cream as his friends laughed.

"Brat," Jimmy rolled his eyes and bumped her hand, tapping Megan's chocolate ice cream into her nose and she giggled.

147

"Y'all ready for tomorrow night?" Brad whooped, "We're gettin' ripped!"

While everyone boisterously agreed, Jimmy shot Brad a scowl, shifting his eyes quickly towards his sister and back. Brad offered an apologetic grimace and Megan shook her head, focusing on her ice cream and refused to look at her brother. Everyone was enthusiastic for the following night, and it certainly didn't sound like they were just planning on cruising to Sheridan for midnight breakfast at the truck stop.

"Alright," Jimmy tossed his half-eaten cone in a nearby garbage bin, "I'll see you assholes tomorrow, let's go, Megan."

She kept her well-earned treat as they got in the Oldsmobile, unlike Dan, Jimmy didn't mind if she ate something messy in his car. Megan's focus stayed out the window as they drove down the street, unsurprised when Jimmy cleared his throat and spoke endearingly.

"Hey, do me a favor," he began, and she knew what the favor would be, "Don't say anything to Dan, huh? They're gettin' messed up 'cause school's over and graduation's tomorrow, but I'm not gonna drink," she scoffed with disbelief and Jimmy urged, "Seriously, we're just celebratin'."

"What're you celebratin'?" Megan sneered, immediately regretting her words when she saw a crease of pain in Jimmy's face before his eyes narrowed.

"Nice," he scoffed and stared out the windshield silently for the rest of the short trip home.

Megan's stomach turned with guilt. Jimmy wasn't angry, he was hurt, and that was worse. She knew for as much as he'd chosen to leave school on his own accord, it was perpetrated by his constant struggle with tests, leading to an eventual lack of motivation to do homework since he'd always fail the exams anyway. He'd said he'd know the material, even understood it, but sitting down to take a test made everything vanish from his mind. Megan didn't fully understand the pressure her brother had tried to describe of how he just got anxious and mad, often unable to even complete a test in the given time, but knew from watching him struggle for years it was very real. When they pulled in front of their house and Jimmy threw the sedan in park, Megan had to say something.

148

"I'm sorry, Jimmy," she barely more than whispered, but his hand halted on the door, "I didn't mean it."

"Then why'd ya say it?" he asked pointedly.

"I dunno," she shrugged sadly, "I just wish you wouldn't drink so much."

He sighed, softening his expression, "I don't drink that much, babygirl, and I'm just goin' to hang out tomorrow, if I have any it'll be maybe one or two, I promise."

"Okay," she nodded, knowing better than to believe him, but tried to be hopeful.

"C'mon," he jerked his head at the house and shoved his door, "I'm gonna grab a nap before I gotta head to work."

"Can I go play with Sam?" she asked, crinkling the cone wrapper and dropped it on the floor of Jimmy's car.

"Yeah, just stick around, those clouds are gettin' dark," he said, raising his voice as she ran across the yards, "Be home for dinner, Megan!"

"Kay!" she yelled, brushing a few raindrops from her bare arms, and hurried to Sam's front door.

"Hey," Sam smiled, but quickly returned to his video game, when she burst in without knocking, "How was the doctor?"

"I'm five feet tall now," Megan announced, plopping on the floor beside him in front of his PlayStation 2 console.

"Congrats," Sam nudged her, "Gotta ways to catch up with me."

She laughed, "I'll never get that tall."

"I'm the same height as my mom," Sam shrugged, his eyes on the television, "And Dan 'n Jimmy are really tall."

"Yeah, but their dad was really tall," she reasoned, "My dad's, like, maybe Jimmy's height."

"And about four times as wide," Sam scoffed and Megan tackled him playfully, earning his mildly amused plea, "C'mon I just got this, I just wanna set up my car."

"Can we play Madden?" she asked, still laying on top of him.

"Yeah, fine," Sam appeased distractedly, "When I'm done."

Satisfied, Megan sat cross-legged on the carpet just behind him, leaning against the coffee table. Darlene wouldn't be home until late, she always closed Pederson's on Fridays, and, like most weeks, Megan asked Sam if he wanted to come over for dinner that evening.

"You guys fed me last night," he said.

"Whatever," she giggled, "Your mom gave us so many extras we still got leftovers."

"Yeah maybe," Sam glanced at the steady streams running down the window and returned his attention to the television, "Gettin' kinda shitty out though."

Rain started to pepper the windows, drumming lightly on the roof as she watched him take a painstakingly long time configuring his car before starting his first race, which Sam promptly failed, miserably. Megan couldn't help laughing, but a sudden boom of thunder and rain hammering the roof stopped her amusement.

"I should go," she said, wishing she hadn't left her jacket in Jimmy's car, "You comin'?"

"Naw," he paused his game, "I'm gonna make some mac 'n cheese and play this."

"Dork," she joked, "I'll see you tomorrow."

"I'll be the one chokin' at the podium," he muttered, walking her to the door.

"Shut up," she slapped him lightly on the arm, "You're gonna do great."

Sam grinned, opened the door and Megan ran as fast as she could through the sopping grass, up the slick porch steps and into her house, leaning dramatically against the door as it shut. Her drenched clothes stuck to her skin uncomfortably and, in the one step she took on the small patch of tile, her sneakers squished.

"Shoes off," Dan hardly looked away from the pot on the stove while issuing the orders, "Go put on somethin' dry, we're eatin' in a minute."

Megann didn't need him to tell her that, she didn't want to sit around in wet clothes, and went to her bedroom to change without a word.

Leaving her wet jeans and t-shirt on the floor, she slipped on a pair of warm sweatpants and a long-sleeved t-shirt before rejoining Dan in the front room. Jimmy walked out of his bedroom as she dropped onto the couch and turned on the television, sheets of rain poured down the window behind it.

"Dan, you seen my work shirt?" Jimmy asked, grabbing a soda from the fridge.

"Hangin' up in the basement," Dan said, taking the pot off the stove and set it on an oven mitt in the middle of the table, "You eatin'?"

"What'cha got?" Jimmy nodded curiously at the hot oven his brother was opening.

"Frozen lasagna 'n mashed potatoes," Dan said, sliding a foil pan off the rack and onto the empty stovetop.

"I'm in," Jimmy said, grabbing plates from the high cabinet.

"Megan, turn the TV off," Dan said, "Dinners ready."

"Two minutes, it's almost over," she answered, barely looking away from the screen.

"Wasn't a request," his tone was simple, but firm, and she clicked off the television, "Thank you."

Megan bit her lips to avoid scoffing 'whatever', but wasn't able to suppress a hidden eye roll, and slumped onto her chair at the table. Jimmy set a glass of milk in front of her and took a plate of steaming lasagna from Dan to his seat. Dan put a plate in front of Megan and she immediately plopped a large helping of potatoes on the empty side before handing the serving spoon to Jimmy. They'd both started eating by the time Dan joined them, adding a modest serving of mashed potatoes to his plate, despite only one, large spoonful remaining in the pot.

"How'd everything go at Doctor Summers today?" Dan asked.

"Not a single tear," Jimmy reported with a smug grin, "Think she's ready for her first tattoo."

Megan giggled, but Dan complimented her proudly, "Good job, sweetheart."

"Thanks," she shrugged, brightening with her suddenly remembered news, "I'm five feet tall!"

Dan's eyebrows raised, "Really? I guess, yeah, you're about that."

"Exactly," she informed him pointedly.

"On the dot," Jimmy agreed in the same moment he finished swallowing a bite of potatoes, "She's growin' up, man."

But, before Dan could agree or disagree, thunder cracked loudly above the roof, making Megan jump in her seat, and both brothers chuckled.

"Little ways to go," Dan grinned, "D'ja get ice cream?"

"Yeah," Megan replied excitedly, "And Brad 'n Travis were there, and Travis hates needles too, he said his dad and two nurses used to have to hold him down for shots."

"Jeez," Dan scoffed, "I'm glad you've never been that bad," Megan's eyes widened as lightning flashed outside the windows and he shook his head, "Still not a fan'a storms."

"Only weirdos are fans of storms," she smirked and Dan laughed.

If the wind wasn't blowing towards the front of the house, the oldest would sit on the porch and watch a storm for hours. Sometimes Jimmy joined him, but Megan had never understood the fascination.

She jumped again as a louder boom of thunder rattled the windows, but, this time, neither brother laughed and Dan looked at Jimmy with his most serious expression.

"You be careful," he said firmly.

"I will," Jimmy nodded, looking at the soaked window with more annoyance than concern.

"You need new tires," Dan said, shoving a forkful of lasagna in his mouth and Megan watched Jimmy roll his eyes.

"They're fine," he insisted, but relented to a sideways glance from Dan, "I'm savin' for a new set."

"What do you do with all your money, kid?" Dan's question instigated an increase in the speed of Megan's fork, badly wanting to get away from the brewing argument.

"Hey, man," Jimmy began defensively, "I've offered to give you more-"

"I'm not talkin' about that, Jim," Dan interjected calmly, though the agitation growing in his tone was clear, "You're always good with that-"

"Then why's the rest'a my money your concern?" Jimmy argued angrily.

Megan was eating her lasagna so fast she nearly choked and another flash of lightning lit the yard outside the window.

"Jimmy," Dan repressed a growl, "Your tires are the only thing between your car 'n the pavement," Jimmy's head rolled dramatically with his eyes and Dan's narrowed threateningly, "Get'cher head outta your ass, y'know I'm right."

"As always," Jimmy grumbled, shoving the rest of his lasagna in his mouth and cleared his plate as he chewed.

"Jimmy, stop," Dan stood from his mostly finished dinner, towering over his brother as another crash of thunder shook the house, "I'm not lookin' for a fight. I'll help you get some Goodyears on it, but those things were bald when I flipped the alternator a couple weeks ago. It's not safe, bud."

Jimmy's scowl slowly faded into a forgiving smirk. Dan only called him 'bud' once in a while, but Jimmy always seemed to concede when he did.

"Yeah, well," Jimmy shrugged, "Maybe you could get me some prices at work tomorrow?"

"Done," Dan nodded, retaking his seat and scraped the last of the mashed potatoes onto his plate.

Megan regretted plowing through her dinner, relieved there hadn't been much of an argument, but the rapidly eaten pasta entrée bloated behind her ribs. Another burst of lightning was followed only seconds later by a crash of thunder, even louder than the last, and Megan jumped again.

"Hey," Dan got her attention, "Why don't you go pick out a movie for us."

Megan left the table and her empty plate, pulling open the wide drawer of VHS tapes at the bottom of the television stand. She ran her finger over the colorful, plastic covers of Disney cartoons she still secretly adored, but landed on one of her more recent favorites. Tugging the tape from between a few others, she set it on top of the VCR and closed the heavy drawer with her feet.

"Alright, I'm outta here," Jimmy shut the basement door, buttoning his work shirt through the front room and twisted his feet into his boots.

"Be careful, Jimmy," Megan said, but, as he turned with near exasperation, another flash of lightning was quickly followed by a crack of thunder and she whimpered, "Please."

"I will, babygirl," Jimmy crooked a finger, but Megan was already rushing him, and he wrapped his arms around her, "It's just a storm. Okay?"

She nodded into his work shirt, but only to appease him.

"You goin' to Sam's graduation tomorrow?" Dan asked, rinsing the dishes in the sink.

"It's at noon, right?" Jimmy pulled on his heavy, hooded sweatshirt and zipped it up to his neck.

154

"Darlene said I can go with her if you don't wanna," Megan said and Jimmy pretended to be offended.

"Don't wanna?" he gasped, "I've put blood, sweat 'n tears into that kid's speech! I'll be damned if I ain't gonna hear it."

Megan giggled and wrapped her arms around Jimmy again in a silent thank you. She wouldn't have minded going with Darlene, but Jimmy was always her first choice.

"There's a strong chance you're gonna have to wake me up though," he warned with a funny smirk.

Jimmy threw his hood up and she heard the rain get louder for a moment when he opened the door, the broken screen door barely audible over the storm. Dan kicked the dishwasher shut and turned to his sister as lightning flashed across the kitchen window.

"Wanna get it set up?" Dan wiped his hands on his pants, moving towards his bedroom, "I'm gonna throw some sweats on."

Megan nodded as thunder boomed and she couldn't help the spastic tension raising her shoulders, but breathed a little calmer when Dan pulled her close.

She'd always hated storms, when she was little she'd find her way to her brothers' room to curl up next to one of them. Neither ever minded, but constantly tried to remind her she was safe. It had been years since she'd left her bed when wind and water beat against her window, but her natural reaction to sudden rattling thunder couldn't be helped.

Dan returned to the living room in gray sweatpants and a regional champions shirt, the numbers 1995 cracked over a faded football, but Megan could remember when it was new. His junior year, before he was captain, but his first season as starting quarterback, the next year they'd won state.

There had been quite a celebration after winning the coveted, Illinois high school title, it seemed the whole town was at the party, shutting down the main street in front of Dr. Summers's office and the pizza place. The football team had ridden in on the back of pick-up trucks, and Megan remembered standing on the curb with Jimmy, yelling louder than anybody when they'd finally seen Dan, smiling modestly while his teammates hooted and stomped in the bed around him. People had pulled Dan in so many different directions that day it was hard for Megan to find him, but, when Jimmy had met a few of his friends and she'd gotten bored watching them crush cans in an alley, she'd gone searching. Being barely more than waist tall in a crowd that was riddled with the same football jersey had made it difficult to navigate, but she hadn't seen number 32 and continued slipping through the sea of legs. Two men in dark suits had been speaking enthusiastically to Dan, who'd looked like he was trying to find an escape, but Mr. Olsen had had a grip on his shoulder while eagerly nodding along. Becoming impatient, Megan had peeked around the broad football coach with a goofy grin. Dan's surprise had seemed annoyed at first, but he smiled back and pulled her to his side. Then he'd said he had more important things to do than play football anymore.

"Alright, what're we watchin'?" Dan plopped on the couch and Megan hit play on the VCR, having already fast forwarded through the previews.

"Meet the Deedles," she landed next to him on the worn cushions.

"Again?" he joked, "Startin' to think you gotta thing for Paul Walker."

"Which one's that?" she asked.

"That one," Dan pointed at the television as the beginning credits started and a handsome young man appeared on screen.

"He's really cute," she giggled, laughing harder when he tickled her side.

"I told you," Dan teased, "Ya can't think boys are cute 'til you're twenty and ya can't date 'til you're thirty-five."

The loudest crash of thunder yet halted their amusement as the lights and television went out, leaving the room in almost complete darkness. Megan whimpered, grabbing Dan's shirt and buried her head in his chest, practically crawling onto his lap. His hand rubbing her back helped a little, but losing power always scared her the most, a promising sign of a nasty storm.

"It's okay," Dan whispered, patting her behind gently, "Lemme up, I'll grab the flashlights."

156

Begrudgingly, she sat back on the couch, hugging a pillow as a terrible replacement for his comfort and squeezed her eyes shut as lightning shot across the sky outside the window. A crash of thunder rattled the house barely moments after the blue flash and Megan knew the storm was close. When she was little, Dan had taught her to count the seconds between lightning and thunder. It was a comforting habit when she could count over three, but, when the thunder cracked before Megan could even start, it was not helpful. He flipped on a flashlight in the kitchen, returning to the couch with a smaller version of the one he carried and handed it to her.

"I was just thinkin'," Dan began, "Have ya read any'a those stories in the book Mr. Glasby gave you?" Megan grimaced apologetically in the dark and shook her head, but he shrugged, "Might be a good night to check it out."

"Will you read?" she asked, getting off the couch and used the flashlight to direct the routine path to her bedroom.

"I was thinkin' you could read to me," Dan said, "But if ya want."

She found the antique hardcover between colorful paperbacks on her bookshelf and returned to the living room, handing it to Dan. Megan loved to read to herself, and aloud in class, but, sometimes, she still missed her brother reading to her before bed, his deep voice lulling her to sleep.

"Can you read this one?" she pointed to The Little Match Girl in the table of contents he was shining the flashlight on.

"You sure?" Dan hesitated.

"I've never heard it," she insisted.

"It's, uh," he grimaced, but nodded, "Okay, yeah, this one."

Dan lifted his arm so she could lean against his side and see the pages, even though there weren't any pictures, it was how he'd always read to her.

He began a story about a little girl wandering shoeless in the streets trying to get someone to buy her matchsticks, but everyone ignored her. The little girl couldn't go home to her father without having sold any, preferring to stay on the frozen streets than face a beating. Megan snuggled closer to Dan, unsure how she felt about this story, but continued listening to his, rumbling voice. The little girl was freezing and curled up in a doorway, lighting matches to keep warm, but, suddenly, wonderful things started happening. A Christmas feast, complete with all the trimmings, and a huge tree appeared, and then the little girl's grandmother, the only one who'd ever loved her and she missed terribly after her passing, joined the celebration. Megan wondered how all these amazing things were possible, elated the little girl had found safety, but confused because her grandmother was dead. As Dan continued, she felt a pang of sadness, realizing the little girl had died, frozen to death in the doorway and her grandmother had taken her to heaven. A very unexpected ending to what she'd learned to anticipate from children's stories.

"She died?" Megan asked, knowing the answer as Dan nodded in the dark room, "But she was a little girl."

"Yeah," Dan agreed sadly, "It's not a happy story."

Megan felt bad for the girl in the story, almost understanding the fear she'd had of going home to a father that would beat her. Not that hers had ever been allowed the opportunity, but that wasn't for lack of trying. If the little match girl had had older brothers like Dan and Jimmy she'd be alive, she'd be warm and she wouldn't be afraid to go home. Thunder crashed again and Megan jumped, but Dan held her close, flipping to the next page.

"Hey, this is a good one," he said and she nodded at The Princess and the Pea, settling next to his side again as he began the familiar tale.

Even with thunder booming around them, Megan found peace in Dan's rumbling chest as he read, finding sleep only a few pages into the story.

A loud crash accompanied a bright, flickering light and Megan's eyes burst open, met by a giant, black claw reaching into her bedroom. She screamed as wind whipped around her room, blowing books and trinkets to the corners, the broken blinds twisted in agony around the branch jutting through her window. Megan's door burst open and Dan snatched her off the bed quickly, carrying her from the room as the door slammed shut from the wind. He flipped on the flashlight, pulled open the basement door and she held onto him tightly as he descended the narrow stairs.

Megan was not a particular fan of their basement, bare concrete walls with a bunch of boxes stacked against the far side and the washer and dryer in the center of the large room. She could still see lightning through the window wells, but the raging storm was quieter under the house. Dan sat her on the dryer and ran the flashlight over her arms.

"You okay?" his voice shook.

"Yeah," she sniffled, "But my windows not."

"I can fix the window," he said, but winced and lifted his sock covered foot.

"Are you okay?" she looked down and saw shadowed discoloration on the floor and, when Dan moved the flashlight to examine his foot, she saw his white sock stained red, "Dan!"

"I'm fine. Must've stepped on some glass," he said coolly, drawing a folding chair closer and propped his foot on his knee.

Megan grimaced, but couldn't stop watching as he carefully pulled the sock off his foot with a muffled groan. Pointing the flashlight at the bloody underside, he used his other hand to carefully pick slivers of glass from his skin, setting them in a neat pile on the washer.

"Good thing I had socks on, huh?" he chuckled after gently running calloused fingers over the affected area to ensure he hadn't missed any glass.

"I'm sorry," she couldn't think of anything else to say.

"How dare you let a tree fall through your window," he joked and she giggled, believing him when he said, "I'm fine, kid, tough as nails."

Not long after, the storm subsided and they returned to the main level. Dan told Megan to go sleep in his bed and she complied by lying with the door open, listening to him move about the house. He cleaned his foot and wrapped it quickly, pulling socks and his work boots on with his sweatpants before shutting himself in her bedroom. Megan heard snapping for a few minutes before she saw his outline leave her bedroom with an armful of broken tree branches, then the front door opened and shut and the screen door banged.

An awful scrapping sound outside made her sit up in his bed, followed by a thud before she heard the front door again. The rustling of a plastic bag and rummaging in the junk drawer barely preceded Dan striding back into her bedroom and closing the door. The house was quiet, except for the soft drumming from the end of the storm on the roof, and Megan continued staring across the dark hall, waiting for him to leave her room. She was breathing softly, just falling asleep by the time Dan crawled next to her, kissing her hair before turning towards the other side of his large bed.

# Chapter 8

Megan woke alone in Dan's room from sun streaming through the window. She couldn't help peeking into her bedroom on her way to the kitchen. Damp clothes, books and paper littered the floor, her dresser cleared of most everything that wasn't simply knocked over, and glass sparkled on the carpeting. Her window was covered by a black garbage bag, duct taped to the frame, and seemed to be breathing with the gentle breeze outside.

"Stay outta there," Dan warned from the kitchen, wearing his work uniform, but a glance at the microwave confirmed it was well passed when he should've been there, and Dan was never late for work.

"Why are you home?" Megan asked excitedly.

"I told Jay what happened when I got in this mornin'," he said, expelling a laugh, "He told me I shouldn't've come in and to get done what I got here."

"Cool!" she exclaimed, "You can come to Sam's graduation!"

Dan's face confessed he hadn't even considered that, but nodded, "Yeah, lemme get some'a this stuff done and that can probably happen."

"What can I do?" she asked, it was her room after all.

But Dan grimaced, "There's a lotta glass in there, I got it."

"Dan," Megan whined, "I can help, I'll be careful."

"It's not just on the floor though," he shook his head, "Clothes, toys, your books, I'd just rather I handle it," Megan burst with a frustrated sigh and stomped her foot, earning Dan's sharp interjection, "Hey! Are you really arguin' with me 'cause I don't want you to help me clean your room?"

She knew it seemed silly, but didn't want to feel guilty sitting on the couch, watching television, while Dan cleaned a mess in her bedroom.

"I just wanna help," she pouted.

"Y'know what," Dan said thoughtfully, "I'm gonna have to bust up that branch outside, but if you could break off some'a the smaller bits that'd be really helpful."

"Okay," she agreed, happy to have something useful to do, and turned to her room to change.

"Stop," Dan's demand halted Megan mid-step and she remembered the glass just as he reminded, "Can't go in there without shoes, I'll get'cha some clothes."

He handed her a t-shirt and jeans, along with a pair of socks and underwear, and Megan's cheeks burned with embarrassment, disappearing into the bathroom. The circumstance couldn't be helped, and it wasn't like Dan didn't see her underwear when he washed them anyway, but it had been a long time since he'd picked out her outfit.

Megan stopped as she left the bathroom, scooping her pajamas from the floor and dumped them in the hamper before plopping on the floor to pull on her shoes by the front door.

The tree in their front yard had a fresh split, nearly down to the roots, where one of the largest branches had broken off in the storm. Megan saw imprints of a muddy struggle where Dan had dragged the branch from her window, leaving it where it had fallen, only threatening the grass crushed underneath.

She put her foot on the small log, using her weight to snap the thicker twigs. But the familiar sound of scrapping metal, accompanied by a high-pitched whine, stole her attention as Jimmy parked his Oldsmobile in front of the house, staring slack jawed out his window.

"What the hell?" he breathed, hurrying up the yard.

"It fell through my window last night," Megan grunted, catching herself as the twig she was leaning on broke.

"I can see that," he said slowly at the damage before eyeing her with concern, "You okay?"

"Yeah," she nodded, "Dan cut his foot on the glass though."

"He'll live," Jimmy shrugged, "Is he inside?"

"My room," she said, kicking at a particularly thick branch.

Jimmy took the porch steps two at a time and the screen door bounced in its frame behind him. With only a bag covering the broken window, Megan could hear her brothers clearly when Jimmy entered her room.

"Dude, what the hell?" he scoffed.

"Tell me about it," Dan grumble.

"Want some help?" Jimmy asked.

"Yeah, thanks," Dan said, "There's glass on everything, though, be careful."

"I got it," Jimmy said and Megan was a bit resentful Dan immediately welcomed Jimmy's help, but didn't trust her to be cautious in the same task.

Megan snapped off a twig and chucked it at the small pile she'd started.

"How much is a new window gonna run?" Jimmy asked.

"Couple hundred bucks," Dan said and her stomach twisted.

"Shit," Jimmy sighed.

"Again," Dan chuckled bitterly, "Tell me about it. There's some plywood in the garage, I'm gonna cover it for now, but maybe tomorrow we can head into Yorkville. I called the Menards there, they've got the right size in stock, we could put it in in a couple hours."

"Sure," Jimmy agreed, "I don't work 'til Monday. Hey, I'm gettin' a vacation next month."

"It's a shutdown, you're not gettin' paid those two weeks either," Dan stated.

"Close enough," Jimmy reasoned, "And who gets paid on vacation?"

"Me," Dan said with amusement.

"Dude, seriously?" Jimmy implored, "When was the last time you took time off, and you get paid for it?!"

Megan also thought this was interesting news and silently agreed with Jimmy's outrage.

"It's called vacation pay," Dan informed him, "And I make more money when I'm wrenchin'.'"

"Well," Megan heard Jimmy's tone and their mischievous smirk crept across her lips, knowing his expression matched on the other side of the plastic bag, "Maybe you could take some time while I'm off next month. I mean, Megan would probably love to have us both home for a few days," she nodded enthusiastically, despite being invisible to them, and Jimmy finished his vague suggestion, "Maybe we could go do somethin'."

Megan held her breath, edging closer to the thinly veiled window.

"You'd wanna do that?" Dan sounded surprised after several quiet moments.

"Yeah, man," Jimmy laughed, "I mean, it'd be cool to do somethin' fun, like campin' or somethin', like we used to y'know. I mean, we've just been fightin' a lot lately 'n I, uh, I don't know, just kinda miss my brother."

Again, it took a few moments before Dan said, "Me too, Jim. Thanks, I, uh, know I've been a bit of a hardass."

"And I'm a pain in the ass," Jimmy admitted, "Which is better?"

"Sure don't always mix well," Dan agreed, "That's a great idea, though, I got a few weeks racked up, Jay can afford to give me one."

Megan jumped, quietly celebrating in the yard.

The three of them crammed into a tent and eating food cooked over a fire were some of the best memories she had. Jimmy would try to tell her scary stories, a flashlight nestled under his chin for an ominous look, and Dan would tell him to shut up from outside the tent while he'd sit and watch the embers turn to ash in the chilly, late night air. They'd go on long walks in the forest and swim in the lake, but the evenings were always the most fun, when the entire campsite turned into a party and strangers became friends over a fire and a few stories. Megan had made a lot of short-term friends trying to build sandcastles in the impossibly soft lake beaches, usually ending in a competition of who could dig the deepest hole, since the sand wouldn't stay together, before racing to the campsite playground still wearing their bathing suits. Dan relaxed when they went camping, sometimes he'd even accept a beer from a neighboring camper. It was a break from his normal responsibilities and Megan liked to see her oldest brother enjoying himself.

"So, what time're ya pickin' up Lacey?" Jimmy nearly sang.

"Seven," Dan took a deep breath, "I am insane for doin' this."

"Why?!" Jimmy scoffed, and Megan was glad because she'd nearly yelled the same.

"Dude," Dan sighed, "She's Lacey, I mean she's gorgeous and smart, she went to college, man."

"She ain't there anymore," Jimmy reasoned, "And what the hell does that matter?"

"She only left 'cause her dad got hurt 'n had to quit his job," Dan said bitterly, "She didn't drop out."

"Still though," Jimmy continued, "She's had a thing for you for forever-"

"Bullshit," Dan argued.

Megan covered her mouth on an escaping squawk, shaking her head at the plastic bag and her astonishingly oblivious brother on the other side.

"You're an idiot," Jimmy stated and she nodded in agreement.

"Whatever, dude," Dan said dismissively.

"Who asked who out?" Jimmy challenged.

"I don't know," Dan stammered, "It just kinda happened, Mike told me I had to come out with them one'a these Saturdays and we just agreed on this one."

"So, her sister's boyfriend asks you to go out with the three of them," Jimmy began thoughtfully, "Which I'm sure she third wheels it with them all the time, and I'm guessin' she wasn't exactly fightin' this idea."

"She kissed me," Dan admitted quietly.

"What?!" Jimmy erupted.

"On the cheek," Dan clarified, "It was right after church."

"Dude," Jimmy clearly found this information exciting, "She wants you! As your brother I am incredibly happy for you. But, as a fellow member of the male species, I kinda wanna club you over the head outta jealousy."

Megan covered her mouth again as she laughed at Jimmy's threat, but Dan laughed too so she knew neither had heard her quiet giggling over his boisterous amusement. Jimmy could always make them laugh, how he said things was just funny.

"Seriously," Jimmy chuckled, "If you don't think that girl likes you, you need to have your head examined, but, seein' as we're broke, I'll offer to beat'cha over that thick skull 'n hope it knocks some sense into ya."

"I'm good thanks," Dan said at the end of his subsiding laughter, "What time are you headin' out tonight?"

"Same," Jimmy said and Megan was a bit surprised when he continued with an explanation of his evening plans, "Pickin' up Brad 'n Travis, there's, uh, well there's this party Missy Walker's havin', her parents are gonna be there and everything, but uh, I figured I'd let y'know where I'll be."

She heard their older brother's heavy sigh, "Do I need to ask?"

"I'm not plannin' on drinkin'," Jimmy assured him, "That's why I'm drivin'."

"You're not plannin' on it?" Dan's tone hardened, but hadn't quite reached a warning level.

"No," Jimmy insisted, "I won't, really."

"Same rules apply," Dan said firmly.

"I know," there was annoyance in Jimmy's voice, "If I do, I'll call you."

"Better," the familiar warning tone emerged, "I will actually beat you if you drive home drunk."

"I'm pretty crafty with that club," Jimmy's joke was perfectly placed and Megan heard Dan chuckle.

"Just be safe," he said.

Their conversation trailed off and, since Megan couldn't find any more pieces to break, she brushed her hands on her jeans and hopped up the porch steps. The screen door banged as she walked to her bedroom, keeping her shoes on and knocked on her open door. Her brothers looked up from their bent over positions, picking large pieces of glass off the floor.

"Stay outta here," Dan raised an eyebrow as he stood.

"I got shoes on," Megan waved a foot at him as proof.

"Still don't want'cha in here," he said simply, "We're almost done anyway."

"I'm done," she shrugged, "What else can I do?"

"She's askin' to help?" Jimmy narrowed his eyes jokingly at Megan, "Who are you 'n what've you done with my little sister?"

She giggled and shook her head, "I just wanna do somethin'."

"I appreciate that, sweetheart," Dan smiled, glancing around the room and grabbed the hamper, "Could'ja bring this downstairs for me?"

With a small sigh, Megan took the hamper and slowly walked to the basement door. The stairs creaked as she descended and, in the soft light of the single bulb lighting the room, she saw a thin trail of dried blood on the concrete floor. Megan really didn't like their basement, it was cold and always smelled damp. So, she set the hamper near the washing machine and hurried back up the stairs, shutting the door behind her in the kitchen.

"Hey, Megan," Dan called, "Bring me the vacuum would'ja?"

She grabbed the vacuum from the closet and dragged it to her bedroom, but Dan met her in the doorway. From her obstructed view in the hallway, Megan saw her bedding balled up in the corner of her mattress and everything from the floor that hadn't been deemed garbage was stacked on her dresser. She felt a pang of sadness seeing one of her Fire Fox books, clearly having suffered water damage, and peered around for the others, hoping A.K. Foreman's signature and inscription were unharmed.

"Thanks," Dan took the vacuum and followed her eyes to the book, "That one took the brunt of it, it was on the floor."

"It was on my bookcase," she said irritably.

"Pretty sure the tree took care'a that," Jimmy remarked, shaking her beanbag chair and shards of glass rained on the carpet.

"It's so dark in here," she whined.

"I'm gettin' you a window tomorrow," he promised.

"Thanks," she mumbled guiltily, it wasn't Dan's fault a tree had broken her window, but he would fix it, like everything.

"Alright we got a couple hours 'til Sam's big speech," Dan pointed at Megan and gestured towards the kitchen, "You go have breakfast, Jimmy 'n I'll have this done soon."

"Fine," she sighed, relenting to his request before it became an order.

Dan started the vacuum and Jimmy left the room with the kitchen trash, taking the entire can outside before removing the bag on the front porch. Megan watched him through the screen door until he disappeared around the side of the house and sat on the couch with a bowl of cereal, turning on Nickelodeon. Jimmy's shaggy hair bobbed along the bottom of the window behind the television a few minutes later and Megan put her cereal on the coffee table as she went to investigate. Pushing open the screen door, she saw him drag a piece of plywood under her window, drop two hammers on the grass and dig a box of nails from his hoody pocket.

"Hey," Jimmy spotted her and jerked his head towards the street, "Your jacket's still in my car."

168

"Oh, yeah," Megan hopped down the porch steps and ran to his rusty sedan, wrenching the door open and crawled across the seat to grab her denim jacket bunched in the corner on the opposite side of the bench seat.

"What happened?!" a high, panicky voice called and she saw Darlene hurrying across the vacant yard barefoot in a t-shirt and small shorts, "I just got up and looked out the kitchen window, oh my God! Are you all okay?"

"Holy shit!" Sam exclaimed, stepping onto his porch.

"Samuel!" Darlene whipped around and he grimaced apologetically.

"We're fine," Jimmy said, "Hell, I wasn't even here."

"It must've happened after I got home," she shook her head of disheveled, blonde hair at the split tree.

"Mornin' Darlene," Dan walked out onto the porch, letting the screen door slap behind him.

"Dan, I can't believe this!" she stared between the branch and the crudely covered window.

"Is what it is," Dan shrugged, descending the steps, "I'm gettin' a new window tomorrow, Jimmy 'n I are gonna put it in."

"Can I help?" Sam asked hopefully.

Dan and Jimmy glanced at each other with the same strained grin before the oldest nodded and said, "Sure, kid, that'd be great."

Megan rolled her eyes, knowing if she'd asked to help install the window he'd have found some excuse why she couldn't, but Sam was a boy.

Darlene continued shaking her head and muttering how she couldn't believe it, which no one seemed to find helpful.

Dan carried a ladder from the garage, leaning it against the siding beside Megan's window and Jimmy stomped the bottom rung before beginning his climb. Her brothers always worked well together, like they knew what the other was thinking and who needed to do what when. Megan, Sam and Darlene watched as Dan hoisted the plywood over the outside frame of the window and Jimmy secured the top right corner with three rapidly driven nails before jumping down the ladder, moving it quickly to the other side and repeated the process. Dan picked up the other hammer and helped his brother fasten the board at the bottom.

"That'll be fun to take off tomorrow," Jimmy panted lightly and Megan could tell he wanted a cigarette after the expended effort.

"Gonna have to take the framin' off anyway," Dan said.

"Is there anything I can do?" Darlene asked.

"Yeah," Dan smirked, "Could'ja watch my sister tonight?"

She shook her head with apparent amazement, "You're incredible, Daniel."

His ears tinged pink, turning to grab the ladder and Jimmy followed him to the garage with the hammers and box of nails.

"I should go get ready," Darlene said absently before looking at her son, "You too, go grab a shower. Megan, are y'all still comin', I mean, I can understand if-"

"We're comin'," Megan assured her, cringing apologetically for her interruption, but Darlene smiled.

"We'll see ya there then," Darlene said before striding across the grass.

"She's tryin' to make me wear a tie," Sam sneered when she was out of earshot.

"So," Megan shrugged, "A lotta boys probably will. You're gonna look great."

"Yeah?" he confirmed modestly.

"Sure," she said, "Sometimes Dan wears ties 'n he always looks good in 'em."

Sam seemed hardly reassured, but nodded, "Well, I just gotta get through this crap 'n then we're goin' to the movies."

"I can't wait," Megan agreed excitedly.

"Me either," Sam grinned.

Half an hour before noon, Megan sat on the couch watching cartoons while her brothers took showers and got dressed. She'd already gotten ready, deciding on a green dress she knew wouldn't fit in a few months and dug a pair of strappy sandals from the back of her closet, before waiting on her brothers. Jimmy wore dark jeans and a gray collared polo and Dan decided on a dark blue polo with his jeans, Megan thought they both looked better with their hair fixed and wondered why they did it so infrequently.

Finally, fifteen minutes to noon, they walked out the door and piled into Dan's truck. Their home looked sad with a plywood patch on the front, far too much like the abandoned house next door, covered in broken boards and holes in the roof.

The school parking lot was nearly full when Dan pulled into a back spot and Megan followed Jimmy out the passenger door. Walking between them, she remembered when she was little, how they would swing her by her arms and their mother would laugh, but had always reminded the boys to be gentle, though she'd probably known it was unnecessary. Seeing all the moms and dads walking into the gymnasium, Megan felt a familiar sadness, a void that was always there and occasionally reminded her it would never go away.

Darlene waved at them from the front door as they approached.

"Oh, darlin' I just love that dress on you," she said, reminding Megan it was Darlene who'd given it to her for Christmas.

"Thank you," Megan smiled and twisted a bit so the bottom of her dress swayed back and forth.

"I didn't even know who was on my couch," Jimmy joked, gently shaking Megan by the shoulders.

"Don't look so bad yourself, Jimmy," Darlene said before shifting her gaze, "That's a good color for you, Dan."

"Uh, thank you," Dan cleared his throat hard, opening the door for an approaching couple and they followed into the school.

The gymnasium was full, the expanded bleachers already packed with parents, grandparents, siblings and friends of the eighth-grade graduates. They managed to find four chairs together on the floor and Megan surveyed the faculty behind the podium near the wall at the end of the room. Spotting the typically disinterested blonde, she poked Jimmy in the side and pointed discreetly to the woman after getting his attention.

"That's Ms. Craft," she whispered.

"Looks more like Bitchcraft," Jimmy mumbled, obviously surprised when all he gained was a smirk in response.

"That's what Sam said," she shrugged.

"He did?" Jimmy sighed happily, "I'm so proud."

Megan did giggle that time, trying to stifle it when Dan glanced at them before Darlene pulled him back into a conversation.

The graduates marched into the gym while Pomp and Circumstance played from a boombox, the process was painfully slow and hardly visible since most of the mothers had stood to take pictures. When Mr. Jarsen took the podium, Megan slumped into Jimmy as the principal began yet another rework of the same speech she'd heard Thursday, and at the end of every school year she could remember.

Mr. Jarsen called honor roll awards before announcing the valedictorian and they watched Sam walk to the podium. Megan knew he was nervous, but thought he looked fairly confident on his way to the front of the room, though he could've lifted his head a bit more. Sam turned to the crowd and Megan heard Darlene exhale as her son grinned weakly at the room. She wondered if Jimmy was serious about running through the gymnasium naked, but, thankfully, she didn't have to worry as the shakiness in Sam's voice faded after the first few words.

"Thank you all for being here today," he began, staring mostly at the notecards, "I've been at this school since my first day of kindergarten, like many of my classmates, and have learned a lot both in the classroom and out of it in my time here. I'll never forget building marble rollercoasters in sixth grade science class and making a tiny amusement park right here in the gym. Or our field trip to Chicago in September to see the Shed Aquarium, unfortunately, our chaperones got lost for a little while," a few of his classmates laughed loudly, but everyone chuckled, even Darlene, who'd been furious at the time about Sam sneaking off with his friends during the trip, "I have a lot of memories at this school and will miss my teachers as well as the friends I'm leaving behind," he glanced up and found Megan momentarily before returning to his speech, "We're about to enter high school, a place we've only heard about, and not all good things, but we're ready for the challenge and look forward to the next four years of learning and growing together as the future class of two-thousand-five, but today, we're the class of two-thousand-one, and this school will never forget how hard we rocked. Thank you."

His class cheered and stood, Megan, Jimmy, Dan and Darlene were already on their feet, and several other audience members joined in the standing ovation. Sam's face turned red as he hurried from the podium and back to his seat in the crowd of students wearing the same blue cap and gown. Mr. Jarsen retook the stand and complimented Sam on his speech before announcing the time had come for the diploma ceremony. Jimmy sighed.

The graduating class only had thirty-seven students and Mr. Jarsen didn't take long listing them alphabetically. Each walked to the podium when their name was called and took a rolled-up paper from the principal with an awkward handshake. Megan was glad when Sam's handshake wasn't awkward at all and glanced at Dan, who had a proud look on his face. After Anthony Young returned to his seat, Mr. Jarsen announced the class to another round of applause and thanked everyone for coming. Jimmy was clearly not the only one getting restless and some people were already walking out the door, which Megan thought was extremely rude. She giggled when Pomp and Circumstance started playing again and the class began parading out the way they'd come in while those clamoring to leave early stood awkwardly near the door as the graduates passed.

Sam was by the front entrance when the four of them managed to get out of the gymnasium, he'd already returned his cap and gown and Megan thought he did look nice in a white button down and green tie. She dodged through the crowd and wrapped her arms around him.

"You did awesome!" Megan exclaimed, letting Sam go and Darlene squeezed him so tight it looked like he couldn't breathe.

"You did, baby!" Darlene had tears in her eyes, "It was perfect."

"Good thing too," Jimmy smirked, "Not a lotta runnin' room, would've had to jump over some folks, no one needs that."

Sam and Megan laughed at Jimmy's subtle reminder of his promise, even Dan chuckled, but shook his head at Darlene, silently insisting she'd rather not know when her confused gaze shifted around the group.

"Nice job, Sam," Dan shook his hand proudly.

"Thanks," Sam smiled with shy gratification.

"Really, kid," Jimmy high fived him vigorously, "Knocked it outta the park."

"Thanks," Sam's cheeks were pink and he changed the subject, turning to his mom, "Are we gonna get lunch?"

"Yeah, of course," Darlene said and looked at Dan, "Will y'all join us? My treat."

"We'll join ya," Dan agreed, "But you're not payin' for us."

"We'll argue about it at Sunrise," she said with an indifferent hand wave.

"If ya wanna," Dan raised his eyebrows in feigned warning, holding the door open and they headed to the parking lot.

They weren't the only ones with the idea of celebrating at Sunrise Diner in the neighboring town, but, having left before most of the crowd, they were able to get a table just minutes before the small waiting area was swarmed with hungry families. Megan slid into the booth next to Jimmy, across from Sam and Darlene, and Dan thanked the hostess who brought an extra chair for him to sit at the end of the table, a trend that was being repeated at several booths in the busy restaurant.

Some of the other parents stopped to tell Sam he did a wonderful job with his speech and he maintained a weak smile, but Megan could tell he was only barely tolerating the attention.

When their lunches arrived, Megan caught a look from Dan, reminding her they weren't at home. She rolled her eyes, thinking if he should be giving anyone a warning glance it should be Jimmy. But, with Sam's mom at the table, Jimmy's manners were fairly impeccable, at least he remembered to swallow whatever he was chewing before he spoke. Once they were picking at the last few bits of lunch Darlene excused herself for the bathroom.

"So, you two are goin' to see Shrek tonight?" Dan asked, looking between Sam and Megan.

"Seven twenty-five," Sam confirmed.

"Y'know I heard that's supposed to be really funny," Jimmy said, "It's Mike Meyers."

"Who?" Megan asked.

"Austin Powers," Jimmy sounded shocked, but then smirked, "Oh, right, you can't watch that yet."

"C'mon, Jim," Dan growled, then pointed at Megan as she crossed her arms and sunk into the cushioned backrest, "And you stop, y'know he's teasin'."

"Your birthday's next Tuesday?" Jimmy poked her shoulder and Megan nodded curtly without looking at him, "What's say you 'n me have a movie marathon after I get up? Austin Powers, Waterboy, American Pie-"

"American Pie is rated R," Dan interjected.

"Is it?" Jimmy furrowed his brow and shrugged as Dan nodded slowly, "Okay, not that one."

"Yeah!" she agreed, mentally listing the tapes in the drawer she'd eyed for years, but Dan had never allowed her to watch.

"It's a date," Jimmy grinned and Megan leaned into him.

Darlene returned to the table with a mysterious smirk, "Everyone ready to go?"

Dan nearly glared at her, "You didn't."

"Oh, stop," she said, "I'm so glad y'all came today."

Megan wasn't sure what Dan was upset about, but he was clearly trying not to look as irritated as he felt.

"Thank you," he said, attempting a smile.

"Yeah, thank you, Darlene," Jimmy nudged Megan under the table.

"Thanks," she said quickly, realizing Darlene had paid for lunch.

"You're all welcome," she smiled, "Thank you, seriously, I'd've gotten stuck with that group of gabby moms who complain about how busy they are, but haven't worked a day in their lives."

"Must be nice," Jimmy rolled his eyes and Darlene expelled a harsh breath in agreement.

As soon as they got home, Megan kicked her sandals into the back of her closet while pulling the green dress over her head and dropped it on her floor next to the towel she'd used earlier. She dragged on her old jeans, struggling to get them over her hips, the fastenings refusing to meet each other no matter how much she sucked in her stomach. Exhaling in frustration, Megan fell on her bed, lying flat as she tried to pull the button to its hole. A knock sounded on her door and Dan peeked in, changed into a sleeveless t-shirt and old athletic shorts.

"Hey," he dropped a basket of her clean bedding on the floor, "Get up, I'm gonna put your sheets on."

"I can do it," she said, rolling off the bed, her jeans still unfastened.

"Pants a little small?" he smirked.

"Guess," Megan shrugged.

"Throw 'em out then," Dan said, pulling her fitted sheet from the basket, "I don't need to keep washin' clothes ya don't fit in."

She peeled the faded jeans off with effort, leaving them a crumpled mess on the floor and grabbed a pair that fit, turning to her brother with a slightly timid expression.

"What?" he asked, slipping the sheet's elastic ends under her mattress.

"Sam 'n I were gonna play by the river," Megan's uneasy statement was nearly a question.

"Okay?" Dan urged for understanding of her concern.

"I might get dirty," she warned and saw amusement on his face.

"Be a first if ya didn't," he remarked, "You got a couple new pairs now, though, right?" Megan nodded, he knew she did, he'd bought them, "Make those ones your new play jeans."

Megan grinned, grabbing the slipcover from the basket and wrestled her pillow into it as Dan shook her blanket flat over the clean sheets. Turning to assess the room with his hands on his hips, he rolled his eyes at the black garbage bag in the window frame.

"Not too shabby," he remarked, pulling Megan into his side by the shoulder and earned her attention with a gentle shake, "Hey, be home by five to eat."

"Darlene'll probably make dinner before the movie," she shrugged, slipping around his back to leave the room.

"Megan," she stopped, flipping around in her doorway, and Dan said, "Darlene's fed ya once today. Come home at five for dinner. Got me?"

"Fine," she sighed, turning to leave again.

"Stop," Dan said firmly, forcing her to turn again, leaning in her doorway with a look of exhaustion as he pointed to the too small jeans on her floor, "Garbage."

Megan hopped into her room, gaining a chuckle from her brother as he threw her towel and dress into the empty laundry basket, and she grabbed the faded pants, tossing them into the kitchen trash can before plopping on the floor to slip on her sneakers. Jimmy's door was shut and she remembered to catch the screen door before it banged against its frame. The tree branch was still laying across the grass and Megan stepped onto one end, balancing her way to the other side, as Sam leapt down his porch stairs and grabbed his bike from against the yellow siding. The brakes squeaked when he stopped in front of her yard.

"Home by five, Megan," Dan reminded, appearing on the porch as she grabbed her bike from under the porch overhang.

"I know," she called, racing out of their driveway with Sam.

There were a lot of people by the river when they slowed their bikes at the end of the street, men were fishing up and down the bank while families played in the shallows. Their usual spot was occupied by a woman and her daughter, crouching together in the sandy dirt as the mother helped count every rock the little girl unearthed. Sam rolled his eyes, jerking his head for them to keep riding, relenting their opportunity to check on the baby birds, and Megan shoved away a twinge of jealousy as they left. Once, when her mother had been feeling up to it, she'd taken Megan to the river and helped her count the rocks she'd dug from the dirty sand.

"Ya wanna go to the gas station?" Sam asked, "We can grab some candy to sneak in later."

"Yeah, but I gotta ask Dan," Megan said, she wasn't allowed to leave their neighborhood without permission and certainly wasn't going to screw up her chances of going to the movies, again. Also, she didn't have any money.

They tore back up the street, panting as they pulled into Megan's driveway. Dan's back gleamed with sweat in the hot sun and the ax in his hands swung down on the branch hard. He dropped it to the ground, took off his hat and ran a hand through his damp hair while Megan hurried over.

"Can Sam 'n I go to the gas station and get candy for later?" Megan used her sweetest voice, shrugging her shoulders in a pleading fashion.

"Just be careful," Dan jerked his head towards the house, "Go grab my wallet off my dresser."

Taking the porch steps in twos, Megan rushed into the house, not even taking her shoes off as she rushed to Dan's bedroom and grabbed the brown leather wallet from next to his truck keys and a rarely used bottle of cologne. When she pushed out the screen door, Dan was cross armed with a small smile watching Sam struggle to swing the ax into the deep cut he had started on the branch. Dan chuckled softly when the ax hit with a soft thud and Sam panted, offering the long handle back.

"Are we gonna have a fire?" Megan asked excitedly, handing Dan his wallet.

"We could," he scoffed at the branch and took out ten dollars before shoving his wallet into the pocket of his mesh shorts, "That's for your ticket tonight too so don't go crazy."

"Thank you," she slipped the money into her front pocket and hugged him.

"I'm dirty 'n gross," Dan chuckled, patting her back, "Go on, be safe. What time ya gonna be home?"

"Five," she refrained from rolling her eyes, feeling the crisp bill fold in her pocket while mounting her bike.

"Good girl," he nodded, lifting the ax onto his shoulder and returned to the branch.

A crack echoed as Megan and Sam pedaled out of their neighborhood. The main road wasn't busy, but the speed limit was forty miles per hour so they had to stay close to the gravel shoulder just in case a car drove passed. Only one did before the gas station came into view, a small building with four pumps and a payphone in front of the two, faded parking spots. They set their bikes against the building and Sam pushed open the glass door, a two-toned bell chimed in the store.

"Heya, kids," the gruff voice of the large, balding man behind the counter got their attention.

"Hi, Uncle Bob," Sam and Megan piped up in synchrony, he was neither's uncle, but everyone called him that, it was on his name tag.

"What kinda trouble are you two findin' today?" he asked, leaning over his hefty forearms on the counter.

"Gettin' snacks for the movies later," Megan told him, but Sam shot her a quick glare and she bit her lips.

"Y'know," Uncle Bob began as he usually did before telling them a story, "When I was a kid, my ma would make a couple grocery bags'a popcorn at home, they didn't have the whole overpriced snack bar they got now. What they charge for a pop! Makes me sick, 'n I know what that stuff costs."

Megan and Sam grumbled agreeably, it always seemed to suffice and they hardly ever understood, or cared, what he was talking about. But

179

he was a nice old man, sometimes he'd give them candy that was about to expire, and Megan appreciated he was one of the few people who thought everyone was hard on Jimmy. Uncle Bob always said Jimmy was a great young man who just needed to find his own way in the world, losing his parents, subjected to years of abuse and forever in the shadow of Dan, Uncle Bob thought it was unsurprising he'd found a little trouble, but would argue anyone who said Jimmy wasn't a good kid.

"So, what movie you kids goin' to see?" he asked, ringing up Megan's gummy bears and M&M's.

"Shrek," she said after a quick glance at Sam.

"That's a good'in," Uncle Bob commented, "Took my granddaughter to see it last week, funny as hell."

"Thank you," Megan took her change, shoving the bills and coins into her jeans pocket before taking the bag with her treats and stepped aside so Sam could pay next.

The two-toned bell rang again as they left, waving good-bye to Uncle Bob and grabbed their bikes from the side of the building. Megan looped the plastic bag over her handlebars, same as Sam, and they turned towards their neighborhood. Sam checked his watch as they reached their street, it was nearly five o'clock, and Dan was just finishing the thinnest part of the branch, now a pile of irregularly chopped wood nearby.

"I'm gonna change," Sam kept pedaling when she pulled into her driveway, "See you in a bit?"

"I'll be over soon," Megan said and dumped her bike under the porch overhang as Jimmy walked out the screen door, letting it bang behind him.

"What'ja get me?" he asked, popping a cigarette in his mouth.

"You stay away from my M'n'M's," Megan crinkled her nose and held the bag tightly as he smirked and lit his smoke.

"Oh, I'mma git'em," Jimmy chuckled and descended the steps ominously, but turned to Dan when he reached the walkway, "How's it goin' Paul Bunyan?"

180

Dan wiped his brow again, replacing his cap and scoffed at the diminished remainder of the large branch, "Gonna have a hell of a fire."

"Yeah?" Jimmy raised his eyebrows enthusiastically, "Hey, uh, speakin' of, would you, uh, mind if I snagged one or two'a those fireworks for later?"

Dan looked exhausted and sighed heavily, leaning on the ax planted between his feet, "Bottle rockets or roman candles, nothin' else."

"Yeah, but, dude," Jimmy pushed, "This is a celebration, I mean, just like one'a the-"

"Jimmy," Dan said impatiently, "No, not at somebody else's house. Not without me. Got it?"

"Yeah, fine," Jimmy rolled his eyes and sat on the porch steps, taking a long drag off his cigarette.

Megan sat next to him and fished out the M&M's. Jimmy smiled, pulling her head towards him for a quick kiss on her hair and shook his head at the offered candy. Dan's arms rose and fell with the ax on the last cut of the once threatening piece of tree and he tossed the last small logs onto the pile before approaching the porch with the ax slung across his shoulders.

"That's not mildly terrifying or anything," Jimmy scoffed and took another drag, expelling his smoke forcefully away from them.

Dan grimaced, Megan could tell he was trying not to, he just really didn't like Jimmy smoking, but steadily said, "I gotta grab a shower. You need one?"

"I'm good," Jimmy shook his head, stubbing his cigarette in the grass until it stopped burning and pushed off the porch step to throw it in the outside garbage bin, Dan had hollered at him too many times about butts in the yard for Jimmy to leave one right in front of him.

Dan moved quickly after his shower, starting a pot of water to boil with his hair damp and a towel wrapped around his waist, setting a blue box of macaroni and cheese on the counter before hurrying to his room. Megan sat on the couch watching a Lizzie McGuire marathon, her jeans hadn't gotten dirty so she'd just changed into a cute baseball style t-shirt with pink sleeves. The hissing of water boiling over the pot made her hop off the couch and rush to the stove, turning the burner on low and watched the rolling bubbles subside. Dan was still in his room.

Megan knew it was an important night, Dan never went out and she couldn't remember the last time he'd had a date. Picking up the blue box, she read the back instructions, scoffing at the seeming simplicity, and plucked the powdered cheese packet out before dumping the hard pasta curls into the hot water, watching as it foamed immediately.

"Hey!" Dan barked and Megan jumped, "What'd're you doin'?"

"Nothing!" she squeaked and cleared her throat, "The water boiled over, I just turned it down 'n put the noodles in."

"Oh," his expression softened as he approached, looking from the pot to Megan and grinned a little sheepishly, "Sorry, I just-"

"I'm not four y'know," she said, slapping the cheese packet in his hand.

"I know, sweetheart," he chuckled, tossing the white envelope on the counter, "Really, I'm just a little," he took a deep breath, "My heads all over the place right now."

"Are you nervous?" Megan nearly sang at him, nudging his side with her elbow.

"Maybe," he grabbed her around the middle, tickling her ribs.

"Da-an, sssst-op!" she shrieked through irrepressible giggles and he let go, tousling her hair, "Hey, I just did it!"

"Couldn't tell," Dan joked, pretending to double over when she punched him in the gut, her knuckles more affected by the hit than his solid torso.

He returned to his bedroom, already wearing one his nice pairs of jeans, apparently still deciding on a shirt, while Megan pushed into the bathroom, grabbing her brush from the second drawer and looked in the mirror. Dan hadn't really messed up her hair, but she brushed it a few times anyway and slid on a pink headband.

"Well ain't you cute," Dan smiled behind her in the mirror, wearing a dark blue t-shirt.

182

"Darlene's right," Megan said, sneaking passed him out of the bathroom as he opened the medicine cabinet for his hair gel.

"Bout what?" he asked absently, meticulously pushing his short hair up and to one side.

"That color looks good on you," she said and saw his reserved grin in the mirror.

"Hopefully Lacey thinks so," Dan remarked, drying his hands on the towel hanging over the shower rod.

"She will," Megan smiled.

Dan squeezed her shoulder as he scooted passed into the kitchen, stirring the pasta with a wooden spoon before foam breeched the pot and shut off the burner. Megan went to plop on the couch, but stopped and flipped around.

"Can I help?" she asked, noting his briefly surprised eyebrow raise.

"Sure, grab the colander," he pointed at the bottom cabinet.

Megan grabbed the strainer bowl and put it in the sink like she'd seen Dan do thousands of times, "Can I pour it?"

"Uh," Dan halted with a potholder on its way to the hot handle, "Okay, yeah, just be careful."

Megan took the potholder and Dan hovered behind her as she picked the heavy pot off the stove, quivering slightly on its way to the sink. Just as she'd watched her brother do many times before, Megan tipped the boiling water and soft noodles into the colander and set the pot back on the burner. Dan picked up the colander quickly and shook the water through the small holes before returning the pasta curls to the pot. She handed him a mangled half stick of butter, setting the gallon of milk next to the stove, and watched Dan eyeballed the right amounts of both before ripping the cheese packet open and dumped the powdery contents into the pot, stirring vigorously. Megan poured a glass of milk and pulled herself onto her knees on the counter to grab a bowl from the high cabinet.

"Get down," Dan ordered, it was a frequent warning, followed by the same argument.

"I can't reach," she whined, snagging a bowl before jumping down, so the reprimand wasn't fruitlessly earned, "Why can't you put 'em lower?"

"Where exactly would you like me to put them?" Dan smirked, gesturing to the limited cabinet space, and Megan rolled her eyes as she always did, grabbing the milk and putting it back in the refrigerator, "Thanks."

"Thanks for dinner," she said, "And the money for the movie 'n stuff."

"'Course, sweetheart," he nodded, returning his attention to the pot and scooped steaming macaroni into the bowl.

"I smell mac 'n cheese," Jimmy walked out of his bedroom in baggy jeans and a black t-shirt, his hair swooped to one side.

"Dig in," Dan encouraged as the phone rang.

He slid the pot back on the stove and grabbed the receiver from the wall, "Hello? – Hey, Mike," he paused and chuckled, "I ain't backin' out on ya, I'm pickin' Lacey up at seven- Okay, yeah, we'll see ya there," and he set the handset back in the cradle.

"Lacey worried you're gonna stand her up?" Jimmy joked, grabbing a bowl from the cabinet.

"That was Mike," Dan scoffed.

"Riiiiight," Jimmy nodded slowly, throwing a wink over his shoulder at Megan and she giggled from the couch.

"You two eat'cher dinner 'n shut up," Dan tried not to smile and headed to his bedroom.

Jimmy joined Megan watching television, devouring their cheesy noodles in the living room. She was surprised he didn't try to change the channel.

Dan returned a few minutes later and an unfamiliar, but pleasant, smell reached her nose. Jimmy noticed it too and their eyes met. His lips stretched into their mischievous smirk and Megan returned it, because she always did.

"Eu de hot date?" Jimmy asked in a dramatic, hoity-toity tone.

Dan's ears colored before he turned around, grimacing nervously as he sniffed himself, "Is it bad? I never use it, crap-"

"Jeezus, man," Jimmy chuckled, "I'm havin' some fun, you're fine."

"I like it," Megan piped up.

"Yeah?" Dan confirmed apprehensively.

"Yeah," she assured him.

"Thanks, sweetheart," he smiled, "I look okay?"

"Very handsome," Megan nodded, eating another forkful of pasta.

"Sears is gonna want'cha for their catalog," Jimmy said, earning Dan's mildly amused scowl.

Jimmy finished his bowl first, dumping it in the sink before checking his hair in the bathroom mirror and said good-bye on his way to the front door.

"What time you comin' home?" Dan asked with a little hardness in his tone.

"I don't know," Jimmy shrugged, "I'll call if I need'ja. What time are you gonna be home?"

"Eleven," Dan answered flatly, "I'll come get'cha, even one, Jim, don't drive."

"I got it," Jimmy sighed, "What time we headin' to Menards tomorrow?"

"I'd like to get an early start on it," he said, "They open at eight, we could get there before Megan 'n I go to service and put it in after."

"Shit," Jimmy rolled his eyes, "Well, I'm definitely not drinkin' tonight."

"If that's all it takes, I'll bust every window in this joint," Dan chuckled, but raised an eyebrow at Jimmy's scowl, "Have fun, be smart."

"I will," Jimmy didn't add a snarky comment, gesturing Megan to give him a hug, "Have a good time at the movie, babygirl."

"I will, love you," she mumbled into his shirt.

"Love you, too," Jimmy kissed her hair and smirked at their older brother, "Have fun, be smart."

Dan laughed and Jimmy cracked a smile, Megan didn't understand what was amusing, but appreciated they weren't arguing.

A little while later, Dan walked her to Sam's house, even though Megan had insisted it was unnecessary. The shadows were long as the sun hung low in the sky and he tossed an arm around her shoulders, pulling her into his side. Megan had never seen her brother so strangely anxious, and, for some reason, hoped Lacey was nervous too.

# Chapter 9

Megan and Sam sat in the back of Darlene's Corolla on the fifteen-minute drive to the movie theater in Sandwich. She always played the popular radio stations and Sam blushed when she'd start dancing and singing to herself. Megan, however, enjoyed her live shows, Darlene had a really pretty voice. Years before, Megan had told her she should've been a singer and remembered the thirty-something, single mother smiling sadly as she'd said she would've loved to, if singing had been 'in the cards'. Darlene quietly did all the sections of *Lady Marmalade*, which Megan found most impressive, while Sam tried to distract her by discussing their expectations for *Shrek*.

The parking lot was packed when Darlene pulled to a stop near the front door. Groups of teenagers, families and couples holding hands made their way into the theater as Sam pushed open the rear passenger door for them to slide out.

"Thanks, Darlene," Megan said, following Sam out of the car.

"Thanks, Mom," he called, already pulling Megan towards the entrance.

"I'll be back around quarter to nine," Darlene nearly yelled through the open passenger window, "Have fun!"

They walked through the revolving door into the lobby and got in the back of the line for tickets. Megan couldn't help noticing Josie and the Pussy Cats was starting just a few minutes before *Shrek* and nudged Sam lightly in the side, jerking her head at the menu board.

He laughed, shaking his head, "Dan'll kick my ass."

"No, he won't," she giggled.

"Fine," Sam agreed, "He'll kick your ass. You can't wait like a week 'n a half?"

"It's such a stupid rule," Megan sighed as they took a step forward.

"Don't have to worry about it soon," Sam did not sound very sympathetic and approached the high counter, "Two for Shrek please."

Megan handed him six dollars, shoving the remaining change from earlier back in her pants pocket. A dollar and change wouldn't buy anything at the concession stand, but the candy weighing down the inside of her jacket made her smirk. A couple years ago, Jimmy had taken her to see Tarzan and managed to sneak in McDonald's burgers and drinks for both of them. Megan didn't know how he had the confidence to do things like that while she nervously passed the ticket taker with contraband in her pockets.

Sam bought popcorn and a large drink for them to share, Dr. Pepper was a mutual favorite, asking for easy ice and requesting their popcorn be buttered in the middle. With the specifically created treats in their arms, and the secret ones lining their jacket pockets, the pair made their way to the dark theater at the end of the hall. Megan followed Sam to the back row, scooting passed a few people until he chose a couple of empty seats close to the middle. The lights dimmed and the scrolling advertisements on the screen changed to previews as they munched popcorn and snuck candy from inside their jacket pockets.

*Shrek* well surpassed Megan's expectations for a PG movie, several times laughing so hard she missed the lines following a particularly funny joke. Shrek and Donkey reminded her of Dan and Jimmy, how the ogre was serious and a bit grouchy, while the carefree jackass relentlessly tried to amuse him. Megan was sure neither of them would see the connection, and decided it was a humorous comparison she would keep to herself.

"That was so funny!" she exclaimed on the way out of the theater.

"The gingerbread man was great," Sam chuckled.

"No! Not the gumdrop buttons!" Megan imitated one of the lines they'd found particularly hilarious.

Darlene's Corolla swooped from the back of the lot as they walked to the stairs in front of the main door, still laughing and reminding each other of their favorite scenes. They explained the entire film to the very patient woman on the drive back. When Darlene pulled into the driveway of her yellow house, Megan thought it was strange to see her home so dark, no cars in the driveway or flicker of the television in the front window.

They were still in movie mode, and Darlene made popcorn while Sam set up *Remember the Titans*, fast-forwarding through the previews.

188

Darlene was watching a very dramatic movie on her kitchen television, taking a small bowl of popcorn from the large one she gave Sam to carry into the living room and Megan followed with a soda in each hand. It was a long movie and they'd both seen it multiple times, so they ended up talking through most of it before a heavy knock sounded on the front door.

Darlene must have seen him walking up, because, when Sam and Megan turned, she was already opening the door.

"You're early," she sounded disappointed.

"Two minutes," Dan chuckled, stepping into the house, "They, uh, well, Mike somehow convinced me to have a fire tonight, so, uh, they're all over there," he jerked his head towards their house and smiled weakly at his sister, "What'd ya say?"

"Cool! Can Sam come?" she asked brightly, turning to Darlene when Dan shrugged his indifference.

"It's almost eleven," Darlene said, "Be home by midnight. Okay?"

"Thanks, Mom!" he nearly jumped before wrapping his scrawny arms around her thin frame.

"And I can have the big TV back for an hour," she smirked.

"I'll make sure he gets home," Dan said, pushing open the screen door.

"Oh, he will," Darlene leveled her son with a fairly intimidating look and Sam nodded, shifting his eyes down.

Megan heard unfamiliar voices in her backyard and hung back a little, letting Dan lead them behind their home. Mike was stacking wood around a few pieces of cardboard in the fire pit, Megan liked how the beginning of a campfire looked like a mini teepee, always finding it a little sad to watch the well-designed structure roast in flames. Mike, however, was not as meticulous about the building process as Dan always was.

"Hi, Megan!" Lacey's upbeat welcome startled her focus on the fire pit, she hadn't noticed the older girls in nearby lawn chairs.

"Hi," Megan forced an awkward, tight lipped grin, shuffling a tiny bit closer to Dan.

Her brother betrayed her, however, with two large strides towards the sisters, finding himself somewhere in between the pairs as he acquainted everyone, "Megan, y'know Lacey, this is her sister, Kayla, and this is Megan's best friend, Sam."

"I know you," Lacey smiled at Sam, "Your mom's Darlene from Pederson's, right?" Sam simply nodded in response, "She's a sweet lady."

He added an awkward smile to his nod the second time.

"Dan, got any lighter fluid?" Mike asked, looking up from his finished creation.

"There's some gas next to the lawn mower in the garage," Dan jerked his head, the door was already open, but the light hadn't worked in years.

"So, what'd you two do tonight?" Lacey smiled, more at Megan than Sam.

"Movies," they muttered together.

"Ooh, did'ja go to Josie and the Pussy Cats? I've been dying to see it, I used to read the comics!" she giggled and Megan shrugged uncomfortably.

"No, we're gonna see that in a couple weeks," Sam nudged Megan with his shoulder.

Dan slid a wheeled cooler towards them and Megan and Sam sat down carefully so it didn't flip.

"Megan's got a birthday soon," Dan winked at his sister and a genuine smile crept onto her face.

"How old are you gonna be?" Kayla sat forward on the woven lawn chair.

"Thirteen," Megan answered quietly, unable to help a small scowl when the two sisters looked at each other and giggled.

"So much happens at thirteen," Lacey turned to her with sincerity, "Enjoy it."

Megan just nodded, but glanced uncomfortably at Sam.

The red gas container sloshed as Mike ambled back from the garage. Popping the yellow top off the spout, he went to lift the jug high over the pit, but Dan grabbed it with what Megan recognized as a less than amused smile.

"I was gonna christen it," Mike chuckled.

"I don't need my house burnin' down, I already gotta replace a window," Dan said, drizzling gas over the lopsided teepee of chopped wood.

Mike handed him a matchbook and the corners of Dan's lips curled a little, striking a few at once and tossing them into the pit, followed instantly by a rush of flames before settling into a less intense blaze. Megan sighed happily in the warmth, watching the fire dance, flicker and grow, it was mesmerizing.

"Tonight has been so fun," Lacey broke the silence after a few moments and Megan saw her brother smile humbly when she commented, "I didn't know you could shoot pool like that."

"Who, Dan?" Mike scoffed, patting the nearly broken lawn chair he was balancing on, "Guy's a hustler on the side, that's how he pays for all this fancy stuff."

Dan laughed, taking a seat on a chopping block stump next to Lacey. Megan found it amusing that, even though his seat was several inches lower, he was still taller than the pretty blonde. She, giggled with the others at her own observation, Mike's joke having gone over her head.

"I got lucky," Dan shrugged, turning to Megan and Sam, "How was Shrek?"

"Funny," Megan smiled, "You'll like it."

"I heard that was great," Lacey said brightly, but Megan's smile slowly faded as she awkwardly nodded.

A shrill ringing echoed from inside the house and Dan rolled his eyes, pushing to stand, and Megan heard him stifle a growl as he jogged around the side of the house.

Mike and Kayla were in a private conversation and Megan felt Lacey looking at her. A little timidly, she glanced at the young woman, hiding a relieved sigh when her focus was on Sam instead.

"So what grade are you goin' into?"

"I'll be a Freshman next year," Sam sounded equally proud and terrified as he answered.

"Oh, cool!" Lacey exclaimed, "High school was great, you're gonna love it! Do you play any sports?"

Sam shook his head, "I did basketball, but, uh, I'm not really into sports," Megan knew that wasn't entirely true, Sam loved watching sports and playing for fun, but he just wasn't as good as a lot of the other boys, making competitive events less enjoyable, his excitement for technology, however, was obvious, "I wanna check out computer club, though, sounds kinda cool."

"That must be new," Lacey said thoughtfully.

"Couple years ago," Kayla interjected suddenly, "They were startin' it up my senior year."

"You like computers?" Lacey returned her attention to Sam.

"They're cool," he nodded.

"I hate 'em," Mike joked bitterly, "Every time I gotta use one'a those damn things I end up wantin' to throw it through a wall."

"That's 'cause you're a caveman, honey," Kayla patted his arm patronizingly and the rest of them laughed.

"Sam's a computer genius," Megan piped up, unsure why when the attention was brought to her and her cheeks warmed.

"That so?" Lacey asked Sam in a gentle, teasing manner.

"Not a genius," he refuted, shrugging modestly, "They just make sense."

"He had to fix the school computers," Megan told them, gaining a little more confidence when the conversation hadn't stopped.

"Really?" Lacey sounded impressed and Mike and Kayla shared an awestruck glance.

"Well, yeah, kinda, it was just a miscommunication to the server," Sam smirked, but Megan could tell he didn't mind the attention since the conversation wasn't revolving around his rapid growth spurt.

"Man," Mike slapped his knee and pointed at Sam, "Kid, you know how to do stuff like that, you better be goin' to college! Shit, we're gonna need people like you with all this technology crap they're forcin' on us," he turned to Kayla and Lacey as he continued, "Did y'all hear about this pod thing they're comin' out with?" the girls shook their heads, as did Megan and Sam, listening eagerly as Mike continued, "They're tryin' to git rid'a CD's, it's this thing, like the size of a deck'a cards they said, and you can put like a thousand songs on it, maybe more, I dunno."

"Where'd you hear this?" Kayla scoffed.

"On the radio," Mike said.

"What's it called?" Lacey leaned forward.

"I don't remember," he shrugged as if that wasn't the point, "They kept callin' it pod, or the pod, your pod-"

"Oh my God, I hope it's called your pod," Kayla exclaimed to her sister and they dissolved into laughter, even Mike and Sam joined in, but Megan only smiled, no idea what was so amusing.

Their laughter was just subsiding as Dan emerged from around the side of the house, his jaw set angrily, but trying to force a smile.

"Everything alright?" Lacey asked sweetly.

"Yeah, all good," Dan nodded, but Megan knew better from his tone than to be convinced.

"Was that Jimmy?" she asked without thinking, and her brother turned with a raised eyebrow that caused an immediate shift in her focus to the ground between her sneakers, her cheeks burning.

"Hey, uh, Mike," Sam came to the rescue, breaking the few moments of silent tension, "What station d'ja hear that on? Sounds cool."

"WGN," the barrel-chested young man answered gruffly, "I'm sure it'll find it's market somewhere, but I like my CD's thank you very much."

"It's like you try to sound ninety-years-old," Kayla teased and everyone laughed.

As the conversation and jokes continued, Megan felt less embarrassed over the silent warning, but still wanted to know what was going on with Jimmy. From the moment the phone rang she knew it had been her free-spirited brother calling in the middle of the night, and no one else could cause Dan to have the expression he did when he'd returned to the fire. Her body betrayed her curiosity, however, as a long yawn caught Megan completely off guard.

"Aaaand there it is," Dan chuckled lightly, checking his watch, "Heya, Sammy, ya got about five minutes to get home, kid."

"I'll be early," Sam smiled and stood, offering Megan a hand up, "She'll be shocked."

They all laughed and Megan gave him a quick hug, "Thanks again for the popcorn 'n stuff."

"Anytime," he nodded and turned towards the others, "It was nice to meet you," Mike and the sisters responded agreeably and Sam shook Dan's hand, "Can I still come over 'n help with the window tomorrow?"

"Yeah, kid," Dan said, "Gonna need all the help I can get."

Sam waved as he took off around the side of their house towards his own.

"What a nice boy," Lacey smiled at Megan, but changed her attention to Dan when Megan looked at her feet.

"He is," Dan said, "Genius too."

194

"That's what we were hearin'," Mike commented, "Told him he better go to college with computer smarts like that."

"Oh, he will," Dan sounded sure in his statement then looked at Megan, "Alright, bed, c'mon."

"Now?" she pleaded, resenting being sent to bed while they were still enjoying the fire in the backyard.

"It's midnight, sweetheart," Dan's tone was mild, but she knew that was only because of the surrounding company, "C'mon, please don't argue with me."

She wanted to, she really did, but, looking at his imploring expression, and sure he would eventually lose patience, company or not, Megan sighed in defeat.

"Fine," she grumbled and started to leave in a stifled huff.

"Good night, Megan," Lacey called, "Nice to see you again."

"Umm, yeah, g'night," she stammered, waving awkwardly and shuffled backwards, relieved when Dan put an arm around her shoulders and told them he'd be right back.

Megan took the porch steps with slow, tired feet and Dan held the door open.

"It's a bit passed your bedtime," he patted her back as she passed and closed the door behind them.

"I'm not a baby," she said irritably, "I can get ready for bed by myself."

"I know," Dan said, "But I wanted to say g'night."

"Oh," Megan's pout curled a bit at the corners of her lips.

At the threshold of her bedroom, her stomach turned a little, scared by the pitch blackness before Dan reached an arm over her and flipped on the light.

"It's dark," she said quietly, looking at him pitiably.

"Your eyes are gonna be closed," he smirked, snipping his fingers at the tongue she stuck out, "Alright, PJ's and teeth brushed, let's go."

He shut her door and Megan changed into an old pair of Jimmy's gym shorts and an oversized t-shirt before heading to the bathroom. Dan leaned against the doorway with his arms folded while she finished brushing her teeth.

"D'ja have fun today?" he sounded tired, but had a grin on his face.

Megan nodded before spitting in the sink.

"How was your date?" she asked, shutting off the faucet and dropped her toothbrush back in the cup with Dan's and Jimmy's.

"Good," but the change in his expression told her he was under exaggerating, "Didn't mind they came over for a fire did'ja?"

"No, it was fun," she said as he followed her back to her bedroom, "But Jimmy'll be disappointed."

"Jimmy can pound sand," Dan growled quietly, but sighed when Megan scowled dejectedly, "There's plenty'a wood, we'll have another."

"Why're you mad at Jimmy?" she crossed her arms, conceding when Dan pointed firmly at her bed and climbed under the freshly washed linens, but insisted, "Did he drink at that party?"

The twitch in Dan's jaw answered before he spoke, "Jimmy has a hard time sayin' no, sweetheart."

"Don't'cha gotta go get him?" Megan sat up, wondering why they hadn't left yet, hoping he wasn't planning on leaving her with Lacey.

"Guess most of 'em were drinkin'," Dan said, "Missy's parents set the boys up in the basement, least that's what Jimmy told me."

"He didn't drive," Megan offered a small shrug.

"No," Dan sighed, "He didn't drive, I'm still not okay with him drinkin', though."

Megan shook her head, "Me either."

196

"Alright, get some sleep," he pulled her head close by the back of her neck and placed a quick kiss on her hair, "We got a busy day tomorrow."

"Can we skip church?" she begged.

"Nope," he smirked, chuckling when she fell backwards dramatically on her pillow, "G'night, Megan, sweet dreams."

He flicked off the light and, without her window allowing the soft lights from the street, complete blackness surrounded her as he shut the door.

"Dan!"

"Yeah?" he opened it again, but didn't turn on the light.

"It's too dark in here," she whined.

Dan sighed, "How 'bout I leave your door open?" Megan nodded, "Alright, go to sleep."

She turned over obediently, waiting for him to leave, and, at the sound of the screen door banging, rolled out of her bed and snuck across the hall into Dan's room.

With the window facing the backyard, Megan could hear the conversation outside clearly and chanced a peek through the bottom corner of his blinds, curling her bare legs and feet under his blankets.

Mike and Kayla had returned to a private conversation, talking very close to each other, and Lacey looked bored until something out of Megan's sight caught her attention. She smiled as Dan walked back around the house and took his seat next to her by the fire, then Lacey leaned towards him and he kissed her. Megan's eyes widened.

Lacey's fingers ran through Dan's short brown hair and his hand found her tiny waist before they separated.

"Well, tonight was fun," Mike commented loudly and the others laughed, nodding in agreement.

"Yeah, I'm glad you guys dragged me out," Dan glanced at Mike and Kayla, sweeping his gaze to Lacey and leaving his attention on her.

"I've only been tryin' for six years," she giggled, laughing louder for a moment when Dan tickled her side.

"Seriously," Kayla joined in their joking, "All I ever heard about was Dan, Mister wonderful."

"Shut up," Lacey retorted, but didn't seem very upset by her sister's comment.

"You were datin' John Miles," Dan threw his hands up, but his tone was also amused.

"And that guy hated you," Mike laughed.

"Yeah, he did," Dan chuckled.

"That was mostly 'cause he thought you fought for Collin to be starting receiver over him," Lacey said.

"Collin was a better receiver," Dan justified.

"Yeah, but him catchin' you starin' at Dan all the time didn't help either," Kayla laughed at her sister.

"Probably not," Lacey joined in her amusement.

"I never once saw you starin' at me," Dan shook his head.

"I was very sneaky," Lacey turned to him with a mysterious smile.

"Obviously not that sneaky," Mike said and they all laughed.

Megan put a hand over her mouth to stifle a long yawn, shaking her head from the buzzing exhaustion, and continued watching the scene between Dan's blinds.

"You had a lot goin' on back then," Lacey's sweet tone was more serious, speaking only to Dan.

"Still do," he shrugged.

"Yeah," she inched closer to him, "Maybe you could use some help, or y'know, at least someone to talk to, or not talk."

Megan knew what flirting was, but Lacey's inflection on her final words was an unfamiliar level to the girl who was supposed to be sleeping.

She didn't hear what her brother said, but he pulled the pretty blonde girl towards him by the back of her neck and brought his mouth down on hers again.

Megan knew she shouldn't be watching, she didn't really want to, but simply couldn't look away. Mike and Kayla had found each other's lips as well and the couples in the backyard silently appreciated their partners in a physical manner. Her face flushed, a bit embarrassed by what she was witnessing, and Megan laid her head on Dan's pillow, deciding to take a break from her eavesdropping until she could hear them talking again.

Her room was bright when she opened her eyes to Dan knocking on her door, fresh from a shower with a towel wrapped around his waist.

"Get up, sleepyhead," he rapped twice more on the open door until she looked at him, "Grab a shower, we got a lot to do today."

Megan turned towards the wall and threw her blanket over her head, unsurprised, but annoyed, when it was suddenly ripped away, curling her legs at the abrupt cold.

"Dan, I'm tired," she whined.

"Well, maybe if you'd gone to bed when I told ya to instead'a sneakin' at my window you wouldn't be," he raised an eyebrow and Megan looked away, "Yeah, that's what I thought. C'mon, up 'n at 'em."

He dropped her blanket in a heap at the end of her bed and left for his own room, closing the door behind himself. Megan forced herself off the mattress, stretching her arms high and lifted on her toes as she yawned. Shaking sleep from her head, she went to the bathroom and turned on the water, already warm from Dan's recent shower.

With a towel around her, Megan stopped and grabbed her pajamas off the floor, tossing them into the hamper outside the door on the way back to her bedroom. It was strange to have to turn the light on in the morning, but, with the door shut on the natural light in the hallway, her room was still very dim. She put on her nicest jeans and a violet t-shirt with stars on it. Despite telling her brother she didn't really like the t-shirt options for girls, Dan always bought at least a couple strictly feminine items when they went shopping.

"You look cute," he commented, setting a plate of eggs and toast on the table when she entered the kitchen, "Got breakfast for ya."

"Thanks," she slid onto her seat and took a fork from Dan as he put down a glass of orange juice.

The high-pitched whine of Jimmy's Oldsmobile brought both their attention to the front door and Megan started to get off her chair, but was stopped by a firm finger pointing at her breakfast.

"Eat," Dan said, "We're runnin' late as is."

Megan slumped in her chair and picked up a piece of toast, watching the door for Jimmy as the porch steps creaked.

"Hey," he trudged in looking tired and kicked off his sneakers.

"Ya hungry?" Dan asked curtly.

"No," Jimmy's refusal sounded almost nauseous as he shook his head and took a few steps towards his bedroom.

"We'll be back in an hour," Dan said, "Better be ready to go."

"Dude," Jimmy sighed, turning to his brother with an exhausted expression, "Missy's dad woke everybody up like twenty minutes ago, I'm on like four hours'a sleep."

"That's my problem?" Dan interjected bitterly.

"C'mon, man, I'm sorry," Jimmy implored, "I didn't drive, I know I wasn't supposed to drink-"

"You said you weren't gonna," Dan reminded him.

"Well I suck!" Jimmy yelled, but lowered his voice immediately, "I was havin' fun, everybody was, and when Missy's parents said we could stay, I figured you'd be cool with it."

"Yeah, 'cause that sounds like me," Dan scoffed, but took a deep breath, "Look, I'm glad ya didn't drive, Jim, but I was really hopin' you'd keep your word about not drinkin'," Megan watched Jimmy hang his head, but Dan continued, "I need your help today. You don't have to come with to Menards, but when I get back with that window you better be ready to work."

"Yeah, okay," Jimmy nodded, "I will, but, uh, I'm gonna go back to sleep."

"Take a shower," Dan's order changed Jimmy's course to the bathroom instead of his bedroom.

Megan finished eating quickly and was putting on her shoes when Jimmy left the bathroom, looking far more refreshed, but still exhausted.

"Dan made a fire last night," she said.

"Really?" Jimmy sighed, "What the hell?"

"There's plenty more wood," Dan jogged up from the basement and shook his head at Megan, "Just stirrin' the pot, huh?"

"I didn't do anything," she protested.

"Mike and the girls came over for a little while," Dan shrugged.

"Oh, so that's why you were okay with me stayin' at Missy's," Jimmy chuckled, "Didn't have your own sleepover did'ja?"

"Mike took 'em home," Dan smirked, but looked sideways at Megan as he said, "I had to remove a snoop from my bed before I could crash."

Jimmy too raised an eyebrow at their sister, "Jamie Bond strikes again."

Megan couldn't help giggling at the seldom used nickname. When she was little she'd called the famous movie spy Jamie instead of James and, along with frequently being caught intruding, the name had stuck for a while.

"It was too dark in my room," she pouted and both brothers chuckled.

"You're such a bad liar," Dan tousled her hair and started shoving his feet into his clean boots, "Jimmy, hit the rack, we'll be back in a couple hours."

"See ya," Jimmy disappeared into his bedroom as Megan and Dan left.

The parking lot was mostly full when they arrived and the few people outside were hurrying into the church before service started. Dan kicked open his door the second he threw the truck in park and was already around the back of the bed just as Megan was getting out of the passenger side.

"C'mon, Meg," he urged, "It's startin'."

"Why do we always have to go to church," she whined, following Dan across the parking lot.

"Because we do," he said simply, it was the only response she'd ever gotten to the question.

Their usual pew in the back had space on the end and Dan gestured Megan to sit before sliding onto the edge, taking their seats just as the reverend was welcoming the parish. Megan glanced at her brother occasionally during the service and, as usual, he seemed equally as unenthused as she was, yet every Sunday they were in the same pew. Their mother used to take them, before she'd only left the house for doctor appointments until her untimely death. Megan vividly remembered the first time Dan had driven to church, she was in a booster seat next to Jimmy, and their mom was in the passenger seat, directing her oldest son where to park in the same lot they walked towards when service was over.

"Dan, Megan!" Lacey's sweet call made Dan turn instantly and Megan hesitantly followed, seeing the young woman hurry down the church steps.

"Mornin'," Dan grinned, returning her hug comfortably, Megan was glad they didn't kiss.

"Mornin'," Lacey took a step back and smiled at Megan, "What're you two up to today?"

"Headin' to Menards now," he jerked his head towards the truck.

"Oh, right," she nodded, "Well, I gotta work 'til five, but maybe I could swing by after and bring y'all some pizza?"

"You don't hafta do that," Dan grinned and Megan saw his ears color.

"I'd like to," Lacey shrugged, "They always tell us to take stuff home, better than throwin' it out."

"Can't argue that," he chuckled and asked Megan, "You want pizza later?"

"I always want pizza," she said, a little embarrassed when they laughed.

"Just cheese though, right?" Lacey winked and Megan couldn't help a small smile, surprised the young woman remembered her pizza preference. Lacey turned to Dan and giggled, "I'll be over a little after five then, but I'm warnin' you now, I smell like garlic bread when I leave that place."

"I love garlic bread," Dan shrugged, but his smile faltered slightly and his ears burned red.

"Well, who doesn't?" Lacey squeezed his arm, "I'll see you tonight?"

"Can't wait," he nodded.

"Me either," they stared at each other for a moment before remembered Megan was still patiently standing next to them and Lacey promised, "One cheese pizza comin' up."

"Thanks," Megan mumbled and walked with Dan to the truck.

When both doors had closed and the engine growled, Megan turned to Dan.

"Is Lacey your girlfriend?"

Dan choked on a laugh, "What? No, of course not."

"Are you sure?" she crooned.

"Yes," he chuckled, "We had a good time last night and might do it again, but no, she's not my girlfriend."

"Not yet," Megan mumbled, giggling madly when Dan's hand found her middle.

"How am I supposed to have a girlfriend, huh?" he joked, tickling her sides, "I already got one girl who takes up all my time."

"And I'm your favorite, right?" Megan's laughter subsided and she leaned towards him with a goofy smile.

"Always, sweetheart," he ruffled her a hair and left the parking lot with the line of church goers trying to get on with their Sunday plans.

Yorkville was about twenty minutes passed fields and farms before Menards emerged in a huge parking lot with a Wendy's near the road. Megan almost asked if they could stop after getting the window, but knew the answer was yes, depending on how she acted in the store, and decided to wait until they were leaving, determined to behave herself, regardless of how bored she became.

Dan parked in the middle and tossed his arm around Megan's shoulders on their way into the huge store. She thought his old GMC looked well suited in the lot full of work trucks, not paying attention to where they were going and felt Dan's hand firmly pull her close as he suddenly recoiled. A minivan, they were about to walk behind, had started backing up much faster than it should have and Megan's stomach lurched at the close call. Dan's jaw twitched as his eyes narrowed at the driver when the minivan screeched to a halt, the woman behind the wheel offering barely an apologetic grimace. Megan felt Dan pull her along again and joined him in giving the woman an angry glare.

The large glass doors slid open as they approached and Megan led Dan through the turnstile, being drawn immediately to the section of light displays. For some reason, Megan found it satisfying when she'd spot two ceiling fans spinning in sync, it was surprisingly rare.

"C'mon," Dan gave her a gentle push to walk with him and they continued passed plumbing and flooring to the window department.

"Hello, can I help ya find somethin'?" a gray-haired man in a green smock looked up from his podium when they approached.

"Yeah, hi," Dan began, "I called yesterday about needin' a double-hung window, twenty-four by thirty-six."

"Dan?" the older man asked.

"Yes, sir," Dan nodded.

"Kris," he extended his hand as he walked around the podium, "I'm the one ya talked to, yeah I got a few of 'em," Megan followed Dan, who followed Kris, further into the aisles of windows, hearing him ask, "Storm get'cha?"

"A tree fell through my window," Megan said, but her lips and grimaced at Dan, but he smiled.

"Sure did," he scoffed lightly.

"Oh, jeez," Kris shook his head, "That must've been scary."

"Kinda," she shrugged.

"Well, I got a few options in that size," he returned his attention to Dan, "I'm guessin' we're just lookin' for the most economical choice."

"Yeah," Dan nodded.

"Need an install?" Kris slid a large, flat box from the bottom shelf.

"Naw, my brother 'n I are gonna put it in."

"Yeah, it ain't that hard," Kris grunted, struggling to lift the packaged window, but Dan stepped forward, leaning down and taking the heavy box effortlessly from him. Kris chuckled as he stood up with a hand on his back, "Thanks, son, I'm gettin' a little old for this."

"Thank you, sir," Dan said, situating the window under one arm.

Megan followed him to the checkout lines, trying to keep her eyes averted from the display of candy, but a milk carton of Whoppers stood teasingly on the shelf closest to her. She found her finger edging along the top of the package, tracing the letters on the logo before she even realized what she was doing and shoved her hand into her jacket pocket. When it was their turn, Dan flipped the flat box to find the barcode so the young cashier behind the register could scan it and Megan watched the girl's eyes flick repeatedly while her cheeks pinkened.

"That's, uh, one-eighty-three-twenty-four," she smiled shyly, taking the two hundred-dollar bills Dan handed her with a tiny, nervous giggle.

"Thank you," he said, taking the change and quickly shoved it in his pocket before hiking the window back under his arm and jerked his head at Megan, putting his free hand on her shoulder as they walked through the automatic doors, "Stay close to me."

Megan sighed, but held in her retort about not being a little kid when she eyed the Wendy's again, "Can I get a Frosty?"

"Yeah, sure," he nodded, "Didn't knock anything over or wander off, I think that deserves a Frosty."

Dan got one too, plus what he called 'hangover food' for Jimmy, and they shared a large fry, dipping them into their chocolate shakes, on the drive home with her new window in the truck bed. Dan had teased Jimmy about his dip choice for Wendy's fries for years, but, when his younger brother had finally gotten him to try it, Dan had had to accept his initital assumption about the sweet and salty combination had been unfounded.

Jimmy's door was still shut when they got home and Dan left to change out of his church clothes, returning a few minutes later in athletic shorts and his 1996 state champions t-shirt, faded and a bit snugger after five years.

"Hey," he tapped Megan on the head, tearing her attention from the television to his wicked grin, "Go get Jimmy up for me."

Megan smiled, hopping off the couch and rushed to Jimmy's door, stifling a giggle as she slipped into the dusky room. The lump under his blankets started with a mess of dark, shaggy hair and ended with his long, bony feet sticking out at the end of his bed.

Megan took a few silent jumps and then launched herself on top of him, yelling, "Hey, Jimmy, get up!"

He yelped and turned over quickly, glaring at her, but his expression quickly softened and Megan sat back on her heels.

"Oh, you're gonna get it," Jimmy promised lightheartedly.

"C'mon," she urged, pulling on his arm, "Dan got'cha Wendy's."

Jimmy grinned and swung his legs off the bed, pushing Megan onto a pile of dirty clothes.

"Hey," she giggled, taking his offered hand and let him lift her to her feet.

"That's what'cha get, kid," he chuckled, patting her behind as he picked a pair of athletic shorts off the floor, "I'll be out in a minute."

Megan shut his door as she left, returning to the couch and channel surfing, not having found anything worth watching.

"Is Jimmy up?" Dan asked, walking up the basement stairs with a basket of laundry.

"Yes, Jimmy's up!" Jimmy yelled behind his closed bedroom door.

"Good, it's only noon!" Dan joked loudly, dropping the basket on the couch next to Megan.

"It's eleven-forty-five!" Jimmy called and his door lurched open, smiling at his brother, "I heard you got me food," Dan jerked his head at the Wendy's bag on the kitchen table and Jimmy folded his hands, bowing dramatically, "You are my savior."

"Eat up, kid, we got a lotta work to do," Dan laughed.

"How was Menards?" he asked, snatching the burger, stripping the wrapper and took a bite in nearly the same moment.

"Expensive," Dan muttered, "I'm gonna get ready to take that board off, come out when you're done."

Jimmy simply nodded, his mouth too full of cheeseburger to even attempt a verbal response.

"Can I help?" Megan asked as Dan opened the front door.

"It's, uh," he grimaced a little, "It's dirty 'n sweaty, I'm gonna be rippin' the trim off the house, just a lotta gross man work."

"You told Sam he could help," she pouted, crossing her arms.

Dan glanced at Jimmy, but Jimmy shrugged, still devouring the burger, and managed a very muffled, "Fee's afkin' t'elp, take a'van'age."

"Alright," Dan conceded with a sigh, "But change, you're not gettin' those jeans dirty."

Megan happily hopped off the couch, hurried to her room to change into her newly dubbed play jeans and rushed outside after slipping on her sneakers, the screen door slapping behind her.

Dan was opening the garage, bending to grab the handle and hauled the steel door up in one motion, the wheels screaming in the tracks begged for lubrication.

The one car shelter was cluttered with boxes, old toys and stacks of things they didn't need but couldn't throw out for sentimental reasons. An assortment of tools was well organized against one wall in a black Craftsman toolchest, taller than Megan, but she could finally, almost, see over the top. It had been Dan and Jimmy's father's and her oldest brother treasured the tools and their solid steel home.

"Are those the fireworks?" she pointed to the cardboard box on the workbench.

"Yeah," Dan grabbed an old coffee can next to it and handed it to her, "Maybe when we're done with the window you 'n Sam can figure out which ones ya want me to set off next week."

"Awesome," Megan nodded, shaking her hands and watched the bent and rusty nails half filling the can jump around on each other.

"Careful," he gave her a sideways glance while grabbing both hammers, using them to gesture out of the garage and hiked the ladder under his free arm before he followed.

Megan didn't say anything, but rolled her eyes as she walked ahead of him towards the front of their house. When they turned the corner, Jimmy was stretching his arms over his head on the porch and descended the steps with a little bounce.

"Feelin' better?" Dan smirked, dropping the ladder in the yard.

"Like a million buck," Jimmy grinned goofily and took the hammer his brother offered.

"Alright, then," Dan surveyed the boarded-up window and flipped the hammer in his hand, "We got our nail collector," Megan shook the can again, "Let's get this board off."

It was a well-choreographed dance, familiar steps even while performing an unfamiliar task. Neither brother was ever in the other's way, moving at nearly the same speed, though Dan was a bit faster at removing the nails. They worked their way up from the bottom on either side, wiping sweat from their brows with their forearms identically, and Megan made sure every nail made it into the coffee can.

"Okay," Dan picked up the ladder and set it against the siding, "I'll hold it while you get those top ones out."

Jimmy was halfway up the ladder before Dan finished, the claw of his hammer wedging around the nail in the right corner.

Within minutes, the board had been tossed to the ground and the black garbage bag again breathed with the breeze.

"You wanna do the outside trim or inside?" Dan asked.

"I'll take inside," Jimmy said, jogging up the porch steps and let the screen door whack its frame behind him, emerging moments later as he peeled the bag away from the window, "Y'know, we should leave your bookcase over there, ya got too many books to move it again."

"No, I like it under the window," Megan stuck her tongue out and Jimmy mockingly returned the gesture.

"We'll worry about redecorating when we get this in," Dan shook his head, "Be careful takin' that trim off, Jimmy, I'm reusin' it."

Dan began gently prying the trim from the siding while Jimmy did the same inside. Silently, and diligently, they pulled the wood surrounding her window from the house, Dan's focus hardly shifting to take the pieces Jimmy handed through the gaping hole and carefully dropped them on the grass.

"Hey!" Sam called as he rushed across the small yards.

"Hey, Sammy," Dan looked up briefly, "Perfect timing, I got a job for you two," Megan smiled, happy he'd included her and watched as her oldest brother took the pieces of trim to the porch steps, setting them on the ground in a line, "Meg, go grab a couple more hammers outta the garage," he jerked his head and she took off around the side of the house, returning quickly with the requested tools and handed one to Sam, "Alright, you two gotta be real careful here. Take your time and go easy," he knelt beside a piece of trim and tapped the pointed end of a nail until it popped out the other side, tossing it in the coffee can.

Sam and Megan set to work, performing the task exactly as Dan had showed them, ensuring each nail made it in the rusty can.

"Hey," Jimmy got his brothers attention with an eager smile, "We ready?"

"Oh, yeah," Dan mirrored his enthusiasm, scooting passed the younger two up the porch steps and into the house.

Megan wondered what they were doing, but the loud ripping sound moments later, followed by a chorus of laughter and pieces of painted wood flying into the front yard, was answer enough. She and Sam took a quick break to watch Jimmy and Dan pry the old window frame from the house. Neither was being gentle and she smiled seeing her brothers enjoy the destruction together.

# Chapter 10

It hadn't taken long to install the new window. Dan let Sam and Megan tighten a few of the bottom screws with his power drill, then he and Jimmy reinstalled the trim pieces inside and out. Jimmy opened the brand-new window and flattened his face on the screen with a goofy smile.

"Hey this thing's pretty sweet. How 'bout we put one in my room."

"Not much to worry about breakin' yours," Dan smirked, "And if you break it, I'll break you."

"Yeah, yeah," Jimmy mumbled, shutting the window and disappeared.

"Hey," Megan turned to Sam, "Wanna bike to the river?"

"Not 'til you're done helpin' clean up," Dan said and she dropped her head exasperatedly, "What? You wanted to help."

Megan rolled her eyes, but picked up the coffee can of old nails and her hammer. Sam went to grab the mess of broken wood below the window, but Dan stepped to the pile first.

"I got this, Sam," Dan extended his hammer, "Put this away for me will ya?"

Jimmy walked out the screen door, swinging the hammer around his finger, "This one too, huh?" he pretended to toss it at Sam, earning a giggle from the younger two and a scowl from his older brother.

"Hey, what're we doin' for dinner?" Jimmy bent down to help Dan pick up the splintered wood.

"Lacey's gonna bring pizza over," Dan said, but Megan didn't hear anything else as she and Sam made their way to the garage.

She set the coffee can on the work bench, dumping her hammer next to it, and Sam shook his head, picking it up and hung it with the others on the peg board. Megan grabbed the fireworks, grinning mischievously, and set the cardboard box on the ground.

"Dan said we could pick a few out for the party," she declared.

"Awesome," Sam crouched next to Megan and joined her in poking through the fireworks.

"Put 'em back, Meg," Dan said as he and Jimmy passed the garage with armfuls of broken window frame, not missing a beat, he turned back to his brother, "Yeah, well, ya weren't wrong."

"I'm never wrong," Jimmy joked smugly.

"Want me to make you a list?" Dan asked, tossing the splintered wood on the pile near the fire pit and peeked back at their sister, "Megan, what'd I just say?"

"You said we could pick a couple out," she reminded, her hands still in the box, but Sam had moved a few steps away and apparently found the lawn mower very interesting.

"I don't want'cha diggin' in there without me," Dan said a little irritably.

"They're not just gonna go off," she scoffed.

"Megan," he raised an eyebrow and growled, "I said not now."

"Fine!" she slapped the cardboard flaps closed and snatched the fireworks off the garage floor.

"Put it back where ya found it 'n get inside," Dan jerked his head at the house.

"Why?!" Megan whined, shoving the box back on the workbench

"It's about to be 'cause'a the attitude," he snapped, "Go vacuum under your window before I move your bookcase back."

Only because Sam was there, she avoided stomping her feet to the front porch and yanked the screen door so it banged louder in the frame than usual. Megan grabbed the vacuum and dragged it to her room, but halted in the doorway.

The room that had been so dark and depressing hours ago was welcoming with light streaming through her brand-new window. She left the Dirt Devil and approached the new addition to her bedroom, easily lifting the glass pane, unlike her old window she'd never

212

bothered struggling with. Megan felt a swirl of guilt as her fingers passed over the smooth, white sill, installed by her brothers' hard work, and wished she hadn't acted the way she had about the fireworks.

Dan's heavy footsteps jogged up the front porch and the screen door slammed.

"Megan," he called, his voice growing louder as he walked down the hallway, "I'm not dealin' with this-"

But Dan's reprimand was interrupted when she met him in her doorway, throwing her arms around him.

"I'm sorry," she mumbled into his sweaty shirt and grinned up sheepishly, "Thank you, I love my new window."

All the hardness in Dan's expression melted as he rubbed a calloused hand on her back, "You're welcome, sweetheart. Looks good, huh?"

"Great," she corrected, rushing to the open window, pulling it closed and pushed it open again, "Look, I can do it!"

He chuckled, "Awesome, but'cha might have a hard time reachin' it with your bookcase there."

Megan looked at the shelf of books shoved in her corner and back at the window, "I think it looks good over there."

"I'm puttin' it back," he shook his head, "Vacuum all that dust up please, I'm gonna grab a shower, don't go anywhere."

"But Sam 'n I were-" Megan let her words trail off as Dan's eyebrow raised slowly.

"Wait 'til I'm out," he said simply and she nodded, resisting an eyeroll.

Megan heard the rush of water when she turned the Dirt Devil off, wrapping the cord sloppily around the handle and carted the vacuum back to the closet by the basement door. Jimmy and Sam were sitting on the middle porch step and turned as she pushed through the screen door.

"Ready to go?" Sam asked.

"I gotta wait for Dan," she sighed, sinking onto the top step dramatically.

"Your life's rough," Jimmy smirked, chuckling at the rude hand gesture she gave him and pretended to take it as a gift, shoving his hand in his pocket.

Megan couldn't help laughing with Sam.

"You stayin' for dinner tonight?" Megan asked.

"Naw" Sam shook his head, "We're goin' to my granpa's in a bit."

"More free pizza for me," Jimmy grinned and descended the stairs, pulling his cigarettes and a lighter from his pocket, but paused his hand and said, "Hey, Sam, your mom's comin' over here."

Sam stood and Megan followed him down the stairs, waving at Darlene. She stopped and smiled, admiring the window.

"You boys did a great job," Darlene told Jimmy.

"Thanks," he nodded, discreetly shoving his cigarettes deep in his pocket.

"Can I steal one from you Jimmy?" Darlene asked, glancing at his pocket, "I've gotta stop on the way out."

"Sure," he smiled, opening his pack for her and taking one himself.

"Thanks," she exhaled and eyed her son, "Sam, we're headin' to Granpa's in twenty minutes go wash up 'n change."

"You said five thirty," Sam complained.

"It's ten after five," she said plainly.

"I'll see ya later," he grumbled, nudging Megan with his shoulder.

"Bye," Megan was equally as disappointed, she hadn't realized it was so late with the sun still high in early summer sky.

"Thanks for the help today, Sammy," Jimmy held up a hand as Sam passed him in the yard.

214

"I didn't do much," he shrugged, completing the high five unenthusiastically.

"C'mon now, we'd still be workin' if you hadn't come over," Jimmy argued and Sam mustered a weak smile before trudging across the yards.

A high-pitched squealing noise grew louder before a small, white Nissan sedan pulled behind Dan's green truck in the driveway. Unlike Jimmy's Oldsmobile, the compact car could fit without the rear bumper overhanging the sidewalk. Megan's stomach twisted slightly as Lacey waved through the driver's window. She waved back, but turned to her brother.

"Pizza's here," Jimmy winked.

"Oh," Darlene had a funny smile and took a drag of her cigarette, Jimmy's was currently resting behind him.

"Hi, all," Lacey waved again as she got out of her car.

"Hey, darlin'," Darlene said, "How's your dad doin'?"

Lacey offered a noncommittal shrug as she approached, "He's tryin'."

"All he can do," Darlene commented sweetly, "I better go make sure Sam's gettin' ready, I'll see y'all later."

Their goodbyes were nearly lost in each other's as Darlene left for her house, cigarette still burning between her fingers. Megan noticed Jimmy's thumb and forefinger inconspicuously rolling between the filter and burning end of his until the ember dropped to the ground and he curled the harmless butt into his fist, all while asking Lacey what they'd done the night before.

"We went to this place up in Plano," she told him, "Mike knew about it, pool, bowling and they had a nice restaurant. The best margaritas. But how was your party?"

"Sounds fun," Jimmy nodded, "It was good, y'know, just messin' around."

The screen door creaked and banged, bringing their attention to Dan, damp-haired, wearing clean jeans and a black t-shirt. Megan saw

Lacey's normally pleasant smile widened and his expression seemed equally enthused.

"Hi," Lacey managed after a moment.

"Hey," Dan's voice was softer than usual.

"Window looks great," Lacey said, hardly glancing at the window.

"Thanks. Took Jimmy 'n I a few hours, but it works," Dan stepped down the porch stairs barefoot and Megan watched Jimmy grind his boot in the grass where the cigarette ember had fallen.

"I helped," Megan interjected.

"You 'n Sam were very helpful," Dan assured her, "Where'd he go?"

"They had to go to his granpa's," Jimmy jerked his head towards the yellow house on the corner.

"Well, are you guys hungry?" Lacey asked and they all nodded.

Dan followed her to her car and, when Lacey leaned through the driver's door to the passenger side, Megan heard Jimmy expel a hard breath. Lacey handed Dan two flat, white boxes and Jimmy tugged Megan's shirt sleeve towards the porch, practically pushing her inside while Dan and Lacey dawdled with their dinner.

"You stayin' home tonight?" Dan asked his brother, setting the boxes on the kitchen table.

"Doesn't sound like anything's goin' on," Jimmy shrugged, "I might head out later, I'm not sure."

"I brought a couple movies," Lacey made her comment mostly to Megan, who forced a smile, "Have you seen Ten Things I Hate About You?" Megan shook her head and Lacey winked, "You'll love it."

"Not tonight, Miss still twelve," Jimmy chuckled, pulling his sister close with an arm around her shoulders and gave her a playful shake.

Megan wrenched away from him and folded her arms.

"C'mon, man," Dan sighed at his brother.

216

"What?" Jimmy laughed, poking Megan in the shoulder, "She's too sensitive."

"Stop it!" Megan whipped an arm at Jimmy, whacking him in the stomach.

"Hey!" Dan barked, but lowered his tone immediately, "Both'a you stop it."

Jimmy rolled his eyes at Megan and headed towards the cabinet for plates and cups. She moved to fold her arms again, but shoved her hands in her pockets, catching Dan's eyebrow raise.

"I'm sorry," Lacey grimaced at Dan.

"You're fine," he sighed, "She's excited to turn thirteen, I kinda got a rule about movie ratings."

"It's a stupid rule," Megan muttered, passing behind him to the bathroom, washing her hands before it became an order.

"I get it," Lacey commented, "I didn't even think, I'm sorry."

"Now you stop," Dan chuckled, "I've never seen that movie either 'n I've heard it's good, for a chick flick."

Lacey giggled and Megan dried her hands roughly on a washcloth, tossing it in a crumbled heap on the sink, instead of folding it like Dan constantly reminded.

Jimmy set plates around the table and Dan was filling three cups from a two-liter of Pepsi, a glass of milk was already sitting in front of Megan's chair.

"I want pop," she said, sliding onto her seat.

Dan stared at her blankly and Megan was sure he would've had something to say if Lacey wasn't there. But she was, and he sighed, reaching across the table for her glass and replaced it with the soda he'd just poured for himself.

That was not the solution Megan was expecting. She actually preferred milk to Pepsi, unsure why she'd made the request, and felt a swirl of guilt in her stomach, worsened by Lacey's clearly unimpressed

217

expression. Jimmy rolled his eyes at her as he took the seat on Megan's right.

"Do y'all say grace?" Lacey asked and Jimmy retracted his hand from a slice of pepperoni he was about to claim.

"We can," Dan nodded, "We don't normally."

"No," she shook her head and grabbed a slice of cheese, "I don't either, I just always see you guys in church."

"Dan says we have to go," Megan said, taking a sip of the soda and cringing at the sweet liquid.

"Yes, he does," Dan agreed, leaning over the table and again switching the milk and Pepsi.

"I go with my granma," Lacey shrugged, "Kayla likes it, I'd rather sleep in to be honest."

Megan nodded in agreement, shoving a large bite of cheese pizza in her mouth. Lacey didn't seem so bad, Megan actually thought she was kind of funny and was happily surprised to find out the young woman was also a fan of the Fire Fox series.

"That's why you went to Milwaukee?" Lacey turned incredulously to Dan, who shrugged ignorantly, "I knew she was in Chicago and was so bummed I missed it, oh Megan that's so cool! Can I see?"

Megan didn't need further encouragement and hopped off her chair, halting at the familiar, low tone.

"Stop," Dan said, "Are ya done?" Megan took the last swig of her milk and nodded, "Wash your hands."

She turned towards the bathroom, before rolling her eyes, and folded the washcloth on the sink when she'd finished.

The second book in the series, Flames, had taken the brunt of the damage when her window had shattered, but Dan had laid it flat to dry and the pages were only a little damp when Megan picked it up off her dresser. She stacked the precious stories on top of each other and returned to the kitchen.

Lacey was leaning against the counter while Dan rinsed the plates and stacked them in the dishwasher.

Dan grinned and asked, "You gonna show Lacey the last one?"

Megan nodded excitedly and set the books on the kitchen table, pushing a mostly empty pizza box aside. She opened the cover of the first book and handed it to Lacey, who grinned while running her finger over the signature.

"This is so cool," she remarked, "Pretty awesome you got to meet her."

"Yeah," Megan smiled at Dan as he pulled the remaining pizza towards himself and a box of tinfoil, "My brother's pretty awesome."

"I'll agree with ya there," Lacey turned to Dan, and Megan saw his ears flush, returning his gaze quickly to the slices of pizza he was stacking on the foil.

"This one's my favorite," Megan flipped open the third book.

"Wow," Lacey's eyebrows jumped and she glanced at Megan before returning to the inscription, "Megan, you must've made an impression."

Megan shrugged modestly, but her grin would not be suppressed, "She was nice, a lot older than I thought she'd be, though."

"Was it a long line?" Lacey asked and, before Megan could even nod, Dan scoffed.

"I'm surprised we're not still standin' in it," he said.

"It wasn't that bad," Megan contended.

"There was a total of three men in the whole place," Dan continued, "Including myself and the security guard."

"You're exaggerating," she giggled.

"Yes I am," Dan chuckled, "It was a good day, besides the line."

"Hey, Megan," Jimmy walked out from the bathroom and leaned on the back of a kitchen chair, "How 'bout you 'n I run up and see Uncle Bob and grab some ice cream for everyone?"

"Yeah!" she immediately hurried to put her shoes on.

"Lacey, ya got a flavor preference?" Jimmy asked, shoving his feet in his beat-up sneakers.

"I'm boring," she said, standing from the table, "But whatever y'all get is fine."

"Jimmy only likes vanilla ice cream," Megan rolled her eyes.

"I'll get'cha chocolate syrup, princess," he said, opening the front door, "We'll be back."

"Drive safe," Dan called over the banging screen door.

Jimmy's car sputtered on with the usual whine and pump of the accelerator before he pulled the shifter down and drove towards the main road. When they got there, however, he turned away from the gas station and further out of town towards miles of corn fields.

"Where are you goin'?" Megan asked.

"Just drivin' around a minute," Jimmy said, "We'll get your ice cream, don't worry."

"Why?" she pestered.

"Why what?" Jimmy glanced over and back at the empty road.

"Why are we drivin' around?" she tossed her arms up in mild frustration.

"Because I said so," he threw his up in joking mockery, "And I'm drivin'."

He turned the radio up, nodding a bit aggressively with the heavy drums. Megan didn't like Jimmy's music, she couldn't understand the screamed lyrics and he always cranked it up too high in the crackling speakers. When one song ended, she reached over and turned the knob down.

"I saw them kissing," she expected him to return their shared smirk, hoping for a little pride in his response too.

Jimmy's reaction was quite the opposite, glancing sideways as he said firmly, "Ya shouldn't've, it's not cool to snoop on people, especially your big brother who never gets a break."

Megan turned to look out the window, hiding a pout and feeling her throat tighten as the truth of his words sunk in. She hadn't been prepared for that reaction, but he wasn't wrong.

"Why'd you do it?" he asked after a few minutes of quiet between them, turning onto another dusty, country road.

Megan shrugged, "I dunno, I just didn't wanna go to bed. You were at a party and they all got to stay out there late, but I," she let her words trail away.

"Look, babygirl," he reached over and pulled her next to him on the seat, "I know ya wanna grow up, but you're gonna have plenty'a time for parties 'n midnight bonfires."

"I'm gonna be a little kid forever," she sighed.

"Naw," Jimmy chuckled, "You're already not a little kid, almost thirteen, goin' into your last year'a middle school, and I don't know a lotta little kids who're five feet tall. Do you?"

Megan couldn't help a small grin and shook her head.

"Don't be so eager to grow up," he said, "It's not all it's cracked up to be, trust me. Enjoy bein' a kid, 'cause someday you're gonna wish it didn't go so fast."

Megan thought that was easy for Jimmy to say, he could drive and stay out with his friends late. But she knew he was at least right about snooping on Dan. She hadn't thought about it at the time, just that she'd wanted to know what they were doing, and her gut swirled with guilt.

Jimmy took another turn, heading towards town on a road that eventually lead behind the gas station. He parked at a pump and Megan followed him into the small store.

"Hey, kids," Uncle Bob looked up from a newspaper as they walked in, "Megan, how'd ya like that movie?"

"It was great!" she smiled.

"Knew you'd like it," he said, "Jimmy, how ya doin', everything good at the factory?"

"Same shit, different day," Jimmy shrugged, heading towards the freezer in the back.

"That's work life, kid," Uncle Bob chuckled, "What're ya up to tonight?"

"Ice cream," Megan told him happily, taking the chocolate syrup Jimmy handed her.

"Well that settles it," Uncle Bob slapped his hand on the counter, "You have the best brothers ever. Don't'cha, little girl?"

Before the pout emerged on her lips, Megan felt Jimmy pat her shoulder and he shook his head.

"Not little anymore, Uncle Bob," Jimmy corrected, "Almost got a teenager on my hands."

"Excuse me," he said apologetically, "Guess I just can't believe how grown up all you kids are gettin', makin' me feel old."

"Tell me about it," Jimmy set the ice cream on the counter next to the chocolate syrup, "Can I get a pack'a reds?"

Uncle Bob tossed the cigarettes on top of the sweating box of vanilla ice cream and Jimmy handed him a twenty, thanking the older man as he took his change. Megan grabbed the plastic bag, swinging it on their way out the door. But Jimmy didn't get in the car, leaning against the store, he lit a cigarette and inhaled deeply.

"C'mon," Megan urged, opening the passenger door and set the bag on the seat, afraid it would get lost in the garbage on the floor.

"I'm smokin'," he waved his cigarette before taking another drag, "Just wait a minute."

"What, ya don't smoke in your car anymore?" she scoffed.

"I'm not supposed to with you," he reminded, snickering at the incredulous look she gave him, "What? I'm thinkin'a your health, babygirl."

"I wanna eat ice cream," Megan whined, slumping against the open door.

Jimmy responded by mimicking a baby's cry and she scowled at him.

"That's what'cha sound like," he said, "Relax, I'm almost done."

"We've been gone for like an hour," she sighed.

"Half an hour," Jimmy remarked, taking another long drag of his cigarette and stubbed it into the overflowing ashtray.

Finally, the Oldsmobile rattled up their street and Jimmy pulled next to the curb in front of their house, but, before he put the shifter in park, he paused in neutral and revved the engine loudly. Megan gave him a questioning look, but Jimmy was already pushing his door open and she followed with the cold bag up the porch steps.

"Wonderin' where you two went," Dan smiled from the sofa, pulling his arm from around Lacey's shoulders as he got to his feet.

"Jimmy wanted to drive around forever," Megan said dramatically, setting the bag on the kitchen table.

"Exactly forever," Jimmy nodded.

"We were gonna set up a movie," Lacey said.

"Can you believe she's never seen Heavyweights?" Dan exclaimed.

"What?" Jimmy laughed, "It's a classic!"

"I'm not a Ben Stiller fan," Lacey shrugged.

"Who is?" Dan chuckled.

"Can we watch it?" Megan asked.

"Yeah, get it set up," Dan jerked his head at the television.

Jimmy grabbed bowls from the high cabinet while Dan peeled off the ice cream lid. Lacey watched them for a moment before turning her attention to Megan, who was working her fingers around the plastic VHS case squeezed into the very full drawer.

"So, it's funny?"

"Really funny," Megan nodded, ripping the movie from between the rest with a dramatic grunt.

Just as Dan sunk the scooper in the ice cream, the phone rang. Jimmy tossed a few spoons on the table, clattering next to the bowls and pulled the receiver from the wall.

"Hello? – Yeah, hang on," Jimmy's noticeable tone change after his greeting told Megan who was on the phone before he turned to Dan, "It's Greg."

She saw Dan stiffen, but he took the phone, jerking his head at the table in a silent request for Jimmy to take up the task, and wedged the receiver between his chin and shoulder. "Hey, thanks for callin' me back," he said before shutting himself in the basement, where he always went when Greg called, and Megan could barely hear his muffled half of the conversation while the spiraled cord swayed between the kitchen wall and the basement door.

Jimmy broke her concentration, "Megan, get the movie started."

"But Dan's on the phone," she said.

"He's seen it," Jimmy raised an eyebrow, looking extraordinarily like their older brother, and Megan rolled her eyes, but pressed play on the VCR.

Dan was in the basement for several minutes, longer than he was usually on the phone with Greg, and Megan was surprised she hadn't heard him raise his voice. She hadn't heard anything since Jimmy made her play the movie. Just as Jimmy was bringing the girls their ice cream, the basement door creaked and Megan looked at Dan, who grinned and gestured the phone in his hand.

"Wanna say hi?" his question was instantly answered as she jumped off the couch and ran into the kitchen.

Dan passed her the phone and ran his hand over her hair as he walked away.

"Hi, Dad," Megan smiled.

"Hey, kiddo. Outta school?" his gravelly voice wasn't slurred, Megan liked when he wasn't drunk, even if their conversations weren't any longer.

"Yeah, I got all A's," she tried not to sound cocky.

"That's what your brother said," his comment sounded almost proud, but Megan wasn't sure, maybe she was just being hopeful, "Good job, keep it up. What else is goin' on?"

"Nothin' really," she wasn't sure what she should tell him, or what Dan already had about the window and decided to avoid the topic, "Darlene's havin' a party for Sam 'n me next Sunday. Will you be home?"

"Couple weeks I'm gonna stop in," he said, "I hope ya have a great birthday."

"Thanks," she mumbled, trying not to sound as dejected as she felt.

"Everything okay there?" he asked, "Dan 'n Jimmy bein' good to you?"

"Yeah, of course," she scoffed a bit at the surprising question, "We're watchin' a movie and Jimmy got ice cream."

Her father chuckled, "Well then I let'cha get back to it. Talk to ya later, Meggie."

Megan cringed a little at the seldom used endearment she despised, but never had the heart to tell him, "Okay, Dad, I love you."

"Yeah, love you too," he said procedurally and the same disheartened feeling that always overcame her after speaking with her father tightened her throat as she hung the phone back on the wall.

"Babygirl," Jimmy called, smiling warmly when she turned around, "Your ice cream's meltin'."

Dan waved her over to the couch and she sat next to him, Lacey was on his other side and Jimmy's long legs were crossed on the chair, his boney knees sticking out over the armrests. She grabbed her bowl from the coffee table and swirled her spoon, combining the melting vanilla ice cream with chocolate syrup more thoroughly. Dan's hand found the back of her neck and kissed her hair before returning to his own desert. She felt a little better from the brief conversation with her father, and shoved a spoonful in her mouth.

The sun set in the window behind the television as they watch the comedy. Lacey laughed so hard at one scene Megan thought she might not stop, it was a very funny part though. When the movie ended it was quarter to nine and Jimmy said he was going for a cruise to see if anyone was around.

"You work tomorrow?" Dan asked.

"Seven PM," Jimmy nodded.

"Crap," Dan said, "Darlene's workin' too. I gotta go to that school meeting."

"She can stay home," Jimmy shrugged.

"I don't know how late it's gonna go," Dan shook his head, dumping the ice cream bowls in the sink.

"I'll be fine," Megan insisted, though she really wasn't a huge fan of staying home alone at night, and offered, "I can go to Sam's."

"Yeah, we'll talk about it," Dan said, "Drive safe, Jimmy."

"Always," Jimmy smirked, shoving his feet in his shoes, "Lacey, thanks again for the pizza, I hope we didn't scare ya too much."

"Anytime," Lacey said and expelled a short laugh, "And you should meet my family."

Jimmy chuckled, tousled Megan's hair and left, the screen door slapping in its frame as he clomped down the porch steps.

226

"Alright bedtime," Dan eyed Megan and jerked his head towards her room.

"But I don't have school tomorrow," she whined.

"Megan," he raised an eyebrow, "Bed, now."

She felt heat creep to her face, a bit surprised he was being so immediately stern with Lacey there, and scowled as she left for the bathroom, but was careful not to shut the door as hard as she wanted to. Megan brushed her teeth and walked to her bedroom, avoiding even glancing towards the living room. Leaving her clothes in a crumpled heap on the floor, she threw on pajamas and climbed into bed, turning towards the wall in what even she knew was a theatrical pout. An expected knock sounded a moment later and Dan entered her room, shutting the door behind him.

"I don't get a good night?" he asked.

"G'night," she mumbled bitterly.

"Megan," he sighed and she felt her mattress sink under his weight as he sat on the edge of her bed, "We had a fun night. Right?" she shrugged under her blanket, "Well, I had a fun night. Why ya gotta get all mad that it's bedtime?"

"I'm not a little kid," she muttered, at the wall.

"Sweetheart," he began, but Megan flipped around, glowering.

"I'm not," she said firmly, "Sam doesn't have to go to bed till ten-thirty 'n that's only when his mom's home."

"Well, Sam's fourteen, baby-" Dan cringed as the word escaped and Megan slammed a fist on her mattress.

"I'm not a baby!" she yelled.

"I know," Dan shushed her, "I'm sorry, I just meant, you're my baby, Megan. Look, how's this? After tonight it's ten. Okay? We'll start a week early, it's summer, I just, can tonight," he sighed and Megan saw the stress between his eyebrows.

"Okay," she nodded, wanting the pained crease to disappear.

"Okay?" he asked.

"Yeah," she said, "Sorry for gettin' so angry."

"I'm gettin' used to it," he rolled his eyes and gathered her in his arms, "Sweet dreams."

"Good night," her words were muffled in his t-shirt.

"I love you, Meg," he said and kissed her hair.

"I love you too, Dan," Megan smiled, no matter how often he said it, it never sounded like an afterthought.

She heard Dan and Lacey's muffled voices in the living room as another movie started playing. Soft laughter peppered their conversation, clearly neither was paying much attention to the show, but soon all Megan heard was the inaudible rumblings from the television as she drifted into a dream.

Jimmy slept the entire next morning, not that Megan minded since she got full control of the remote, but, when Sam walked in at quarter after eleven asking if she wanted to ride around the neighborhood, Megan quietly pushed open her brother's door. His room was dark with the blinds shut tight in the window and the smell of stale cigarettes grew stronger as she approached the shaggy haired lump under the blankets.

"Jimmy," Megan whispered, pushing his shoulder gently, "I'm gonna go play with Sam. Okay?"

"Mhm," he grunted, but didn't open his eyes.

Megan shut his door soundlessly before slipping her shoes on and following Sam outside, careful to catch the screen door before it met its frame.

"Hey, can I come over tonight?" Megan asked as they pedaled down the street, "Dan's gotta go to this school meeting."

"I'm goin' to Matt Weaver's later," Sam said, "His dad got him a pitching machine 'n he invited a few of us to come check it out."

228

"Oh," Megan grumbled, "Have fun."

"Y'know you could if I was home," Sam assured her.

"Yeah, I know," Megan shrugged.

Hoping to check on the baby birds, they raced to the river. Finding the nest empty, however, Megan immediately feared the worst had happened. But Sam confidently contended birds learned to fly early and they were most likely out with their mother.

After managing to find a few hours of entertainment, Sam announced he had to get going and, without better options, Megan dumped her bike under the porch overhang and trudged inside. Jimmy was reclined on the sofa with his bare feet on the coffee table and a bowl of cereal balanced in his lap.

"Hey, babygirl," he glanced away from the television.

"Hey, Jimmy," Megan said, kicking off her shoes and headed to the fridge.

"Pour me a pop would'ja?" Jimmy asked.

Megan grabbed the two-liter of Pepsi with less than a glass swirling around the bottom, but didn't see the milk carton.

"Where's the milk?" she asked and Jimmy responded by lifting his cereal bowl, "Man, I hate Pepsi 'n there's nothin' else to drink."

"Water," he suggested.

"Gee, thanks," she scoffed, shoving the two-liter at him.

"No, thank you," he smirked, and guzzled the last of the soda.

Megan sat with Jimmy watching television, getting up during commercials to recheck the refrigerator from famished habit, not because she expected the contents to change, and closed it in mild frustration every time. Jimmy's suggestion of dry cereal and his offer to heat up SpaghettiOs were bitterly refused, and Megan stewed cross-armed on the couch as her stomach started to rumble. When Dan's truck growled into the driveway, Jimmy got up to dump his bowl in the sink and the empty Pepsi bottle in the trash.

"Hey," Dan said as the screen door banged and he kicked off his boots.

"Hey," Jimmy jerked his head at the couch, "Fair warnin', she's hangry."

Megan rolled her eyes, but couldn't disagree, so she didn't respond.

"What'd you eat today?" Dan asked.

"Cereal," she shrugged.

"She was out ridin' around with Sam all day," Jimmy said.

"So?" Megan challenged and her brothers rolled their eyes at each other.

"Ya want Spaghettios?" Dan asked.

"Tried that," Jimmy muttered while she shook her head.

"Well, what'cha want?" Dan tried and Megan shrugged, "Not helpful, Meg."

"I don't want Spaghettios," she grumbled.

"Want me to heat up some pizza from last night?" his offer was met with an immediate, happy nod.

"I thought you took that for lunch?" Jimmy accosted his brother.

"Not all of it," Dan shook his head, "It's in the foil on the top shelf."

"Hell, yeah!" Jimmy turned to the refrigerator as Megan leapt off the couch.

"You finished the milk!" she accused angrily, pushing between Jimmy and the open fridge.

"Guys," Dan nearly yelled, "There's plenty, relax."

"Yeah, relax, shrimp," Jimmy wrapped his arms around Megan, picked her up, turned around and dropped her behind him, flipping back to the open refrigerator and snatched the foil packet off the shelf.

"Jimmy!" Megan stomped her foot.

"Megan!" Dan barked before lowering his tone, "No one's gonna starve ya, Jimmy's gonna make you a plate. Ain't'cha, Jim?"

"Right here, brat," Jimmy said, tossing three slices of cheese on a plate.

"Thank you," she crooned sweetly, earning another eyeroll from her brothers.

Megan and Jimmy finished the leftover pizza and Dan ate SpaghettiOs before Jimmy started digging through his room on his usual, last minute search for his work shirt and Dan showered. Megan wasn't thrilled about Dan's insistence she had to go with him to the school board meeting, not that she'd prefer to stay home by herself, but if she was stuck reading a book for a couple hours she'd rather it was in her own living room than a bench in an empty school hallway. Unfortunately, her brother was adamant that she accompany him, insisting it might run too late for her to be home alone.

"Jimmy used to babysit me when he was my age," Megan whined on the way to Dan's truck.

"Not late at night," Dan reminded, "I just don't know how long this is gonna go, Meg, it could be a couple hours."

Megan shut the heavy door, expelling a frustrated sigh, and opened Ashes, the third installment of the Fire Fox trilogy, hopeful Mrs. King would be at the meeting and she could show the librarian A.K. Foreman's inscription. She closed it again, setting the book in her lap when Dan accelerated onto the main road, reading in the car always gave her a headache.

The front row of the school parking lot was already full when they pulled in behind a silver Saturn. Dan stopped the truck in a middle spot and Megan followed him to the main entrance. Mr. Jarsen was getting out of his beige Ford Taurus and waved them over as he grabbed his sport coat off a hanger in the backseat.

"Hi, Mr. Jarsen," Dan said and Megan gave her principal a small wave.

"Hello, Dan," he said, pulling on his jacket, "Megan, how's summer so far?"

"Good," she said quickly.

"Jimmy's workin'," Dan explained, "I didn't have anyone to watch her."

"I don't need to be watched," Megan muttered, rolling her eyes at Dan's sideways glance after he turned his attention back on the principal.

"Perfectly fine," Mr. Jarsen chuckled, "These things can get a little longwinded. You wouldn't wanna be by yourself all night would'ja?"

Megan shrugged, shuffling a tiny side step closer to her brother.

They followed Mr. Jarsen through the front doors and into the library. Several of the small tables had been pushed together into the middle of the room with chairs surrounding the massive, make-shift table and a stapled packet sat in front of each spot. Several of the seats were already occupied by teachers Megan recognized, and a few adults she didn't, but, when Ms. Craft met her eyes, she slipped behind her brother's broad back. Her shelter didn't last long, though, because the teachers noticed they'd arrived and most of them got to their feet, greeting Dan with handshakes and smiles.

"Daniel, you look great," Mrs. Tursa said and grinned at Megan, "I'm looking forward to having you in eighth grade with me next year."

Megan nodded as Dan replied, "Thanks, Mrs. Tursa, she's excited, trust me."

"Dan, I'm so glad you came," Mrs. King exclaimed, waddling over behind the rail-thin eighth grade teacher, "Have you spoken with Dotty Clark?"

"Last week," he looked down in a silent request for her not to continue.

"We should get started," Ms. Craft called to the lively room.

Megan watched Mrs. King and Mrs. Tursa roll their eyes as several grumbles could be heard from the adults taking seats around the table. Megan glanced up at Dan and grabbed hold of his shirttail, hoping he didn't leave her standing there, unsure where to go.

"Megan," Mrs. King gestured to her office behind the library checkout counter, "Would you like to read somewhere quiet?"

Dan nodded and gave her a gentle push.

Megan poked Mrs. King's arm gently as they walked and, when the older woman looked down, she opened the front cover of her book with a proud grin. Mrs. King put her hand over her mouth and inhaled softly, leaning down to examine the book closer.

"How was it?" the librarian asked with hushed excitement.

"Awesome," Megan giggled, "She was really nice."

"I'm so glad you got to go," Mrs. King said, opening her office door, "I knew Dan wouldn't disappoint you."

Mrs. King's office was small, but warm and inviting. She had a plushy chair, that was very well worn, and colorful pictures students had drawn for her over the years covering the walls. Megan thanked her, crossing her legs on the chair as soon as Mrs. King shut the door and opened her book, falling back into the familiar story.

It wasn't long, however, before she realized how thin the door between the small office and the large room was, and many of the adults were deafeningly passionate.

"That is not the only issue we're here to discuss, Cheryl," a harsh woman's voice said, Megan was sure it was Ms. Craft.

"I think it's the only one most of us are concerned about," Mrs. King snapped.

"I don't understand what there is to discuss," the first woman spoke again, definitely Ms. Craft, "Illinois education laws require that all students have a parent or legal guardian sign their forms, if neither exists that child must be a ward of the state in which case the state has special circumstances for foster children-"

"She's not a foster child!" Mr. Jarsen growled, "Dan has never forgotten a form or missed a parent teacher conference-"

"He should not be the one attending those meetings," Ms. Craft challenged.

"Well then no one will!" Mr. Jarsen barked, "You don't understand what they're dealing with with her father."

"I can sympathize," Ms. Craft said, and a symphony of frustrated scoffs followed, "But we have deadlines and rules in place for a reason."

"Excuse me," another woman interrupted, "Ms. Craft, what grades have you taught?" a moment of silence followed the question, "So, you must understand from those of us on the front lines that this is a special circumstance and should be treated accordingly."

"With all due respect to you and the other front liners, Mrs. Larsen," Ms. Craft sounded even meaner, if that was possible, "This is a black and white issue. Megan must have her father sign her forms for next school year, I'll consider extending the deadline, but I cannot allow this to continue."

"What if I'm gonna be her legal guardian?" Dan's voice made Megan listen closer, already off the chair with her ear pressed to the crack by the floor.

"Are you?" Ms. Craft asked with the same sneering tone.

"I've started the paperwork," he said.

"Her father will have to agree," her condescension was pointed.

"He already has," Dan growled.

Megan's stomach turned and she sat up on the floor. His words settled, and she understood her father had agreed to relent his parental rights to her brother. It wouldn't change her life at all, but there was still a squirming sense of abandonment in her gut while listening to the excited murmurs following Dan's proclamation.

"We will need that documentation," Ms. Craft said.

"He won't be in town until the end of the summer," Dan said, "But he's agreed. Look, ma'am, I'll get this handled, I promise, I just want my sister to be able to play volleyball with her friends when school starts."

"Of course, she will, Dan," Mrs. Olsen's peppy voice chimed in.

"As long as we have all the proper documentation by the first day of next year," Ms. Craft said, "I'll extend both deadlines."

"Thank you, ma'am," Dan said, "You will."

Megan didn't return to her book as she sat back in Mrs. King's chair, thinking about what she'd just heard while the conversation turned to the need for new text books in the science department. The door opened and Dan grinned.

"Ya ready to go?" he asked.

Megan nodded, sliding off the chair with her book and followed Dan out of the library, absently returning her teachers' waves goodbye.

"You don't have to stay?" she asked when the door shut behind them.

"We can thank Mrs. King for gettin' it outta the way," he said.

"Did my dad really-" Megan bit her lips, but, when Dan stopped, an explanation burst from her lips, "I couldn't help hearing!"

"C'mon," Dan urged gently, "Let's talk in the truck."

She nodded, but fought confused tears through the parking lot, hopping onto her side of the bench seat when they reached the old GMC.

"Okay," Dan sighed after shutting his door, "I just haven't had a chance to tell you yet, it wasn't that I wasn't gonna."

"So, what happens?" Megan asked.

"Nothin'," Dan scoffed lightly, "Least not with you, everything's gonna be the same, but this way I can sign all your stuff 'n put you on my insurance. It's just legal stuff, sweetheart, he's still your dad."

"And he's okay with it?" she asked.

"He understands it makes things easier," Dan said, inquiring further, "Are you okay with it? If I'm your legal guardian?"

"Sure," she shrugged, "I kinda thought you were."

Dan chuckled as he turned the engine over with a loud rumble and left the school parking lot.

Megan thought about what he'd said as they drove home. Dan was right, it wouldn't change anything, except her father might come home even less than he already did. Part of her was saddened by the idea that he was willing to give all responsibility for her over to Dan, but Megan rationally knew there was very little responsibility her brother didn't already have.

# Chapter 11

Darlene was in full party planning mode the entire week and, while he tried a few times to offer his assistance, she repeatedly told Dan everything was under control. He seemed to appreciate her creativity for the upcoming Sunday in the park, but at one point did get a little frustrated when she refused money from him, which Darlene eventually took, despite insisting it was unnecessary.

Megan and Sam were only focused on the games they planned to play and agreeing on the cake flavor. She was fighting for chocolate, but Sam contended more people liked vanilla. Megan didn't understand why anyone would prefer vanilla to chocolate, but Darlene had assured them it could be both, ceasing the debate with an agreeable compromise.

"So, Megan," Lacey began after they'd eaten dinner Wednesday night, she'd brought pizza over again, "What'd you want for your birthday?"

"Nothin' really," she shrugged.

"C'mon," Lacey urged, "There's gotta be somethin'."

"I mean, there's a few books I kinda want," Megan admitted.

"How come she gets the goods?" Dan joked from the sink, "I've been askin' you for weeks."

Lacey shushed him teasingly, "Girl talk."

"Well, excuse me," Dan acted offended and the girls giggled together.

Megan was pretty sure Lacey was his girlfriend, at least she hoped so, it was nice to have another girl around, and she especially enjoyed how much pizza they'd had lately.

"Lacey, thanks again," Jimmy said as he rushed from his room to the front door, buttoning his factory shirt while working his feet into his boots.

"You're very welcome, Jimmy," she repeated, "Have a good night at work."

"I'm sure it'll be thrilling," Jimmy rolled his eyes.

"Hurry up," Dan glanced at the microwave, "You're runnin' late."

"No shit," Jimmy scoffed, grimacing at his words even before Dan raised an eyebrow and hurried out the front door, the screen door banging as he clomped down the porch steps.

"Sorry for that," Dan muttered.

"I've heard much worse," Lacey laughed and turned her attention back to Megan, "Your party sounds like it'll be a lotta fun this weekend."

"Ya wanna come?" Megan asked and Lacey's eyebrows jump with surprise.

"I'd love to," she smiled.

Megan and Lacey talked for a while, Dan hardly getting a word in, though he didn't seem to mind, and just grinned as they chatted. Megan didn't argue when he encouraged her to go to bed at 9:30, she'd have gone to bed sooner if he'd asked, knowing they wanted some time alone.

In the morning, she woke early, too early, and flipped over to go back to sleep, but a feminine giggle in the yard got her attention and Megan rolled out of bed. Peeking through the blinds, she saw Dan kissing Lacey against her car in the driveway and quickly jumped back in bed, but found returning to a dream suddenly difficult.

She heard the squeal of Lacey's white sedan fade, then the slap of the screen door in the frame. Dan walked through the house, up and down the basement stairs and around the front room, eventually peeking in her room to find Megan very convincingly asleep.

Just before the screen door banged again, Megan heard the scratch of Jimmy's wheels. Dan's heavy footsteps thudded on the porch and Jimmy's car door slammed.

"How was work?" Dan asked.

"Same ol'," Jimmy sounded as enthused as he usually did after his shift, "How's your night?"

238

"Good," the small crack in Dan's voice confirmed he was grossly downplaying his evening's events.

"I like her," Jimmy said, "And she feeds me."

"Well, that'll win your heart with anyone," Dan chuckled.

"Is there any left?" Jimmy asked.

"In the foil," Dan said.

"Cool, thanks," Jimmy said and Megan heard him jog up the porch steps.

"Save some for Megan," Dan ordered.

"I won't starve the princess I promise," Jimmy vowed sarcastically and Megan stuck her tongue out in his general direction, "Have a good day at work."

"Thanks," Dan said, "I'll see ya later."

"Later," Jimmy called and the screen door banged a moment later.

Sometime after the microwave beeped, Megan felt her eyelids getting heavy and, when she opened them to look at the clock on her nightstand, it was nearly noon. Her stomach ached, not like she'd eaten something rotten, it was an uncomfortable cramping she'd never felt before, but Megan definitely wanted it to stop. She forced herself out of bed and dragged her feet to the kitchen, deciding she needed to eat something.

A bowl and a half of Cinnamon Toast Crunch later, however, she still had the strange uneasiness in her lower abdomen. Megan set the half-eaten cereal on the coffee table and went to the bathroom, hoping that would help. But when she turned around to flush, her eyes went wide at the splotches of bright red in the water. Megan's stomach dropped and twisted, not at all helping the dull pain still resting below her belly button.

Folding several sheets of toilet paper, she'd heard a few girls at school say they did that when they didn't have anything else, Megan placed them where they needed to be placed and washed her hands thoroughly before leaving the bathroom. Then she stared at Jimmy's closed bedroom door for several minutes, mustering the courage to wake him, and finally, she did.

"Jimmy?" Megan whispered from the doorway, carefully walking around the mess of clothes and magazines, "Jimmy, you awake?"

"Obviously not," he mumbled, "Go away."

"I, uh," Megan felt heat creeping up her neck, "I need your help with somethin'."

"What?" he grumbled, still facing the wall.

"I need to go to the store," she said, hoping he didn't ask why.

"Why?" Jimmy sighed.

"I, uh," she couldn't find the words, tears were filling her eyes as her throat tightened and Megan wasn't even sure of the entire reason, so she just started sobbing from the emotional confusion.

Jimmy flipped upright in obvious frustration and practically yelled, "What the hell are ya cryin' for?"

"I g-ot m-y period," Megan stammered.

Jimmy's jaw dropped open and, for a few moments, the only sound in the room was sniffling as she wiped her face with the back of her hand.

"Ya sure?" he asked finally and Megan narrowed her damp eyes, "Okay, yeah, uh, shit, uh, yeah, I have no idea what to do here."

"I don't really either," she admitted.

Jimmy scoffed lightly, shaking his head and pushed off his bed, "Well, you're growin' up, kid, congrats or somethin', I think."

"Thanks," Megan muttered, her cheeks burning, and followed Jimmy from his room, "What're you doin'?"

"Callin' Dan," he said.

"Why?" she asked, horrified.

"He'll know what to do, I hope," Jimmy added as he picked up the phone and dialed the shop, smirking at the scowl Megan was giving him, "What? He's gonna find out. Or are you plannin' on doin' your own laundry now?" she stuck her tongue out and Jimmy returned the gesture before talking into the phone, "Yeah, is Dan available? – Thanks," there was a few moments of silence and he actively avoided looking at her, "Hey, brother – No, not, wrong, exactly – Well, uh, Megan sorta – Dude, she's fine. She got her uh, y'know, the girl thing, her, uh – Yes! What do I do? – You gotta know! – Yeah, but which one? – That's why I'm callin' you! – Okay. Ya think they got 'em at the store in town? Never mind, I ain't goin' there – Damn straight. We'll go to the Walgreens across the river. Where they gonna be? – Well, damnit Dan you have been no help. – Yeah, thanks. – Alright, I will. – Bye."

"What'd he say?" Megan asked.

"Nothin' useful," Jimmy grumbled, "He says congrats or somethin' too."

Megan just looked down and blushed again, it was not something she wanted attention for, let alone repeated congratulations.

They both dressed and were in the Oldsmobile in a matter of minutes.

"You're not gonna, like," Jimmy cringed teasingly, "on my seat are ya?"

"Shut up!" Megan couldn't help laughing as she punched him in the arm.

"Hey, okay," he chuckled, "Least I know why you've been so moody lately."

"Why?" she inclined her head.

"It's a thing," Jimmy shrugged, "PMS, girls get all pissy 'n cry over everything when they get that."

"Every time?" Megan asked.

"That's what I hear," he said and Megan dropped her head, "Yeah, tell me about it."

They passed the movie theatre on their way and turned into the Walgreens parking lot. Jimmy pushed his door open, but Megan didn't move.

"I ain't doin' this alone," he informed her and she begrudgingly got out of the rusty sedan.

Megan followed Jimmy passed the automatic sliding doors and through the aisles of cards and candy to the pharmacy section. He peeked down one row after another, finally turning when they reached the end. But what they were looking for was not on the shelves of vitamins and supplements. Megan pushed her thumb into her abdomen, it helped a little, but not much.

Jimmy rounded the end of the aisle and continued into the next with Megan shuffling behind. Again, there was nothing related to feminine products among the pain relievers and Megan sighed from frustration and discomfort.

"Relax, we'll find 'em," Jimmy muttered.

"Can I help you find somethin'?" a brunette wearing a white lab coat stopped as she passed their aisle.

"I, uh," Jimmy glanced at Megan, who blushed and looked at her sneakers, "Think we're okay. Just, uh, girl, er, woman, stuff?"

"Come with me," the pharmacist led them away from the pain relievers and smiled at Megan, "First one?"

She nodded, trying to look at the floor, but, when they turned into the next aisle, the seemingly endless choices of brightly colored boxes lining the shelves stole Megan's attention. There were so many choices. Pads or tampons, and then the decision of size! Light, regular, super or super plus, though Megan was at least sure the latter was unnecessary. Heat rushed to her face again as she stared at the rows of options, blinking away the sting of tears and swallowing hard on her squeezing throat.

"Alright," the pharmacist picked one and handed it to Megan, "This'll do ya. How's your stomach?"

"Hurts," Megan admitted.

"Got any Tylenol and a heating pad at home?" her question was directed at both Megan and Jimmy.

"Yeah, somewhere," Jimmy said.

"That'll help," she nodded.

"Thank you," his grin was full of appreciation and embarrassment.

"Not a problem," the pharmacist turned her sincere grin on Megan.

"Thanks," she mumbled and followed Jimmy towards the front of the store.

At the register, he jerked his head for her to put the box on the counter and tossed a Hershey's bar next to it.

"I heard it helps," Jimmy said and Megan leaned into him.

Lacey came over that night. She'd been over every day except Monday since their date, though Megan was fairly certain she'd only spent the night once. If Dan had said something, Lacey did a very good job of acting shocked when Megan told her the news. Somehow congratulations from her was less humiliating than it had been from her brothers.

The young woman shared a few pieces of advice, agreeing with the pharmacist about a heating pad being helpful for cramps, and Megan appreciated everything Lacey offered. She was also grateful her brothers had decided to find something to do in the garage while they talked.

Megan made sure to follow Lacey's guidance over the next few days and was glad when Saturday night proved the situation was over. At least the first one. But Megan was just relieved she wouldn't have to worry about it at her party the next day.

Sunday arrived and Megan woke before Dan, showered and took much longer on her hair than normal, finishing in her bedroom after Dan insisted she leave the bathroom.

Megan changed her shirt three times before deciding on a peasant-style top Darlene had gotten her, for no reason other than she'd said it was in fashion and knew it would look nice on Megan. A quick rap on her door preceded Dan walking in the room, dressed in a white button-down and clean jeans.

"You're wearin' that for football?" Megan giggled.

"No," he smirked, "I'm wearin' this for church, your party's not till one, Darlene's not even startin' settin' up 'til noon."

"Dan!" she whined, sitting hard on her unmade bed and tossed her arms up in frustration, "Just once? Please? Darlene 'n Sam aren't goin' today!"

"Well we are," Dan said firmly, "So let's go."

"I hate church," she insisted.

"We're still goin'," he shrugged and Megan fell back dramatically on her bed, "C'mon, you got a fun day planned, let's not ruin it."

"Okay," she sat up, "Let's not go to church then."

Dan sighed and hung his head before looking back at his sister, "I'm gettin' in the truck, Megan. If you're not out there in two minutes we're gonna have problems."

Megan heard the screen door bang and let out an annoyed growl as she pushed off her bed. She knew Dan didn't enjoy church any more than she did, he was always yawning and never sang with the parish, at least that much Megan enjoyed. Passing Jimmy's closed bedroom door, she stuck her tongue out in jealousy of her brother who wasn't forced to sit through an hour of boring sermons every week.

It was as dull as expected and Megan tried to pull Dan to the truck when service ended, but, as usual, he got caught in conversations on their way. She tried to feign patience, though scowled every time he met her eyes, Megan welcomed the distraction when someone tapped her shoulder.

"Hey party girl," Lacey smiled, "You should be gettin' ready."

"Tell him that," Megan jerked her head at her brother.

"We got plenty'a time," Dan smirked, pulling Lacey into his side with one arm and quickly pecked the top of her head.

Megan saw a few parishioners glance at the pair with intrigue, but, with their eyes locked for those few moments, Dan and Lacey only seemed to notice each other.

"Are you coming?" Megan asked.

"Yeah, of course," Lacey said, "I forgot Kayla 'n I were gonna do some shopping in Yorkville, she's a little salty I ditched her, but she'll get over it."

"Bring her," Megan offered, glancing quickly at Dan, knowing his eyebrow was raised and his expression didn't disappoint.

"I could ask her," Lacey looked questioningly at Dan, who nodded, "Okay, I'll see what she wants to do, but I'll be there either way."

"Cool," Megan said.

"Can't wait," Dan pulled Lacey in tighter before letting her go and saying good-bye as they walked towards the green truck in the emptying lot.

"So," Megan crooned slightly, "Is Lacey your girlfriend now?"

Dan smiled and his ears turned a light shade of pink, "I hope so."

"Me too," she said.

When they got home, Dan shut himself in his bedroom to change, telling Megan to wait for him before running over to Sam's house. She plopped on the couch and mindlessly surfed television channels, wishing he would hurry. Jimmy's door was still shut, he wouldn't be up until the afternoon, but had promised Megan he'd stop by the party.

"Okay, kid," Dan said as he walked back in the front room, "You ready?"

"Been ready," she said, turning off the television and jumped to her feet.

They walked across the short yards to the yellow house on the corner where Darlene was bustling around her kitchen, readying food to take to the park. After pausing a moment to gush over how cute Megan looked, Darlene said Sam was cleaning his room and she hurried out of the way, finding her best friend sitting on his bed listening to his boombox while leafing through a video game magazine.

"Hey," Megan shut the door behind her.

"Hey," Sam sighed, "The party's not even at our house and she's makin' me clean my room."

"Have you even started?" Megan giggled, though had to admit Sam's room wasn't anywhere near as messy as hers usually was.

"She won't care," he shrugged, "It's just what she tells me to do so I stay outta her way."

"Dan's goin' to get his truck in a minute so we can load everything for the park." Megan said.

"Cool," Sam nodded, "I like that shirt."

"Thanks," Megan glanced down at the flowy top, "Your mom got it for me."

Sam helped Dan load the truck bed with coolers, extra folding chairs and the bags of assorted party necessities Darlene had packed. When they finished, Megan begged him to let her and Sam ride in the back on the way to the park. Dan never allowed her to ride in the bed, but it was only a block down the neighborhood street and, with the help of Darlene's instigating shrug, he relented. They climbed over the tailgate before he could change his mind.

The playground was full when they arrived, but the park district had taped red 'reserved' signs on three of the picnic tables near the large field. Darlene pulled the tags off the tables while Dan dragged the cooler and a bag of charcoal next to a square grill, cemented into the ground.

"You're sure it's alright I invited Lacey?" Dan asked as they unpacked.

"Of course," Darlene said, "Now it's not weird that I did too."

Dan chuckled, "Oh yeah, when was that?"

"I eat pizza sometimes too, Dan," she smiled.

"She might bring her sister Kayla," he said.

"Good," Darlene nodded, "We have more than enough food, and it'll be nice to have a few people older than middle school to talk to."

"I'm in high school now," Sam corrected.

"Of course," Darlene rolled her eyes with a grin, "Forgive me."

When their friends started showing up, half of one table quickly filled with gifts for both of them. Megan couldn't help eyeing the growing pile, occasionally, pinpointing a few that were obviously for her, being wrapped in pink with curly ribbons. A few parents hung around a little while, chatting with Dan and Darlene as she continued arranging snacks on the table and he readied the charcoal grill.

Sam grabbed his football, hardly needing to encourage any of the boys to follow him onto the field, and Megan joined immediately, urging the other girls to partake, but only a couple did. Megan didn't get why they'd rather coordinate silly cheer routines than play football, but it was on a long list of things other girls did that she didn't understand.

"Megan," a boy from her class waved her over, breaking his whispered conversation with part of the group, "Can you ask your brother to throw? We wanna play five hundred."

"Yeah!" she nodded, excited by the idea, and ran to Dan by the grill.

"Hey, havin' fun?" he asked, but inhaled nervously when she skidded to a halt in the gravel by the picnic tables, "Careful."

"Will you throw for five hundred?" she panted.

He looked at the recently lit grill and shrugged, "Sure, these gotta burn a bit."

"Thank you!" she jumped, bolting back to her friends and Dan followed, at a normal pace.

Sam tossed him the ball and Dan stretched his fingers around the laces with a small grin. Megan moved backwards with the others, proud they all knew what to expect when her brother threw a football, and he didn't disappoint as the first toss launched high into the air and Dan yelled, "One hundred!"

The adolescent herd ran towards the spiraling football and two of the boys collided as one of them folded his arms around the pigskin before they toppled to the ground. Both jumped to their feet laughing while the one who'd successfully caught the ball held it triumphantly in the air.

"I got one hundred!" he yelled, throwing the ball back to Dan.

"C'mon, Dan!" Lacey called, crossing the field with Kayla, "You can throw farther than that!"

"Yeah!" the boys cheered encouragingly, running towards the end of the field while waving their arms.

"Alright," Dan chuckled, "Jackpot!"

A few kids gasped at the prospect of winning the game in one catch, readying themselves for the opportunity. Dan took a few steps, his right arm stretched behind him and then snapped over his shoulder. The football soared high over Megan's head and she watched it sail passed the group who'd retreated, landing at least twenty feet beyond them.

"Still got it," Lacey smiled.

"Barely," Dan scoffed lightly, putting an arm around her when she was close, "Hey, Kayla, glad you could make it."

"Yeah, for sure," Kayla said.

Dan threw a few more reasonably distanced passes, abandoning the game as soon as one of the boys had caught enough to add up to the five hundred points needed to win, and returned to the grill. Megan knew he wanted to give Lacey his attention, but was sure Dan had purposely aimed the last couple passes towards the kid who'd won.

A familiar whistle stole her attention from the reforming game and Megan ran across the field towards Jimmy. He crouched as she got closer, hunching in a tackle position and she lowered her head to charge, but Jimmy grabbed Megan around the middle, swung her over his boney shoulder and started spinning around wildly.

Megan laughed, lightly peppering her fists against his back, "Jimmy put me down!"

248

"What?" he asked, tickling her side and held tight as she wiggled, "I can't understand ya when you're laughin'."

"Jim-mee!" she gasped through uncontrollable shrieks of laughter.

"Oh, I'm sorry. Did you want me to stop?" he teased, leaning forward until her feet touched the ground and Megan stuck her tongue out at him. Jimmy grinned, jerking his head towards the picnic tables, "Food ready? I'm starvin'."

"Almost," she said, "Lacey 'n Kayla are here."

"Kayla?" Jimmy whispered, "She's a bitch."

"She seems okay," Megan shrugged.

"I knew her in school," he said, as if that settled the matter.

"Megan!" Sam called from the field, "You playin'?"

"Go," Jimmy encouraged, yelling as she ran towards the game, "You boys better watch out for my sister! She'll kill ya!"

Megan blushed and shook her head, pushing into Sam before steadying next to him in starting formation. As the game continued, and all the kids were laughing and falling on top of each other, the rest of the girls from Megan's class decided to join, though they actively stayed away from the football.

Darlene called everyone to eat a short while later and the sweaty group lined up with paper plates along the picnic table. Dan was sliding the last few burgers onto buns on a tray and Lacey had filled a few plastic cups with soda while Jimmy made up funny names for the snack foods, earning giggles from all the kids. Megan glanced at Kayla, grinning with mild tolerance as Darlene tried to make conversation.

After eating, almost everyone agreed to take a break from football and the party dispersed around the park. Megan climbed the jungle gym with girls from her class, letting their legs dangle, each perched on a crossbar, and kicked at the boys trying to grab their feet. It wasn't long, though, before the two sodas she'd had took their toll and Megan slipped through the bars, running towards the park bathrooms.

"Megan!" Jimmy waved from where he and Dan stood by the picnic tables, "Gimme a hug, I'm headin' out."

"Thanks for comin'," she said, hugging him quickly, bouncing on her toes from the urge to pee.

"Be safe, Jim," Dan said, but Megan didn't hear Jimmy's response as she bolted towards the bathrooms.

The park bathroom always had a musky smell and the florescent, ceiling light fixtures were full of dead bugs. The woman's bathroom had three stalls while the men's room had two and a urinal. Megan only knew that because when she was potty training she'd had to use it once, Jimmy had refused to go in the women's side.

She sighed with relief behind the closed stall door, reading graffiti on the walls, most of it familiar, though a few new additions were clear in fresh permanent marker. Megan always forgot to bring a marker, though probably wouldn't know what to write if she had. Jimmy was better at that stuff.

The bathroom door opened as she zipped her jeans, but Kayla and Lacey's voices made Megan soften her breathing, unable to help overhearing.

"-happy for you," Kayla was saying, "Seriously, Dan's about the best guy there is."

"But," Lacey encouraged her sister to continue.

"But he's got a lot goin' on," Kayla said, "Yeah, sure, Jimmy'll be outta the house soon, but Megan?" Megan's ears perked at her name, "Lacey, she won't be eighteen for five years and you'll be twenty-seven. I'm just sayin, you wanna do the whole marriage 'n kids thing, but Dan's kinda already got a kid."

"Kayla," Lacey began, "I know, but I'm okay with it. I like Megan 'n Jimmy-"

"How can you like, Jimmy?" Kayla scoffed and heat pounded in Megan's ears.

"He's a sweet kid," Lacey said, "And Megan," she sighed, "she could use a female in her life."

"Pretty sure the cougar next door has that covered," Kayla laughed and so did Lacey, Megan didn't understand the comment, but their amusement made her even angrier.

"You're terrible," Lacey's giggling subsided.

"I'm right," Kayla said confidently, "I just don't wanna see you waste your time, or get sucked into the drama of that family."

Megan couldn't hear anymore and pulled the stall door open, glaring at the surprised young women in the mirror.

"Megan," Lacey breathed in quiet shock.

She was afraid simply opening her mouth would result in escaping sobs and, before the building tears could fall, Megan ran from the bathroom. Not stopping when her friends called her name, running passed the playground and towards the river as fast as she could.

Megan jumped down to the bank and stepped one foot in front of the other on a narrow strip of sandy dirt, her sneakers dampening as small waves lapped her toes. The noise of the party faded as she walked, trying to push Kayla's words from her mind, but they continued echoing anyway. Jimmy was right, Kayla was a bitch.

Finding her way to the tree she and Sam always climbed, Megan wiped her cheeks and hoped the baby birds were in their neighboring nest. Maybe they'd even look like birds this time.

"Megan!" she heard Dan's deep, distant call.

But Megan didn't turn, breaking into a jog in the last few feet, and leapt into the tree, scaling the branches quickly. She didn't want to tell him what happened, she wished it hadn't and didn't want to talk about it. Scooting carefully across the branch towards the nearby tree, her chest was ready to explode, only contained by the tightness in her throat and a shred of remaining will-power. The baby birds would help, though, she was sure of it.

"Megan!" Dan was agitated, and closer, but her focus was on holding back tears while peering at the nest, praying for a moment of solace.

A single, tiny brown bird chirped, fluttering its wings happily as its mother returned and both birds took flight across the river. Megan's throat constricted painfully as tears filled her eyes.

"Megan!" Dan barked, jumping onto the bank and glowered up at her, but, in hardly a second, his expression and tone softened, "Sweetheart, what's wrong?"

"There's only one bird," she cried, shaking her head, "There were two!"

"What?" Dan tilted his head in confusion.

"There's only one!" she sobbed.

"Okay, c'mere," Dan's tone lowered and Megan climbed to the branch nearest him, making eye-contact before he continued, "Why'd ya run off? I know it wasn't about some birds."

"Ask your girlfriend," Megan muttered, wiping her tears.

"I'm askin' you," he said firmly, putting his arms up, "C'mere."

Megan slipped off the branch, dropping into her brother's arms, and immediately burst into sobs on his shoulder.

"I'm sor-ry," she cried.

"Why?" Dan was practically pleading, "Megan, talk to me. What happened?"

"I was in the bathroom," she began after a few deep breaths, wiggling in his arms until he let her down, "And, Lacey 'n Kayla came in. Kayla was sayin' how like, y'know, you got a lot goin' on with me 'n Jimmy, and Lacey wants to get married and have kids, but you, already, got 'em," she sobbed again, "I'm sorry, Dan, I got mad, and just ran outta there. They saw me, but I couldn't listen to it anymore," she cried into his shirt, "I'm sorry."

"What on earth are you sorry for?" Dan asked, crouching to her height and wiping her tears with his thumb, "I'm sorry you had to hear that. Of course, you got angry, but you didn't do anything wrong, sweetheart. They shouldn't've been sayin' that stuff, not here anyway."

252

"Are you mad?" Megan asked timidly.

"At you?" Dan chuckled, shaking his head, "Not even a little bit."

"At them?" she clarified.

"I'm not happy about what'cha heard," he said, "But I can't blame Lacey for understanding the truth," Megan looked at him curiously and Dan smiled, "You are not a burden to me, Megan, never will be, but you are my responsibility and that's not gonna change."

She wrapped her arms around him, mumbling into his t-shirt, "I love you."

"I love you, too," he rubbed her back, "Wanna head back or do you need another minute?"

"I'm okay," she said.

They walked back towards the park together, but Megan's stomach twisted seeing Lacey approaching them. She shrunk into Dan's side, finding some comfort in his encouraging shoulder squeeze. His expression was neutral as Lacey got closer and Megan wished she could be anywhere else.

"Megan, I'm so sorry," Lacey insisted, her puffy eyes and pink cheeks betrayed recent tears.

"Lacey," Dan's tone was almost cold, "We can talk about this later."

"Dan," she raised her eyebrows challengingly, "I'm sorry for everything my sister said, but it's Megan I need to say that to first," and turned an imploring gaze on Megan, "If you'll let me."

Megan looked at Dan, who nodded, but didn't relent his grip on her shoulder.

"Megan," Lacey began after a shaky breath, "My sister talks a lotta crap, she always has. I've learned to ignore it and just let her say what she wants instead of getting into a pointless argument."

Megan shrugged to let Lacey know she'd heard her, even if she hadn't quite understood, but listened as she continued.

"I told her she was wrong and to go home," she said, "I shouldn't't've just let her keep talking like that and I'm so sorry you had to hear it."

"Not far off though," Dan added, "My life ain't normal and it never will be."

"I don't care," Lacey said flatly, "I know what I'm gettin' into here, so don't think I share any'a my sister's opinions. I like you, Dan, I like your family, and I think you're one'a the strongest and smartest people I've ever met for holdin' them together how you have. I'm not lookin' for normal, or perfect, I just want you, and everything that comes with you."

Megan watched the grin on Dan's face grow as Lacey's passionate frustration subsided into quiet panting.

"Megan, I'm truly, so sorry for what my sister said," she repeated, her anger instantly replaced with remorse when their eyes met.

"Jimmy said she's a bitch," Megan mumbled without thinking, her eyes widening just after the word slipped out.

"Megan!" Dan's response instigated a hasty step away from him.

"Jimmy's right," Lacey scoffed lightly, "She is a bitch, sometimes."

"Still doesn't give you the right to say that," Dan scolded Megan, "You know better than to use that word."

She nodded, deciding not to argue how Jimmy used that word, and worse, with little to no repercussions. Megan tried to suppress a smile when Lacey caught her eye and stuck her tongue out at the back of Dan's head.

He whipped around just as the pretty blonde's smirking lips hid the offending culprit, but her cheeks turned a renewed shade of pink. Dan shook his head at both of them before chuckling and walking towards the park. Megan and Lacey giggled together as they trailed behind.

"Megan," Lacey whispered, "I hope you know I'm not like my sister. I like your brother, a lot, and I like you 'n Jimmy, I think it's really cool how you've got two big brothers, and they both love you to death."

"I know," Megan said, "Dan likes you too, and Jimmy thinks you're awesome."

"And you?" Lacey's attempted smile was more a grimace of anticipation.

"I like you," Megan giggled, "I kinda like havin' a girl around sometimes, and you're pretty cool."

"Cool," Lacey beamed.

It was late by the time they made it home with armfuls of leftovers and gifts. Many of the parents had stuck around when they'd come to pick up their child and watched the short fireworks display. Dan had even brought bottle rockets for the kids to set off.

Jimmy's car was parked out front when Dan pulled into the driveway with Lacey behind him in her white sedan. She didn't stay too long after helping them bring everything in and giving Megan her own gift. A hardback copy of the Fire Fox book that had been destroyed.

"But, if you're gonna go see A.K. Foreman again," Lacey said, "Can I come?"

"Yeah!" Megan scoffed, squeezing her gratefully around the middle.

"You'd fit better in that line than me," Dan mused.

"Thank you," Megan said, releasing Lacey and hugged her new treasure.

"You're so welcome," Lacey smiled, but her eyes were misty.

"Alright, Meg," Dan clapped his hands, "I'll put away the food, you take all this stuff to your room."

"I should get goin'," Lacey said.

"You don't wanna watch a movie?" Megan asked.

"It's quarter to ten!" Dan laughed, "And how are you not exhausted?"

Megan shrugged, unable to stifle a yawn as soon as he implied it and Dan smirked knowingly.

She said good night to Lacey, gathering her gifts of books, CD's and clothes, and went to her bedroom. Megan heard the screen door slap in the frame as Dan walked her to her car. It banged again a few minutes later, right before he entered Megan's bedroom.

"Well," Dan sighed, "I think all in all it was a successful day. D'ja have fun?"

"Yeah," Megan smiled.

"You okay about what happened?" he raised his eyebrows curiously.

"Yeah," she grinned, "Jimmy'll think it's funny Lacey agreed with him."

Dan scoffed and shrugged, "Yeah, well, ya can't pick your siblings. Just gotta love 'em anyway."

"It's a good thing I'm perfect, right?" Megan joked with a goofy grin.

Dan laughed, "Yeah, you're perfect and Jimmy's next in line to be the Pope."

"All 'cause'a you," she giggled, returning the hug he pulled her into.

"Alright, my little saint," Dan patted her back, "Bed, let's go."

Megan had no interest in arguing and slipped under her blanket.

"G'night," he kissed her forehead, "I'm glad you had a good day, but, uh, do me a favor and stop growin' up so fast, huh?"

She stuck her tongue out, giggling when he snatched at it. Dan chuckled and turned off her nightstand light before leaving the room.

Megan was exhausted and it didn't take long for her to fall asleep. But a repeated shrill ringing woke her just passed midnight.

She dragged herself out of bed and trudged into the hallway, blinking in the sudden light when she opened her door. The ringing had stopped and she heard her oldest brother's tired voice.

"Yeah Andy, what's up?" Dan grumbled into the phone as Megan snuck into the kitchen, "What'd he do this time? – Andy, just say it." he became rapidly agitated, the muscles in his bare back clenching, "Why? – Andy, tell me!"

Dan's shoulders dropped and Megan was chilled by the silence engulfing the room.

"Where is he?" Dan asked, then screamed, "Andy! Where the hell is he?!"

Megan let out an unexpected sob, hearing a desperation she never had in his voice, and Dan turned, his face white.

"Get your shoes 'n jacket on!" he ordered, returning to the phone, "I'm on my way," and the receiver slammed on the cradle, "Now, Megan!"

His barked command made her jump and drop on the floor near the door, shoving her bare feet into her sneakers. Dan stalked to his room, returning only moments later in jeans and a hooded sweatshirt, slipping his beaten-up sneakers on as Megan pulled on her jacket.

"Dan? What's going on?" she tried, but he didn't even look at her while wrenching the door open and pushed through the screen door so hard it slapped the siding before returning to its frame like a crack of thunder.

She stared across the truck's bench seat, seeing concern etched in his features.

"Dan, please," Megan begged, "Is Jimmy okay?"

"I don't know," he said quietly, slamming the accelerator on their street, much faster than he'd ever driven in the neighborhood.

Megan wanted to ask where they were going, but Dan just stared straight ahead at the road as he pushed his truck to higher and higher speeds. Her stomach twisted anxiously, wishing she at least knew why Dan's cop friend, Andy, had called about Jimmy at midnight and why they were headed out of town.

But, when they continued after passing Yorkville, Megan couldn't take it anymore.

"Where are we going?" she demanded.

"Aurora," Dan said simply, his eyes never leaving the road.

"Why?" Megan pleaded.

Finally, Dan's gaze faltered and his head drooped as he sighed heavily, hardly more than whispering, "Jimmy was in an accident."

Megan felt nausea swarm her insides as her hands went cold, holding her breath and waited for Dan to continue, urging when he did not, "What happened?! Is he okay?!"

"I don't know, Megan," Dan gritted his teeth, gripping the steering wheel tighter, "He's at the hospital, that's all I know."

Tears stung her eyes and she turned towards the window to hide her face, though in the darkness all she saw was a reflection of her own misery. Megan sniffled quietly, she hated hospitals, nothing but awful things happened in the overly clean, yet disease filled buildings. Thinking of Jimmy being in one made her throat tighten agonizingly. Folding her hands together and squeezing her eyes shut, Megan silently prayed as hard as she could, begging God for her brother to be alright.

Dan pulled into the mostly empty hospital parking lot, the truck's tires squealing on the blacktop as he maneuvered to the nearest spot by the emergency entrance. They both pushed open their doors as he threw the shifter in park and Megan sprinted after Dan, passed the sliding glass doors, and skidded to a halt at the check-in desk.

"Can I help you?" a woman in scrubs barely looked up from her computer.

"My brother," Dan panted, "He was in an accident, Jimmy, his name's, Jimmy Murphy, James, Officer Andy Switzer called me-"

"Dan," Andy walked around a corner behind the desk, waving his hand at the registration clerk, "I'll take 'em from here, Jody."

She shrugged as if it made no difference to her and returned her attention to the screen. The officer's shoulders were slumped in his uniform, his blonde hair disheveled from running his hand through it repeatedly and Megan was surprised he didn't look at her. Andy always smiled when he saw her, but he wasn't smiling at all.

"Andy," Dan sighed with relief, "Where is he? Is he okay?"

"C'mon," Andy said, leading them around the corner he'd come from.

Megan curled her fingers into the back of Dan's sweatshirt as they passed a set of heavy, automatic doors. Andy looked sad, definitely paler than usual, and he took a deep breath as the doors clanged behind them.

"Jimmy, Jordan, Travis 'n Brad were drivin' around Yorkville," Andy began, "Just late night coffee 'n smokes at the diner, y'know?" Dan said nothing and the officer continued after a shaky sigh, "They got hit on their way back. Drunk driver. Yorkville cops called us seein' as all the boys are from our town, figured we could get a hold'a everybody faster."

"Where's my brother, Andy?" Dan growled impatiently.

"Down here," Andy gestured towards the row of doors and Dan immediately continued his rapid pace, shrugging off his friend's hand when Andy tried to stop him, "Dan, wait."

"Why?!" Dan barked, but Megan heard his fear and tears blurred her eyes.

"He's not," Andy tried, "He didn't," he took a deep breath, "Dan, Jimmy didn't make it."

"Fuck you, Andy!" Dan shouted, "Where's my brother?!"

Megan's chest was caving in, she couldn't breathe. The world went quiet, but her feet followed them automatically, stopping outside of room 104. Andy was not even allowed the opportunity to grab the handle as Dan rushed into the room.

"Megan," Andy put a hand on her shoulder, "You shouldn't see this."

She said nothing, but ripped herself from him, stopping short of the bed, behind Dan. Megan felt her insides freeze at the lump of white sheets and all hope shriveled as Dan gently pulled the linen from their brother's battered face, folding it down to his bruised shoulders.

A scream reached Megan's ears and she felt strong arms wrap around her tightly, lifting from the ground she'd fallen to when her knees had given way.

"No!" Megan cried into Dan's shoulder, hitting his arm with a tightly balled fist, "JIMMY!"

She stopped hammering his bicep, grasping Dan's t-shirt while sobbing mercilessly and felt him shaking with his own grief. Dan never cried, but, as they clung to each other over Jimmy's lifeless body, the oldest did not hide his agony.

Megan prayed to wake up from the nightmare, sure that's what it was, it wasn't real. Jimmy couldn't be dead.

# Chapter 12

Travis had been driving, Jordan was in the passenger seat with Jimmy behind him and Brad next to him in the backseat. They'd been going west through a green light when a pick-up truck ran through the stop light in the south bound lane, colliding directly with the rear passenger door.

The driver of the truck had nearly three times the legal limit in his system, apparently it wasn't his first offense for the crime either. Not one of the boys had been drinking. Whether it had been on the agenda prior to the crash or not, the four young men had been stone cold sober when it happened.

Jordan was in intensive care, badly injured, but with a hopeful prognosis. Brad and Travis would be held a day or two for broken bones and concussions, but overall, they would be fine. Jimmy had taken the full hit from the out of control truck and died on impact.

Megan faintly heard these pieces of conversation between the police and Dan as they sat in a small, private room with soft couches and several boxes of tissues. Huddled under a hospital blanket between an overstuffed armrest and her brother, Megan colored. One of the nurses had offered her a very used box of pencils and a few books, admitting they may be too childish, but Megan needed something to do, something to focus on other than the words echoing around her, and thanked her quietly.

She didn't know how long they were there, three full pages at least, but Megan forced her concentration on the mindless task in front of her, not on Andy and another officer in a different uniform, or on the parents of the other boys who came in with condolences, or the priest who offered to pray with them, silently appreciating that Dan sent the priest away. She didn't feel like praying, she'd never feel like praying again.

Whether Megan walked to the truck or Dan carried her she couldn't be sure, suddenly finding herself next to him on the bench seat. The hospital's coloring book and pencils still in her hands.

"I have these," she said in a small voice.

"Did'ja hear the nurse when she said you could keep 'em?" Dan asked and Megan shook her head, tears stinging her eyes, "Well she did, it's okay."

"No, it's not!" a wet sob broke passed Megan's lips.

"No," Dan agreed solemnly, "It's not."

They were all wrong, Megan was sure they had to be wrong. That wasn't Jimmy. Besides the dark, shaggy hair and slight resemblance, that bruised up boy could be anyone's brother. It wasn't hers. It couldn't be. It wasn't fair.

Jimmy would come home, like he always did, maybe still a little drunk from the night before, but he'd come home. Megan opened the coloring book and continued her fourth page as Dan drove home with the morning sun behind them.

It was a quiet drive and, just as she'd abruptly found herself in the truck, Dan was suddenly helping her up the porch steps, holding the pencils and coloring book in his other hand.

Megan robotically kicked off her shoes and walked across the front room, pushing open Jimmy's bedroom door. The comforting smell of stale smoke surrounded her as she navigated the mess of dirty clothes to his bed. Climbing under the blankets, Megan's throat closed painfully again, trying to hold back a sob. Because if she didn't cry it wasn't real, he wasn't gone. But she couldn't stop herself, letting tears fall on Jimmy's pillow as she curled into his comforter, inhaling his scent with every unsteady breath.

Dan approached the bed and Megan tried to plead with him not to make her move, but all that came out was a pathetic wail. He did move her though, a bit closer to the wall as he laid down, pulling her tight to his chest and smoothed her hair while she sobbed on his sweatshirt.

Her eyelashes stuck together when she woke in her bedroom, a blanket had been tossed over her window to shield the brightness outside, making the walls a dim orange. Megan wiped her eyes, unsure why'd she'd been crying, and peered at the clock on her nightstand. It was afternoon. Why had she slept so late?

Her stomach twisted nauseously as the events of the night before crashed into her mind. But it had to be a dream. A nasty nightmare, sad and horrific, but nothing more. Megan reassured herself as she threw her blanket off and left her room.

Dan was at the kitchen table with Darlene and Lacey. They turned to her with red eyes, even Dan's, glistening with fresh tears, and Megan stopped.

Without a word, she pushed into Jimmy's room, expecting to see her brother reclined on his bed, smoking a cigarette and skimming through a magazine. But he wasn't there.

Dan walked in behind her and shut the door, putting a hand on Megan's shoulder as she sunk on the empty bed and sat beside her.

"Where's Jimmy?" her question was hushed, not wanting him to answer.

"Do you remember last night?" Dan asked softly.

Megan shook her head vigorously, tears stinging her eyes as she forced words passed quivering lips, "It was a nightmare."

"Yeah," Dan agreed, and his own voice broke, pulling her close, "But sometimes nightmares are real."

Megan sobbed, her chest about to explode from agony.

"Megan," Dan said after a few minutes, brushing her hair from her face and she saw tears streaking his cheeks, "Can you try 'n eat somethin'?"

She shook her head, pulling away and laid on Jimmy's blanket, "I wanna stay here," and wait for him, but she didn't vocalize the last part.

"Sweetheart," Dan sighed, but bit his lips, "I'll be back to check on you."

Megan hugged Jimmy's pillow, inhaling his scent despite the growing ache in her heart with every breath. She ignored the conversation in the front room, barely hearing the screen door bang occasionally, followed by the addition of a new voice. Some were inherently familiar, like Mrs. King, but most she didn't bother trying to recognize. She was buried in dark thoughts, suffocating in grief.

No one stayed long and, when Darlene departed, the house was silent for a few minutes before Jimmy's door opened and Dan maneuvered through the dark room without turning on the light. Megan didn't move.

"Sweetheart?" his tone was light, but pained, "C'mon, come eat somethin'."

"Don't want to," she mumbled, barely lifting her face from the pillow.

"You got to," Dan said sympathetically, sitting on the edge of the bed and gingerly dragged her next to him.

Megan didn't fight him, but she didn't help. Her chest was sore, her tears had run dry and her head was pounding. Dan held her close and Megan let him, finding her agony renewed as he shook.

"It's not fair," she whispered, hugging him tightly around the neck as another sob crushed her heart.

Dan just cried and held her on Jimmy's bed. A bed his little brother would never sleep in again.

The next day, Megan shut herself in Jimmy's room as soon as she woke in her own, furious at Dan for moving her again. But, with his voice breaking in pained anger, Dan threatened to lock her out of it if she didn't eat and Megan relented, stomping to the table and slammed into a chair. He ignored it and set bacon, eggs and toast in front of her with a glass of orange juice.

"Hey, Megan," Dan started, trying to force a grin when she glared at him, "Happy birthday."

Her stomach churned and her chest started aching, she was thirteen and had forgotten. Tears filled her eyes and Megan curled her legs, hugging her knees as she cried.

"We- were- Jimmy- movies," was all she could manage between sharp, panicked breaths.

Dan crouched next to the chair, trying weakly to hush her cries, but his own pain was breaking through.

"I forgot," Dan whispered, "I'm sorry."

Megan wanted to tell him it wasn't his fault. Not the promise of watching PG-13 movies with Jimmy all day, not that it was her birthday, not Jimmy. None of it was Dan's fault. But all she could do was shake her head and sob.

"I'm so sorry, Megan," he buried his face in his hands.

"Dan, it's not your fault," she forced the intendedly comforting words passed her squeezed throat.

Her brother broke. Megan had never seen Dan so tortured. Even when their mother had died he'd only shed a few tears, remaining the ever-solid foundation for his distraught siblings. But he dropped to his knees on the linoleum and Megan wrapped her arms around his shaking back, trying to give him the comfort he'd always given her, knowing she'd never relieve him of this suffering.

More people came and went as the day progressed. But Megan didn't hide in Jimmy's room and, while she hardly spoke, stayed by Dan in the kitchen as friends and acquaintances stopped one after another to offer condolences and food. Everyone brought food.

Darlene came over again, bringing Sam this time, and, despite Dan's half-hearted protests, she set to work packing the abundance of meals for the freezer. Darlene wiped her cheeks occasionally, yet never stopped fussing with one thing or another, as well as having appointed herself the house handler. At least that's what she reminded Megan of when she gently ushered a few people, who'd stayed a bit too long, out the front door, just like at A.K. Foreman's book signing. She was glad to have Darlene there.

Sam didn't say much, but sat next to Megan and squeezed her hand for reassurance under the table, his eyes were glassy. Megan suspected that Sam and Darlene didn't want to cry in front of her and Dan, but she wouldn't blame them if they did.

"I'm, sorry," Sam managed and Megan forced a tight lipped grin at him.

"Thanks," she said, Dan had told her that was the appropriate response, even though it's not their fault, that wasn't the point.

"Uh," he grimaced uncertainly, "Happy birthday."

"Thanks," Megan nodded, swallowing hard on her raw throat.

She was glad Sam didn't say anything else, Megan didn't feel like talking, but appreciated that he didn't leave her side.

When Lacey arrived in the late afternoon she brought pizzas, but Megan wasn't interested in her favorite food, pushing her plate away after two obligatory bites. Dan didn't insist, hardly eating any of his either.

"Dan?" Darlene began, "Is there anything I can do? I know you said you got it, but really, honey, this is a lot. I'm here for anything you need."

"I know," Dan nodded, "Thank you, I, uh, I got," his voice cracked and he hung his head over the mostly untouched plate of pizza.

The room was silent as Dan bit back his emotions and Lacey put a hand on his shoulder. He reached up and Megan thought for a moment he might refuse the comfort, but he folded her hand between his own and looked over with a teary, but grateful, grin. Lacey covered her mouth with her other hand as a sob escaped, throwing herself at Dan and wrapped her arms around him.

"I'm so sorry, baby," she cried quietly.

Dan held her tight, his face buried in Lacey's neck for a moment before letting go and she kissed his cheek.

"I could maybe use some help," Dan admitted, his wet eyes on Darlene.

"Anything," she said.

Lacey stayed the night at Megan's insistence, something about having someone else in the house made if different, like she was still dreaming and would wake up to Jimmy clomping up the porch steps after work, complaining about his job. She silently held onto the useless hope while the three of them settled on the couch and watched television until they fell asleep, the girls curled on either side of Dan with his feet on the coffee table.

The growl of the semi-truck should have woken them. Or the heavy footsteps on the porch. But it wasn't until the front door opened and the screen door banged that Dan jumped from the couch, startling Megan and Lacey awake.

Her father's bulky form in the doorway registered slowly as Megan's eyes adjusted in the dark room.

"Greg," Dan's surprise was obvious, "What're you doin' here?"

"Dispatch girl tracked me down after you called," Greg said, "Megan? How ya holdin' up?"

"Bad," she whispered, curling into the warm spot Dan had abandoned on the couch.

"I bet," Greg nodded, crooking his finger and Megan obliged, trudging across the living room and let his large, unfamiliar arms press her into his protruding gut, "Who's this?"

"Hi," Lacey hopped off the couch, extending her hand to Greg.

"This is Lacey Peters," Dan said.

"Girlfriend?" Greg asked Dan, releasing Lacey's hand as absently as he'd taken it.

"Yeah," Megan offered, dipping her head from Dan's gaze, even in the dark she could see his raised eyebrow.

"Nice to meet'cha," Greg turned again to his stepson, "Ya got everything handled?"

"Yes, sir," Dan responded automatically, "Are you, uh, stickin' around?"

"Think that's best," Greg said curtly and Megan saw Dan's shoulders raise, "I'm goin' to bed, long drive."

Greg ruffled her hair and left for the bathroom. Megan and Lacey both looked at Dan, waiting for him to speak, or move, but he didn't. A minute later, they watched Greg walk down the hall, shutting himself in Dan's room.

Megan's stomach turned, expecting her brother to storm in and drag her father out, but Dan shook his head with an exhausted sigh.

"I should go," Lacey said.

"It's really late," Dan commented, but didn't urge her to stay.

"I'll be fine," she assured him, "Call me tomorrow, I'll stop by if it's okay."

"Thanks, Lacey," he said and they kissed.

"I'll see you soon," Lacey promised, giving Megan a tighter hug than usual.

"Drive safe," Dan said as she left and shut the front door, the screen slapped loudly in the dark silence.

"Dan?" Megan whispered, leaning into his side.

"It's gonna be okay, sweetheart," his tone was hardly convincing, but the arm he squeezed around her was a small comfort, "You should get in bed."

"Where are you gonna sleep?" she asked, glancing at Jimmy's closed bedroom door.

"I'm okay out here," he said, dropping on the couch.

"Can I stay?" she asked, plopping next to him before he could answer.

"Sure," Dan nodded after a thoughtful moment, pulling the blanket off the back of the sofa and stretched across the cushions.

"Why is Greg here?" she crawled beside him and felt Dan tense at the name.

"I don't know," he grumbled.

Megan didn't ask any more questions, snuggling into his side and closed her eyes. The pain in her chest started again, but she took a few labored breaths, trying to calm her tears before they started. Dan's hand moving from her shoulder to her elbow and back helped Megan eventually drift into sleep, praying Jimmy would be home when she woke up, not her father.

Megan was alone on the couch the next morning, yawning awake and her stomach twisted immediately seeing her father at the kitchen table. He caught her eye and Megan knew she couldn't pretend to still be sleeping. It was strange, normally Greg being home would excite her, at least at first. This time, however, she wanted nothing more than for him to leave. How dare he show up now, while they grieved Jimmy, a stepson he'd shown nothing but contempt and abuse.

"Mornin'," Greg said, sipping a cup of coffee.

"Mornin'," Megan mumbled and retreated to the bathroom.

She took a while, washing her hair twice and stood under the water until it went cool. The television blared on the other side of the wall, much louder than usual, and she hoped it was a sign her father was going deaf.

"What're you doin' in there?" Greg called and Megan took a deep breath before walking into the front room, "Took ya long enough."

"Is there breakfast?" she asked, noticing a pan on the stove.

"I just made some sausages 'n toast," he said, hardly glancing from the television.

Megan was angry at herself for the tears that stung her eyes. She was perfectly capable of getting her own breakfast, at least warming frozen waffles or pouring cereal, but she'd smelled sausage and knew Dan would've had a plate waiting for her.

"Where's Dan?" Megan realized her tone was accusatory and her stomach twisted as he turned, lowering the television volume.

"Hospital, funeral home," Greg shrugged indifferently, "Said he had some errands to run."

"Why didn't he wake me up?!" she cried, running towards her room to change.

Dan should have taken her with him. Why hadn't he taken her with him? She should be there. Tears welled in her eyes as Megan pulled on a pair of jeans from her floor and riffled through a basket of clothes for a t-shirt, barely remembering socks before she rushed to the front door for her sneakers.

"Where'd ya think you're goin'?" Greg chuckled.

"I can ride my bike into town," Megan said confidently, it was partially true because Dan would let her if she was with Sam.

"I think you mean, can I ride my bike into town," Greg sat forward on the couch with his forearms on his knees, "And the answer is no."

"Why?!" she yelled.

"Because Dan's busy," Greg raised his voice, but, from previous experience, Megan knew he wasn't yelling, "He doesn't have time for you to be runnin' around him right now," Megan bit her lips, her chest swelling painfully, and her father slapped the couch cushion next to him, "C'mon, watch some TV with me."

She glared at the ground, too afraid to shift her angry, hurt gaze at her father, and stomped once before remembering who she was with, taking the remaining steps to her room quietly. Curling on her bed, she hid her face in her pillow and cried, almost thankful the television volume raised again.

It was afternoon when she heard the sweet growl of Dan's truck and jumped off her bed, wanting to hug him as much as she wanted to hit him. Greg was napping on the couch and Dan was just getting out of his truck when Megan leapt down the porch steps, the screen door whacking its frame behind her.

"Megan-" Dan's chastisement on her descent was interrupted before he'd hardly sighed her name.

"Why didn't you take me?!" she exploded, tears dripping down her cheeks, "Why couldn't I come?! You left me with-" Megan's throat tightened too much to complete the allegation and she shrugged her brother's hand off her shoulder, snapping viciously, "I woke up and you were gone!"

Her knees went weak from the following torrent of sobs and Dan disregarded her feeble fight, holding her close and sunk onto the porch steps.

"I'm sorry," she whispered after a few deep breaths.

"Don't be," Dan shook his head, "But I couldn't put you through that, sweetheart, it was hard enough alone. I couldn't've dealt with you seein', and hearin' all that. If I'd known before we went to the hospital-"

"Ain't you a little big to be sittin' in somebody's lap?" Greg chuckled from the porch, the screen door banging loudly.

"She's fine, Greg," Dan growled.

"You would say that," her father scoffed and her brother tensed.

"You wanna elaborate on that?" Dan asked calmly.

"You baby her," Greg laughed again, "Always have. She's a young woman now. Isn't that right, Megan? Heck, there's girls in the world her age been married a few years 'n already got a couple kids."

Dan patted Megan to hop off and stood, turning on his stepfather, "Is that what you want for her?"

"What?" Greg scoffed, "That's stupid, 'course not! All I'm sayin' is she ain't a little girl anymore, ya ought'a stop treatin' her like one."

"Greg," Dan's tone was steady, but Megan heard his words shake, "I realize that what happened doesn't affect you one bit, but if you can't see how much your daughter is hurting, you are goddamn blind."

Megan stood close to Dan, trying to prove their solidarity, while gripping the tail of his shirt.

Greg stared at Dan for a few moments before offering a curt nod, "I know it ain't easy," and turned back into the house.

"I hate him," Megan muttered as the screen met its frame.

"Don't say that," Dan said.

"Why?" Megan wiped away a few stray tears, "It's true."

"He's your dad," Dan shrugged.

"So?" she challenged, "He's never here, he's mean when he is, he doesn't like me, or wanna know anything about me," tears started streaming furiously down her cheeks, "I wish he'd died and Jimmy was still here!"

Dan didn't say anything against her statement and simply rubbed her back as she cried, soaking the front of his t-shirt. Megan was sure she was running out of tears.

"Hey," Dan got her attention gently when she'd calmed down, "Dotty's comin' over."

Megan forced a smile, she liked the social worker, but wasn't feeling up to more company. Although, Megan assumed Dotty's visit was not purely to extend her condolences. A loud growl from her stomach, however, immediately changed the subject.

"What'cha eat today?" Dan asked.

"Nothin'," she mumbled and he sighed.

"C'mon," he jerked his head and led her into the house.

Greg was reclined on the couch with his boots on the coffee table, but he turned down the volume when they walked in and set his feet on the floor. Dan grabbed the pan off the stove and tossed it carelessly in the sink.

"Want some'a that lasagna Mrs. King made?" he asked and Megan shook her head, "How 'bout a small piece with some Jell-O salad?"

"Okay," she agreed and Dan slid the tray from the shelf.

Greg scoffed blatantly, but Dan ignored him. Megan poured a glass of milk and sat at the table with her back to the living room, trying to pretend her father wasn't behind her.

"Ya said that social worker lady's comin' today?" Greg asked.

"Dotty Clark," Dan nodded, keeping his attention on the lasagna he was scooping onto a plate.

"Good," Greg said.

"I have the paperwork," Dan said, "I told you, you just gotta sign. Courts on Monday, but you don't have to be there."

Greg snorted and Megan turn in her seat to see him shaking his head with a nasty smile as he stood from the couch.

"You think I'm still okay with that?" he sneered at Dan, who narrowed his eyes, but said nothing as Greg continued, "No, I've let you take the reins around here long enough 'n look what happened."

"What?" Dan whispered in disbelief.

Megan's stomach lurched.

"What?" Greg scoffed, "This is my house, my kid, 'n I don't need you messin' her up like the other one."

"Jimmy was in an accident!" Dan yelled.

"That kid was an accident!" Greg expelled spitefully.

Megan leapt off her chair as Dan lunged at Greg, flattening her back against Jimmy's door.

Greg shoved his bulky weight into Dan and they knocked into the arm chair, sending it crashing to its side. Dan took scarcely a moment to find his balance, but Greg stole the opportunity and punched his stepson in the face.

"Stop!" Megan screamed, watching blood spurt from Dan's nose.

But neither paid attention to her screams. Dan wiped his face with the back of his left hand as his right fist sunk into Greg's amble gut. He doubled over, gasping in pain, and Dan shoved him backwards. Greg landed on the floor in front of the couch, his arm smacking hard on the coffee table.

Dan's shoulders heaved as he took a few steps back from his stepfather, his glare madder than Megan had ever seen.

273

"Ya think this'll help your case?" Greg spit with a mean laugh.

"How're you gonna take care'a her?!" Dan shouted, "You're never here!"

"Well, that ain't your problem!" Greg argued, getting to his feet.

"Like hell it's not!" Dan yelled, "She's always my problem!"

"I'm her father!" Greg barked.

"Since when?!" Dan screamed frantically.

Greg hurtled at his stepson, who was already in a defensive position in front of the open front door, but his full mass barreling into Dan sent them both flying backwards. The screen door cracked against the side of the house and Megan heard more thuds, nearing the altercation just as Dan flung Greg down the porch steps.

Greg unsteadily pushed himself off the ground, hollering rabidly, "Get out! Get the fuck outta my house!"

Megan froze beside Dan, staring in shock at her enraged father on the ground, oblivious to the red Honda pulling into the driveway, and the screen door hanging sideways by its bottom hinge.

# Chapter 13

"Get out!" Greg raged, ignoring the thud of a closing car door in the driveway.

Megan twisted her fingers into Dan's shirt, stiffened by fear as her father's words gained meaning.

"What's going on here?" Dotty asked, approaching the porch.

"Are you the lady with DCFS?" Greg rounded on her, but Dotty was clearly unimpressed with his anger.

"Dotty Clark," she nodded, "We've met."

"Yeah, yeah, I remember you," Greg muttered.

"I expected you would only be signing the guardianship papers-" she began.

But Greg interrupted with a hard laugh, "That ain't gonna happen."

Dotty tilted her head and narrowed her eyes, "You've changed your mind?"

"Got that right, don't I?" he growled, jerking his head at Dan, "Like I got the right to kick shitheads outta my house."

"Sure," Dotty nodded, "I have to ask, though, considering your line of work, how do plan on getting Megan to and from school? Or making sure someone's here when she's home?"

"Ain't your concern," Greg scoffed.

"Actually," Dotty smirked, "Since Megan's been on my case list for the last four years, it is."

A low, frustrated rumble grew from the back of Greg's throat, scowling at the social worker before offering an answer he'd clearly just concocted, "I got a buddy with a kid about her age who stays on the road with him, does the homeschoolin' thing."

Megan felt the color drain from her face, curling her fingers tighter into Dan's t-shirt and leaned as close to him as possible. Her father couldn't be serious.

"You can't be serious," Dan scoffed.

"It definitely ain't any'a your concern!" Greg snarled back.

"This is her home!" Dan raged desperately, but gently held Megan to his side, "Her friends live here! Her school is here! Her life is here!"

"She's my kid!" Greg shouted, "Her life is wherever the hell I want it to be!"

Megan sobbed, wanting to run away, but there was nowhere to go. Her father blocked the walkway and she'd be trapped inside. Lacking an escape, she just sobbed.

"Homeschooling is rigorous," Dotty seemed to be forcing steadiness as she spoke, "And will be overseen."

"We'll be fine," Greg disregarded.

"Mhm," Dotty was obviously not reassured, "I will be seeing you at the court hearing Monday morning then?"

"The what?" Greg furrowed his brow.

"Dan's guardianship hearing," Dotty said plainly, "It's part of the proceedings for him to take custody. Since you're so difficult to get a hold of the judge was going to evaluate and approve, simply pending your signature."

"We don't need to do that anymore," Greg scoffed, "I ain't givin' up my rights."

"They'll want to know why," she continued, "It's unusual for a parent to agree and then retract, especially one with your, history."

Greg's shoulders raised, glaring at the social worker, and Megan's stomach flipped, but her father expelled a defeated breath and dropped his head.

"Dotty," Dan gained her attention softly, "Can we," his question trailed as he jerked his head, silently requesting a private conversation.

"Of course," she nodded.

"You need to get your ass outta my house is what'cha need to do!" Greg spat.

"He can't!" Megan screamed, wrapping her arms frantically around Dan.

"It's not up to you Meggie," her father tried to sound tender, but she snarled.

"I hate you," Megan whispered bitterly, finding confidence in his widened eyes and screeched, "Go away! I hate you!"

"Megan," Dan crouched, wiping her cheeks, and hushed reassurances, "I love you, I'm always gonna be here," hearing Greg scoff, she sobbed, but Dan lifted her chin so their eyes met, "Even if I'm not here for a little while, I'm always close, you always have me. I'll always be your brother, sweetheart."

Megan shook her head, terrified of being alone. First Jimmy, now Dan.

"You can't," her quivering lips barely formed the protest while her fingers curled tighter into his shirt, refusing to surrender, "You, can't, leave."

"It won't be for long," he promised, but she heard doubt.

"You can't!" she screamed as he tried to pull away, shrieking when her father took a step towards the porch, "No, not you!"

Greg's looked instantly wounded, then irritated, but stopped his advance, "Megan, I'm your dad."

"No, you're not," she whimpered, clinging to Dan.

"Megan, sweetie," Dotty's gentle voice earned Megan's attention, "Let's talk, okay? You 'n me?"

"And Dan," Megan sniffed.

"And Dan," Dotty agreed.

"Daniel," Greg said threateningly, "I'm not messin' around here-"

"For Christ's sake, Greg!" Dotty snapped, "Didn't nobody think you were! I need five minutes with them, and then sir, I'd like to have a long conversation with you 'bout your plans with this girl. So, I suggest you take this time as an opportunity to actually make some."

Greg's eyebrows raised in shock, though recovered quickly into a scowl before he stomped up the porch steps and slammed the front door. But a deafening absence lingered in the brief silence and Megan noticed the screen door, hanging by its bottom hinge, sideways on the porch.

Dan lowered the tailgate of his truck and helped Megan onto it, sliding next to her as Dotty leaned on the hood of her red Honda.

She shook her head and glared at the front door before softening her gaze on them and took a deep breath, "I can't tell you two how sorry I am," Dotty's expression broke and she put a fist to her mouth while tears filled her eyes, "Jimmy, was a great kid. Oh, Megan, Dan, I don't even know what to say."

Dan slid off the tailgate when Dotty opened her arms, his own eyes damp when their embrace ended.

"Megan," Dotty pulled her into a hug and Megan did her best to return it, "You poor thing. Both'a you, just."

"Thanks, Dotty," Dan said sullenly as her condoling statement faded, "Can't see how things could get much worse now."

"He can't make you leave," Megan linked her arms around Dan's elbow.

He sighed and Dotty bit her lips sadly.

"He can, Meg," Dan whispered and she shook her head, "Megan," his finger caught under her chin and tugged her face to look at him, "This isn't gonna last, okay, trust me. But can you be strong until I get it figured out?"

"No," she sobbed, squeezing his arm tighter, "You can't- you can't leave me!"

Tears spilled onto his cheeks at her broken plea, but he cleared his throat and said, "I'm never gonna leave you, Megan. Ever, I promise."

"I don't wanna be homeschooled," she sniveled, pinching snot from her nose, "And I hate his truck."

"Don't worry," Dotty said confidently, "I'll do everything I can to make sure that doesn't happen. In the meantime, though, Dan, do you have somewhere to stay?"

"I'll be fine," he brushed off her concern, focusing on his own, "Do I have any chance'a fightin' this?"

Dotty frowned, "It's up to him. We can just hope he'll see sense."

Megan expelled a hard, cynical laugh and Dan squeezed her shoulder, but she wasn't reassured. The foundations of her life were crumbling.

Dotty accompanied them into the house, joining Greg at the kitchen table with a blank expression, while Dan returned to the pan of lasagna on the stove.

"Dan-" he began sharply, but his stepson flipped around furiously.

"I'm leavin', Greg!" he snapped, "But Megan hasn't eaten yet today and I'm gonna fix that first! So back off!"

"She can heat up her own damn food!" Greg argued and hatred surged through Megan.

"Greg," Dotty said firmly, "I need your attention now. Don't you be worryin' about them."

He leveled her with an aggressive stare, but Dotty seemed unaffected and began peppering him with questions about his plans. Starting with how he intended to take care of Megan from the moment Dan walked out that door.

"What'd you eat today?" Dotty asked flatly.

Greg scoffed, as if the question was hardly relevant, but, when Dotty blinked vacantly, awaiting a response, he said, "I made a couple sausage patties 'n some toast. What of it?"

"What'd you feed Megan?" her question was plain, but deliberate.

Megan leaned even closer to Dan, his hands gripping the counter's edge with his back to the table, and she wished the microwave worked faster.

Greg expelled a hard laugh, "She laid in bed 'n then spent an hour in the bathroom," Megan could feel her father's eyes hot on the back of her head as he continued, "Am I supposed to guess what she wants?"

Dotty didn't say a word, but Megan recognized her typically dissatisfied 'mhm' while a pen scratched a notepad.

"She ain't a little girl," Greg growled, "She can get her own breakfast, and heat up her own lunch! Do they need to be here for this?"

Megan jammed the button, popping the microwave door open seven seconds early. Dan squeezed her shoulder and Megan saw his face contort with agony before he expelled a quiet breath. But, too quickly, Dan walked away.

Megan grabbed her plate and snagged a fork from the drawer, hurrying to follow. She wasn't supposed to bring food in the bedrooms, but doubted Dan would care this time.

After kicking his door closed with her heel, Megan carefully climbed onto Dan's unmade bed, a sure sign he hadn't woken in it, and watched him riffle through his closet, grabbing his old football duffel bag.

"You're not really leavin', right?" Megan stabbed at her lasagna, but couldn't bring herself to eat.

"I have to, Meg," Dan said, opening the bag on his bed.

Megan's throat constricted and she simply shook her head until gentle fingers gripped her chin. Dan had tears staining his face, but forced a smile.

"We'll get through this," he promised, "I don't know how, but we will."

Megan nodded, badly wanting him to be right.

She couldn't think of a time Dan hadn't been able to fix a problem. But now, between Jimmy's unexpected passing and her father's irrational demand for Dan to leave, Megan couldn't find any hope to hold onto.

Slowly, she ate her lasagna while Dan packed his clothes and necessities, only eating to satisfy her brother, Megan couldn't even taste it. He zipped the bag with effort and slung the strap over his shoulder, sighing deeply before forcing another grin.

"We're gonna be okay," he repeated.

"Okay," Megan managed a tiny raise in the corners of her lips, finding little reassurance in his words.

She followed Dan into the hallway, finding Dotty and her father still at the kitchen table. Greg looked decidedly more nauseous than angry, not even glancing at his daughter and stepson.

"Dotty," Dan interrupted the awkward silence, "You can reach me at the shop if ya need to."

"I will," she said, her expression softened dramatically the moment her focus changed, "And I'll see you soon."

"Yes, ma'am," Dan's eyes shifted to Greg, "You will."

Megan heard her father's low growl and dropped her plate into the sink.

"You leavin' now?" Greg's words were more of an order than a question.

"Yeah," Dan scoffed, "Grabbin' some stuff in the garage and I'll be outta your way."

"Better not be any'a my stuff," he grumbled, but Greg's surprise was obvious when Dan uncharacteristically sneered.

"What, besides that piece'a shit lawn mower is yours in there?" Dan's angry laugh was nothing Megan recognized, growing more anxious as she watched her brother lose control, "Everything in that garage belongs to me! You can't even name half my father's tools! I've been livin' here for twelve years and you don't have the right to throw me out without thirty days' notice!" Greg was about to refute, but Dan roared, "I've been waitin' for this, asshole! I know the law! You want me outta here? Fine I'm not arguin'. But you touch my shit, we're gonna have problems!"

Greg scoffed, but had clearly lost confidence in his argument, narrowing his eyes and said, "Don't worry, boy, I ain't gonna touch your daddy's shit."

Dan moved towards his stepfather, who flinched slightly, as if forcing himself not to lean back.

Scarier than Megan had ever heard, Dan barely more than whispered, "You lay a finger on my sister. I swear to God, Greg, you hurt her in any way, it won't be a legal thing. I'm just gonna kill you."

Greg's nostrils flared and Dotty stared slack-jawed. She'd certainly never seen even-tempered Dan so threatening, but her expression settled into understanding more than disbelief.

Dan glared at Greg until, apparently, he felt his message was understood, then turned away and tore open the junk drawer, handing Megan a plastic sandwich bag.

"Mind grabbin' my toothbrush for me?" he asked, halting her first step to the bathroom with a quick squeeze around her wrist and Megan appreciated the tenderness after witnessing him behave very unlike the brother she knew.

Megan reached for Dan's toothbrush in the cup, but her hand stopped, noticing the blue one next to it, Jimmy's. Her throat closed again and guilt swirled in her stomach as she remembered, despising herself for the moments she'd forgotten. But deep, shivering breaths brought a temporary calm Megan was grateful for, she was tired of crying.

Shoving Dan's toothbrush into the clear bag, she rolled the handle, wrapping it in the plastic on her way out of the bathroom. Dotty met her eyes as she snapped her leather case shut and offered an encouraging grin, but Megan found it impossible to return and hurried out the door.

It was strange not to push the screen and she looked despairingly at it, laying on its side, hanging by a badly mangled hinge. A crash behind the house, however, stole her attention, and Megan jumped down the porch steps, sprinting towards the garage.

But, when she rounded the front of the GMC, and the green obstacle wasn't blocking her view, Megan froze, staring at her brother, hurtling the tools he treasured so much at the garage walls.

Compared to his recent explosion inside, Dan's rage had grown into obviously blind fury as he assaulted his prized possessions. The garage, while never pristine, had suffered significant abuse in very short time and Dan wasn't stopping, cracking the workbench savagely with a pipe wrench before chucking the heavy instrument towards the back wall.

Megan turned at the sounds of rapid footsteps and saw Dotty snatch Greg's arm, hissing in his ear.

"Everything in there is his," she reminded, "You let that young man be, he ain't hurtin' nothin' a yours."

Greg stared at Dotty, then at the garage and finally Megan, before returning his nasty sneer and brushed the social worker off, disappearing around the corner towards the porch. Dotty waved sadly at Megan and she returned it the same way, shifting closer to the garage as Dotty turned to her red sedan at the end of the driveway.

Dan hadn't seemed to notice his brief audience, or that one of them was still watching. But he'd stopped attacking his things and was leaning over his forearms, his head dipped so low it rested on the workbench beneath quivering shoulders.

The box of fireworks had been moved to on top of the lawn mower. Neither had been touched, unlike everything else in the garage, and Megan couldn't help her curiosity, wondering why the contents hadn't been littered all over the floor in Dan's rage. One flap hung outside the box and she lifted the other.

Her heart squeezed painfully as her eyes settled on Jimmy's distinctive, uneven handwriting, scrawled in black ink on a sheet of torn notebook paper.

*Not without me - Got it?*

A shiver reverberated down her spine and Megan felt nauseous, staring at her brother's words from beyond the grave. Understanding the state of the garage as she listened to Dan's quiet sniffles and tried to tear her blurred gaze from Jimmy's last request.

She'd stayed in her room, refusing to eat when her father had told her to join him, thankful he didn't insist.

And, the next day, he seemed to have forgotten Megan was even there, curled miserably in her bed, broken inside. Nothing was right and she missed her brothers so much her chest ached, but she had no more tears to cry. Jimmy's happy laughter haunted her ears and Megan wished she could go back to when he was spinning her around at the park. She'd have held onto him and never let go. Never let him get in that damn car.

The addition of Dan's absence was crippling. Watching him leave had left Megan with a sense of cold abandonment.

The television blasted on the other side of her wall, but Megan hardly paid attention as she stared at her new window and contemplated what life would be like with her father, without Jimmy, without Dan. The idea of living out of cheap motel rooms or the sleeper cabin of his semi-truck was awful, terrifying even, and she pulled her faded blanket tighter around her shoulders.

Megan watched the sky turn dark before dawn slowly brightened it, hours of thought with no sleep left her with a warm, nauseous feeling in the back of her throat. Rest was fruitless. Her mind hadn't stopped considering every scenario she could concoct, which was a surprising amount, even to Megan. At some point the television had turned off, but she was too lost in concern to notice.

Based on her unfortunate, yet likely, assumptions, Megan's mind was made up. She would not live with her father, helpless to his whim and unprotected from his wrath for the next five years.

Sliding silently onto the floor, Megan slipped on jeans, a t-shirt and socks from the basket Dan had left on her floor. Turning the knob without a sound, she pulled her door open only as far as necessary to sneak through and returned it to the latch with the same stealth.

Greg's snores echoed from Dan's room and Megan's face burned with anger. She'd found comfort in that room many times, always being welcomed with open arms, but Dan wasn't there, and the man who was had never opened his arms to her.

Megan tip-toed down the hallway and peeked at the microwave. It was nearly seven o'clock. Dan would be at the shop soon, and, while Megan had never made the trip on her bicycle, she was confident she could get there just before he started work. Unlocking the door, Megan realized she didn't have a key. She did somewhere, but had lost it, someone was always home so it hadn't mattered. Considering the house was hardly safe anyway, she scoffed quietly and left the front door unbolted.

A pick-up rumbled by as Megan crept down the porch steps, but nothing else on her street stirred. Still being careful to not make a sound, she snuck her bike from under the porch overhang and took off down the street.

Jimmy's Oldsmobile sat by the curb as a cruel reminder he wasn't at work, he wasn't driving his friends around, and he wasn't home. Dan's truck, the always faithful GMC, was gone without any true promise of return. And, down the street, by the vacant lot, so the neighbors didn't complain, she passed Greg's semi-truck, squat and fat without a trailer, dirty, old and unreliable. Megan held up a rude hand gesture and pumped her legs harder, turning towards town when she reached the main road.

The gas station was open and she caught a glimpse of Uncle Bob restocking shelves, remembering the last time Jimmy had taken her there, now understanding he'd been giving Dan and Lacey some time to themselves. Guilt swirled Megan's stomach, thinking about how she'd whined at him for driving around so long and then her chest ached again, knowing they'd never drive around together again.

Her legs were sore by the time she reached town. The street wasn't busy, the pizza place hadn't yet opened for the day, but the manager of the Ace Hardware waved at Megan when he walked outside to light his cigarette. She waved back, unable to help herself wondering if he'd heard about Jimmy.

Finally, Jay's Lube 'n Tires came into view and the unmistakable, green truck sat on the side of the shop. Relief washed over Megan at the promise of seeing Dan and she forced her exhausted legs to pedal feverishly.

The garage doors were still shut and the open sign wasn't lit, but Megan heard a familiar grunt as she dropped her bike by Dan's truck and followed the noise to the back of the brick building. Her brother was piling tires as a burly man rolled them to the end of his open box-truck.

"Last one, Dan," he sighed, hardly assisting the tire's bouncing journey.

"Thanks, Bill," Dan caught it, his back to Megan, but Bill smiled at the intruder.

"Hey," he got Dan's attention and jerked his head, "Think ya got a visitor."

Dan turned and her stomach flipped, suddenly worried she shouldn't have come, but, when he beamed in surprise, Megan quickly closed the distance between them. Dan hardly had time to toss the tire aside before she wrapped her arms around his middle.

"What're you doin' here, sweetheart?" he asked, brushing hair from her face.

"I missed you," she admitted and he tightened his grip around her.

"I missed you, too," Dan said.

"This your little sister?" Bill asked.

"Yeah," Dan pulled Megan to his side, gesturing to the older man, "Megan this is Bill, he drops the tires off with me every Friday."

"Hi," she offered a tiny grin before looking at her sneakers.

"Hey, girly," Bill smiled, "You're up early for summer vacation."

She nodded, leaning closer to Dan.

"Does your dad know you're here?" Dan's question caused a painful squeeze in her throat.

Megan shook her head, expecting his heavy sigh.

"Dan, lemme straighten these for ya," Bill gestured the stack of tires.

"Thanks, Bill," he said, gently pushing Megan through the back door.

She'd been to Jay's shop many times, but never before it was open and found the unusual silence chilling. A large sedan was suspended several feet in the air on one of the two hydraulic lifts and Megan shuffled towards it, craning her neck to see the exposed undercarriage, but Dan tugged her away.

"So," he began, steering her into the front office and closed the shop door, "Wanna tell me what happened?"

"Nothin'," she shrugged, again finding interest in her sneakers.

"Megan," Dan sighed, tipping her chin up, "What happened? Did he say somethin' to you?"

She shook her head.

"He didn't-" Dan scowled and Megan shook her head more adamantly before he could finish the question.

"No, he didn't touch me," she said, "I just don't wanna be there."

Dan grimaced, "I know, but you don't have much of a choice, sweetheart."

Megan's eyes stung with tears, turning away from him as her chest constricted painfully.

"For now, okay," he insisted quickly, halting her mid-pivot.

"Are you gonna try 'n make him sign those, papers?" Megan asked, suppressing the excitement she felt at the idea.

"If I can," Dan sounded disheartened, but attempted a hopeful smirk as he continued, "Dotty 'n I are tryin' to make it near impossible for him to take you on the road. Don't say anything, we don't know how it's all gonna work out, but she says we've got a chance."

"I don't wanna live with him here either," she muttered.

Dan chuckled lightly and shook his head, "I'm doin' my best here, kid."

"I know, I love you," Megan wrapped her arms around him, the comforting smell of his t-shirt flooded her nose.

"I love you, too," he said and kissed her hair.

Dan walked behind the counter and reached for the telephone, cradling the handset between his shoulder and chin as he dialed.

"What are you doing?" Megan asked in hushed disbelief, knowing exactly what he was doing.

"He's gonna be worried, Megan," Dan said simply.

And she jumped over the front of the desk, knocking over a coffee mug of pens and slammed her finger into the cradle.

Dan gaped and his eyes went wide. Megan's face flushed, retracting her hand slowly, her anger vanishing into deep mortification.

"What the hell, Megan?!" Dan barked, slamming down the phone.

"Please don't call him," she begged, "I hate him."

Dan bit his lips and took a deep breath, "Sweetheart, I have to."

Megan stared at him, her chest caved while numbing abandonment returned more painfully than before. She didn't want to go back to the house she'd just fled, but, when, Dan picked up the handset again, Megan resigned to one of the worn waiting chairs.

"Hey, Greg, it's Dan," he sounded far away, "Just wanted to let'cha know Megan's safe, I got her," there was a pause before Dan scoffed lightly, "She rode her bike over here, I'm just waitin' for Jay to get in and I'll drive her home."

The word 'home' stabbed Megan's already aching chest. The empty house she'd ridden away from was not a home.

"Okay, well, when're ya gonna be back?" Dan asked, "Yeah, I mean, I'm workin' and later I gotta stop by the funeral home, don't really wanna bring her if I don't have to- No, I know she can, Greg, that's not the point," he growled quietly, "Alright, y'know what, just don't worry about it, I'll take care of her."

He slammed the handset even harder than before and Megan jumped.

Dan took a deep breath before raising his head to meet her eyes and smirked, "Wanna hang out with me today?"

Megan grinned.

"C'mon," Dan jerked his head and she followed him through a door behind the front desk, immediately leading up a steep, narrow staircase.

A damp smell grew stronger with each creaky stair to the landing that housed an old, office door. Inside was a small room with filing cabinets along the walls, some stacked so high with boxes that the ceiling tiles had been lifted a few inches into the unsettling darkness above. A two-seat sofa sat under the only window in the room and Megan recognized the duffel bag nestled in its corner.

With trepidation and disbelief, she turned slowly to meet Dan's eyes.

"Jay's lettin' me stay here, 'til I get everything figured out," he answered the unasked question.

"You can't fit on that," Megan pointed angrily at the loveseat.

"It folds out, Meg," he chuckled, "Here," Dan pulled an old television from a cluttered desk and situated it on an upside down milkcrate that was serving as a pathetic coffee table in front of the sofa, "If ya mess with the antennas you might be able to get more than three channels."

He dusted off the tiny screen with his sleeve and turned the channel knob. The screen brightened into fuzzy, zig-zagging lines, but Dan flipped the knob and the outlines of people slowly focused.

Megan curled up next to his stuffed duffel bag and absently commented, "Sam's granpa still has a TV like that, but it's bigger."

"This came outta a Chevy Astro van," Dan shrugged, "There's a chance it'll stop workin' for no reason, just be gentle with it. I gotta start work, but I'm gonna take you home later."

"Can I stay here?" she figured it couldn't hurt to ask, but knew the answer.

His sigh began the expected response, "No, sweetheart, but your dad's got some stuff goin' on today, so you can hang out 'til I can get outta here."

"Pederson's havin' a special?" Megan's comment earned a short, yet hearty, laugh from Dan, but, without Jimmy to repeat it to, she didn't feel the pride she usually did after a well-delivered joke.

"I really don't know what his plans are, Meg," Dan lied.

"Kay," she mumbled and pretended to be intrigued in the morning news program.

"I'll get lunch for us," Dan promised, "If you need me, come down 'n tell Jay. Okay?"

"Yeah, fine," Megan shrugged and kept her eyes glued to the unfocused, colorless screen as he left, latching the door before his heavy steps faded down the stairway.

Greg's plans undoubtably included a corner seat at Pederson's bar. She wasn't thrilled about spending her day in the foreign upstairs of Jay's shop, but really didn't want to be alone in an empty house, waiting for her father to arrive in an unknown state of inebriation. She appreciated that Dan hadn't allowed the option, even if she was mad at him over the promise to take her back later.

The shop noises were muffled in the upstairs office, but Megan could hear metal grinding and deep voices shouting conversationally while she flipped through dated car magazines from a stack on the floor, paying them very little attention, and absolutely none to the fuzzy television. Her thoughts strayed to the house she'd left, her father's plans to drag her around the country in his smelly semi-truck, and the most painful. Jimmy. His empty bedroom, his Oldsmobile sitting abandoned on the street and the ghostly echo of his laughter she'd never hear again. Guilt absorbed Megan every time she tried to stop thinking of Jimmy, but thinking about him was agonizing.

She tossed the third *Car and Driver* she'd skimmed the pictures of to the other side of the tiny sofa and slid her feet to the floor. There wasn't a bathroom upstairs, so Megan crept down to the lobby where Jay was sitting behind the front desk.

"Hey there, Megan," he turned with his crooked, yellow smile, "I heard we had company. How ya doin'?"

"M'okay," she shrugged, Jay's eyes were sad and Megan anticipated an obligatory apology for Jimmy's unexpected passing, hoping he wouldn't.

"Got a lot goin' on, kid," the corners of his mouth turned down behind his gray scruff, "I told Dan, anything I can do let me know, goes for you too."

"Thanks, Jay," she forced a grin, turning her toes towards the small bathroom, "I just gotta-"

"I won't keep ya," he swung his desk chair and returned to the computer.

She closed the bathroom door quietly on her way out, but Jay swiveled at the nearly nonexistent sound.

"No chance I could get ya to help me with somethin'?" he asked.

"Sure," Megan nodded, welcoming a distraction of any kind.

Jay jerked his head at three filing cabinets lining the wall between the front desk and waiting area. A Valvoline box, overflowing with papers, sat on the middle cabinet.

"Okay," Jay sighed, hauling the box to the floor at Megan's feet, "I'm a little behind on my filing."

"What do I do?" she asked, overwhelmed by the seemingly infinite forms.

"It's easy," he promised and his grin was encouraging.

It didn't take her long to understand Jay's system and began sorting the mess. Megan didn't mind how much louder it was than upstairs and, even though they didn't talk, Jay was good company.

The whirring from the shop became louder for a moment and a familiar chuckle tore Megan's eyes from the repair order in her hand.

"Y'know, there's laws about child labor," Dan leaned against Jay's desk, smirking, and winked at her.

"I'm buyin' lunch," Jay retorted with sarcastic indignity.

"I'm kiddin' around," Dan shook his head.

"Still buyin' lunch, so figure out what'cha both want," Jay said, continuing when Dan began to protest, "Don't argue with me."

"Why not?" Dan laughed, "I've been winnin' lately."

Jay scoffed and returned his attention to the computer screen, but was only trying to pretend he wasn't amused.

"You hungry?" Dan asked and Megan nodded, "What'cha want?" she shrugged and Dan dropped his head dramatically before looking at Jay, "Three times a day with this."

"She's a cute girl," Jay grinned at Megan, "She's allowed."

"What'd ya eat last night?" Dan asked and Megan shook her head, unsurprised at the crease of concern deepening between his eyebrows, "Did you eat at all yesterday?" she shook her head again and Dan closed his eyes a moment, releasing a quiet sigh, "Ya want pizza?"

"Sure," Megan said, her stomach was painfully empty, anything would've been acceptable.

"I'll call it in," Jay said.

"Mind doin' half cheese?" Dan asked, jerking his head at Megan.

"She can get her own pizza for helpin' me with that, hell, I'll buy her three," Jay laughed, "Hey, Meg, want one'a those big chocolate chip cookies too?"

Megan smiled, but it fell quickly. She loved those giant, warm cookies, but had always shared them with Jimmy when Dan would spring an extra few bucks for dessert. Her throat tightened and Megan shook her head, focusing on the repair order in her lap.

She didn't listen to the hushed exchange between her brother and his boss, her ears buzzing from the pressure of forcing herself not to cry.

An unmistakable increase in noise from the shop didn't escape Megan's ears, however, and she glanced up when Dan's bent knees entered her blurry vision. He crouched in front of her, his greasy hand grazing her shoulder, and Megan tossed the forms aside as her feebly contained tears broke free.

She buried her face in Dan's shoulder and hoped Jay wasn't watching, but, when Megan relented the comfort of his work shirt, she was relieved to see they were alone.

"I'm sorry," she sniffed.

"No reason," Dan shook his head, halting his dirty thumb before wiping her cheeks and grimaced lightheartedly, "I don't wanna make ya look like a football player."

Megan forced a pathetic attempt at a giggle, sniffling hard and wiped her tears dry with the back of her hands.

"I gotta keep goin' on this Impala," Dan stood, asking, "You gonna be okay?"

"Yeah," Megan lied.

"I'm just in the shop if you need me, and we'll go pick up lunch soon," Dan said, backtracking to the shop door.

Megan nodded to let him know she'd heard, picking the discarded form off the grimy tile floor, but a high-pitched ding whipped her attention to the door. An elderly woman she recognized, but not by name, walked into the office, her hand shaking on her cherry-red cane. Megan was relieved when Jay returned from the shop at neary the same time.

"Mrs. Sullivan," he smiled, taking faster steps than usual and gestured one of the worn chairs, "I didn't hear your horn."

"Oh, I don't wanna do that, Jay," she scoffed, shaking her head as she eased carefully onto the seat, "I can park my car and walk in here like everybody else."

"Never said ya couldn't Mrs. Sullivan," Jay's tone was light and Megan hid a smile when he rolled his eyes at her while the old woman wasn't looking, "But we don't mind, really. Next time just pull up to the garage door 'n honk. We'll come out, and you don't have to walk across the lot."

"You act like it's a Walmart," she laughed hoarsely, "I see you got a little helper."

Megan's ears burned, but she kept her focus on the papers, pretending she hadn't heard.

"I need it," Jay said gratefully, "Megan's Dan's little sister, she's helpin' me get back on top of all that filing I hate doin'."

"Danny's sister?" Mrs. Sullivan stared at Megan, who couldn't pretend she hadn't heard Jay, and raised her eyes, offered a small, very forced grin before dropping her focus again to the form in her lap, but heard Mrs. Sullivan continue, "Didn't Danny's brother-"

Jay cleared his throat, shifting slightly to block her view of Megan, "You got your keys, Mrs. Sullivan? Just the oil change 'n rotate today, right?"

Megan heard the old woman stumble a little over her words and the jingle of keys being passed from one hand to another. Then the door chimed again, leaving the room in awkward silence.

"I am so sorry about your brother," Mrs. Sullivan said, compelling Megan to meet her sad eyes.

"Thank you," she muttered the all too familiar response, wishing Mrs. Sullivan wouldn't continue.

"I lost my brother too," a pained grin crept across her wrinkled lips.

But Megan just nodded, keeping her head down while swallowing hard, barely helping the raw soreness in her throat. She didn't want to hear about Mrs. Sullivan's dead brother and she certainly wasn't going to talk about Jimmy.

When the shop door opened and Dan walked in Megan couldn't have been more relieved. He, however, scrunched his eyebrows at her fresh tears, but his attention was quickly diverted.

"Danny," Mrs. Sullivan called, waving the hand that wasn't still firmly latched to her cane.

294

"Hello, Mrs. Sullivan," Dan said, "How are you?"

"Oh, my life doesn't change," the old woman said and Megan's throat throbbed painfully when she continued pitiably, "I heard at my women's club yesterday, I'm very sorry about your brother. Such a shock, and so sad."

"Yeah," Dan stiffened, but he politely said, "Thank you, it was. Jay's pullin' your Buick in right now, Armando's gonna take care of it today."

"Armando?" Mrs. Sullivan openly grimaced, "Is that the Mexican fella I've seen around here?"

"He's Puerto Rican," Dan stated flatly, "And yeah, he's worked here for two years. Lucy's in good hands."

Mrs. Sullivan further proved her ignorance to his tone in her sweet response, "If you say so, y'know I trust you and Jay."

Dan forced a grin and nodded curtly, crooking his finger inconspicuously at his side. Familiar with the gesture, Megan slid the forms from her lap to the floor and followed. Before slipping into the shop behind Dan, Megan gave Mrs. Sullivan a tiny wave. She didn't want to be rude, even if the old woman had been.

"Hey, hey, mija!" a portly man with a wide smile and a faded tattoo poking out of his t-shirt collar shouted from the other side of a beige Buick in the small shop.

Megan immediately brightened, she'd met Armando a few times and he was always smiling. Dan had told her he was born in Puerto Rico and moved to the United States alone when he was fourteen, working every job he could get. He'd only been a year older than Megan, in a new country, barely knowing the language and entirely by himself. She'd always found his story impressively terrifying.

"Hi, Mondo," she smiled, surprising her unsuspecting lips, but his beaming expression was contagious.

The nickname started because she'd had a difficult time saying Armando, but he insisted he preferred it, even after she'd been able to correctly pronounce his name.

"Mrs. Sullivan knows you're workin' on it," Dan humorously warned.

"Crusty old white lady?" Armando chuckled, "Tell her she don't need to worry, I'mma fix Lucy up good. Lower her a bit, put some spinners on there with the hydraulics. She gonna love it."

Megan had no idea what Armando was saying, but knew it was a joke and laughed with Dan and Jay. Her chest felt a little lighter afterwards.

"We're gonna go grab lunch," Dan announced, leading Megan to the rear shop door.

"Jayman, you get me lunch too?" Armando's sarcastic plea caused Megan another quick burst of amusement.

"I got two large pizzas 'n breadsticks," Jay scoffed, "Pretty sure there's enough."

"I don't know man," Armando patted his ample middle, "Sounds like a single serving for me."

Megan's giggling earned a wink from the stocky jokester. She liked Armando and appreciated his comic relief more than ever, certain he knew about Jimmy and glad he was acting like he didn't.

"Why's she call her car Lucy?" Megan asked on the way to Dan's truck behind the shop.

"It's a Buick Lucerne," Dan rolled his eyes, "She's just one'a those people, I guess."

"Weird?" Megan offered.

"Yeah," Dan agreed, "And thoughtless sometimes too."

Jay's shop was down the street from the pizza place and Dan parallel parked his GMC in an empty spot out front.

"Is Lacey working?" Megan asked.

"I'm not sure," Dan said.

The smell of warm bread and onions filled Megan's nose, welcoming them at the threshold, and her eyes found Lacey smiling behind the counter.

"I was wonderin' who Jay ordered all that pizza for," she giggled, leaning on her forearms and brushed against a rack of snack-sized chips.

"Got a surprise visitor at work today," Dan winked at Megan.

"And now I got two," Lacey beamed, "Pizza's almost done."

"Good, I'm starving," Megan intended her remark to be lighthearted, despite its truthfulness, but a sad smirk flashed across Dan's face and guilt thumped an uncomfortable rhythm in her gut. She hated making Dan feel bad.

"Well, we can't have that," Lacey snagged a bag of potato chips from its clip on the counter display and offered them to Megan, giving Dan a wink, "My treat."

Megan could tell he wanted to argue, but, in the few moments of hesitation, she offered her familiar, sneaky grin while inching her hand towards the bag, pinching it between her fingers and cradled the gift dramatically against her chest. Dan expelled a short laugh and Lacey giggled. Megan was pleased by their reaction to her impulsive, comedic move and knew Jimmy would be proud when she had a chance to tell him.

Then her chest caved in again.

"Hey, Megan," Dan's voice was far away, his hand on her shoulder equally as distant.

How could she smile and joke when Jimmy was dead? How could she forget Jimmy was dead? The lack of contents in Megan's stomach was a small blessing as nausea forced hot acid through her impossibly tight throat and tears poured down her cheeks. The foil bag crinkled in her twisting fingers and Megan had the urge to hand them back, and refuse the pizza too. Jimmy wouldn't ever eat again, it wasn't fair.

"Megan," Dan snapped, but only enough to get her attention and wiped her tears as he hushed encouragement, "Breathe, sweetheart."

Dan's comfort helped and she sniffled hard after catching her breath. Megan burned with embarrassment, turning her watery eyes on her brother, and hoped Lacey wasn't staring at her pitifully. She wasn't, having snuck into the kitchen to give Dan and Megan some privacy.

"I'm sor-" her whimper was directly interrupted.

"Shh," Dan held her tight and whispered reassurance, "Got nothin' to be sorry for."

Megan shook her head, pushing away from him, and took another shuddering breath before blurting the confession, "I forgot!"

"What'd you forget?" Dan tipped her chin, but Megan couldn't meet his eyes.

"That, Jimmy's," her throat squeezed again, refusing to say the word and she ground her teeth on an escaping sob.

"Me too," Dan admitted.

"Really?" Megan sniffled earnestly.

"Few times, it hurts worse every time," Megan nodded in agreement and Dan said, "Don't feel bad about it though."

Dan's resolve sounded like he was trying to set his own guilt at ease as much as Megan's.

"C'mon," he patted her on the back and Megan wiped her nose with the back of her hand as Dan stepped up to the counter, calling into the kitchen, "Hey, Lacey, how're those pizza's comin'?"

"Done," Lacey answered brightly, walking around the kitchen corner with three flat boxes and slid them across the counter, "Here, Jay paid over the phone."

"Thanks, Lace," Dan grinned, taking the stacked pizzas and gestured Megan towards the door.

"Will I see you later?" Lacey asked, leaning so far across the counter her feet couldn't possibly still be on the floor.

"I'll call ya either way," Dan promised, pushing the door open with his foot.

"Bye, Megan, I'll see you soon," Lacey waved.

"Bye," Megan forced the corners of her lips upward for a second before leading Dan out to his truck.

Her stomach still swirled with guilt, absently climbing into the passenger side of the green GMC while pressure pounded her head, but Megan wouldn't stop thinking of Jimmy, afraid she'd forget again.

"Hey," Dan patted her knee, "It's gonna be okay."

She nodded, but didn't believe the placating lie, and stared out the passenger window.

# Chapter 14

The afternoon passed far too quickly for Megan, dreading the moment Dan would take her back to the house, Greg's house.

When he stopped at the funeral home Dan insisted he would only be a minute, leaving the keys in the truck for Megan to listen to the radio, but she didn't want to. Every song had a way of bringing Jimmy's face to the forefront of her mind, lingering there with his joyful, sneaky smile.

Dan could've been gone a few minutes or an hour, Megan was trapped in grief, staring out the open window. Birds sang to each other, fluttering from tree to tree and her thoughts trailed to the nest and the missing baby robin. Her eyes brimmed with tears, unsure if she was crying for the bird or Jimmy or both. But the green GMC was rumbling out of the lot before Megan even realized Dan was behind the wheel again.

"You okay?" Dan asked, dragging Megan from her daze.

"No," she said simply.

"Yeah," his agreement was nearly inaudible, "Me either."

"I don't wanna go back there," Megan repeated.

"I know," Dan said sadly, "I wish I didn't have to take you."

"You don't," she crossed her arms, turning towards the window.

Dan just sighed and kept driving.

Greg's semi-truck was still parked in the same place down the street, though he was most likely still at Pederson's. Since it was less than a mile away, he'd often make the trek on foot if he couldn't con someone into a free ride. But Jimmy's Oldsmobile wasn't on the street.

"Where's Jimmy's car?" Megan already assumed the answer, her question propelled by angry disbelief more than confusion.

"I've got an idea," Dan growled, jamming the shifter into park.

"He can't!" she exploded, slamming her fists on her knees, "That's not his! He can't! It's Jimmy's car! It's not his! It's not his!"

Megan's chest was going to burst, her entire body shook with rage, but she couldn't fall apart, Dan needed her to be strong.

"No, he can't," Dan whispered, "It won't happen again, don't worry."

Megan was worried. She'd never been so worried in her whole life, but she'd always had her brothers to take care of everything. Jimmy was gone and Dan was stripped of his only family as well as his home. She was alone, forced to live with a man who had proven his unpredictability and hateful nature at every opportunity.

Dan grabbed her bike out of the truck bed, propping it against the wobbly railing post and followed Megan up the porch steps. But he paused, shaking his head, and sighed at the screen door, still holding on by one bent hinge.

"Are you stayin'?" Megan begged.

"Just 'til Greg gets home," Dan said, thumbing his keys in one hand, but Megan grabbed the handle and pushed open the unlocked door.

Dan scoffed and shook his head, tossing his keys on the counter, like he always did, and pulled open the junk drawer.

"What're you doin'?" Megan asked.

"I don't need you trippin' or cuttin' yourself on this," he kicked the broken screen door gently, crouching in the open doorway and unscrewed the last of the fastenings holding it to the frame.

He didn't have to, but he would anyway. He hadn't had to sacrifice his own future to make sure she had one, but he had. His little brother, who he'd shared a childhood, the loss of both parents, and years of abuse from their stepfather, was gone. Megan had no doubt, despite an unbearable hollowness growing inside, Dan's pain was greater than anyone's, but still, his concern for her didn't waiver.

Megan put her arms around Dan's shoulders and said, "I love you."

"I love you, too, sweetheart," he patted her forearm, "Why don't you find somethin' to eat and I'll get it goin' for ya?"

"I can make my own food," she mumbled sadly.

"I like makin' you food," Dan shrugged, returning to the stubborn screw.

Megan opened the refrigerator and pulled out the foil covered lasagna on the bottom shelf. Greg had obviously helped himself to the condolence casseroles and hadn't even bothered to cut uniform pieces, leaving a jagged square in one corner. Megan hopped onto the counter, snatching a plate quickly from the cabinet before dropping almost silently to the floor. Dan's smirk proved her attempt to be sneaky failed.

"Better grab me one too," he said, focusing again on the hinge, and Megan repeated her acrobatics on the counter.

They ate in the living room with the television on, though neither was watching, and Megan took slow, deliberate bites, hoping Dan wouldn't leave if she never finished. It was a silly, childish ploy she knew she should be too old to consider, but couldn't help it.

Megan couldn't help curling next to him on the couch either, a familiar comfort in a suddenly unfamiliar world. The sky darkened outside and, despite trying to stay awake, her full belly encouraged a betraying yawn. She leaned closer to Dan.

"Hey," he nudged her shoulder, "Get to bed."

"You're gonna leave," she didn't mean to whine, but she did anyway.

"I'm not gonna leave you alone," Dan promised.

"I'm alone when he's here anyway," Megan mumbled, pushing off the couch and headed to her bedroom, but the distinctive sound of scratching rotors and squealing brakes halted her step.

Dan stood from the couch and jerked his head down the hall, "Go, you don't have to deal with this."

Megan took a step towards the hall, but stopped again, looking at Jimmy's closed door and then at Dan. She couldn't let him deal with Greg alone, Jimmy never had. But Jimmy wasn't there, Megan was, and she stepped up to Dan's side.

302

"You don't have to deal with this," she corrected, doing her best to hide the anxiety tumbling in her gut.

Her father's heavy footsteps on the creaky porch steps turned the tumbling into flips, but Megan took a silent, deep breath and narrowed her eyes on the opening front door.

"Waitin' up for me?" Greg scoffed, leaning exhaustedly against the door even after it latched.

"Wasn't about to leave my sister alone," Dan spat through gritted teeth.

"Cut the cord, kid, she's thirteen," Greg chuckled, but abruptly snarled, "And what the hell're you doin' here, huh? I told'ja to get out! I'll call the cops!"

"Don't worry, I'm leavin'," Dan challenged, "But be careful with your threats, especially when you drove a stolen car drunk."

"Stolen?" Greg laughed, though it faded when Dan stuck out his hand.

"That title's in my name," he said simply, "It's insured under my policy."

Greg slammed the Oldsmobile keys into Dan's hand, growling, "Wasn't like it's doin' any good just sittin' out there. How's'bout you get your piece'a shit off my property then?"

"Wasn't aware you owned the street," Dan remarked snidely.

Greg pushed passed Dan into the kitchen, expertly steadying himself with the back of a kitchen chair and set his irritated gaze on his daughter, "What the hell're you still doin' up? Get t'bed."

Megan looked at Dan, who nodded, but she lurched as Greg exploded.

"NOW!" he barked, "I'm the dad! I'm in charge! Not him!"

"Don't yell at her!" Dan stepped between them and Greg halted his advance, "And don't you dare touch her!"

"I've never laid a finger on her!" Greg asserted.

"Only 'cause we didn't let'cha!" Dan argued.

"You 'n yer brother deserved every beatin' I ever gave you!" spit flew from Greg's mouth as he yelled.

"Yeah?!" Dan moved intimidatingly towards his stepfather, "I remember how I deserved that broken arm. Or wait, that time was an accident, right? But what about our mom? What did she do, huh?"

"I never touched your mother," Greg grumbled with much less conviction than his claim of never hurting Megan.

Bitter laugher escaped as Dan shook his head and said, "Your ability to convince yourself of your own lies will always astound me."

"Get out!" Greg's voice shook through his clenched teeth.

"Megan," Dan said, never taking his eyes off his adversary, "Go to bed, I'll be here at nine to pick you up."

"I'll take her-" Greg began.

"You're not goin' anywhere near my brother's funeral!" Dan snapped.

Greg glowered, but said nothing, and shut himself in the bathroom, slamming the door so hard the frame rattled.

"Don't, please," a scared sob broke passed Megan's lips, but she knew Dan couldn't stay, or take her with, and fear churned her stomach, dreading the moment she'd be alone with Greg.

Dan crouched, pulled her into his arms and whispered, "Go to bed. Lock your door. He's not gonna do anything, but just in case. Okay?" Megan nodded, "I'll be here early and we'll go get breakfast. Sound good?" again she nodded and Dan kissed her hair, "Okay, I love you. Go, I'll see you tomorrow."

"I love you, too," Megan whispered, squeezing him until he insistently patted her back and pulled away.

She locked her door and collapsed on her bed, sobbing when the thud of Dan's truck door reached her ears.

Darlene knocked early the next morning. She had a new black dress, sweater and shoes for Megan, who was relieved, but further pained. She'd hardly slept, burdened by one anxiety after another, though only minorly concerned about not having anything appropriate to wear for the day, futilely wishing she didn't need a mourning outfit at all.

Greg insisted it was unnecessary, emerging from Dan's room shirtless and scratching his pale, bulging gut. Megan didn't miss Darlene's momentary disgust before assuring him she was more than happy to help, adding how important it was to her that Megan was receiving love and support. Greg grunted agreeably while burying his head in the refrigerator.

Megan thanked her, promising Dan would be by soon, and left for her bedroom before Darlene closed the front door, deserting Greg in the kitchen.

"I'm changing," Megan called in response to a sharp knock on her door.

"It's wrong of your brother to keep me from Jimmy's service," Greg said bitterly, "Y'know that, right? It's just wrong."

Megan didn't say anything. Her mouth was dry and her stomach twisted uncomfortably, wondering for a moment if he was right. Vigorously shaking her head as the memory of Greg kicking Jimmy on the kitchen floor played in her mind. He didn't deserve to be anywhere near his memorial.

"I know you think ya gotta be on Dan's side with everything," Greg continued contemptuously, "But he's in the wrong here, Meggie-"

"Go away!" she snapped with far more confidence than she actually felt, "And my name is Megan!"

A heartless scoff preceded a loud, sharp crack as his fist connected brutally with the other side of her bedroom door. Megan's arms instinctually wrapped around herself, staring at the door, and sighed with relief when he stomped away.

She changed quickly, even though there was more than enough time, and leaned over the top of her bookshelf, watching impatiently out her window. Her fingers traced the bottom of the frame, remembering when her brothers had replaced it, Jimmy's hands right where hers were.

The distinctive growl of Dan's truck interrupted her brewing tears and Megan sniffled hard before bolting from her room. Greg didn't say good-bye when she ran passed him in the living room, only slowing at the porch steps, unsure of the new shoes, but safely in sight of the truck.

"Look at you," Dan praised as she slid onto the bench seat.

"Darlene brought it over," Megan tugged the hem over her knees and clicked the toes of her new shoes.

"Well, that was nice of her," Dan said, backing out of the driveway, "No problems after I left?"

"No," she shook her head, deciding not to worry him with the brief altercation between Greg and her bedroom door.

"You hungry?" he asked and Megan shook her head, far too nauseous to eat.

They spoke less the closer they got to the funeral home. A long ramp wrapped around one side of the renovated Victorian house and paint peeled from the siding. Megan's nose wrinkled at the stale smell in the foyer and her stinging eyes found the ugly, floral carpet while she followed Dan.

The funeral director greeted them, though Megan barely looked up from the distressed roses, her throat closing painfully as the reality of the day sunk in. The man briefly ran through the morning's itinerary and Dan's hand absently gripped her shoulder, reminding Megan he was just as scared to be there as she was.

Darlene, Sam and Lacey arrived with poster boards covered in pictures and Megan studied a cluster of geraniums, she knew what memories the photographs had captured. But, passing the visitation room, she caught sight of Jimmy's school portrait. Megan thought it was strange since she didn't remember any of Jimmy's school pictures being framed, let alone purchased.

Sam sat next to her on the couch in the private room every time Megan snuck away from the visitors, which she did several times in the few

306

hours they were there. Dan didn't seem to mind and Lacey hadn't left his side other than to check on Megan the first time she'd disappeared. Megan appreciated every gentle back rub and shoulder squeeze she saw Lacey give Dan. He had never looked more beaten despite his neutral appearance.

Everyone was sorry. They all offered to help in any way they could and commented how well she and Dan were holding up. Jimmy's normally boisterous and care-free friends were huddled in tight groups, crying on each other, while they pointed out pictures of themselves on the poster boards. Some of Jimmy's co-workers filtered through, but only a few stayed for his eulogy.

During the service, Megan was absorbed in memories of fooling around with Jimmy during countless sermons of the same reverend who was droning on next to his ashes. Dan kept his arm around her and Megan leaned into his side, having no idea how to give him the support he needed, but she was the only one who understood his pain.

When the preacher announced that Mr. and Mrs. King would be offering lunch to whoever wanted to join at Pederson's, she looked at Dan, but he didn't seem surprised. It was the only restaurant in town besides the pizza place and McDonald's, but Megan's stomach twisted with the immediate image of her father sitting at the familiar bar. Whether Dan understood her silent concerns or not, the arm he kept around her shoulders on the way out of the funeral home was wholly welcomed.

"Do you think Greg'll be there?" she asked after shutting the truck door.

Dan sighed, "I hope not."

He wasn't there. But Megan still glanced at the door every time she heard it open, until Sam repeated his insistent request to play shuffleboard and dragged her away from their table.

Dan, Lacey, Darlene, Mr. and Mrs. King and several teachers were sipping drinks and exchanging stories about Jimmy around a few pushed together tables in a secluded corner. Megan didn't want to listen and was unsure why she'd refused Sam's initial suggestion, though she had no interest in the games they usually enjoyed.

Others came and some left, but Megan and Sam only stopped sliding the little weights across the gritty surface when they were interrupted by someone's goodbye, and the repeated condolences Megan wished would stop.

Mr. Glasby, Jay and Armando had just excused themselves from their short visit when an unwelcome salutation got Megan's attention. Sam's hand gripped her arm, but she hardly noticed his thoughtful hinderance, scowling hatefully at the intruder.

"Bob, Cheryl," Greg greeted Mr. and Mrs. King with civil disdain before turning to Dan, "Good service?"

"It was fine," Dan said quickly.

Megan noticed a short moment of unbalance in Greg's brisk nod, less than what she expected, but enough to confirm his activities had followed their usual course. When his glazed eyes fell on her, Megan turned to the dartboards against the back wall, pretending she hadn't seen.

"We playin' darts now?" Sam asked indifferently.

Megan shrugged.

"We can play pool," he suggested.

She briefly considered the billiard table in the bar, hidden from the dining side, and shook her head, "I wanna stay around Dan."

Whatever Sam planned on saying was interrupted as their attentions spun towards a chair clattering to the floor. Having only ever known Mr. King to be kind and reserved, Megan was stunned by his furious tone and unexpected aggression.

"You need to leave!" Mr. King shouted, towering over Greg with every inch of his minor height advantage, "You will not speak to my wife like that!"

"Your wife's been stirrin' shit up in my house for years!" Greg's expression was threatening, but he increasingly backtracked from the attacker he'd provoked.

Dan jumped to his feet, but Lacey seized his wrist.

"You wanna blame somebody you don't need to look any further than a mirror, Greg!" Mr. King was completely oblivious to his wife's gentle tugs on his sport coat as he took another looming step towards the drunk, and Mrs. King relented her hold to avoid toppling out of her seat.

"Bull!" Greg spat, his eyes darting desperately around the group, but avoiding his assailant's, "This whole damn town's been against me since Lisa died! The hell was I supposed to do with three kids by myself?!"

"Don't flatter yourself, Greg," Darlene interjected, bitterness building with each word, "You've never done a thing to help those kids. And we've all hated you since way before Lisa passed."

Megan glanced at Sam, his eyes were wide at his mom, who was smirking at Greg, as if baiting him to respond. His shoulders heaved with palpable anger, but snapped his lips shut every time he opened his mouth. Finally, Greg's attention shifted from Darlene and nausea boiled in Megan's gut when their eyes locked.

"Megan, we're leaving, now!" his demand instigated her instant retreat, but quickly realized she was trapped when her back met the dartboard machine.

"Leave her-" Dan began to argue.

"You stay outta this!" Greg snapped and returned his fury, "Megan, let's go!"

"I don't," tears blurred her vision, but Megan looked pleadingly at Dan.

"Greg!" Darlene's chair hit the floor when she jumped to her feet, "She's playing, leave her alone!"

"Megan, we're goin' home, now!" Greg yelled, entirely ignoring Darlene, and pointed an unsteady finger at his target, then the floor in front of him.

"You go home!" Darlene shouted, lowering her voice, but not her tone, with the promise, "I'll drop her off tonight."

"And give ya more time t'poison my kid against me?! Megan, now!"

The moment Greg took an advancing step, Dan shook free of Lacey's grip and rammed him against a wall. Mr. King snatched Dan's upper arm and tried to pull the young man off his stepfather while Lacey, Mrs. King and Darlene earnestly protested Dan's readying fist. Megan vaguely noticed Sam's arms around her as crushing sobs wracked her chest.

"Do it, you little shit!" Greg raged.

"Dan!" Mr. King snatched his wrist, "He's not worth it!"

"Y'all think I'm the problem?!" Greg laughed manically, "Look at this kid! He's crazy!"

"Dan, please!" Lacey's emotional plea broke the snarl on his face.

Dan's fist relaxed, but he pushed roughly off Greg, growling, "Go."

"Not without my kid," Greg's resolve churned Megan's rising nausea.

"Leave her alone! You're drunk!" Dan's plea was buried under enraged fear.

"I am not drunk!" Greg tried to hide a badly timed stumble by leaning on a table, resentfully insisting, "And I didn't drive here anyhow, so try again, smartass!"

"After what we had to do today?" Dan was beside himself and pointed intensely at Megan, "Look at what she's wearing! You're not makin' her walk all the way home! It's not happening!"

Greg's eyebrows elevated and he chuckled sinisterly, keeping his contemptuous glare on Dan as he turned his head towards the bar side of Pederson's.

"Hey, Artie," he called the bartender with sinister amusement, "Mind gettin' the cops down here? Havin' a little domestic dispute."

Dan's badly contained fury instantly reignited and Mr. King, again, snatched his arm, struggling to hold him back.

"For Christ's sake, Greg!" Darlene exclaimed, marching towards the bar and hollered to her coworker, "Artie, we're fine-"

"Like hell we are!" Greg scoffed, blocking Darlene's course, "I don't need you takin' my kid home, or buyin' her clothes. What I need is for y'all shit stirrin' busybodies to get outta my business."

"It is my business, Greg," Darlene snapped, "I've been there for those kids! I love them, something I don't think you're even capable of!" her voice lowered, hissing pointedly, "Lisa was one of the dearest friends I've ever had and there is nothing you could ever do to redeem yourself for the hell you put her through. You don't know the half of what I know about the monster you are."

"You don't know shit," Greg bore down on Darlene, but she didn't move.

"We all saw the bruises on those boys. But Lisa," Darlene paused, leveling him with scornful disdain, "You low life, disgusting excuse for a man, don't think I don't know exactly what you did."

Crushing silence followed her vague, yet obviously heinous, accusation and Megan's mouth went dry, acid bubbling in the back of her throat. Whether it was then or later, she'd end up alone with him, and that imminent truth sent cold shivers down Megan's arms. Greg had never hit her, but Dan and Jimmy had always been there to protect her from the occasional attempt. And suddenly they weren't. Megan's terror of the changes looming in her uncertain future encumbered the weight progressively swelling in her chest.

After several, awkward moments, Greg swept his attention from Darlene, his eyes shooting daggers at the others before settling on Megan.

"You comin'?" his commanding tone bore little question.

Megan contorted her arid mouth, stammering, "I, I, don't wanna, walk."

Greg's cautionary glower lingered and Megan feared she would vomit. Then he disappeared around the corner to the bar and, a moment later, the steel door slammed.

A shuddering, wet sob escaped and trepidation rolled inside Megan like a storm. She took a hesitant step forward, but stopped, unsure of the safest direction. When a familiar hand touched her shoulder, the fear flashing inside sparked and a thundering rage broke through.

311

"Why'd you do that?!" she flipped on Darlene with panic-stricken rage.

"Megan-" Darlene began gently.

"No!" Megan screamed, "You don't have to go back there!"

As the fearful admission left her lips, Megan dissolved. Overwhelmed by the dreaded anticipation of being alone with Greg after his public humiliation.


Megan apologized to Darlene on their way out of Pederson's, but she insisted Megan had no reason to be sorry, and admitted she hadn't considered the current situation while attacking Greg, offering a sincere apology of her own.

The drive to their street was somber, and far too quick. Sam forced a grin when their eyes met, but Megan couldn't return his artificial serenity, turning her attention out the window.

"Do you want me to walk you in?" Darlene asked, stopping her car where Dan's truck should have been.

Megan shook her head, her throat too tight to attempt a verbal response.

"Here," Darlene dug in her purse and handed Megan her cell phone, "Call the house. Even if it's three in the morning, Megan. If you need me, call."

Megan's appreciative grin and promising nod as she took the phone seemed a satisfying enough response for Darlene.

"Don't beat my Snake score," Sam's joke won a short laugh from Megan and she leaned across the backseat, savoring his embrace before thanking Darlene and sliding out of the car.

Her heart hammered harder on each porch step until Megan assumed her chest would explode at the front door. Instinctually, she reached for the screen door handle and expelled a bitter scoff, certain Greg hadn't even noticed the broken obstacle's absence. Gripping Darlene's cell phone tightly in one hand, Megan hid it behind her wrist and pushed the front door open.

Her father was reclined on the couch with his boots on the coffee table, but shut off the television and sat up, setting his beer where his feet had been. Megan leaned against the front door until it sunk into the frame, the latch produced a deafening click in the silence.

"You 'n I gotta have a talk," Greg was clearly curbing his festered irritation.

She dragged her feet to the armchair without taking her eyes off him.

"I know you've had a rough week," he began, "And I'm sorry for that, I am, but you need to figure out real quick who's in charge around here, 'cause it's not Dan, and I ain't about to let what happened earlier slide again. Got it?"

Though anger thumped in her ears, Megan obliged a tiny nod, but only to appease his demand and end the uncomfortable lecture. His equation of Jimmy's accident to a 'rough week' echoed ruthlessly as Greg continued.

"Things are gonna change around here," he said firmly, "Startin' with you listenin' to me. Are we clear on that?"

Megan drew her gaze from her thumb rubbing across the buttons of Darlene's phone to Greg, her raw throat made it nearly impossible to plead, "I don't wanna move."

He expelled a cruel laugh, "Well, if that happens it's not gonna be up to you-"

"My friends are here!" she wailed pathetically, "And Dan-"

"Dan's got nothin' to do with this!" Greg slammed his fist on the coffee table.

Megan burst into tears, jumped to her feet and bolted to her room, skirting around her father's burly arms snatching at her over the back of the couch.

"Megan!" Greg roared, but she slammed her door as he started pounding down the hall.

The lock was hardly reassuring, she'd seen him bust down Jimmy's door without effort, and Megan shoved her dresser, but already knew she couldn't slide it in front of the door. Her options were desperately limited.

She sunk to the carpet, flattening her back against the door, and braced her new shoes on the footboard of her bed as the first thundering strike fell.

"Open this goddamn door, Megan!" Greg yelled, his fist hammering in quick succession.

Megan's cries warbled with the violent vibrations, fully aware she wasn't prepared to undertake the siege alone, but she was alone. The cell phone blurred while tears swam in Megan's eyes and her stomach twisted, Darlene would probably make it worse than she already had anyway.

"Megan!" Greg's fury was growing and she whimpered when the door bowed and snapped against her head.

Nervously, she thumbed through Darlene's phone book. Jay's shop was one of the few stored numbers Megan recognized, but the shop was closed on Sundays, even if Dan was there, the likelihood of him answering was slim. Lacey's number wasn't there and Megan dropped her head as another hard hit shook the door.

"I'll take this goddamn door off the hinges 'n then you won't have one!" Greg threatened, rattling the handle.

Megan didn't care about the door, or her room, or the house. Greg could take all the doors he wanted. She just wanted her brothers back.

Pounding thundered again, but she didn't shake from the force, and then the doorbell chimed. Relief brought fresh tears to Megan's eyes as Greg's weight lifted from her bedroom door, but she swallowed hard, resisting vulnerable sobs, and listened attentively through the wall.

"Evenin', Greg," Andy's familiar voice was muffled, but clear.

"What can I do for ya, officer?" Greg asked impatiently, apparently not recognizing the young man who'd grown up with his oldest stepson.

"Well, y'know, it's a nice night," Andy continued, "I was drivin' by with my windows down and thought I heard some yellin'."

"Is that a crime?" Greg asked flatly.

"Depends on how it ends, sir," Andy said politely.

"Get off my porch," Greg growled, "There's nothin' here for you to worry about."

"Of course," Andy's tone remained light, but firmly insisted, "I'd just like to hear that from Megan and I'll be on my way."

Bitter understanding filled Greg's laugh, "I know you, yer Dan's buddy. He ask ya to circle the place? 'Cause that's harassment!"

"As I said, sir," Andy repeated calmly, "I'm on patrol and heard yelling when I drove passed. I'll be on my way just as soon as everybody in the house tells me there's not a problem."

After a brief hesitation, and without hiding his annoyance, Greg called, "Megan, c'mere!"

Andy was one of the only people whose presence Megan trusted enough to risk surrendering her single, protective barrier in the hope he'd offer more. After a shivering breath, she left her room.

Ignoring her father, she dragged her gaze from Andy's boots to his badge and then his usual smile, but it faltered. Megan knew, in that fleeting change, Andy understood her fear.

"Hey, Megan," Andy maintained his professional tone, but snuck a concerned eyebrow raise as he asked, "Everything alright?"

She thought she'd said something, at least nodded or made a gesture in the direction of a response, but, when Greg snapped his fingers sharply, Megan wasn't sure how long she'd been standing there, silent.

"Ye-ah," she managed with a weak nod, praying Andy didn't believe her.

His smirk was proof enough he didn't, but his expression calloused when he looked at Greg, "I'm on patrol all night."

"I better not see ya circlin' around here," Greg growled, "Or I'll be callin' yer captain."

"I'm sure Chief Matthews would be happy to hear from you," Andy allowed a layer of cynicism in his comment and Greg's eyes narrowed.

"Matthews is in charge now, huh?" he scoffed.

"Over a year now," Andy confirmed, "I'm sure he remembers you."

Greg stalked to the refrigerator and lurched open the door, snarling, "If ya don't have any more reason to be here, I need to feed my kid dinner."

Andy's smile returned when his eyes met Megan's and he gave her an encouraging wink, "I'm around all night, call the station if you need-"

"Ain't nobody gonna need ya, kid!" Greg snapped from the kitchen, "Now kindly get the hell outta my house."

Andy glared at Greg, who's attention had returned almost convincingly to starting dinner, but, as he left, Andy made an inconspicuous gesture with his pinky and thumb. Megan nodded, silently promising to call if she needed him, and Andy pulled the front door closed. The screen door's absent slam resounded in the silent house.

Megan's heart pounded, afraid to look at her father, but she twisted instinctually towards the danger. Greg couldn't completely hide his suppressed rage, but jerked his head at the open refrigerator.

"What'cha want for dinner?" he asked flatly.

"I'm not hungry," Megan said, she was still full from Pederson's.

"You're eatin'," he growled, "Pick somethin'."

Tears stung her eyes, but Megan blinked hard, refusing to look at him as she slid onto her seat.

"Green bean casserole it is," Greg said.

"I hate green bean casserole," Megan grumbled, her brothers knew that and never would have bothered to offer it.

"Then what'd ya want, kid?" Greg asked shakily, clearly exerting effort to maintain control of his anger.

"I'm not hungry," she repeated, "I ate at Pederson's with Dan."

Greg growled, shaking his head and his fists in frustration, but his feet remained planted. Megan held her breath, scooting to the edge of her chair while her father threw a stifled fit. He slammed the refrigerator door, ending his tantrum with dramatically heaving shoulders.

"Fine," he bit out through gritted teeth, "Just go to bed then."

Surprised, but without hesitation, Megan slid off the chair, blindly shuffling backwards until she reached the hallway, and hurried to her room, shutting the door quietly.

She'd never felt so alone, staring out her window and grazing her fingers along the edges Jimmy had helped install. Megan's chest contracted in familiar pain and it was suddenly obvious her heart had broken.

Unfamiliar, hard knocking startled Megan awake, opening her eyes just as her door flew open.

"Up 'n at 'em," Greg said, "Runnin' late."

She nodded, but, as soon as he walked away, turned towards the wall and shut her tired eyes on the bright room. It seemed only seconds later his booming voice shook her awake again.

"Megan! Up, now, c'mon!" Greg cracked his hands together.

"I'm up," she insisted, shuffling her legs just enough under the blanket to show she had intentions of getting of her bed.

"Ya said that five minutes ago," he growled, "Get dressed, we gotta go."

"I need to shower," she whined, throwing off her blankets, but not yet vacating the safety of her bed.

"Should've woke up on time," Greg shrugged, "Ten minutes, Meg, I'm pullin' the truck around."

She rolled her eyes at his back and still sat on her bed for a few minutes, swallowing bitter frustration and anger. Even if she had gotten up when he'd first knocked on her door, there was not enough time to shower and dry her hair. Megan's teeth clenched, letting terrible hopes for her father overtake her thoughts, absently grabbing the green dress from the few clean clothes she had left.

Greg returned and called twice for Megan to hurry, though the second time she didn't respond, afraid her voice would crack over the lump residing in her throat. She brushed her hair into a greasy ponytail and wiped away tears, taking a deep breath before leaving her bedroom.

"Cute dress," Greg smirked, leaning against the counter in ill-fitting khakis with a dingy, white button down and a wrinkled tie that stopped midway down his protruding gut.

"Thanks," she mumbled, moving habitually towards her chair at the table.

Greg scoffed hard, "We gotta go, kid, we're already late."

Megan gaped and her stomach twinged with hopeless anticipation, but she followed his insistent gesture out the door. Reminded by the chilly breeze she'd forgotten her jacket, but Greg was locking the deadbolt and she didn't bother to ask if she could grab it.

The semi-truck wedged in the driveway further infuriated her, Dan's truck should've been there. The cab smelled like stale food and Megan hated climbing onto the rickety passenger seat, always afraid she would fall. But on their hurried drive to the courthouse, Megan didn't express her hatred for the truck, not wanting to give Greg any excuse to speak to her.

He tried though, just a few times, and gave up when Megan offered no more than indifferent shrugs.

"Y'know," he sighed on his final attempt, "You can ignore me all ya like, but someday you're gonna have kids and understand that sometimes ya gotta make the unpopular choices."

Megan blinked back tears while staring out the passenger window, hating her father more with every ache in her chest.

Dan's truck was already in the parking lot of the judicial building and Megan spotted Dotty's red Honda while Greg made his way to the far back. He maneuvered the overbearing truck across three spots in the rear corner and Megan was out passenger door in the same moment he pulled the air brake knob out of the dashboard.

She ignored his repeated requests to wait, walking ahead of him to the entrance, but, when her father barked threateningly to slow down, she did, furious at herself for lacking the courage to defy him. Together they entered the courthouse, moved through the metal detector and Megan followed Greg down the long hallway.

Her brothers had been there before, but Megan had never followed the brass framed signs towards 'Family Court'. She rubbed her hands on her green dress, but they were still clammy.

"There she is," a familiar women's call reached her ears and Megan saw Dotty wave, Dan stood next to her with his hands shoved in the pockets of his black slacks.

Megan couldn't've cared less about the well-dressed professionals' scowls, or the guard warning her not to run, dodging recklessly around them into Dan's arms. Squeezing tightly around his neck as tears spilled down her cheeks, Megan begged him to come home, hoping even for a pacifying promise.

Dan said nothing, but tightened his hold when his shoulders quivered.

"Megan, you ready?" Dotty's question wasn't impatient, but she had an unmistakable cringe when checking her watch.

Megan nodded, but looked at Dan and asked, "Can we get breakfast after?"

Dan's brow furrowed, turning disdainfully towards Greg, but his scowl vanished when his attention returned, "We'll see," and then asked Dotty, "We got two minutes?"

"Only two," Dotty raised a cautioning eyebrow, tapping her silver wristwatch.

"Yes, ma'am," Dan said, tweaking Megan's shoulder gently before jogging away, a silent promise he would be right back.

"If you'd gotten yourself up earlier we would've had time," Greg said indifferently.

"That's why you're the dad, Greg," Dotty said dryly, "When you have to be somewhere important, it's your job to make sure that happens."

"Yeah, well," Greg fumbled before bitterly retorting, "Ain't no point in bein' here anyway, waste'a time."

"I'm sorry that's what you think," Dotty's sarcastic pity included an arched eyebrow, promising a fight if Greg continued.

The solid, wood door they'd gathered in front of swung open, ceasing the unpleasant conversation brewing between Dotty and Greg. A heavyset man wearing a guard uniform and a scowl blocked the doorway, but his expression brightened when he saw Dotty.

"Ms. Clark, I didn't see your name on the list today," he smiled.

"Tim, how many times do I gotta tell you to call me Dotty?" she chided playfully, "I'm just sittin' in as a courtesy."

He smiled, "If only everybody at your department worked as hard as you."

"Yours too," Dotty's comment produced a short chuckle from the guard as he gestured them into the office.

She put a hand on Megan's shoulders, guiding her into the room towards a glossy, wood desk and four, straight backed chairs facing it. Megan hesitated at the far-right seat Tim offered when Greg dropped onto the one next to it.

"I wanna sit by Dan," she told Dotty, who nodded empathetically and pointed to the two empty chairs on the other side of Greg, settling herself on the one Megan had refused.

Briefly, Megan considered sitting in the furthest chair, but that would force Dan next to Greg. So she slid onto the chair next to her father without the tiniest glance in his direction, rubbing her hands over her upper arms, wishing she had her jacket.

"Thought this started at nine?" Greg grumbled, shaking his shirt sleeve over his watch before crossing his arms again.

320

"Probably best the judge is givin' us a few extra minutes," Dotty's words and tight-lipped grin were dripping with derision.

Greg didn't respond, but Megan felt his irritation burn and dreaded the moment they'd leave together. When she'd be alone.

Every head swiveled towards at the soft knock on the door to the hall and Tim strode from his station by another door at the back of the small office and let Dan into the judge's chambers. He handed her a foil packet of Pop-Tarts, sidestepping between the chairs, and took his seat on the far-left.

"No eating in the judge's chambers," Tim demanded with brisk simplicity.

Megan looked sadly at the package she'd just ripped open, the smell of artificial strawberries reminding her how hungry she was, but a pleading look at Dan resulted in nothing more than an apologetic grimace.

"She hasn't eaten today, Tim," Dotty said piteously to the guard, "She'll put it away as soon as Judge Mendoza's here."

Tim and Dotty shared an expression that made Megan think of the silent understandings she had with Dan, and had had with Jimmy. The guard leveled a brief scowl at Greg before his eyes shifted to Megan.

"Be neat," Tim said with a small smirk.

Megan nodded earnestly and carefully shoveled the vending machine treat between her gnashing teeth, hoping to finish both Pop-Tarts before the judge arrived.

She'd just broken off the first bite of her second pastry when a soft tap echoed into the mostly quiet room and Tim raised his eyebrows at Megan, reaching to open the rear door next to him. Dan snapped his fingers softly and, begrudgingly, she handed over the Pop-Tarts, watching them disappear stealthily behind him on the chair.

"The Honorable Judge Mendoza presiding," Tim's voice boomed as a thin woman with dark, graying hair walked in, her black robes billowing around her short frame.

Judge Mendoza's piercing, brown eyes swept the room and the corners of her lips tugged upward at Dotty as she took her seat behind the large desk, setting the files she was carrying on the glossy surface.

"Alright, is everyone present?" Judge Mendoza asked.

"And then some," Greg grumbled and Megan caught the judge's brow twitch upward.

"Ms. Clark, are you representing for a minor today?" she asked.

"If need be, your Honor," Dotty nodded in Megan's direction, "But I'm here as a professional witness, and moral support."

"A professional witness?" Judge Mendoza flipped the top file open, scanning the contents before asking with surprise, "This was set as a guardianship change, correct?"

"Yes, your Honor," Dotty answered.

"But, obviously, we aren't here for a cut and dry closing to that pending case," Judge Mendoza's gaze moved from Dan to Megan to Greg before landing back on Dotty.

"No, your Honor," Dotty shook her head, "There should be a recent petition-"

"Very recent," the judge commented flatly, studying the rather weighty file.

After several, awkward moments, Dotty persisted, despite her intended audience remaining head bent over Dan's desperate petition, "I've been assigned to Megan's cases with DCFS since February nineteen-ninety-seven and just wanna help look out for her best interests however I can."

Judge Mendoza nodded as she raised her eyes and focused on Greg, "State your name, please."

"Greg Connor," he said stiffly.

Megan wasn't prepared for the judge's gaze to land on her and blurted her name out as the intimidating woman was repeating her request. Mortified, Megan covered her mouth seconds shy of the outburst. But

Judge Mendoza didn't yell at her like Judge Judy would have, and Megan actually thought she caught an amused smirk before the judge turned to Dan with the same request.

"Dan Murphy, your Honor," he said.

"You're the brother who was seeking guardianship?" Judge Mendoza asked.

"Yes, ma'- your Honor," Dan stammered over his address, grimacing nervously at the judge, but she hadn't seemed to notice.

"And Mr. Conner," she flipped her attention while asking, "You were going to release your parental rights to Mr. Murphy?"

"Was," Greg scoffed, continuing when Judge Mendoza stared at him blankly, "He called me and said her school was havin' issues with the paperwork 'cause I weren't there to sign somethin', and goes on about how it would be easier for me if he could handle that stuff legally, and at first, I'll be honest, it sounded fine. But then I find out he lied to me, tellin' me I'll still have all my parental rights, but I find out from a buddy who had somethin' like this happen that I won't have any rights-"

"I never said-" Dan interjected, but, when the judge whipped a hard look at him, he bit his lips together.

"So," she turned her attention back to Greg, "Your concern was losing all parental rights over Megan?"

"That, and her safety," Greg sneered over Megan's head and she watched Dan's fingers curl next to his leg.

"What made you concerned for Megan's safety?" the judge's question hung heavy in the air and Megan dreaded the answer that would fly from her father's cruel tongue.

"His little brother, Jimmy, ya probably got a whole file on him," Greg scoffed at the desk, "He was out cruisin' with some buddies last weekend, got hit 'n died. Ya think I can trust my only daughter to the kid who let his brother go around drinkin' and drivin' underage-"

"Jimmy wasn't drunk or driving-" Dan snapped, his nostrils flaring when another quick look from the judge forced him to halt the resentful protest.

"You can see he's got a temper. Danny here even put me in the hospital once," Greg jerked his head at his stepson and Megan scowled at him with every ounce of the hatred she felt in her broken heart.

But her abhorrent trance broke when Dan tugged her hand. Megan eagerly accepted his comfort and squeezed his fingers, offering the most hopeful smile she could muster. She knew it was a pathetic attempt, but seemed enough to make the hidden rage fade from Dan's eyes.

Judge Mendoza flipped a few pages, leaving them in another minute of silence, and finally nodded while bringing her eyes back to Greg, "Yes, I see there was an incident in ninety-ninety-eight. Would you like to speak to that, Mr. Connor?"

"Sure, well, I was good enough not to press charges," Greg said haughtily, "Still can't hear outta my right ear like I used to, though."

"And what was the motive for Dan's attack?" the judge asked simply.

"I'm sorry, uh, what, your Honor?" Greg sat up a bit straighter in his chair.

"His motive, Mr. Connor," she repeated.

"Why's that matter," Greg asked, crossing his arms over his chest while snarling in confused irritation, as if insisting the judge's questioning was out of line.

"People don't typically attack people for no reason," Judge Mendoza explained plainly, "And if they do, they are not someone most people would continue to keep as the primary caretaker of their child," she waited for his mouth to snap shut twice before adding, "Allow me to remind you, Mr. Connor, you said you'd like to speak to the incident."

"It's irrelevant," Greg said, agitation bubbling in his voice, "I, honestly, don't know why I'm here your Honor. He's got no right to take my kid from me! He's an adult, I don't have any more obligation to keep him housed or fed or clothed-" Dan expelled a laugh and Greg's hardly held composure cracked, shifting almost off his chair as he barked, "Ya got somethin' to say smartass?!"

"Mr. Connor," Judge Mendoza' sharp, scolding tone earned everyone's attention, "This is the only warning you will get about language and shouting in my chambers."

"My apologies, your Honor," Greg mumbled, dipping his scowl until his overextended self-control could hide his outrage.

"You're here, Mr. Connor, because when parents with a history in our system," the judge lifted the file slightly and continued, "have agreed to waive their parental rights to a fit guardian and suddenly change their minds we have an obligation to that child to look into it," she held up a form and said, "Mr. Murphy's petition to alter this guardianship hearing to a request for visitation rights, while highly unusual-"

"He doesn't have any rights to visitation! He's her half-brother for Christ's sake!" Greg erupted, causing Megan to shrink into Dan and Tim to move from his post by the door.

"Mr. Connor," the judge warned, holding a hand up for the security guard to wait.

"I'm sorry," Greg expelled a shaky breath, though his indignant scowl remained as he spoke, "But, your Honor, he's got no right to ask for that-"

"And you've got no right to take me away from my home!" Megan burst, covering her mouth over the interruption as much as the sobs trying to escape, but, when Dan squeezed her hand in his, she let the other fall and whimpered, "I'm sorry."

Judge Mendoza nodded, her expression blank, and turned back to Greg, "How long have you worked on the road, Mr. Connor?"

"Seventeen, almost eighteen years now," he said, drawing his shoulders back.

"And what's your schedule like?" the judge asked.

"I do the long hauls," Greg grinned pompously, "US to Canada, keeps me on the road few weeks at a time."

Megan scoffed at her father's downplayed portrayal of the time he was gone, but Dan's quick squeeze reminded her not to say anything.

"Have you always done the long hauls?" Judge Mendoza asked nonchalantly.

"Mostly, yeah," he shrugged.

"And how old was Megan when Mrs. Connor passed?" her expression was stone and her tone matched.

"Five or six, I think," Greg said, obviously confused by the abrupt change of questioning.

"Prior to her passing," the judge continued coldly, "Did Mrs. Connor require care or was she relatively healthy?"

Greg's sad sigh was barely believable, "The last year was rough, she hardly got outta bed."

Dan squeezed Megan's hand and she squeezed back, unsure if his had been intentional comfort or a reflex of bottled anger, but she didn't know how else to let her brother know in that moment she loved him.

"And how much time did you take off following her passing?" Judge Mendoza asked.

"I was home for a while," Greg considered, "Maybe two, three months."

"How old was Mr. Murphy at that time?" her question fired the moment Greg responded.

"Uh, I'm not," he looked inquisitively at his stepson, "I think fif- no, sixteen, he'd just started drivin' that gas guzzler."

Silence settled when another question wasn't peppered at Greg, but the judge stared emotionlessly at the subject of her interrogation for an uncomfortable amount of time. Greg, however, had found a convenient hangnail to distract himself, until her commanding voice forced his returned attention.

"So, in the six years since your wife's passing, and the year prior that you state she was medically incapacitated," Judge Mendoza seemed a bit baffled, "During the, in your words, weeks at a time, that you're on the road. Who has been the primary caretaker of your daughter?"

For a moment, Greg's fermenting anger stretched his nostrils, but he cleared his throat and weakly admitted, "Dan."

"Mr. Murphy?" Judge Mendoza clarified.

"Yes, your Honor," Greg's teeth clenched through his compelled agreement.

"Then we are here, Mr. Connor, to discuss the petition for visitation from Megan's primary caretaker," Judge Mendoza decreed, shuffling a few papers and held up a postcard sized form, curiously mentioning, "I have the signed receipt for the certified letter you received Thursday informing you of the change."

Greg shrugged hard, his arms tight across his chest, "I skimmed through it, lotta legal jargon."

"I'm sorry if it was difficult to understand," the judge maintained her icy indifference, but condescendingly pointed to the form while saying, "We do provide a number to call if you need more information, or would like to refute the petition before the stated date."

"Didn't get a lotta time, did I?" he asked defensively.

"You received the letter at eight thirty-seven Thursday morning," Judge Mendoza pointed again to the official document, never taking her challenging gaze from Greg, "You didn't have any time between then and close of business Friday?"

"Well, I understand now," his words finished with a growl and Greg cleared his throat, imploring with slightly less frustration, "But your Honor, with all due respect, this is ridiculous-"

"I don't waste my time on ridiculous things, Mr. Connor, I assure you," Judge Mendoza said simply and turned to Dan, "Mr. Murphy, this is your petition. I will say, it's a new one for me. So, what reason do you have for the court to mandate visitation with your half-sister, Megan Connor," she paused briefly to recheck the papers in front of her, "Every Sunday morning?"

"Every Sunday morning?!" Greg exclaimed furiously.

"Mr. Connor," Judge Mendoza hardly raised her voice, but trained a hard warning glare on Greg, gaining direct compliance, before turning back to Dan, "Go ahead, Mr. Murphy."

"You're Honor," Dan squeezed Megan's hand again before letting go and straightened in the chair, with a deep breath, he began, "I've been taking care of my brother 'n sister a long time. Jimmy 'n I were little when we lost our dad, and my mom, well, she took it, bad. So, I got used to takin' care'a, him, 'cause she needed my help. Then when Megan was born," Dan turned a pained grin on her for a moment before continuing, "They found a tumor. It was blockin' her from, y'know. And all these doctors were yellin' how Megan wouldn't make it much longer, it was really scary, and they had to do an emergency C-section, but, uh, that's how we found out our mom was sick. It was blessing, 'cause if Megan hadn't been born they never would've found it and we wouldn't've even gotten the few extra years we did," he paused a moment, taking a shaky breath, "My mom, she took us to church every Sunday, even when she got really bad, she tried to make it, but I still took Megan 'n Jimmy, 'cause she asked me to. The last promise I made her, I promised to take Megan to church on Sundays, at least until she had a valid and well-researched argument not to," Dan smirked at the memory of their mother's single exception to the vow he'd made.

Megan suddenly remembered all the times she'd complained about going to church, badly wishing she hadn't, and raised remorseful eyes. Dan smiled, meeting her gaze, and quickly turned back at the judge.

"That's an admirable reason, Mr. Murphy," she said, a hint of sadness on her face, "I am sorry about your brother, as well as your parents."

Dan's throat bobbed when he swallowed, blinking his misty eyes, and simply offered a nod as thank you.

"And Mr. Connor," Judge Mendoza returned her attention, and blank expression, to Greg, "What is your objection to the arrangement Mr. Murphy is requesting?"

"Cause I can't promise I'm always gonna be in town to let him take her," Greg tossed his hands up, landing on his knees as he sat forward, "Your Honor, as I've said, I'm gone for weeks at a time."

Judge Mendoza's eyebrows rose, "Are you intending to continue your current work lifestyle, with Megan, on the road?"

"I gotta a buddy, his kid does the homeschool thing," Greg said.

"While I won't venture to assume the circumstances around your, friend's, situation, Mr. Connor," she said, removing half the file's contents and waving the stack, "I have a pile of letters from her teachers expressing Megan's intelligence and how well she thrives with other students-"

"Busy bodies, town's full of-" Greg interjected contemptuously.

"Do not, interrupt me, Mr. Connor," Judge Mendoza snapped intimidatingly and Megan grinned, "Call them what you like," she continued, "But I rarely see this kind of support from adult members of the community for a child lacking a stable parent in the home," she held up a hand to halt Greg's attempted protest, "Stable parents are with the child on a daily basis, Mr. Connor."

Greg closed his mouth, leaning back in the chair and crossed his arms again, rage exuding from him.

"I wasn't able to get through all of them, but I see a theme," Judge Mendoza commented to Dotty.

"Mrs. King tried to pry your number outta me," Dotty smirked.

"Is that the seven pager?" the judge ended her question with an amused smirk when Dotty nodded, "You can tell her I read that one thoroughly."

Dotty had a satisfied expression, offering Megan and Dan a quick, encouraging smile, and returning Greg's glare before the judge regained their attention.

"There is understandable concern, Mr. Connor," Judge Mendoza said, "That Megan might not excel as much with a fairly unregulated home-schooling program as she has in a conventional school environment."

"She's smart," Greg reasoned indifferently, "She'll be fine."

"She is," the judge agreed, "So, do you contribute Megan being generally happy and well cared for to her grades and friendships?"

"Well, uh," Greg fumbled, his neck turning red as he deflected the question, "Sure, that's part'a it, she's always been smart, just a sharp kid, your Honor."

"Is Megan's opinion something you're taking into consideration with these changes?" she asked flatly.

"Well," Greg trembled with bottled rage, "I gotta work, I mean, I don't know what ya want me to do. I gotta feed the kid-"

A quiet, but audible, scoff dragged everyone's shocked eyes to Tim, still standing by the door, and he aimed an embarrassed grimace at Judge Mendoza. She simply nodded at Greg to continue.

"I know it's not ideal," Greg admitted irritably, "But it's what I do."

"I understand, Mr. Connor," Judge Mendoza said, "But what I asked was, are you taking your daughter's feelings into consideration? Have you spoken to her about what's going to happen?"

"I tried to," Greg sneered, "She went runnin' in her room, locked the door, and then his cop buddy shows up, had him circlin' the block. Harassment, that's what it is, that whole town!"

Megan glanced at Dan and the tiny upturn of his lips was enough to tell her he'd had some influence over Andy's patrol route the previous evening.

"Did the officer approach your door?" Judge Mendoza asked, leaning forward with intrigued contemplation.

"Sure did," Greg nodded curtly.

"What was his reason for approaching your residence?" she inquired.

"Harassment, like I said," he sounded much less enthusiastic about the accusation the second time.

"What's the officer's name?" she asked, waving for Tim to approach, "I'll have someone call their precinct-"

"No, that's, I'm sorry, your Honor," Greg grimaced and rushed to explain Officer Andy's stop, "I don't need any more'a them gettin' involved. No, the cop came up 'cause we were gettin' kinda loud. She's not happy about this, I know that, I was tryin' to talk to her, I'm a loud guy, y'know. But that kid cop was told, by someone not on the force, to bother me," he glared at Dan while emphasizing his words, but managed nearly pleading eyes at the judge as he said, "I'm just doin' my best."

Judge Mendoza nodded slowly at him before asking, "Do you mind if I ask Megan a few questions?"

Greg obviously stiffened, but shrugged after a moment and said, "Sure."

Megan's mouth went dry, terrified she would interrupt, or forget to call her 'your Honor', or start crying. A hidden, deep breath hardly helped to calm her nerves.

"Megan," Judge Mendoza's eyes weren't harsh and Megan was relieved, "I have your report cards here from the last few years, looks like all A's to me."

"I got a B in math last year," Megan said, clapping a hand over her mouth in angry disbelief of how soon she'd interjected.

Judge Mendoza, however, stifled amusement and continued, "Looks like you've improved then, that's what counts. Do you enjoy school, Megan?"

"Yes, your Honor," she said, twisting her fingers absently in her lap.

"What are some of your favorite things about school?" the judge asked.

"Well, volleyball's a lot of fun," she began, "I really like English class 'cause we get to read stories, and gym's kinda fun, as long as we're not playing dodgeball 'cause the boys always go for the girls first," Judge Mendoza's smile encouraged Megan to go on, "I go to the library a lot, Mrs. King's okay with it during lunch."

"She mentioned," Judge Mendoza glanced warmly at her desk and returned her attention to Megan with a nod to continue.

"Well, this year," Megan started excitedly, "We made roller coasters in science class to learn about centrifugal force 'n stuff. Just like little ones, with a marble, y'know, but I had the best one when we showed them off in class. Dan 'n Jimmy helped me and it," Megan's words dissolved as she choked on a fresh flood of memories.

She knew it wasn't the place to cry, but her vision blurred anyway, mildly alleviated by recognizable comfort squeezing her shoulder.

"You're okay," Dan said reassuringly and Megan sniffled hard on the sobs still trying to escape.

"Megan," Judge Mendoza said kindly, "You don't have to talk about anything you don't want to."

Stray tears ran down Megan's face as she weakly admitted, "I miss Jimmy."

"Have you always been close with your brothers?" the judge asked and Megan nodded, "Both of them?"

Megan looked at Dan, his smirk said she'd better tell the truth, and, coyly, she replied, "Well, Dan's kinda bossy, but I know it's 'cause he loves me."

Judge Mendoza allowed a singular giggle, inquiring, "What's Dan do that's bossy?"

Megan shrugged, twisting her fingers again as she explained, "Y'know, he tells me to clean my room, and when to go to bed, and do my homework 'n stuff."

"What time do you have to go to bed?"

"It was nine thirty," Megan divulged, aiming a grin at her brother, "But I just turned thirteen, so it's ten now," shifting her gaze warily to her father, Megan added a disheartened, "I think."

"Well, happy birthday," Judge Mendoza continued, "That's a big age. I bet you've grown a lot lately," Megan nodded proudly, "When you need new clothes, who takes you?"

"Dan," Megan said without hesitation, unsure why she let a sad truth follow, "Jimmy would come with sometimes."

Judge Mendoza nodded and then turned her attention to Dan, "Mr. Murphy, you work at a mechanic shop, correct?"

"Yes, your Honor," Dan was surprised by her change in focus, but answered quickly.

"And about how much money has Mr. Connor provided you this year to care for Megan?" she asked, keeping her eyes on Dan and ignored Greg's flushed, contorting face.

"He, uh, he used to give me more," Dan answered, "Since the beginning of this year he's given me maybe a grand-"

"I sent you two hundred bucks through Western Union just for that medicine she needed after New Year's!" Greg protested.

"I'm countin' that, Greg," Dan spat through gritted teeth.

"Mr. Connor, it is not your turn," Judge Mendoza snapped impatiently before turning again to Dan, "Mr. Murphy, do you pay the mortgage on the property?"

"It's owned outright," Greg said bitterly, "By me."

"Mr. Connor, this is your final warning," the judge trained her fiery scowl on Greg, jerking her head in Tim's direction, and raised a cautionary eyebrow.

"It is, in his name," Dan agreed resentfully, "Our mom's life insurance paid it off. I pay the bills, taxes included, but we've always made it work, your Honor."

"And your brother, Jimmy, how old was he?" she asked gently.

"Eighteen," Dan's eyes fell with his weakened tone.

"You took care of him too?" Judge Mendoza's question was more of an insinuation and Dan simply nodded, "These letters I've gotten, all the ones I've read so far anyway, say that you had your pick of colleges after graduation on a football scholarship. Why did you decide against that opportunity?"

Dan's damp eyes rose, accompanied by a grin and a lighthearted joke about his reality, "You just said it, your Honor, I had two kids at home."

The hint of a smile faded as the judge turned to Greg, "Mr. Connor, did you know about Mr. Murphy's scholarship offers?"

"A few of 'em," he admitted gruffly.

"And why not at that point take your daughter into your daily care?" she asked plainly.

"What'd ya mean?" Greg scoffed.

"I mean," Judge Mendoza said, "Mr. Murphy has sacrificed life changing opportunities to care for Megan, and now, years later, you're deciding to take his responsibility over her away. I'm curious why their brother's unfortunate passing, which from the police report, I'm seeing was nothing more than an unforeseen tragedy that claimed that poor, young man's life. So then, why is that the sparking force behind your decision?"

Greg stared at the judge, gaping a moment before he snapped his jaw shut.

"Mr. Connor," she insisted.

"I don't know," Greg spat in frustration.

Judge Mendoza's eyes narrowed, "You don't know why you want to disrupt your daughter's life more than it already has been recently? And in spite of the evidence that she's thriving under Mr. Murphy's care?"

Megan stared at her father, waiting for an answer.

"She's my kid," Greg shrugged, certifying his cold indifference towards his daughter as simply a contract of ownership.

"She is," the judge agreed, "And being her father, it is your responsibility to ensure she's healthy, happy and allowed the opportunities to grow into a successful woman. That includes structured education, balanced meals and social relationships with her peers. Do you believe you can provide those things better than they've already been provided for Megan?"

Greg leaned back in his chair, deflated. But, after a few moments of internal contemplation, he turned to Megan, whose distraught scowl

334

was still trained on him, but softened in surprise at her father's sincerely heavy sigh.

"What would I do with you on the road anyway?" he smirked, "I do love ya, Meggie- Megan, I really do. Just, y'know, I wasn't plannin' on havin' kids, but that doesn't mean I don't love you," Greg sighed again and stared at Dan before looking at her with a compassion she'd never known from him, "Stay with your brother."

As his proclamation settled in the room, Megan's eyes widened in elated disbelief. Dan's hand gripped her shoulder and she clutched it instinctively, her awed expression still on Greg, sure she hadn't heard him right.

"Mr. Connor," Judge Mendoza gained everyone's attention, but Megan didn't relent Dan's hand, "Are you deciding to relinquish your parental rights over Megan Connor to Daniel Murphy?"

Megan squeezed Dan's hand, holding her breath in the agonizingly long seconds before her father answered.

"Well," Greg expelled a hard breath, "If I'm doin' what's best for her, that's probably it."

A relieved sob burst from Megan's lips as Greg confirmed his decision. She lost her balance on the chair while leaning towards Dan, but his strong embrace didn't let her fall.

"Thank you," Dan barely more than whispered.

"Yeah, well," Greg cleared his throat hard, "How long'll this take, your Honor?"

Judge Mendoza pulled a familiar, yellow envelope from under the file, "Just a few signatures and you'll be on your way, Mr. Connor."

He nodded, turning regretfully towards Megan, "I wasn't thinkin' about'cha, I'm not used to havin' to. But I do want you to be happy, I really do."

She patted Dan's arm to let go and took a couple steps in front of her father, wrapping her arms around his neck.

"Thank you, Dad, I love you too," Megan insisted gratefully.

He patted her back and wiped his face as Megan retreated blindly until she reached the comfort of Dan's welcoming hug.

"You gotta pen, then?" Greg asked and Judge Mendoza laid a silver pen on top of the yellow envelope.

# Chapter 15

Sunlight poured through the window, but Megan's face was partially buried in her pillow, trying to find another few minutes of sleep. Until a knock on her door dragged her tired eyes to the intruder.

"Mornin' sleepyhead," Dan stepped to the end of her bed, holding a towel around his waist, and rubbed his other hand vigorously over his damp hair.

"Stop!" Megan giggled, ducking under her blanket to avoid water sprinkling her face, unsurprised when the warm shield was tugged away.

"C'mon, we're goin' to Menards after service," he patted her door frame on his way out of the room.

Megan kicked off her blanket and stretched her arms over her head as she yawned. The urge to complain about church rose, but she instantly shook her head of the thought, remembering Dan's words from the week before about the promise he'd made their mother.

When they'd left the courthouse together, watching Greg leave in his semi-truck alone, Megan had asked why he'd never told her before. Dan had simply said talking about their mother was hard for him and he hadn't thought the information would do anything but upset Megan and Jimmy. She understood and had vowed to herself not to argue with Dan about church, purely thankful just to go home with him.

Darlene had cried when they'd pulled into the driveway in Dan's green truck, bolting across the lawn with her hands holding her head in exalted amazement. Megan had thought Dotty's reaction outside of the courthouse had been passionate. But Darlene's powerful, half-minute hug had outdone even the social worker's rib-crushing embrace.

Despite Jay's insistence he take the week off, Dan had gone back to work Thursday, after being sent home Tuesday morning and warned not to show up before Friday. Megan had asked Dan if he was worried about money, since he'd missed so much work, and was surprised when he hadn't brushed off her question with the usual assurance of his ability to 'figure it out'. Instead, he'd told her Jay was compensating him, but admitted he felt guilty being paid and not working. Megan had then suggested they clean the garage, it was basically work.

And it had been, but together they sorted the mess. Several apologies had mumbled passed Dan's lips, his ears burning at the disaster he'd created, until she'd snapped. Reminding him there were countless tantrums he'd never held over her head and listed a series of irreplaceable objects that had gotten in the way of her warpaths. Megan finished her rant by loudly insisting that his reaction was more than valid and, if it had been her, she'd have lit the lawnmower on fire. Dan laughed heartily, making giggles erupt from Megan, and, when they'd returned to the task, his apologies ceased. The box of fireworks, and Jimmy's note, were carefully placed on a shelf to remain untouched.

Sam was been a good distraction while Dan was working, but every evening they had dinner, whether Lacey joined them or not, there was a painful absence at the table. Neither would open Jimmy's door, leaving his room exactly the same, as if he would walk in again, kicking his boots off while the screen door banged behind him. But the screen door was gone, Jimmy's work boots sat unmoved on the mat, and his Oldsmobile waited by the curb for a driver that would never return.

Megan stared at his closed bedroom door, a new ritual before every shower, knowing Jimmy wasn't behind it and tried to rid herself of the hopeless wish. At least Megan had stopped pausing at the hamper on her way out, listening for snoring she wouldn't hear.

"How's it comin'?" Dan asked, popping his head in Megan's bedroom.

"I'm ready," she said, finishing her ponytail while following him into the front room, "Why're we goin' to Menards?"

"Screen door," Dan said, pulling on his clean boots.

"Can we get Wendy's?" she asked habitually, wriggling her feet into her sneakers.

"Sure," he smirked, pulling open the front door, and gestured through the gaping hole.

Sunday service was predictably dull, but Megan tried to pay attention, reminding herself why they were there.

Leaving church took much longer than usual. Mr. and Mrs. King, especially the latter, wanted to express their congratulations to Dan and Megan on the outcome of their court visit. Mr. Glasby and his wife also stopped to comment how happy they were to hear the news, followed by a few cheery parishioners who'd overheard. Megan sighed with relief when Lacey approached.

She, Kayla and Mike stopped on their way into the next service and Lacey promised to bring pizza over later before stealing Dan's attention from continued congratulations. But the well-wishers dispersed and, when she caught the young woman's eye, Megan scowled bitterly at Kayla, finding some satisfaction in her apologetic cringe. The peck Dan and Lacey shared prompted goodbyes from the rest.

"Seems like everybody's pretty happy you're stickin' around," Dan smiled, shaking Megan gently by the shoulder on the bench seat and turned over the truck's ignition with a growl.

"Not as happy as me," she declared.

"Ya got competition, kid," Dan teased, smirking at her confusion, "Me."

Megan stuck her tongue out and Dan pretended to snatch at it, but his hand shot to her side, causing an outburst of giggles.

Occasional laughter offered a moment of decreased pain, but Megan's bliss over her life going back to normal was plagued by the constant reminders that it never really would. She felt less guilty during rare, happy moments when Jimmy would cross her thoughts, but wondered if that sensation would ever completely fade.

Dan parked near the front of the lot when they arrived at Menards and Megan glanced at the Wendy's nearby, suddenly angry at herself for suggesting it. She kept forgetting about things that reminded her of Jimmy, but just about everything reminded her of Jimmy. Dan said that was normal and time would make it hurt less, but Megan didn't believe him, she didn't think he even believed him.

Dan led her to the back corner of the store, passing a display of expensive doors to the aisle behind. A man in a green apron asked if they needed assistance, but Dan said he knew what he was looking for, thanking the man as he pulled a torn corner of paper from his pocket. Megan watched him check the scribbled measurements and stayed quiet while he examined the storm door options, fiddling with the frayed edges of a broken box marked 'clearance'.

"Alright, what'd you think," Dan said finally, pointing out two of the cheaper options, "Fifty bucks more for the one you just have to pull the glass down for the screen, or do we go old school and flip the screen in for the summer?"

Megan scrutinized both doors, knowing it was a question he would've asked Jimmy, and wanted to be sure she gave Dan her best assessment.

"Well, with the sliding one we can open it whenever," she offered, "You always complain when it's cold at night and hot during the day."

"That I do," Dan admitted with a small chuckle, sliding the boxed door she'd chosen out of its spot.

Two employees offered their help on their trip to the register, but Dan insisted the awkwardly shaped box wasn't heavy and carried it all the way to his truck, sliding it carefully into the bed.

Megan didn't remind Dan about her request for Wendy's, but he headed towards the drive-thru anyway. Part of her feared ordering fries and a Frosty, while another part insisted on the tradition. Too quickly, a young woman's greeting echoed from the intercom.

"What'cha want?" Dan asked and Megan stared at him, her vision blurring with fresh tears.

Dan ordered her a junior sized burger, fries and a Frosty, getting himself the same in a larger size. Megan wasn't sure if she'd grinned or grimaced in appreciation, but, when she wiped her eyes, he was smiling, clearly understanding of either response.

"Sweetheart," Dan said after a few minutes of driving in silence, a bag of food untouched between them and melting Frosties in the cupholders, "It's okay to enjoy the things we used to with Jimmy, it's a reminder of the time we had with him."

Megan started to nod, but shook her head, contending fruitlessly, "We should've had more time."

Dan nodded, "Yeah, we should've," he bit his lips hard before continuing, "But Jimmy would want you to be happy," Dan paused again and glanced at her with misty eyes, "Megan, he loved you so much. Jimmy, he wanted nothing but the best for you, hell, most'a his fights with Greg started 'cause Jimmy told him he was a bad dad," he winced, shaking his head earnestly, "Don't think I mean it was your fault, it wasn't, Megan, not even a little bit. I'm just sayin', Jimmy loved you, more than I think he ever loved anybody, just know that. Know that he'd want you to be happy. Always."

She wiped her cheeks, her voice cracking through the confession, "Sometimes, I still yell at him to come out of his room."

Dan expelled a hard breath, tears dropping down his face, "I knock on his door every day, and every day I remember, and it hurts."

"I knock on his door too," Megan admitted and reached a hand to his shoulder.

Dan clutched her unspoken comfort as if he depended on it.

For at least half the drive home, they sat in silent understanding of each other's pain, until a crinkling paper bag broke the stillness. Dan popped off the lid of his Frosty and dug his hand in the open bag for a small handful of fries, holding them out to Megan. His urging nod while dipping his fries in the chocolate shake made her mimic the action.

Dan scraped off the excess ice cream, lifting the chocolate soaked fries, and said, "To Jimmy."

A sad smile crept onto her face as Megan repeated, "To Jimmy."

A tap of their sweet and salty treats concluded the toast, and they ignored the few drops of ice cream that fell on the truck floor, devouring their brother's signature combination.

Dan put his hand on her knee, looking at Megan the way he always did when he'd make a promise, and said, "We're a little broken right now, but we're gonna be okay."

Megan trusted his words. Dan had earned her unwavering faith. Her life had mutated, shattering the simplicity she'd been sheltered by, but strength she didn't expect budded in her relentlessly pained chest, vowing she would return the support her brother had always provided. Outside the window, a semi-truck passed in the opposite direction and Megan was glad to see it disappear in the side view mirror.

## About the author

Mollie McGrath was born and raised in Elgin, IL with an older sister and younger brother. Writing was a passion from a young age and she studied creative writing at Western Illinois University from 2007-2010 before returning to Elgin.

Contact:   little.broken.book@gmail.com

## Cover Art

Created by Eddie Morales, an Elgin based tattoo artist who shares his talents with Chicago convention shows and showcases at shops in the Southwest region.

Made in the USA
Monee, IL
19 May 2022

96710230R00204